PRAIS

T0270175

Third Cla

"I read Elizabeth Genovise's *Third Class Relics* with tears in my eyes all the way through. This book is so masterfully crafted that it is impossible not to feel the message that pounds like a heavy heartbeat in each line. This novel is a call to action, and that action is love. If only we could love others for who they are and not who we selfishly need them to be . . . It is imperative that we start now."

—AMY WILLOUGHBY-BURLE, author of *Out Across the Nowhere*

"With lyrical language that often reads like luminous incantations, Elizabeth Genovise crafts a saga of shattered children cleaving to one another in the shadow of broken parents, all salvaged by a savior unexpected and delightful. Here is a book sometimes quirky, often quite funny, but always profoundly insightful. It's a novel that belongs on that rare shelf alongside unmatched wonders like *The Heart is a Lonely Hunter* and *Housekeeping*. *Third Class Relics* is tragically lovely, brutally true, miraculously devastating."

—NEIL CONNELLY, author of *In the Wake of Our Vows*

"A portrait of brothers and sisters who turn against one of their own, *Third Class Relics* is a poignant novel whose characters traverse the full spectrum of emotions from fury to grief and at last to burgeoning joy."

—KAYE PARK HINCKLEY, author of *Birds of a Feather*

THIRD
CLASS
RELICS

for Silas

CONTENTS

THIRD CLASS RELICS

(a novel)

I.

MY COUSINS AND I spent our childhoods in an unincorporated area just north of Two Rivers, Wisconsin. Our houses backed up to state-owned land, a swath of dense forest through which the Ice Age Trail wandered until it spent itself in the sands of Point Beach. As a child I had no idea that this trail was the product of thousands of years of continental glaciation, but in another time, massive formations shape-shifted and grappled with one another as if vying for the attention of God. In their vengefulness and confusion, mountains subdued their brothers and rivers submerged their sisters. Long stretches of silence would follow these calamities, the air cold and still, until in their guilt and shame the same stones would stir again, spurring a fresh war as though one loss could redeem the other. These battles bruised the earth, opening deep moraines and raising drumlins and eskers all across the state until at last, perhaps through sheer force of will, the land came to an accord like a pair of clasped hands to form a passage through the wilderness.

A two-mile hike along this healed scar led us from our backyard into a marshy low-lying forest fragrant with cedar, then through a red pine grove where the boles were spaced cleanly apart and seemed to replicate into infinity. Beyond the grove, where the needle-beds at our feet gave way to sand, a faded boardwalk traversed chains of dune ridges that left further evidence of all that ancient violence. Swales between the ridges would sometimes flood to form shallow pools that nourished fragments of maritime forest—balsam poplar, quaking aspen, yellow birch. Marram grass waved along the foredunes and sand reed swayed in the slacks. Slowly the dune ladder descended, its rungs carpeted in juniper and bearberry, searocket and sand cherry, low hardy plants that stitched the hillocks together and colored in the sands with emerald and crimson and white. Down at the waterline the level beach was scourged clean by wind and snow. On halcyon days when the spindrift was light as lace, the Lake could seem almost ingenuous, but in truth its shoaled depths were a graveyard for wrecked vessels dating back over a hundred years. Each morning driftwood gathered where the chevron pattern of wave met land, and in its silvery whiteness was like the bones of men who had journeyed through terrors and been stripped bare of all triviality.

The business of the real world was remote, even surreal to us. We had few neighbors, and beyond those cabins there was little save an expired lighthouse abutting a ranger's station and a shuttered Slavic monastery that had kept silent vigil over the Lake for decades. On foot, it was a two-mile trek into Two Rivers along the back roads. Our parents claimed to love the freedom of such isolated living, this approximation to what they'd known back in the communes, but they were impatient with rural Wisconsin's sleepy towns, its poky farmers and quaint cafes. Even in middle age they were like cut flowers, living off the scent of their formerly vibrant lives.

My Madison-born grandfather was a writer who abandoned his family in his thirties to pursue his calling. My father, Jude, and his sister Lissa were left with their mother to fend for themselves, until Lissa fled to a commune in California. There she met Lonnie and his sister, Taryn, who were also on the run from Wisconsin. Meanwhile my father escaped to an apartment in Chicago with several other would-be writers who pooled their money in a paroxysm of faith in their own latent genius. In the end it was need that landed them back to Two Rivers where Lonnie and Taryn's childhood home awaited its heirs: their favorite communes had broken apart, my father's cohort couldn't make rent, and without employment references, nobody knew where to start. Taryn and Jude eventually settled into the Cape Cod next door, a foreclosure purchased for pennies.

The four of them considered themselves artists, and their property served as a barricade against the prosaic demands of the ordinary world. My father was an aspiring author who buried himself in a tiny study where plywood shelves groaned beneath the battery of books my grandfather had bequeathed him decades earlier. "Once he made his big break, he didn't need anything that had been written before," my father explained, and it seemed that he too strived for some sphere in which the old voices would become immaterial. He worked in local real estate, selling cabins and old vacation homes to retirees and moony tourists, though by his own admission he spent most of that time daydreaming about his imminent breakthrough. My aunt and mother were painters who shared a studio in my cousins' attic the way two pigeons might share a rafter: you didn't want to go up there for fear of being splattered with something. Both knew yoga and massage therapy but cited our steady government aid as reason enough not to turn those skills into dependable employment. My uncle played bar gigs in Milwaukee and otherwise worked resentfully at a Garden Center in Manitowoc. Sometimes, in the middle of pacing the yard or smoking his dope, he'd go saucer-eyed and say, "The lyrics just came to me," and then he'd bolt to the den where he kept his instruments, as though the words and the melody were in danger of missing each other at a train station.

My father was responsible for naming four of us, Aunt Lissa three. I suppose we were lucky in this (Lonnie would have named everyone after different species of marijuana, and my mother was fond of dreamy nature-monikers like Meadow and Sequoia). My cousins were Frida (Kahlo), Andrei (from *War and Peace*), Marcus (a compromise between Chagall and the emperor Aurelius), Pablo (Picasso), and Jeffrey (after the singer Jeff Buckley, who ended up drowning three years after my cousin was born). Jeffrey was what my aunt called her surprise baby, arriving nearly eight years after Pablo. Technically, though, it was Marcus who'd been the surprise, because Frida and Andrei were adopted—that is to say, lifted off the hands of a friend of Lissa's who wanted to return to commune life baggage-free—back when my aunt and uncle thought they couldn't conceive. I came along about the same time as Marcus, my little brother Rafe (Raphael) in tandem with Pablo. As for my name, my father plucked *Abra* from a Steinbeck novel he later admitted he hadn't even finished reading. We never understood why they borrowed our names from artists, from authors or their characters. They owned books about those giants, but our parents' work seemed a deliberate effort to snub all that had preceded their own creative efforts. It was as though they'd named us against their own judgment.

As far back as I can remember, our property was a study in chaos. The backyards were jungles of uncut grass, and sometimes the weeds would grow so tall they'd sprout strange flowers and lilt forward like despairing souls walking into a hard wind. Raccoons and hedgehogs routinely snacked on our trash and loitered on our porches. Our furniture was always off-kilter, our plates and cups chipped and mismatched; anything our parents hadn't inherited had been purchased at the Christian Center Thrift in Two Rivers. We had a TV in each house but got no channels and could only watch movies on a VCR. Our parents claimed that once upon a time, they'd gathered woodland strawberries and blueberries, made tea out of sarsaparilla, even fished with bamboo poles and kept chickens for the fresh eggs, but they must have gotten lazy after we came into the picture. In place of wild harvesting, somebody would drive into town each week and come back with a big box of dry goods from the food pantry and a sack of frozen meals from the Dollar Mart. Our parents were allegedly opposed to eating meat, so we never ate fresh chicken or beef, but for some reason it didn't count if it was processed, so there were always plastic blister-cases of baloney and squat cans of Spam. If Uncle Lonnie or my mother made the trip to town, there'd be marijuana somewhere in the car, too, as well as incense sticks and musk oil from a tiny shop called Gaia's Truth they'd discovered on a backstreet of Manitowoc.

When we were small, our parents wandered into our rooms or followed us outdoors as if hoping our antics might stir the pot of their ingenuity when they were bored. This ceased as we approached puberty, from which point on they mostly ignored us. At first we told ourselves that they wanted us to make up our own games and find our own dinners because these things would nurture our creativity, but we quickly realized it had more to do with their conviction that we were talentless and thus completely in the way, not even useful as soundboards for their ideas. So in the state forest we built hideouts and dug holes and climbed trees. We explored little eyots on Molash Creek and fished with sticks baited with hot dog pieces. We prowled through our neighbors' trash and dared each other to steal small items from their porches or yards. There were only two such neighbors on our gravel road—Mrs. Hambly, a fifty-something widow who kept to herself save to bring over the occasional misde-livered mail (a favor we never returned, since we let our own mail pile up by the kitchen door until its contents became irrelevant or else a crisis), and a young Scotsman in the cabin on the other side of my cousins' house. When he first moved in, the Scotsman made a pact with my uncle in which neither would call the police no matter how loud the other's music became. He failed to tell my uncle that it was the bagpipes he played, but when those first notes seared the air a few days later, it was too late to renege on the deal. Those bagpipes became the soundtrack to our group hikes to Lake Michigan, the notes forever following us like drifting balloons.

Each day was provident only to itself. There was never talk of saving or preparing for anything, and there was just enough income in both houses to keep the utilities paid. If something broke or somebody picked up a cold or flu, both the leaking freezer and the sneezing child went unattended for weeks. Later, when the plumber's instructions were dis-regarded, the penicillin forgotten halfway through its recom-mended course, it was always the fault of the technician or doctor, never our own. "Jackass set up the air conditioner to break again," was something we heard often, or, "If you're still sick, he didn't diagnose you right . . . he just wanted his office fee." There were always emergencies. Pablo once fell through an iced-over pond in the woods and would have frozen his leg off had Andrei not dragged him out just in time. When she was ten, Frida climbed onto the roof to try her first cigarette, but a gust of wind swept the burning butt through an open window in my parents' house and set the carpet on fire. Andrei and little Rafe put out the fire with Kool-Aid while our parents went on smoking their pot or whatever they were doing on the front porch. When I was eight, I found an old kite in the street and scavenged some string out of the garage so I could fly it.

Marcus saw me from an upstairs window and came tearing out of the house, screaming at me to drop it, it was going near the power lines . . . I dropped the kite seconds before it hit a wire and exploded. Later, Marcus cut open the string to show me its metal core. "You would have died," he panted. We were always cheating death or injury this way, perpetually saved by accident or luck, the right person being there at the right time—though that person was never one of our parents.

Spouses and friends assume that it was in rebellion against our tumultuous upbringing that we took on the most stolid, practical professions imaginable. Frida makes custom window shutters out of old barnwood. Andrei is a furniture maker and carpenter, Pablo a plumber. Marcus is an auto mechanic, Rafe a home inspector. And I work as an optician, fitting glasses over people's eyes for a living. But people don't understand how long it's taken us to arrive at our stability. Most of us are relatively new to our professions. We're all in our late thirties or early forties now, two of us divorced. My cousins' sons and my niece are all toddlers, save for Pablo's firstborn, whose mother took off shortly after his birth.

Now, all four of our parents have passed: Lonnie of a heart attack, Lissa of lung cancer, my mother in a car wreck on a backcountry road. My father was the last to go, and tonight, the night after his wake, we've gathered in my cousins' old house which has been Andrei's for years. As of this week the old Cape Cod next door belongs to Rafe and me, but neither of us has spoken of it yet. Our handling of the funeral and wake was efficient, the talk strictly of paperwork and payments. If Rafe has wept, he's done it alone.

The dining room table is so pocked and scarred from the decades of our eating that it's tempting to search out words in the weathering. The same stained-glass hooded light that was there when we were children trembles when Pablo knocks into it, and I wonder if anyone else is sensitive to the faint aroma of stale musk oil competing with that of the vinegar and baking soda scrub Andrei always mixed as teenager to save us money on household cleansers. This battle of smells—the feral contending with the antiseptic—is age-old in both houses.

Frida, the only one who can cook, passes around bowls of spaghetti and salad while Marcus tinkers with a broken toaster. Rafe hunches over in his chair with Andrei's adopted cat, Balthazar, on his lap. A beat passes before Marcus starts a prayer dating back to high school: "Bless us oh Lord, for these our parents' gifts . . ."

". . . which we'll never receive," we continue in unison.

". . . and for thy bounty—"

" . . . which they cannot afford—"

" . . . for shit's sake, amen."

And then, God love them, they all begin to talk. It's the sort of loud, everyone-at-once conversation that's been our refuge for most of our adult lives, and tonight, they're performing it for my sake and Rafe's. Hilarious and haphazard to a stranger, in truth our talk is an art, comprised of elisions and evasions we've practiced to perfection like dedicated students of an inflected language. We've each had a spouse at some point in time sit agape at a table, helpless to keep up. It's why Pablo, Rafe, and Marcus suggested their wives head home with their children just after the service, why Frida's husband up in Green Bay offered to repaint the porch for her while she was in Two Rivers for the funeral and wake. I know they feel like strangers when the six of us are together in one room. We all got married late in life, and there wasn't much time for our spouses to adapt, much less understand.

Christmas Eve at Frida's six years ago, Andrei's then-wife yanked on her coat and said, "You all talk like kids on a merry-go-round. You ride the outside so hard, a person's got to wonder what's in the middle, the thing that sets you off but you won't ever touch." Andrei glanced at me, his face plaintive and open. Then he said to her, "Do you really want to know" "I don't," Merry responded. "I'd like to get home before the snow starts."

Nobody's eating much, but the bowls keep moving around the table. Marcus, lover of odd factoids, tells Frida that magenta is the only color without a frequency. "It's a fake color," he says. "An impostor. Can you think of anything more sinister?"

"If it's fake, how can it exist?" Rafe breaks in.

"Exactly."

"So who made it, then?" Pablo wants to know. "Who woke up and was like, 'I know; fake color.'"

"That I don't know, but I'll find out."

"And what was the motivation," he continues. "I mean what do you accomplish with a fake color?"

Marcus says, "Personal satisfaction knowing that fools everywhere are using and wearing your color."

"I was in a thrift shop last week," Frida says, "and I saw some of those old-school wooden tennis racquets, like from when we were kids. I mean can you believe people used to play with those? Wood's too hard."

"That's what she said," Pablo says.

"Tennis is for the rich," Rafe adds.

Marcus sets aside the toaster. "Can we go back to the no frequency thing? How do you prove a color doesn't have one?"

Ignoring him, Pablo starts telling us about an old movie called *Soylent Green* he saw on cable a month ago, a film he found both disturbing and hilarious. We discuss Charlton Heston, collectively appointing him the honor of Sexiest Man Who Ever Lived, and Andrei admits that if he swung the other way, he'd go for it. We all laugh. Rafe glances up and says, "Wait, wasn't he the one in *Ben-Hur?*", then stops short.

It's as if an alarm has pealed through the kitchen. Frida stands up and asks if anyone needs more of anything. Marcus coughs and asks for ice. Then the chatter resumes, charting its customary zig-zag course high above an undercurrent of fear.

Somehow the topic shifts to apocalyptic disasters. "How do you know when things are bad enough that it's time to bug out?" Marcus wonders, and Pablo responds with, "My metric is when canned ravioli is no longer available at the grocery stores."

"Okay," I say, "top three items you put in a backpack if the world's coming to an end, and you have to run for it."

Andrei says, "Anything?"

"No," I say hurriedly, "just food. Your top three food items."

"The perch sandwich at Waverly's, extra tartar sauce, twice," Rafe said. "Then a hot fudge parfait at Dairy Queen. If I'm in Two Rivers for some reason, that's what I always go for. I mean technically it's the birthplace of the ice cream sundae, right?"

I say, "I don't think you understand the game. That stuff's not going to *keep*. You're going to put perch sandwiches and ice cream sundaes in a backpack?"

"Canned ravioli," Pablo says. "Velveeta. Velveeta."

Frida pretends to hurl into her hands. "So you'd eat the Velveeta straight?"

"Of course. There's no other way to appreciate it for what it is. It's like toothpaste you can swallow."

"You're sick."

Ticking off fingers, Marcus says, "Cheetos. Slim Jims. Those little chocolate cupcakes with the white wiggly frosting on the top. See, they're good picks not just for taste. They're *survivors.* They're the cockroaches of the snack-food world. I ran one over with my car once and it instantly recovered."

Rafe says that his daughter wants a guinea pig for a pet and Pablo comments that guinea pigs would make for decent survival food in the event of a disaster. "You could grill them, broil them, or make guinea jerky," he suggests. My brother wraps his arms around Balthazar, making an expression of mock horror, and the cat wriggles out of his lap onto the floor and stalks off.

"Oh my God," Frida yelps. "Remember the hamster incident?"

A collective moan. Pablo and Rafe once stole a pet hamster from their first-grade classmate on Show-and-Tell day, smuggling it home in a lunchbag, and Marcus had adopted it. About a week later, the hamster suddenly keeled over as if from a heart attack, and Marcus made a racket that brought us all upstairs to his room where we found him doing chest compressions on the dead animal with his fingertips.

"The CPR," I say. "Oh, man."

Pablo shakes his head. "Fucking Marcus kneeling on the floor counting out *one, two, three, four* . . . "

"Even Andrei lost it," Rafe says. "I remember it. He was punching the wall by Marcus' door. I think he was crying, he was laughing so hard."

"Marcus was the crying one," Frida points out.

Marcus, denying nothing, shrugs and helps himself to more salad. "I still don't know what was wrong with him. I fed him and everything."

"It was the shock of realizing he was in the wrong house. The worst house possible."

The talk spools out, meandering to other topics. Andrei just listens, his calloused hands folded on the tabletop in front of his plate. I tune out for a while the way one might take a nap on a train or bus. When I come back, they're talking about saints and reliquaries.

"Every legit Catholic church has a piece of a saint lodged in its altar somewhere," Frida says. "You guys did know that, right? Like a bone or a piece of hair. Those are called first-class relics and apparently you have to have one if you want your church to be the real thing. So there's quite a market for them. If you knew a saint, you could make an eBay storefront." She snorts.

"First class? Like on a plane? Is there a second class?" Rafe wants to know, sitting up. He's smiling too brightly; I know he's been struggling to keep it together all week.

"Oh, yeah. Second-class relics are things the saint used all the time, like a Bible or a rosary, most likely to, you know, communicate with God. And third-class relics are objects that *touched* the second-class relics."

"What?" Marcus chokes on a mouthful of salad. "*What,* now?"

"So, let's say a saint touches his rosary to a roll of toilet paper," Pablo says. "Now there are a shit-ton of third-class relics just in that one roll. I mean every square counts, right?"

Everyone bursts into thunderous laughter, even Andrei. But as the laughter peters out, he leans back in his chair and says quietly, "We've got a whole room full of third-class relics here, don't we."

No one else seems to hear him. Some other nonsensical topic has already come flying out of the ether. But against my will I meet his gaze, and reflected in the forest-pool hazel of his eyes is the image of my father a few nights ago at the awards banquet, where he was to receive an honor from the Milwaukee Arts Council for the novel that had eluded him most of his life. By his own admission, this book was not *edgy* or *irreverent* as he used to describe his work. Nor was it, as one editor had pronounced a much earlier attempt, *a mess of abstractions, an unmitigated study in arrogance.* We were all there at the venue, dressed in the nicest clothes we owned, making an effort. As the emcee stepped up to the microphone, Marcus leaned in and whispered, *good thing the rest of our parents are gone, or they'd kill him for this.* My white-haired father sat across from me at our linen-draped table, humbly content in a way I had never seen him. His head tilted in response to the emcee's voice. Then a startled look passed over his face, quick as a bird's shadow, and he slumped to the floor. Panic erupted and someone called out, "Call 911!" A terrifying silence stifled the banquet hall. In the space of that silence, my father's stricken mind cast into the waters of memory for the one name that mattered, then reeled it into the open. When he cried out the name, the timbre of his voice was awry like a deaf man's, but my cousins and I knew. We've always known, but we have refused to speak that name in front of one another for twenty years. When my father's cry faded out, none of us could bear to lock eyes, not even Andrei and I . . .

"Who is that?" Marcus is asking. It's the same question people asked at the banquet. *Who* is *that?* But Marcus is only peering over Rafe's shoulder at Rafe's phone.

"Just Mandy," Rafe says. "She wants me home early." His relief is palpable. Like the rest of us, he's never understood how Andrei could live in this house after our aunt and uncle died, and he's in no hurry to walk through our parents' home even to claim what's rightfully his.

Reading my mind, he glances at me. "I know I should stay and—go over there with you. But I think Mandy's afraid I'll get all emotional and decide I want to move us into the Cape Cod or something."

"Is she, really?" Frida asks, frowning. What she means is, *then she still doesn't know you at all, does she?*

Rafe ignores the question. "I told her you'd probably sell the house, Abra, since you're the executor, but then she was worried we wouldn't get as much money for it if you did all the work."

"That's ridiculous. You'll get your half no matter what. Even if I moved in,"—and a flicker of surprised alarm circles the table—"even if I did that, I'd pay you your half of the house's worth. Honey."

"I wouldn't let you. I wouldn't want—" He stands up, shoving the phone into his pants pocket. "I better go, guys. Thanks for, you know. Thanks for cooking, Frida."

"Of course. You know where to find us if you need us."

"Yeah."

As he passes my chair, I reach for his hand and hold it awkwardly against my forehead. "Love you kiddo."

"Don't be a drip." We're still learning these gestures of open affection, and his discomfort is no less acute than mine. He pauses. "Me too." And he's out the front door, leaving a rush of cold air in his wake.

The silly banter resumes. Even as they laugh and chatter, I can feel them watching me, protecting me as they protect themselves. Somebody keeps my wine glass full, somebody else picks up my napkin when it falls to the floor. We finish dinner and then dessert.

When at last we clear up, Pablo knocks over a plastic decanter with his elbow and starts a small waterfall off the side of the table. "Good thing it's not glass," he says as Frida hands him a roll of paper towels.

"Glass is stupid," I say. "Planned obsolescence."

"Planned break-o-lescence," Frida nods.

"Amen to that. We use all plastic at home."

"Better get moving, everyone," Marcus calls, peering out the living room windows. "There's a storm rolling in."

"How can you tell? It's pitch dark out there."

"My elbows are acting up. And I can smell it through the windows. Trust me, major skyarrhea is coming."

Andrei finds Balthazar and carries him off to his donut bed. Marcus comes back to the kitchen to help Frida spoon leftovers into plastic containers, complaining all the while about Andrei's mismatched Tupperware. "It's a travesty," he insists, shuffling through the cabinets. "None of these lids go with the bowls. How can anyone live like this?"

"Buy him a new set for Christmas, then, if it's so traumatizing."

"It is traumatizing. I can't *think* of anything more traumatizing."

My cousins go home, Frida an hour north to Green Bay, Pablo and Marcus forty minutes south to Sheboygan to their wives and little boys. Everyone has to be up at six for work. My apartment in Chicago is waiting for me at the end of a three-hour drive, but so is the old house next door. I dally as long as possible, volunteering to help Andrei with the mountain of dishes even though I'm as uneasy inside these walls as the rest of them.

As teenagers we must have stood together like this a thousand times, side-by-side at the kitchen sink washing dishes for a horde of people. If we'd not done it, our siblings and parents would have eaten their meals off food-crusted plates and sipped their instant coffee from mugs veiled over with old grape soda. We don't speak, our hands moving in the familiar synchrony as we squint into the indigo darkness beyond the kitchen window. We're still sequestered as ever out here, the old tract of forest obstinate in its constancy, and it's too easy to imagine the seven of us hiking down the path, calling out to one another as we trek to the Lake. Frida, then Andrei and me, followed by Marcus, Pablo, Rafe, and then—

My unconscious supplies the seventh name, the wrong name. God, even now . . .

"Jeffrey," Andrei says softly, correcting what I have not said.

Turning from him a little, I slap a clean bowl onto the drying board and say to the backsplash, "How do you go on doing it? Living in these rooms. Working wood. Walking the beach . . . I still don't understand."

"You know how. I do it the same way he kept that caterpillar box next to his bed."

"I still say it's beyond me." My voice breaks. "It's superhuman, Andrei."

He shakes his head and we resume scrubbing, our hands brushing beneath the soapy water.

Andrei says, "You should have taken off your watch."

"It's waterproof. So, I was thinking I'd give Goodwill a call in the morning. Or the Christian Center. They'd take most of the furniture and whatever else is still there. Wouldn't they?"

"I'll come over and help you. It's a lot of work, deciding what to keep and what to let go. I've been there."

I withdraw my hands from the sink and turn away, reaching for a towel.

He says, "Or if you're not up to it, you could stay here a while."

Drying my hands becomes a protracted, complex activity, a stalling tactic. I'm thinking of what happened the last time we were alone together in this house. Finally I say, "No. I need to get over there and I need to do it alone."

"Are you going to sleep there tonight, then?"

"I think I have to. I have to do this now, in the next few days, or I might not do it at all. I told my boss I was going to use up the rest of my vacation time for this." It embarrasses me to add, "That was the only way I knew I'd hold myself to it."

"I get it." He hesitates. "If you change your mind, if you want help, I'm right here. Rap on my door in the middle of the night if you need to."

I try not to hear the need in his voice. I say, "Okay."

I pull on my jacket and let myself out the back door onto the old path between the houses. It's late October, the eddying winds off the Lake crisp and bearing the scent of copper. In the box of light cast by Andrei's windows, leaves spin themselves into small cyclones like spirits struggling to reclaim corporeal form, and two owls call out to each other from somewhere in the trees, insistent questions met with patient answers. With an unsteady hand I key my way into the Cape Cod.

The grandfather clock in the living room, which tolled reliably when we were children thanks to Marcus' many attentions to it, should be chiming for ten at night but is stalled on 5:15. I hear the ghost of the old notes anyway, and they follow me up the narrow staircase to the bedrooms. Here is my parents' on the left, and mine and then Rafe's, much smaller, tucked into alcoves on the right. I go into my parents' room first and sprawl face down on the floor.

As in Andrei's kitchen, the carpet's scent is complex yet familiar. Who on the outside would appreciate its manifold elements? There are top notes, those of the world we all fought to create after death shook apart illusion, but below this, the dark and musky aroma of the life we inhabited before we learned. Andrei told me years ago that there was no going forward without both, that it would do no good to pretend away the latter, but I have resisted—we all have—even as we've reformed ourselves from the outside. And so we could not meet one another's eyes at the banquet when my father cried out that name we loved above all others.

I turn over and face the ceiling. With the curtains drawn, the darkness here is dense and damp, and all I want is to sleep. I let out a long, defeated exhalation. How can I get up, turn on the lights, move through these rooms? How can I relive it all as Andrei has? I am certain that I cannot. But our wizened neighbor, the Scotsman who's never left his cabin all these years even when his children tried to coerce him into a nursing home, takes a huge breath just after I release mine, and presses his lips to the chanter. The bagpipes' cry spears the night air, two courageous notes, and all I hear inside them is—*Rupert.*

II.

THE YEAR AUNT LISSA WAS PREGNANT with Jeffrey, we played Jeff Buckley's cover of "Hallelujah" hundreds upon hundreds of times in both houses. Nobody understood the lyrics, but it didn't matter. We listened to the song on CD boomboxes and on a chipped Discman Frida had stolen from God knew where, and we hummed snatches of it as we wandered the woods on weekend afternoons. Together we were wildly out of tune, but I preferred this to singing alone, because I could always pretend it was somebody else's fault that the song came out all mangled.

Frida was nearly twelve, a beauty with burnished brown hair, olive skin, and catlike green eyes. She spurned all things artistic and seemed determined to defy our mothers' conception of beauty, keeping her hair short, wearing bras before she needed them, and concocting makeup out of whatever materials she could find. I recall that she got on the bus for her first day at the junior high wearing a perfume she'd made by mashing up crabapples and rainwater in a peanut butter jar. Lissa called her "my little klepto," because whatever irresistible fad was going around at school—sparkly pencils, cheesewedge erasers, jelly shoes—Frida waited for her moment and pounced, taking what she liked. Everyone in her class despised her for it, but she didn't care. She would come home smug and mirthful, as if she'd beaten them at their own game, then add the coveted object to the pile of booty in her dresser drawer.

At ten, Andrei was the family caretaker. He had Frida's coloring but his face was a counterpoint to hers, open and waiting where hers was closed and cagey. He was the one to load the washing machine and scrub the dishes and shovel snow off the driveway, though I have no memory of anyone asking him to do these things. Thanks to books or else to his natural resourcefulness, he had a thousand tricks for saving both households money. He attached draft stoppers to our doors and taped plastic wrap over the windows to hold in heat during winter, rolled toothpaste tubes around pens to squeeze out every last drop, put rock-filled soda bottles in the toilet tanks so that we flushed less water. He did what he could to help the rest of us fit in at school, though we were forever pariahs there, friendless because we were grubby and because our lives were nothing like the others', those children of farmers and nurses and foundry workers. Most of our clothes came from the back room of a used bookshop where a Christian couple invited Andrei to fill a plastic bag with gently-worn clothing for two dollars. "They're good people," he told us, as if we cared. "The clothes are even cheaper than the books." He shopped there for all of us, stuffing sweaters and pants and jackets into grocery bags and hauling them home on his back like Santa Claus.

Sometimes I wanted to slap him for his dutifulness, that incorrigible urge he had to bring order out of our chaos. But Andrei had a secret—a sturdy blue duffel bag he kept stashed under his bed, packed for a midnight flight. It was crammed with clothes, granola bars, a flashlight, a tarp, some money in a plastic sandwich bag, and a myriad of other supplies he'd scrounged. I found it by accident when I was eight or so, and every so often I'd sneak into his room and check the bag's contents to find that he'd updated the clothes to larger sizes or switched out the snacks to ones with a later expiration date. This continued into his late teens. I never told him that I knew, but sometimes I dreamed of him standing at the end of the driveway with the duffel in hand, about to take that first step onto the road and away from us. The look on his face would be one of pure torment. Then I'd wake up and hear him outside raking leaves or up on the roof pulling birds' nests out of the gutters.

When he wasn't struggling to put one house or the other in order, he was always on the hunt, combing the beach for wreckage after a thunderstorm or prowling through my father's old books. Up in his room he'd whittle the bits of driftwood he salvaged from Point Beach into owls or turtles, his hands working of their own accord while he read some smuggled novel or anthology of poems held open with one of Marcus' spring clamps. If we spent the night in one of the living rooms, he'd recount stories of Narnia or Tolkien's Middle Earth, throwing cushions at me if I started to drift off. "This is important," he'd say, or, "Come back on board, Abra," as though we were about to be transported off-planet. I'd hoist myself on an elbow, redoubling my effort to absorb whatever it was he'd found so inciting. I was his only partner in these adventures, after all; Frida decried all fiction as babyish, a waste of time, and Marcus habitually dismissed anything that lacked practical import. Andrei's dream was to become a poet, but he was a slow reader, mildly dyslexic, and my father had told him years earlier that he would never be a writer. "Know your limits, kiddo," he told him. "Don't try to fit a square peg into a round hole. That's just a sad thing to watch someone do."

Marcus and I were nine. He loved cars and all things mechanical. This was his singular joy; he otherwise wore an impermeable air of dejection for which even his classmates teased him ("How's Eeyore today?" they'd ask as they passed his locker). He tended to our clocks, toasters, and VCR's, brusquely waving us off if we distracted him from his project. Neither house had ever had air conditioning, and when Andrei approached Marcus with a vague design for a unit we could make ourselves, Marcus shot first to the local dump and then to the Scotsman for parts. A few days later we had two handmade units pumping away (one in the upstairs of each house), consisting of frozen water in a big bucket topped with a scavenged fan. Later that year, he dug a 1970's minibike out of our parents' garage and asked Uncle Lonnie if he could tinker with it. Lonnie, a little stoned, waved his hand to indicate he didn't care either way, and Marcus set to work that same night. After some finagling he replaced the minibike's lawn-mower engine and disabled the governor so he could race it as fast as he liked. To make it snow-worthy he removed the front wheel and attached a wide strip of welded metal, like a ski, that he'd scavenged out of a junkyard. Until Pablo stole it and crashed it into a fence, it was Marcus' pride and joy; he'd zoom all over the snowbanks, his gangly awkwardness momentarily vanishing as he flew.

He kept a pair of plastic safety glasses under his pillow, and on the nights I slept on his floor, I'd watch him read auto manuals from behind those glasses, his flashlight trained on nebulous illustrations of mechanical innards. I don't know why he did his studying at night, since our parents had no objection to the trades even if they were disgusted by the idea of regular employment. Once they'd divined our lack of talent, the implicit understanding was that this was precisely the sort of track on which we all belonged.

In my own secret reading I delved mostly into books about famous painters, the glossy pages bright with reprints of their work. I admired fiction when it was pretty, and I liked the escape it proffered me, but writing was no temptation. It seemed unglamorous in contrast with the easy vibrance of our mothers' work up in the attic. You could cover gallery walls with your paint and have a crowd of people mill around them, but words were trapped dully on paper, meant for the eyes of just one at a time. And while my father made a show of cursing and toiling away in his study, my mother and aunt flung paint onto canvas as breezily as they might have tossed a pizza.

Vincent Van Gogh above all others suffused my childhood dreams with sun-yellow and cobalt blue. I once stayed up all night pencil-tracing a still life of his onto thin paper, and as I worked on that tracing, I projected myself into a future so romantic that even Andrei's poems and fairytales paled in comparison. The truth was that I shared our parents' disgust for the nine-to-five. Whenever I imagined such a life, I saw only closed doors, heard a voice saying with drab finality, "you are just this now; you can no longer be *anything*." But when my mother saw what I'd done, she told me that a real artist never traced, that she was purely original from the start. She patted my shoulder and said I'd do better with a job in math or computers.

Later, I heard Aunt Lissa deliver a similar condemnation to Pablo, whom she'd caught paging through an old text on Picasso.

"But you *named* me for him," he said, falling into the same trap each of us had at one point or another—the hope that seeded in our names was the promise of singularity, like a violet crystal trapped in a geode.

"Oh, honey," Lissa said, snapping the book closed. "You know that man Henri who comes to fix our toilet when it breaks? How his name is stitched on his shirt? Henri Matisse was an artist, but that doesn't make Henri the toilet-man a painter."

My brother had a similar moment, with Lonnie. When he was six, he climbed onto the piano bench and began pressing keys. The notes were timid and random, creating no song to speak of, but Rafe's face went slack as though someone were massaging his back. He practically purred with pleasure. Then Lonnie stepped in and said, "Kid, even with lessons, it's never gonna happen. You either got it, or you don't."

It was only natural that at seven years old Rafe and Pablo rolled up pretend cigarettes out of dead leaves and tried to act like streetwise thugs. If another boy had something they wanted, they didn't steal it, like Frida would have; they destroyed it. In their wake they left dismembered toys and shattered Lego houses and smashed apple hand-pies crafted by doting mothers who were nothing like our own. They took special pride in finding ways to damage humbly useful items like light bulbs and mailboxes and pencils, as if they were offended by anything with a whiff of industriousness to it.

And yet, when no one was looking, they fed baby raccoons and petted the furry backs of bees, left out cheese for the mice in our walls. The urge to spoil any valued object was native to them, but their fingers never effaced butterflies' wings and their shoes never quashed the slender grace of grasshoppers, however much pleasure their peers took in these small cruelties. But their teachers didn't know that. "Little savages," one of them remarked once within my earshot, and fairly enough. We were all train wrecks in the classroom, intractable and unfocused. It was the system's fault for not appreciating us. We'd learned this easy answer from our parents, who commanded us to "follow our feelings" and who scorned the schools, the government, any institution they saw as critical of their ventures. Like them, we took pride in our indifference to anything that impressed anyone else. If ever we did love or admire something, it was safer to encase it irony—even when we were alone.

So how was it that *Hallelujah* had captured our collective imagination and held it? How were we able to hum it together without fear of mockery? Why is it that from the chaos of my childhood memories, those opening eight notes as I first heard them emerge so luminously that I cannot detach them from an image of tall white candles in a line, one tiny flame leaping up after the other?

We played it practically every night those last two months before Jeffrey was born. One Saturday when we were all sprawled on the living room floor, listening, Aunt Lissa's patience snapped. "I'll throw myself in the lake if I hear it one more time," she cried, punching the STOP button on our boombox. "From now on, it's on the Discman or never, you got me? It's *disruptive*."

"Such a teacherly word," Andrei muttered, then, "As if it's *ever* quiet around here."

"There's only one Discman," Frida said.

For good measure, Lissa yanked the boombox cord out of the wall socket. "When Jeffrey gets here, you people might have to try to be quiet for once in your lives."

There was a stunned silence. Lissa started toward the kitchen, then turned back, puzzled. "What's the matter? You all look like you've seen a ghost."

"*Jeffrey*?" Pablo echoed, letting his fake cigarette fall out of his mouth.

"Yes. Jeffrey. This one." Lissa pointed to her swollen belly. "Barely two months to go here if you haven't noticed. You can't be blaring music twenty-four-seven if you don't want to hear a baby screaming all night."

"Is he named for—for *him*?" I asked, fighting to control my voice. "For Jeff Buckley?"

"Yep."

After Lissa had left, we all sat there motionless. Andrei said tightly, "So she hates the song, but she's naming the baby after it."

"*That's* nice," Rafe muttered. "*That* makes sense."

"It's ours," I thought I heard Marcus say from where he lay face down on the couch.

Frida grabbed the television remote and punched the power button. Nothing happened. "What the fuck. Why isn't this working?"

Marcus reached into the cushions and tossed a second remote at her. "Use this one."

Frida keyed up her movie and pumped the volume. Nobody said much the rest of the night.

Sunday morning, the whole lot of us hiked down the beach. It was rare that all six of us went anywhere together, but there was a restlessness in both houses, a feeling that no one had slept. We'd all been awake for a two A.M. thunderstorm, and when Andrei said he wanted to sift around in the washed-up rubble, everyone went in search of shoes. We found them neatly lined up in the garage where Andrei had treated them with a can of waterproofing spray he'd purchased for ten cents at one of his resale haunts.

When we left the house, my mother was barefoot in the side yard performing yoga in one of her skimpy outfits while the Scotsman licked his lips from behind his window. Marcus, who always mocked yoga, mumbled, "She's doing the Flying Toaster again. Or else the Horny Mailbox." Lonnie was relaxing in a wicker chair on the back porch with a bottle of vodka in one hand and a fat candy bar in the other. He took a sleepy bite of chocolate, losing some of it in his beard, then roused himself when we passed. He said to Andrei, "You mowing later? I almost stepped on another snake yesterday."

Andrei had been borrowing the Scotsman's push-mower on the weekends in an effort to clean up the yards. Testily he said, "Yeah, I am, but it takes hours with that thing. It's not really the highlight of my day."

"You're young. It's not gonna break your back."

"Would it be so hard to get a real mower?"

"That ass at Discount Hardware won't sell to us," Lonnie said, flicking his wrist in the direction of Two Rivers. "One bad check and he holds a grudge forever."

"Yeah, he's selfish as hell," Andrei responded, but Lonnie was already drifting back to sleep.

"We going or what?" Pablo called from the tree line.

Andrei nodded, adjusting the big canvas knapsack he always carried down to the water on his wood-scavenging trips. Lonnie was right—a push-mower wasn't going to break his back. Even at ten years old he was broad-shouldered with slender but ropy arms, a born athlete. More than once I'd spotted him standing at the fence around the school baseball field, watching the other boys, but Andrei never played.

"You think Lonnie really stepped on a snake?" I said as we crossed the backyard.

"I've stepped on whole nests of them where the grass is really high. I had to mass-murder them with a shovel. That's why I asked Bagpipes for the mower."

Rafe was interested. "You get bit?"

"Yeah, but I had pants on. It didn't draw blood or anything."

"Cool."

"Not cool. Rafe, if you ever get bit, don't be an idiot. Come find me so I can fix it up."

Rafe shrugged and drifted back to Pablo's side.

Marking our entrance to the woods was an old green sled (originally stolen) that was currently a weed-garden and come winter would be an iced pond. It was always so heavy with the wilderness and weather that had settled into its plastic depths that even Andrei had given up trying to move it. "We should try putting a fish in there in like November,"

Pablo suggested. "Then it will freeze and we can look at it all the time through the ice." Nobody responded as we entered the trees in a big clump.

As the trail narrowed, we were forced to hike single file. The forest between our houses and the water had a pattern: tightly clustered young trees on our side of Molash Creek deferring to cedar, tamarack, and spruce as the forest turned wet, followed by the vast red pine grove. The conifers became massive where the trail turned sharply waterward. A line of these giants stood guard at the sand's edge, and beyond that, only a few of their kind dotted the dunes like rogue wanderers from some forgotten age, or else like fiercely devoted shepherds, sentinels of the younger trees whose aspen souls were newer to those shores. Andrei once had a nightmare that the guardian conifers walked inland, abandoning the beach, and that the coast then fell into the sea.

As we hiked, my cousins kept taking turns humming little snatches of "Hallelujah," only to stop suddenly as though someone had clamped a hand over their lips. The third time this happened, Andrei came to my side and said softly, "Funny how nobody can sing it all the way through now."

Molash Creek was thick with skunk cabbage, palpitating with the frantic business of water bugs and the blue music of dragonflies. The previous night's rain was steaming back up in the burgeoning heat of the morning, and the air smelled of leaves and mold and worms as we picked our way past greasy boulders shaggy with moss. I stayed quiet. When Andrei had a certain look in his eye, it was best not to encourage him. Sometimes I got lucky and he either lost his train of thought or decided not to pursue it after all.

But he continued, "She had it right for once. Disruptive was a good word."

I kept my voice down: "What do you mean?"

"I was thinking about it all night. About the song. I think there're different kinds of disruption. Like there's the kind that's just annoying pointless noise, like a vacuum cleaner or something, and there's this other kind that sort of shakes you up and makes you feel things."

"Andrei, what are you talking about."

He let out a little puff of air. "I don't know. It's like the second type is the good kind. You hear it and you want to go *through* it. Whenever we play it I start thinking about all these scenes in *Lord of the Rings,* like Sam going through Shelob's tunnel, or when Aragorn has to take the Dimholt road . . ."

We moved into a patch of deep shade beneath a clump of red and silver maples whose exposed roots cradled shallow pools of rainwater. A startled blue heron flew in a low, straight line past us back to the creek, and in the wake of its flight, Rafe hummed *Hallelujah's* refrain. The old feeling unfurled again within the basket of my ribs. When my brother stopped humming, it hit me that Lissa was really naming the new baby after the song's maker.

"It's not fair," I blurted out.

Andrei nodded bleakly. "I know."

"It's crap," Pablo said from behind us.

"What is," Marcus said, then, "Oh." We were collectively scandalized, too aghast to speak of it, but the question must have been on everyone's lips: why should this stranger lay claim to what was ours to hoard?

Frida, who was in the lead, was using a stick to thrash random trees as she walked. Suddenly she turned and sniped over her shoulder, "You shrank my favorite shirt in the wash, Andrei. Are you brain-dead? That's the second time now."

"I couldn't have, I always wash on cold. It's cheaper. But you could do your own laundry sometime, Your Grace."

Frida smacked a birch with her stick and said, "I'm not washing clothes. I'm nobody's maid."

No one pointed out the illogic of her remark. I figured some new torment had found her at school, where she was teased mercilessly. They called her a hippie-tramp and put garbage in her locker, once even stuffed a dead bird into her desk. We all knew our turns were coming.

As if reading my mind, Frida said, "It's been a shit week, okay?"

Marcus said, "Was it another dead bird?"

"Maybe they'd leave you alone if you'd quit stealing things," Andrei muttered.

Frida folded her arms but slowed her walk. "Everyone at school knows about Andrei and me. That we're adopted."

Rafe said, "How do they know?", his voice overlapping with Pablo's: "What do they care?"

She flashed us a bitter smile. "From me. I started signing my homework with 'Two for One.' And Miss Malone wanted to know what it meant, so I told her. I said, I was a two-for-one. My mother wanted to give up Andrei right after he was born, and I was almost two years old, and she realized she could get rid of us both at the same time so she could go back to her hippie-camp without any, you know, *inconvenience*. So she added me in. Like a two-for-one deal at McDonald's."

There was a pause.

"I didn't even have a name," Frida continued. "She—my mother—was calling me *Girl*. So that was convenient, too." With strained casualness she adjusted a tangle of rubber bracelets on her wrist, a pink and gold set she'd swiped from somebody.

Andrei got in front of her, forcing her to stop walking. "How do you know all this?" he demanded, standing there sweating under the pines with the neck of his knapsack strangled in his fist.

"Mom told me. And, oh yeah, it's freaking obvious?"

"What else did she say?"

Frida looked blankly at him. So did we. "What else did she say about what?"

"Did she say anything about our father?"

"Father," Frida repeated, as though he'd spoken of unicorns or aliens. "Yeah, okay." She moved around him, and we resumed our hike.

At the beach, Andrei delivered his requisite lecture: "Don't freaking step on the dune plants. They're holding the dunes together, and this is the only place in the world some of them exist, and you'll kill them with your stupid feet." Then we left the boardwalk path and wandered our separate ways. Everything looked wind-bruised and wan in the wake of the previous night's storm. The low-lying shrubs and grasses were bent westward from the force of the winds and the flood-pools were clogged with twigs that turned in endless slow circles like broken compass needles. At the waterline, Andrei began dismantling a thicket of driftwood and other debris, attacking the chaos with ferocity. I watched this for a while from my post on the spine of the last dune, in the scanty shade of an aspen whose leaves clattered in the breeze. He didn't let up, didn't speak, for several minutes. Nothing in the pile seemed to please him. He was humming broken bits of *Hallelujah* the whole time, his soft muted tenor incongruous with his gritted teeth.

A solitary dead alewife lay at the base of the driftwood pile, glinting silver in the sun, and Andrei somehow managed never to step on it. His conscientiousness irritated me. Finally I said, "You looking for something in particular, Andrei?"

He loosened a grimy old net from the pile and flung it aside as if it disgusted him. "Yes. Even though I know that's not how it works. You never find anything good when you go in with an idea already of what it should be. But I can't help it."

I slid down the dune and studied the driftwood heap. "What about this?" I fished out a long, twisted piece like a wizard's staff. Wind and water had tempered its skin to blue-grey and some creature had tunneled through it, leaving thousands of tiny worm holes in its wake.

"Hm. Let me see." He took it and turned it beneath the burgeoning light. "Actually . . ."

"Actually, you love it," I said.

His eyes softened. "It does look kind of Tolkien-ish."

I knelt in the sand and dipped my fingers into the water. I was wearing a mood ring I'd stolen from my mother and I wanted to see the color shift. When the turquoise blue behind the nub of glass faded to a sickly brown, I said, "I think this ring is defective. They're not supposed to turn this color, are they?"

Andrei talked over me: "Something kind of sad happened the other day." He was still appraising the wizard's staff, but I knew that tone.

"I don't want to hear about it," I said.

"It's about *your* brother." He knelt beside me and ran the staff through the water, cleaning it. "When I was folding the laundry, I found this thing in one of his pants pockets." From his pocket he removed a little wooden keychain, a two-dimensional house with the windows and doors drawn on with colored marker. "We all made them—remember? It's one of those things everybody does in preschool."

"Yeah, so?"

"Well, he was carrying it around. I thought that was weird, so I just asked him. He acted like he didn't recognize it.

I said, is it okay if I keep it then? And he said fine, why would he want it? The windows were drawn on so bad it looked like a monkey did it. That's what he said."

"And—?"

"If you'd just let me finish." He tugged off his sweater and started drying the staff with it. "I started walking off, and he grabbed me, and he said, 'Take care of it, though, it's sad.' And he looked like he was going to start bawling. And then he ran off somewhere with Pablo. And I couldn't leave it alone, because it was so familiar, and then I remembered. He tried to give this to your mom on her birthday the year he was in preschool. I remember his face, like he thought it was a work of art. And she just laughed."

I glanced backward. Rafe was taking a piss over a creeping juniper while Pablo made obscene gestures with a stick he was holding to his crotch. "He looks fine to me," I said dryly. "You obsess over the weirdest things, you know that?"

"Probably." He took the keychain back.

A throng of migrating Canada geese passed honking overhead, then vanished behind us. I said, "*This* is what you're thinking about right now?" What I really meant was that if Andrei were uneasy about anything, it should be Jeffrey— the interloper whose arrival was now just a month away.

"No," he said as he maneuvered the Tolkien stick into his backpack. "It's not all I'm thinking about right now. I'm not sleeping so great."

"I know." Through a chink in his doorway I'd seen him re-packing that duffel of his just a few nights earlier, at two in the morning when I got up for a glass of water. This new baby would not be a little brother for him, but just another, bigger responsibility than the dishes or the yard. Already Andrei looked pale and flagged, like a young father who'd been up all night with a crying child. He wiped sandy water across his forehead as if to cool it, then started back up the first dune with his pack slung over his shoulder.

"You don't have to take care of it, you know," I said, following him. "The baby. It's not your problem. Hell, technically it's not even your blood."

"Isn't it, though? That's what I've been trying to figure out."

"Your problem, or your blood?" When he didn't answer, I said, "It's only your problem if you make it that way."

But Andrei wasn't paying attention. He was rerouting a clunky little sand beetle who'd wandered onto his arm as they often did. "No, buddy," he said softly. "You can't come home with us. You'll die."

"You and beetles."

"How can you not love them. They're so dumb." He walked the creature over to a patch of beach pea and deposited it in the shade.

Just then Marcus drifted over to show us a huge rusty nail he'd found tangled in the marram grass. "From an old shipwreck, I bet," he said. "I might be able to use this for something."

"Hammer it into your dumbass brother's head," Frida called from where she sat tossing corn chips at a herring gull. "He's going to tell the priest he stole eagles' eggs. Lamest shit we ever thought of."

"Oh, crap," I said. "It's Sunday."

Andrei checked his wristwatch. It was a prize of his, a miracle resale find with a built-in illuminated compass and an air of military competence that beguiled him. He said, "Time for confession . . . our favorite."

We followed the sound of the Scotsman's bagpipes home, where Lissa waited beside the van with her hands on her hips.

As a household we had no religion of substance, though there was a time when everyone save my mother and uncle made a weekly pilgrimage to Catholic Mass. Aunt Lissa, who often carried little saints' medals in bizarre contrast with her crystal pendants, insisted upon it when we were kids, as she insisted on the mealtime prayer when she was in the mood. My uncle had no interest in "that guilt crap," missing the fact that none of us felt remotely guilty at any time. My mother flirted with a new religion every year, running the gamut from Hinduism to astrology, so it was a given that she would not attend. She was a believer in signs; she had a Magic 8 ball she consulted, and sometimes she'd point to a blue jay or an oddly-shaped cloud and tell us in her faraway voice what it meant for her, as though every anomaly in the sky had been placed there to highlight her own singularity. As for my father, he'd sit there expressionless during the homily, and later when Andrei and I did laundry, we'd find his Communion wafers curled up in his pockets like the husks of insects. In a rare confiding mood, he once told me that Mass had been the only constant in his and Lissa's chaotic upbringing, but Andrei had another explanation for Lissa's strange habit: adherence to the rituals of Mass meant she could bypass the more vigorous labors of self-review.

Of course, he didn't put it in precisely those words. But at ten years old Andrei was already asking questions. The rest of us easily wrote off the idea of God, because where had we ever glimpsed any proof of a larger purpose, be it religious or natural? Our world was one of entropy, of senseless mistakes on repeat. It was all as random as the palm-lines my mother sometimes read for us. If ever there was something unnerving in our palm-maps, my mother would assure us that "nothing is permanent, and in a way, it could mean anything." Randomness was what we knew, and perhaps randomness was what we preferred. There was something consoling, like a lullaby, about those glib palm-readings—just as there was for Aunt Lissa in the mindless routines of church. But Andrei bought himself a used Bible and paged through it as if searching out words in a dictionary, ignoring my aunt when she snapped at him, "You don't need that. That's what the priest is for." Sometimes he used me as a soundboard for ideas he wished to tease out, but for a long time it was hard to say whether it was affirmation or repudiation he hunted for. He'd say to me, *This Trinity stuff doesn't work . . . how can God and Christ be the same being when the Old Testament God is a totally different person than Jesus in the New Testament? It's total schizophrenia, it's impossible* and I would tell him I didn't know, none of it made sense, when what I really wanted to say was, *who the hell cares? It means whatever you want it to mean.*

Lissa made us go to confession once a month. She never entered the box herself but stood there with her arms folded as we filed in and out. It never occurred to us that we had anything real to confess, so it became a contest among us to see who could make up the most audacious sin. In that confession box, we stole boats and kidnapped fishermen, we tricked out the neighbor's car so it would explode upon ignition, we set fire to Port-o-John's. We stole vegetables from Mrs. Hambly's garden and launched them through people's windows, calling it *drive-by cucumbering.* Marcus, who believed that "logically, there has to be a God, but no way is he interested," liked to pose difficulties for the priest when it came to assigning the proper penance. He once told the man that he'd climbed a fence into a dairy farm and spray-painted all the cows pink, for the sake of providing God with a little visual variety. Didn't He get a little sick of all the green in Wisconsin? Wasn't it like watching the static fuzz on a TV that didn't work?

We were the last to line up for the confessional that Sunday morning after our hike to the beach. As I waited my turn it occurred to me that technically speaking, I did have a venial sin to confess—an impulsive theft, committed the previous Wednesday at school when another girl flashed around a doll her parents had just ordered for her. "I had to get one hundred percent on everything," she claimed, "and do double chores, for *months*." Contemptuous, I peered over shoulders to see what she'd slaved away for. The reward for all the vacuuming and weeding, for all the ridiculous A-pluses, was a chubby, dully wholesome doll dressed in a blue flowered dress and apron and leather work boots. Her hair was in tight braids beneath a checkered bonnet. She looked about as romantic as a dairy cow, and I was just short of rolling my eyes when I noticed one little dab of the fantastical on her person— an amber heart necklace strung on brown ribbon, glowing on her calicoed chest like a captured bead of lamplight. It stopped my breath. I waited my chance, as Frida would have, and had it in my pocket by lunchtime.

But I didn't mention the necklace to the priest. I made something up, and when I'd finished, I made no attempt to hide my effort to hear what else was going on in there. I listened to Pablo confess to the federal offense of heisting an eagle's nest (to make himself a headdress, he said), his small face still appropriately grave when he exited. Rafe said he was selling gateway drugs to the local deer. Marcus, who mumbled something to me about how these priests could serve the world better by fixing water heaters or laying pipe, went in next and said he'd gone into a grocery store parking lot and replaced people's back tires with personal flotation devices. "It was a selfless act, even if I sold the tires for profit," he added. "If there's a flood like last year's, they'll still be able to drive. I'm saving lives. How do I do penance for that?"

Frida went in next. She skipped the rote "bless me Father etc.," and said, "I have hate." The priest murmured a question, and Frida responded, "My selfish cunt of a mother. My real mother," and then her voice dropped so that I couldn't hear the rest. When she came out, she wore her usual expression of bored hauteur, as though whatever fatuous counsel the man had fed her was simply to be expected.

Once Frida was through, Andrei told the priest that he wished he had a real father because there was no one to tell him what to do. "There are things I need to *know*," he said, and then, "I don't understand the rules. Or even if the game's worth playing. I mean, is anything ever going to come back to me, is it worth it, or is it always going to be like this?" The priest said that God was everyone's father, but that he, the priest, was here to tell him what God wanted him to do. And if he came to church more often and paid attention at Mass, he would come to understand the rules for right behavior . . . had he heard the homily last week? Andrei came out of the black box with his jaw clamped tight.

Sardine-packed in my uncle's van on the way home, we were mostly silent save for when Marcus hummed a bar or two of *Hallelujah,* then stopped. This triggered something in Frida, who straightened her shoulders and remarked that there were too many children in this family.

My father glanced at her in the rearview mirror but kept his face impassive. Lissa said, "I didn't plan this one. You understand how that happens, don't you?"

"Where are you going to put it? All the bedrooms are taken."

None of us had thought of this.

"You're all pretty much already sharing anyway," Lissa pointed out. "You're all over the place."

"But we all have our own, except Marcus and Pablo," Frida persisted. "I'm not sharing. I'm not putting a fucking baby in my room."

My father, who'd been staring vaguely out his window, said, "Quit yammering already. I've got a passage finally coming together in my head."

"Oh yes." Lissa rolled her eyes. "Big Pulitzer Prize winner over here, can't have his thoughts interrupted."

"Because *you're* such a scintillating success story," my father muttered.

Lissa sped up for a yellow light, then returned her attention to Frida: "You're a worrywart, girl, you know that? We'll figure it out. It's weeks away yet."

I turned to assess the younger boys' reaction to this. Rafe looked horrified. He was possessive of his alcove—we each had so little that was our own—and it wasn't beyond the realm of possibility that my aunt and uncle would ask my parents to house the new baby somewhere in the Cape Cod.

Andrei said, "Shouldn't we be putting together a crib or something?"

Nobody answered. Lissa steered the van into a Dairy Queen lot, claiming she needed a sundae, and a smoke, after all that church.

That Sunday night, Frida found a big bottle of maple syrup in my parents' pantry and took it back over to her house. While my aunt and uncle were smoking on the porch, my uncle's stentorian voice booming in its description of his latest musical breakthrough, Frida went into their carpeted bedroom where she scooped up all the clothes that lay on the floor and tossed them onto the bed. Then she upturned the bottle. With the syrup she traced an intricate labyrinth until the entire carpet was covered. Pablo and Marcus watched this in fascination and called me up to see the final product. When she had finished, she tossed the plastic bottle aside as an arsonist might toss his lighter after the building has exploded in flames. She flashed us a triumphant smile, crossed the hall into her room, and closed her door. She was as pleased with herself as she'd been when she replaced a teacher's ginger ale with green Listerine.

"Shit," Marcus breathed. "Mom's gonna flip. It's not a bad maze, though. If it had structural integrity, it'd be something."

Andrei appeared at the top of the stairs. "We need to have a talk," he said. He looked at me. "Can you get Rafe? Meet back in my room?"

"Sure."

Five minutes later we were all congregated in Andrei's room under the eaves, sprawling on discarded sleeping bags and knocking over old water glasses and pop cans as we shifted around. Somebody else sat on a half-full package of cheese puffs and we all snorted when the bag let out a toot. Pablo retrieved the bag and tipped its stale contents into his mouth.

"What's this about, Andrei," I said.

Before Andrei could speak, Marcus said, "Shit might hit the fan soon, just so you know. Frida just syruped Mom and Dad's room."

Frida, looking coldly feline curled up on the window seat, just grinned. Andrei didn't ask for a definition of this new verb. He said, "We need to talk about the baby. Who's going to take care of it. And where we're going to put it."

"The garage," Frida said. "Even better—the attic. He can sleep in a hammock strung between two easels and nurse from an oil paint tube." Andrei ignored her.

"Jude's study," Marcus offered. "I mean does he need a whole room just to type in? And one whole wall's all books he never even reads."

"Of course he doesn't read them," Andrei said with a smirk. "If he did, he couldn't be so *original*."

"You guys are dreaming," I said. "Trust me, my dad's not putting anything in that room but himself."

"Of course he isn't. That's why we're having this conversation. It's got to be one of us."

Rafe glanced at me, wide-eyed.

I was thinking of the one thing that was really mine—my dollhouse. The top floor held a princess' bedroom and an artist's atelier, a paradise for my avatar. I imagined a toddler smashing up those rooms, shoving the miniatures into his mouth. There were exquisite little books Andrei had found for me, with faux-leather bindings and real, blank pages he told me I should write in if I could find the right pen. I had a tiny globe, a thing of beauty, that I'd found in an arts and crafts store in Manitowoc one Saturday when my mother had accidentally left me there after buying herself some new paintbrushes. I said, "Our rooms are tiny. Smaller than yours. If anyone's taking a baby in, it's one of you guys."

"*We* can't," Marcus said, gesturing to include Pablo. "There's no room."

"And it smells like a fart sandwich in there," Frida added.

Marcus went on, "Plus we're already feeding Stewie." Stewie was a mouse who came up through a hole in Marcus and Pablo's room to nibble the scraps they left him on a paper plate. He wasn't the first rodent we'd befriended. Frida had run through two, and Rafe and I once fed a shrew for six months before she disappeared.

"His lifespan can't be much longer," I pointed out. "When he goes, you can just stuff the hole."

Marcus glared at me. "Either way, it's not gonna work. And we all know that if we put a baby in Frida's room, she'll just kill it." He adjusted his glasses, the drugstore kind whose prescription was so off that he constantly had headaches. "It's got to be you, Andrei."

"Duh," Frida said. "Could've told you that ten minutes ago."

Rafe let out a little exhalation.

Andrei stood up and walked the perimeter of the room as best he could without stepping on one of us. When he paused to lift the sash of his window, cool air rushed into the room. "Damn," he said. "I missed some." Gently he pinched up a little handful of dead ladybugs from the sill. Every year when they squirmed through our screens, he gathered them in cups and deposited them outside so they wouldn't get trapped and die. "They're so dumb," he sighed.

"*Andrei,*" Frida said.

He turned back to us. "Could some of you take a few of my things out of here? Could you make room for my stuff?"

There was a chorus of enthusiastic assent. Taking in Andrei's desk or his wicker basket of used books versus a screaming baby was a hell of a bargain.

"If somebody takes the dresser, you could put the crib next to the window," Marcus said helpfully, pointing. "Or actually, you might be able to get the dresser into the closet. Let me get my measuring tape."

Andrei turned to study the spot for a moment. When he turned back, his eyes were pleading. "We're all going to have to help," he said. "You know they're not going to do anything. You guys have got to help me feed it and stuff. I mean, while we're at school, it's not in our hands. But after. And on the weekends."

Through cheese-powdered lips Pablo managed to say, "Diapers and shit?"

"Abra and I can take care of that." Andrei nodded at me. "Right?"

"Yeah." I thought I might throw up.

"But while we're at school . . ." It was Rafe, speaking up from his corner. "What if nobody comes up here to see him and he's just alone, crying or something?"

I looked at him in surprise.

"It's called *self-soothing*," Frida said dryly. "Ask either of our mothers."

"Look, we just do what we can do," Andrei said. "We need to take turns with some things, after school. Like you can't just go to the beach whenever you want, unless you know somebody's watching him."

"This is fucked," Frida pronounced. "I'll go when I want to. I'm not the one having a baby. Why should we have to do anything for *Jeffrey*? Did anybody take care of us? I mean, what the hell makes him so special?"

The emphasis she placed on the name rekindled our sense of outrage. I pursed my lips. Marcus, who recoiled from physical touch even more than the rest of us, crossed his arms and said, "No way am I picking up any baby. It's not our job."

Pablo said flatly, "I'm not touching it." He glanced at my brother.

Rafe, altering his stance, mimicked him: "No way. The whole thing is fucked."

In truth, there was nothing unfamiliar about this pow-wow. There was a reason Andrei and I did most of the laundry, the dishes, the cleaning-up of vomit or blood or anything else that resulted from some accident. Andrei just did it, and I helped because he trusted me to. By the time Uncle Lonnie came upstairs for something and walked across Frida's syrup maze, it was settled: this baby was Andrei's and mine to look after whether we wanted him or not.

We waited breathlessly for my uncle's reaction to the syrup. But he only plodded back down the stairs, his shoes making squelching sounds against the carpet, and called out to Lissa, "It's not up there—must be next door in Jude's study. Ass is always stealing my things." He hadn't even noticed.

"Dad," Frida barked.

Uncle Lonnie turned halfway around. "Yah?" Something from dinner was caught in his beard.

"Just a quick question." She was fighting to keep her voice coolly indifferent, but it came out as a snarl: "Why does someone like you keep having babies?"

We all sat there agape. You did not address any of the parents in that tone, ever. We may have been a family without discipline, but our parents' pride was formidable. Uncle Lonnie came back up the stairs, bringing with him a belated stench of marijuana. "Excuse me?"

"Why," Frida went on with barely-restrained fury, "did you all have so many kids."

My uncle considered, tapping his knuckles on the banister. "Children are like lovers, Frida," he said at last. "They keep things from getting stale." He paused. "And down the road, when your brain starts working and you're not spending all your time playing with make-up and trainer bras, you might understand that."

Frida slammed into her room. Uncle Lonnie grinned and went downstairs.

Later that night, after spending a few hours trekking through the woods with Andrei and Marcus, I staggered up the stairs of my parents' house and heard a voice coming from Rafe's bedroom. I stopped to listen, then nudged open his door. He was standing at his window with the Discman stuck into the waistband of his pants, the headphones clamped over his ears. He was singing along to Jeff Buckley: *maybe there's a God above, but all I ever learned from love was how to shoot somebody who outdrew you.* He was rocking his hips side to side, and when he turned slightly, he had in his arms an old baby doll of mine that had lived in the upstairs closet for years. It was a pitiful thing, just a white pillow body with a bald plastic head and limbs. My brother didn't see me.

His dance veered him away from me again and he went on singing, out of tune but right on rhythm.

I closed the door. I went into my own room and lay down on the mess of blankets under the window. A single star winked in the blue ether.

Our parents did little to prepare for Jeffrey during those final weeks before his birth. Somebody found an old carrier and a shabby crib in one of the basements; somebody else bought a closetful of diapers; my father went to the food pantry and hauled home a stock of cheap formula. My mother made a kind of mobile out of twine and quartz shards ("For happy energy," she explained), which Lissa loved until my father pointed out that the pieces were sharp and therefore unsafe for a baby to reach up and touch. Arguments ensued; the mobile met a dramatic end; my parents didn't speak to each other for a week. Lissa, too heavy to climb the stairs, lived on the couch while Lonnie languished on the porch as if hoping he could sleep through it all.

But there was a frenzy of activity up in Andrei's room every afternoon when school let out. He reorganized his books, designating the fiction and poetry as baby-appropriate and the more scholarly volumes as his territory alone. He removed everything he thought he could do without, vacuumed his floor, even washed the window. He came back from the lakeshore with backpacks full of fresh driftwood and at night he whittled toys from it, boxy little train cars whose wheels could not rotate. All this lucubration left a pleasant scent of wood and lemon in its wake, so that Andrei's room seemed fresher than the rest of the house which forever stank of pot and cheese-puff snacks and the bloated sturgeon Pablo and Rafe sometimes brought back from the Lake to be dissected in the sinks.

Aunt Lissa went into labor on October 30th and delivered sometime after midnight. When the doula finally left, everyone was asleep, scattered like passed-out drunks in bedrooms that weren't theirs, and no one heard her close the door behind her. I was on Marcus' floor with a stolen book on my chest when Andrei shook me awake.

"Come downstairs," he whispered.

Marcus' digital clock read 5:15AM, and only the faintest blue light filtered through the window. I started to protest, but Andrei put his finger to my lips. We were a family that rarely touched, and his gesture was so surprising that I climbed to my feet without a word. I followed him down the carpeted stairs into the living room, where my aunt and uncle were sleeping soundly on the sofas.

The only light was that of the stained-glass-hooded lamp above the enormous dining room table. Something was perched on the table, centered in the circle of that soft glow. It was the baby carrier my parents had dug up for my aunt and uncle. Andrei urged me forward, keeping one hand on the small of my back as we approached the table.

Two wide blue eyes blinked up from a nest of pale blankets. Tiny fingers stirred and reached. To this day I swear that I heard the first eight notes of "Hallelujah" clear as bells as I squinted into the light. Andrei must have heard them, too, for he hummed the answering twelve notes as if in a dream.

Like young lovers hardly believing how their world has changed, we leaned forward, and put out our hands.

III.

RAIN TAPS AT MY PARENTS' WINDOW. I pull myself up off the floor and switch on their bedside lamp. My eyes are bleary, but there's no missing the tiny drawing on the wall just behind the table—a beetle with a clunky shell and two antennae stretched high in a posture of joy. This drawing is ubiquitous in both houses, inescapable. It's etched into doors and carved into tables, and after a hard rain, it still appears in the condensation on the windows. I pass my fingertips over the drawing, then walk across the carpeted landing into my old bedroom.

There's not much left here save the bones of my childhood bed and my dollhouse. The dollhouse is empty of furnishings now, its rooms glowing an eerie grey with moonlight filtered through its plastic windows. I kneel in front of it. Even now, I can feel the ghost of old desire the moment I reach into one of the rooms to caress its wooden walls. How I ached with yearning back then, those long afternoons when I'd hole up in here and play out my stories. Later, when I was too old to play with dolls, I went on rearranging and redecorating like an interior designer never quite satisfied with her results. Always I preferred the fantasy to the reality, the hours of pushing around tiny beds and dressers in a house I never could inhabit. There was even a mock-gallery in there, a room I'd dedicated to the display of a series of miniature paintings I'd done on index cards taped to the walls, and I loved to imagine huge crowds of people packed into that room, everyone fighting for glance. If one of my cousins so much as bumped into the house, I'd order him out of the room with the indignation of an insulted queen. Once, when Rafe was really little, he begged me to let him play with it and cried when I told him no. To placate him, I told him that he could at least live on the block. I set an empty shoebox on its side and donated some furniture, the plastic pieces I didn't much care for anyway.

I tried therapy several years ago, when I was still married and living in Milwaukee. I only made it through one session. When I got home, my husband Gary was sprawled on the couch in front of the TV. He asked me how it went and I told him I wasn't going back. He asked why not, but he was asleep before I could answer, his head lolling to one side. I covered him with a blanket and made his work lunch for the next day. I cleaned up the mess from his dinner. Then I went out on our little concrete balcony, slid the glass doors closed behind me, and called Andrei.

He answered immediately. "Hey," he said. Crickets were strigulating in the background. "It's funny you called. I'm outside, can't sleep."

I said, "Me either. I'm out on the balcony." I tracked the lights of an enormous cargo vessel that trawled along the black horizon of Lake Michigan, which in the dark was blissfully anonymous. It could have been farmland or an expressway for all anybody knew, and the moon above was a blind eye, filmy with cataracts. I said, "I went to that psychiatrist this afternoon. It didn't work out."

He waited.

"I didn't have the energy to tell her what things were like . . . before. Before Rupert. But I knew she had to know. And then I realized, it didn't matter, because I couldn't tell her about Rupert himself, or what happened to him, and if I couldn't do *that*, what the hell was the point?" I took a breath.

"Tell me something. Have you ever tried? I mean, to tell a single person?"

A quiet, pained laugh. "You know I haven't."

"No. I can't either." I glanced back through the glass doors at my sleeping husband. Gary was a landscaper, sweet-natured and a little helpless. He spent most of his paychecks on smokes and on accessories for his truck, and most of his spare time napping or watching movies. He could do this because I uncomplainingly paid the bills and looked after all his affairs. I said, "How is it possible to be married to someone who doesn't know something so big about you? It's like being married with half your life. The other half . . ."

Andrei said, "You're always jagged. You're always afraid of cutting someone else up with your own ragged edges."

"So you wrap them up, over and over again in so many blankets no one knows they're there at all."

"And the longer they think you're all softness and warmth, the closer you come to suffocating to death."

There was a long silence. I listened to him breathe. Finally I said, "I can't go back to that shrink unless she can time-machine herself to 1994, and just watch. When the tape got to 2001 I'd say, 'pay attention, freeze the frame, because Rupert's about to be born.' And she'd say, *who?*, and five minutes later she'd be making frantic notes trying to pin some eight-syllable disorder on me."

"Abra, if you knew you couldn't tell the truth . . . what did you think she could give you? Anesthesia in a pill?"

In fact, that had been precisely what I'd wanted. I said nothing, unwilling to admit to it but also unable to lie to him.

Andrei said, "I'm sorry."

"It's all right."

"Are you going to bed soon?"

"I think so."

"Me too. Meet me at the shore?"

It was something between us alone. I told him I'd be there, and then I hung up.

What *would* a therapist have said, if she'd been there to observe us over the first seven years of Jeffrey's life?

She might have summed up our parents' case as one of classic arrested development. My uncle, kicked out of four bands by players who could no longer abide his attitude, was beginning to drink heavily. Somehow he'd held onto part-time hours at the Garden Center, but he was always finding creative ways to cheat restaurants out of food or stores out of merchandise, and he'd boast about these conquests, insisting that only an idiot would work a nine-to-five when it was so easy to load up. Aunt Lissa had a series of affairs that left her frazzled and restless; she spent weeks after each breakup chain-smoking and studying her aging reflection in mirrors. Her painting became more erratic, her visits to church more frantic. One Sunday she came home and ranted to my mother as we tried to make ourselves lunch (nobody else was attending Mass anymore). The priest had tried to coax her into the confessional, implying that she might be in need of absolution. What did he know?, Lissa squawked. What had *she* done wrong?

My father continued to accumulate publishers' rejections, and his anger was infestive as vines, crawling the walls. He declared to the family that he was finished reading other people's work, as though this act of rebellion would dowse their lights so that his might finally shine brightly enough for others to notice. As for my mother, she became involved with a kind of part-time cult, desultory hippie-types who traveled to sweat lodges in the Dakotas now and then to have transformative experiences. She came back from these trips all red-eyed and shaky, and on one occasion told Rafe and me that she'd done some drugs she hadn't tried before and had gone a little overboard. "You should know that I couldn't help it," she said. "It's genetic. It's easy for us to get addicted, and that's not our fault. But sometimes it's worth it, for the kinds of things you can *see*." Neither the retreats nor the drugs brought her any peace, even when she claimed to have been initiated into some new, heightened state of being. Once she was back at the house, something as simple as one of us eating a Popsicle she'd set aside for herself in the freezer was enough to set her off, and she'd be icily silent for days. Sometimes my parents went weeks without sleeping in the same room.

If the shrink were interested in Frida, Pablo, or Rafe, her report would be a study in death drive. She would note the tiny cuts that embellished Frida's arms the year she finished high school with her 1.5 GPA, or the way the boys chain-smoked in the woods and experimented with whatever cheap alcohol or marijuana they could find. She might point to Frida's loss of virginity at the age of fifteen, also in the woods, or the way she paraded coldly through both houses in an effort to conceal her hurt and regret. There was Pablo's fascination with pornography, Rafe's habit of vanishing at night to sleep on the beach, and the seething resentment both boys harbored toward the classmates who ostracized them. I once heard that a group of boys had hauled Rafe into a Dumpster, closed the lid over his head, then sat on it for an hour. When Pablo went to hoist him out, the same boys dragged him into the woods behind the school and took his jacket and cigarettes. Later that year, a classmate invited them to a party on the condition that they brought pot. Once the pot was handed over, the classmate's older brothers ran them off the property like dogs.

If the therapist were watching Marcus, who caught mononucleosis freshman year and was ill for months due to our parents' failure to seek proper medical care, she'd be appalled to learn he'd been set back a year at the high school and lost what few friends he'd had there. He was teased endlessly for faking injuries so he could sit out gym class; even at home, he limped in the mornings before school and cringed when he sat down to eat his cereal. Silent and more dejected than ever, he kept his door closed. There were no more sleepover nights in his room. Pablo slept in Rafe's room most nights.

Unquestionably she would have sensed the rising desperation in Andrei as he struggled beneath the weight of caregiving when he should have been enjoying teenage self-absorption. His jaw was forever in lock-mode, and in secret he went on updating the contents of that blue duffel bag under his bed even as he stuck band-aids on Frida's arms, bought condoms and left them where his siblings could easily find them, anticipated household needs the way he always had. At night he read to Jeffrey, a captive audience. In his slow voice he relayed chapters of Tolkien and C.S. Lewis—the sorts of stories he'd now abandoned for theological texts—or else verse from Coleridge or from Eliot's *Four Quartets* ("only for the sound of it," he told me, as if he could convince me that he felt nothing for those writers whose slim volumes he'd rotated under his pillow for years). As a baby Jeffrey had no toys save for Andrei's wooden freight cars and birds, along with a blue plastic rattle Rafe bought at a yard sale and slipped under Jeff's blanket one night. He denied having done it, but I knew.

I took on more of the housework to counterbalance Andrei's perpetual exhaustion. He was trying to raise his grade point average in hopes of attending a community college for job training, and three afternoons a week he worked on his dyslexia with a volunteer tutor at the high school. He took great pains to conceal this from our parents, not that anyone even noticed he was gone those afternoons. *Why not tell them?*, the therapist might ask. The answer is that he could not have borne their condescension had he put so much effort into this, and failed. If he came home and still got his letters scrambled, how they'd laugh . . . *Don't try to fit a square peg through a round hole . . . that's just a sad thing to watch someone do.*

Everyone's ego hung by a thread. Certainly mine did. In middle school, kids had shoved my head into bus windows, stuck gum in my hair, and thrown my backpack into puddles. High school girls looked askance at me as though I were a rat that had skulked into their territory, and otherwise ignored me entirely. I didn't even register on the radar, wasn't worth the time it would take to tease or torment. Like the boys who tormented Pablo and Rafe, they traveled for sports and ran for Student Body office and walked across stages on Awards Night clad in the on-trend outfits their parents had purchased for them; they managed to seem smug even as they completed math quizzes or sat eating sandwiches in the cafeteria.

It never occurred to us that those self-assured, well-adjusted kids had good reason to cast us out. Instead we nourished a belief that some were randomly elected into a world of good things while others were not, and this allowed us to feel righteous about our membership in that latter group, as though victimhood alone made us heroes. So if say a distracted queen-bee-type left a textbook or a calculator behind in class, I'd toss it into the trash. Marcus made rounds through the high school parking lot to let the air out of tires. Frida's shoplifting had evolved from swiping trinkets from classmates to pinching makeup and jewelry from Schroeder's, the only department store in Two Rivers, or from the Manitowoc mall. Pablo and Rafe slunk out of the house at night to commit random acts of vandalism all over Two Rivers, spray-painting street signs and parking lots and people's fences, sometimes even ripping up flower gardens. They paid special attention to Neshotah Park, where tourists picnicked, and to the beautifully manicured homes along Zlatnik Drive on the waterfront. Not even Andrei was immune. Outside the high school auditorium, I once saw him tear down a flyer that advertised a reading for the students who'd been published in the school's literary magazine.

He was not immune, and yet he had a curious power to jolt me out of complacence. Most days I wanted only to disappear, join a caravan or cult, hop a plane to Paris where I'd live as a painter-princess occupied only with my own glory. Had Lonnie and my mother made marijuana seem more attractive over the years, I probably would have chased the same highs Pablo and Rafe did as a means of easy escape, but pot left them all soporific and slow, and Andrei had such disdain for it that it never even occurred to me to try it myself. In any case, I didn't need it. I entered fantasies all on my own, and would sit cocooned in soft shimmering mist until Andrei dispersed the clouds by calling me downstairs to finish my homework or help him with some chore. Whatever irritation I felt waned to a curious sort of submission that reminded me of how I'd felt in a doctor's office once as a little girl, when a kind physician wrote down instructions for how to take my Strep medicine and tucked the paper in my shirt pocket as if understanding that my parents would never remember. He was trusting me to do right by myself, and though I'd hated him for sticking that depressor down my throat a few minutes earlier, I was grateful.

The truth was that alone in my foggy worlds, I turned and turned as if in a maze, but with Andrei I felt a propulsion just behind me, like fan blades stirring water. I would feel this when we carried Jeffrey into the woods out back to show him ghost pipe flowers or snowberries, or on rainy nights when we rocked him in front of the living room windows. As Andrei murmured verse over us both, fantasy and jealousy and vengefulness would scatter from me like startled seabirds, leaving behind only the surf music of Jeffrey's breathing.

Sometimes I would compensate, assuring him that he'd hurdle his struggle with words and become the writer he'd always hoped to be. "You can, and you will," I'd say to him after he'd flung his pen to the floor. Once, little Jeff crawled over to the pen and handed it back. I said, "See? Even Jeffrey knows." But these moments came rarely, and as Jeffrey grew from toddler to child, even Andrei's affection for him faltered. At the end of those first seven years, any outsider would have seen that the sting of envy we'd all felt back before Jeffrey was born had blistered into full-out fevered resentment. It was inevitable. After all, the most dangerous element you could introduce into a household of frauds is the real thing, and that's exactly what Jeffrey was.

Of course, we didn't fully understand yet that our parents were frauds, nor did we realize that they were not so much disappointed as deeply relieved that we, too, were ungifted. But *they* knew. I believe it was not only their accumulated failures—publishers' indignant rejections, expulsions from bands and venues, disinterest from gallery owners and fellow painters—that exposed this to them. It was something in their own hearts that had begun to clamor and protest. I know very well that even the most elaborate self-deception will not keep limbs from flailing as the soul asphyxiates.

When he was four, Jeffrey asked to be taught piano. Vaguely amused, my uncle complied for a week before pawning Jeffrey off to our neighbor Mrs. Hambly who taught out of her living room. "She's a damn widow, bored out of her mind," was Lonnie's reasoning. He was right, because Mrs. Hambly thought Jeffrey was the sweetest boy she'd ever seen and called to say she'd teach him for free.

I was the one who had to listen to her rhapsodize over the phone as I knelt beside the fridge trying to kill a roach with one of Andrei's shoes. "He's so *overcome* by music," she gushed. "He found a tape of that Jim Henson movie, where Kermit sings that song on a log? It just *took* him. He wants to learn the piano accompaniment like his life depends on it." Having succeeded in splattering the tile with roach guts, I resisted the urge to tell Mrs. Hambly what we all thought of that song (Pablo had declared it "gay," Marcus and Frida had rolled their eyes, our parents found it nauseating). Instead I said that she was nice to call, but that I needed to go. So nobody had a clue that Jeffrey was gifted until he was five, when he sat down at Lonnie's piano and picked out a tune that was so haunting and spare that everyone who happened to be there froze. Our horror mounted when Jeffrey revealed that he'd composed the tune himself.

"After I heard Satie," he added, as if this explained everything.

"Liar," Rafe said, then turned on his heel and walked out.

Another afternoon, I came back from school to find my parents having one of their hiss-and-curse fights in the kitchen, the kind that always ended with them not speaking to each other for a week or my mother leaving for another of her retreats. A freshly painted canvas sweated on the breakfast table between them.

"You said it just to insult me," my mother was saying. She was in one of her thin floor-length sundresses, a getup Marcus referred to as the Lookaway because the worn material made her habitual bralessness more noticeable than usual. She continued, "You always pull that shit. Act like it's all innocent when really you're trying to tell me—"

My father held up both hands. "Taryn, I swear . . . oh, hell, what does it matter? Why am I defending myself? You're putting words in my mouth because it's what *you* think and you don't want to admit it."

"Oh? And exactly what is it I don't want to admit, Jude?"

"That this kid has got it on better than you do. Looks like *self-trained* isn't working out for you after all."

"And it's working out for you, college dropout? Still can't catch up to Daddy even with all the time in the world on your hands." She was seething, her nostrils flaring.

My father walked out before she could unleash further wrath on him. She turned it on me instead: "You want to add something? Miss I-Couldn't-Even-Do-Papier-Mache-For-Eighth-Grade-Art-Class?"

I lifted the canvas by the edges. Jeffrey had captured a belted kingfisher eyeing a pool of water from atop a narrow branch, and bird was *alive,* its breast feathers trembling in the wind. I pushed the canvas away. I said, "He just got lucky. Don't you tell us all the time that they have kids' exhibitions even at the Art Institute? It's just kids playing with paint, and they get lucky."

I found myself perpetually disquieted in his presence. He played strange games and couldn't have cared less whether anyone else participated. He built intricate fairy worlds inside old cookie tins, filling them with moss forests and little stone pathways glued down with Elmer's, then twisting together bread ties to form fences around gardens where upturned lids from various jars served as ponds. Pablo and Rafe destroyed these dioramas whenever they could, but Jeffrey was wily, finding subtler venues for his little worlds. I once found in the crotch of an oak an abandoned bird's nest Jeffrey had filled partway with soil and then stabilized with braided vine. Into the soil he'd stabbed a circle of pale white stones like a miniature Stonehenge, and guarding this tiny cemetery or holy place was a curlicued gate made of sapling twigs. When one of his teachers let him take home a plastic bag of wiggly-eyes left over from some class project, Jeffrey pasted the eyes onto acorns, then tucked the little faces into the hollows of trees along the Ice Age Trail. Every so often one of us would be hiking along and glimpse a tiny acorn forcing eye contact like a teacher seeking a response to a hard question.

Trailing us to the Lake on weekend hikes, he'd make strange comments about the wind tasting blue or sounding like silver violins. Listening to a movie soundtrack, he might narrow his eyes and say, "So many *triangles*," or, often in response to the film's closing track, "Circles. All circles now. Everything's all right."

Over breakfast he'd describe the dreams he'd had the night before—complicated narratives full of mountains and rivers, dark caves and deep pools, dragons and stair-cases and mysterious trees. There were heroes journeying through tunnels and white horses appearing ghostlike in forests and fallow kingdoms restored to their glory through eleventh-hour intervention. We all feigned indifference, but I couldn't help listening with mounting distress. "I'd sure like to know how he gets to all those magical worlds without help," my mother commented once. She was smiling tightly, her voice acid: "I'd sure like to know how that little trick works." Sometimes Jeffrey's dreams were about us, and while it was usually impossible to make sense of them, their telling left us uneasy.

One night when Andrei was up late with his books, he woke several of us with a loud stream of epithets followed by the thump of something flung into the kitchen trash. Downstairs the next morning, Jeffrey told me what he'd dreamed after hearing Andrei's little explosion: "He was in a church and they were going to have a crafts show," he said. "Andrei was in charge of making all these little ornaments to sell. There was a huge table covered in these wooden pieces to make ornament-men. There were heads and legs and everything kind of like Lego pieces but nothing was connected. And Andrei was sitting there trying to screw together a man while all these people were watching, telling him to hurry up, the show was about to start, but none of the pieces fit, and he kept getting upset and throwing them across the room, and he was getting angrier and angrier but he kept trying." He paused. "I was there, too. I just wanted him to throw all the pieces out."

I lifted the lid of the kitchen trash. No wooden ornaments, just a couple of damp books still bearing yellow stickers from the used bookstore. One of them had John Calvin's name on it and the other was some tedious-looking discussion of the Protestant Reformation. I let the lid drop.

"Anyway," Jeff continued, "I watched him til I couldn't take it anymore and then I told him he didn't have to make his guy out of *any* of those pieces. Then I got him to leave the church with me."

"Morning," Andrei said gruffly from behind us. He went straight to the sink to do the previous night's dinner dishes and said nothing else.

Jeffrey was also moved or troubled by the strangest things. I remember that he'd watch the opening two minutes of *Beauty and the Beast* over and over again, his arms visibly pebbling. And after discovering *E.T.* on VHS, he walked around in a pensive daze for a week, until finally Andrei got sick of it and reminded him E.T. had never existed. Jeffrey turned and said, "Yes he did." When Andrei pursued it—"What the hell is so sad?"—Jeffrey said, "I can't explain. But every time I watch it, I feel all shaky inside, like it's more important than it looks."

I recall an Easter weekend when Andrei had begrudgingly promised to take Jeff to the community center in Two Rivers for a sandbox egg hunt. Jeff came to get me when he found Andrei asleep on top of his algebra book. "Can we still go?" he asked timidly, as if afraid of me.

I went to wake Andrei, then decided to let him be. I could take one for the team, couldn't I? So I walked with Jeffrey into Two Rivers via the old back road and took him to the community center. We stood in a long line of kids waiting to climb into a deep sandbox and dig out their prize-filled eggs. Bored and put out, I stood there with my arms crossed as one kid after another dug frenziedly through the sand and loaded a basket or an upturned shirt with plastic eggs. But when it was Jeffrey's turn, he moved slowly through the box, a faraway look on his face like he was listening for something. He was in there forever. Finally he surfaced with a single blue egg cradled in his hands. Outside, I wanted to know why the hell he hadn't tried to get a heap of them, since we'd walked so damn far.

"I only wanted the one," he said, prying it open. Inside was a cheap plastic bunny figurine, the eyes painted on all lopsided, but Jeff held it to his chest like he'd just signed adoption papers.

"How'd it go?" Andrei asked when we returned. "I'm sorry I fell asleep."

"Fine," I said shortly. "Fine. He got a stupid plastic rabbit and then we walked home."

He blocked my bedroom doorway. "Something's wrong. Tell me."

I told him.

He wasn't surprised. "Were you here that day he followed me into town, to that discount tool place? He followed me into this place and I pointed to a Ryobi saw and made some comment like, those are trash, it's not a good brand, you want to avoid it if you can save up for something better . . . and Jeff gets that look like he's going to cry, and he wraps his hands around the saw like he's covering its ears or something And then he says to me, 'he doesn't *want* to be junk, so don't say things like that where he can hear you, or he'll think he doesn't have a choice.' And then he gets all teary-eyed. And people are looking at us like, what's wrong with this kid, and I'm trying to haul him out of there before he breaks down over the idea of something being on *discount* for God's sake."

Jeffrey had skipped a grade, and still his teachers sent home radiant reports hinting that my aunt and uncle should consider putting him in a gifted program. When no one responded to the notes, one of those teachers took the initiative to come out to the house. It was Mr. Sundahl, the third-grade teacher we'd all tried desperately to impress. He was one of those fatherly types even the worst kids—perhaps especially the worst kids—intuitively wanted on their side. Frida, who even at that age believed she had to flirt to get what she wanted, only put him off. When I was his student, he wrote on a report that I was "unfocused" and "not a team player," and Marcus' extreme reticence unnerved him. Pablo and Rafe made a brief effort to win his affections, too, but they were so far gone at that age that he only noticed them when he had to send them to the principal's office. So we were all stone-faced, fighting to suppress a sudden recrudescence of yearning, when that same wizard-like man rang the bell and asked to talk with Lonnie or Lissa about Jeffrey, "that marvelous little boy, Jeffrey."

All of us save the parents were home that day. "They're not here," Frida said shortly.

"And he's not a genius," Pablo added. "We would know. We live with him."

Andrei just stood there looking wan.

"I can wait," Mr. Sundahl offered, not to be cowed so easily. "I can just wait outside if they're due back soon." Jeffrey had written him a little essay, he said. Not a homework assignment, but something of his own volition. The writing was simply incredible. Almost a poem. It was an analysis of, wait, he wanted to quote it just right—*the scene in Star Wars where the triangles are loudest.* The scene where Skywalker fought a hallucinatory Darth Vader deep in a swamp cave, only to find that when he slashed Vader's head from his body, the melted helmet revealed Luke's own face. In this moment (Jeffrey had written), Luke was starting to see just what kind of triangle he was living in.

"He's seen that movie too many times," Andrei said. "He watches it like he's hypnotized."

"Star Wars is just a babysitter," Frida tossed in, a line we later declared brilliant.

I told Mr. Sundahl to try some other time and then I bolted the door once he'd gone. I was already beginning to worry the word *volition* in my mouth like a sore. When I turned back, Frida said, "Maybe he'll remember that the place smelled like pot and he won't come back."

"Oh, he'll be back," Andrei said flatly.

Shortly after his seventh birthday, Jeffrey recited a John Donne poem from one of my high school English textbooks, and he read it the same way he played the piano: the silences speaking as loudly as the words, the accented syllables taking on a life of their own. *Dull sublunary lovers' love, whose soul is sense, cannot bear absence, for it doth remove that which elemented it* . . . Andrei listened to this with an expression of such pain that Jeffrey noticed and stopped.

Over time, Andrei's habit of using me as a soundboard for questions and ideas began to change tone. There was an urgency to it now, like he was frantic to prove to himself that he understood what he read. If Jeff happened to wander into the room. Andrei would freeze mid-sentence, even hide the book behind his back. "Hey, Jeff," he'd say with forced lightness. "What can we do for you?"

Christmas Eve that year, Andrei and I stood outside in our coats and studied a vertiginous sky spattered with stars. "Does it ever seem kind of horrible to you?" he murmured. "I mean, just the huge waste of it, all these empty stars and planets where nothing lives, and then us just kind of stuck randomly into the mess."

"It's not horrible," I said. "It's kind of a relief if you think about it."

Andrei misheard me. "A reprieve?"

I didn't answer, but Jeffrey did; he'd slipped onto the porch behind us. He started telling us about an ornament he'd seen on the Christmas tree in Mrs. Hambly's house, a blue translucent star with a pinwheel nested in its heart. "The wheel moves when the lights heat it up," he said. "She always puts it right in the middle of the tree, and then she hangs her most boring stuff around it. Like just red and green balls and these plastic candy canes she has a million of."

Andrei glanced at me, then back at Jeff. "And you're telling us this because—?"

"Maybe that's why we're all alone." Jeffrey nodded at the sky. "We're supposed to be like this, so we'd know that we mean something to whoever started us spinning."

The hair stood up on the back of my neck. Andrei shoved his hands deep in his coat pockets, then crunched down the porch steps into the snow. "I'm going for a walk," he said. "Go to bed, Jeff. It's freaking late."

It was no different with the others. Marcus, pale and thin, watched one Saturday morning as Jeffrey took apart and put back together a radio. "We should send him to the tech school in Sheboygan," my uncle joked as he walked by toting his guitar. "They'd give him a full ride." This had been Marcus' dream for years. My cousin watched Lonnie exit the house. He looked back at Jeffrey and waited until he met his gaze.

"Is that what you want?" Marcus asked gently. "You want to work on cars and stuff?"

Jeffrey was surprised. "I don't know."

"Don't," Marcus said, his blue eyes intense. "Don't, Jeff. Please? You won't like it. You'll be so bored."

"Okay. I won't." Jeffrey glanced at me. As with the poem incident, he looked frightened. "I won't, Marcus. I promise."

"Okay."

I followed Marcus to his room. "You can still go," I said.

"I'm a year behind. And how can I save enough money? I tried—" He sat down heavily on his bed. He really had tried. He'd worked as a fuel attendant and grocery stocker, but both times, his illness or its aftereffects had come to haunt him, so that he'd fall down bone-tired when he got home and sleep right through dinner. When Lissa or Lonnie teased him about faking it, he simply rolled over and stuffed his face into his mattress.

"I'll help," I said. I was babysitting regularly by then, for a big family down the road that was even more slovenly than ours and didn't seem to care what I did with their kids as long as nobody got killed.

"You can't make money babysitting. Not real money anyway." Marcus took off his glasses and rubbed at his nose. "I'm a shit human being."

"What, why?"

"Because I hate him sometimes." He didn't have to say who. "Because I keep wishing he'd just disappear."

Frida resented even the abuse Jeffrey received, for it infuriated her that she lacked the power to upset our parents. Neither the cutting nor her promiscuity fazed them. She'd gone so far as to lay little traps for Lissa, pitiful attempts to snare her attention—birth control pills forgotten on the sink, obscene notes from boys left out on the kitchen table, one-sided phone calls staged within Lissa's earshot—but Lissa stepped through them every time.

There was a girl in Frida's class whose parents bought her a glass bird every year on her birthday. It was a tradition, Frida explained to me, pronouncing the word with a certain reverence. They took their daughter to a little glass-blowing shop in downtown Manitowoc and let her choose one bird every year. She'd brought a few to school, sparkling robins and orioles strung from twine. Frida was enamored with one in particular—a hummingbird with cerulean and emerald wings. It wasn't the first time she'd gotten hooked on someone else's *tradition*. Christmases, she was obsessed with the fat cellophaned gingerbread cookies everyone at school got from their parents; they were almost shapeless, but bigger than your hand and sleeved in a richly colored decal of St. Nicholas carrying a sack of gifts. She'd eat the stolen cookie over the course of a week, then stash the decal in her top drawer with its fellows.

One night she told me the whole glass-bird story a second time while Aunt Lissa fussed with something at the kitchen counter. Jeffrey was there, too, sitting at the other end of the table with one of Andrei's books. Anytime Andrei finished something, Jeff would find the book and immediately start on it like homework. "It's obnoxious," Andrei said to me once. "He tailgates me, he won't let me have five minutes to try and understand something before he takes it over." I never voiced the suspicion that it was Andrei, not the texts, that Jeffrey was trying to understand.

"It's just a small thing, and not very expensive," Frida said loudly. "If I had something like that, I'd take very good care of it." Lissa glanced over and said, "If you like it so much, steal it," then headed upstairs to her studio. Frida sat there for a moment, motionless, then lifted her chin the way she did whenever she was struggling not to cry.

A week later Jeffrey knocked on her bedroom door and presented her with a tiny origami bird balanced on his palm. He'd used colored pencil to shade in the wings with blue and green. Even from down the hall I could see that it was a thing of beauty, impossibly intricate.

"What is this," Frida spat out. "Am I supposed to be impressed?"

"It's a hummingbird," Jeff started to explain, his palm still out.

This further incensed my cousin. "You think I want a fucking paper bird?" She crumpled the paper in her fist and threw it back at Jeffrey. "You think you're so smart. But paper isn't glass now, is it?"

In the fall of eighth grade, Rafe walked into the band room and said he wanted to try out. The instructor asked him what he could play and Rafe responded nothing, but he still wanted to try. Everyone laughed. A flutist suggested to the instructor that Rafe could play the triangle—did they have one in the closet somewhere? My brother walked out, stone-faced, and later that week sneaked back into the rehearsal room and tore the place apart. His classmates called him Triangle Boy for weeks.

I didn't believe for a minute that Rafe was really interested in band. But then one morning I caught him listening to Jeffrey at the piano, and the look on his face was a precise antonym for the expression he'd worn back when he pressed down the ivories for the first time as a little boy. The muscles were all twisted, his mouth a thin line, and I was certain that he'd strike at me if I touched him. At that moment, Jeff noticed Rafe standing there and immediately ceased playing.

As for our parents, the more Jeffrey's latent gifts revealed themselves, the more panicked they became. They sabotaged each other—Lissa spilling coffee on my father's computer or my mother erasing a voicemail for Lonnie from an old friend looking to play a venue. They sniffed around each other's projects like exterminators scanning for anthills, wary of any sign of progress. Worse, they made a habit of trapping one or two of us in a room where they'd talk interminably about their projects, and if we so much as glanced away, hardness would overtake their faces like disease. Then came the eruption. The best way to put an end to it was to reroute their frustration to Jeffrey, which was all too easy. When he entered a room, it was as though someone had led a kingly horse into a kennel of mutts; he made us notice our nappy hair and yapping voices, our tawdry little dramas and our limited choices. Our parents' eyes would narrow at him until our shared resentment had restored a slippery sort of peace. The conflict having petered out like a drained geyser, we'd watch the pocked earth of our floors for tremors, and somehow it was always Jeffrey standing in exactly the wrong place for that next explosion.

There was an especially bad weekend in late April of that seventh year. I was jarred awake Saturday morning by the roar of Andrei's voice down on the back lawn: "I *knew* it was you, I knew it, you royal piece of shit . . ." I opened my window and leaned out in time to see Andrei slam Pablo into a tree. Pablo just grinned and returned his cigarette to his mouth. Quick as a snake Andrei slapped it away. Even from two stories up, I recognized the look on his face; it seemed he could do anything. "Hey," I shouted. "What the hell, you guys?"

Andrei didn't respond, but he let Pablo go. Being Andrei, he paused to stomp out the burning cigarette before he stalked back into his parents' house.

I hurried downstairs and followed a trail of glass clippings into Lissa's kitchen. Since we all had a habit of leaving doors and windows hanging open, the seasons always passed through our homes this way, leaving slush or leaves or dandelions in their wake. Sometimes birds flew in and banged around the downstairs rooms for an hour or so before they found their way out again. It was always Andrei who'd get up on a chair afterward to bleach away the droppings they'd smeared along the walls or ceilings.

I found him at the sink, attacking the electric teapot with a Brillo pad. The stove was on the fritz, and people had been trying to boil eggs in the kettle. I said, "What's going on?"

He scrubbed harder. "*He's* the one who dumped my books into the marsh. And he blamed Jeffrey."

"Your books—?"

"Do you ever listen? Those *beautiful* books I found last week. I *said* they were valuable, I wasn't going to let them mold over like your dad does, and, you know, Pablo has a special fucking radar for anything that might be *important* to someone, so he had to drown them, because that's what you do when you're diseased like he is, you drown anything that has any value—"

Through the open windows of my parents' living room came the sound of something shattering, then my father's voice. Ten seconds later he was in the kitchen, staring wildly about. "Five thousand words," he shrieked. "Five thousand fucking words deleted. I know it was him—I found him in the middle of the night sitting at my desk and there's no other reason why he'd be there. Now tell me. Where. Is. Jeffrey."

Jeffrey had a strange penchant for studying our things when we weren't around, as if trying to decipher some code. I could have explained this to my father, told him that whatever he'd seen was probably innocent. Instead I said, "He's upstairs."

My father stormed up the stairs. For several minutes he raged at Jeff about the importance of his work before we heard him pound his way up another flight into the attic. When he came back into the kitchen, he was carrying my mother's newest painting, a big globby mess of red and pink dappled with turkey feathers. We followed him into the bathroom where he dumped the painting into the shower stall and turned on the water full force. We stood there watching as oil paint ran out all over the tile like blood.

"That'll make a statement," my father said through his teeth. "Maybe it *was* Jeff, but we all know that Little Miss Freewheeling doesn't handle it real well when somebody else makes something *worth* a damn." He let the shower run until the turkey feathers formed a clump around the drain.

"That probably wasn't a good move," I said at last.

"Remember what she did last week, when I was finally getting somewhere with that other story?"

My mother had told Rafe and me that under no circumstances were we to answer the phone for the next three hours. Then she went into Lissa's house and dialed our home number every five minutes—purely to break my father's concentration, if not to drive him mad—until he tore the cord out of the wall.

It was sheer luck that she was spending the weekend at some camp and wouldn't be home until Monday. But it wasn't even lunchtime when the next explosion hit: Lonnie bellowing at the top of his lungs about someone breaking his guitar strings. "It was fine last night . . . I pick it up this morning, it's dangling strings like dental floss. I'm going to use them to string somebody up, I swear to God . . ."

Rafe came slinking into the kitchen, avoiding eye contact. "It was probably Jeff," he said. "He's always hanging around by your stuff."

Lonnie charged up the stairs. Rafe nuked himself a Hot Pocket and ate it over the counter as Lonnie lit into Jeffrey. When Andrei said, "I'd bet the farm you're the one who ripped up those strings," my brother just shrugged, then let himself outside to have a cigarette with Pablo.

"It's not the first time," Andrei said to me. "I think he's got a fetish for sabotaging instruments. I heard he fucked up somebody's trumpet at school, like he poured juice into it or something. He's not very original."

My uncle was still yelling when Lissa came downstairs in her bathrobe. "What is it now?" she moaned. "Can't a woman get some sleep around here? My head is killing me." She went for her recent breakfast of choice, a frozen Snickers bar.

From behind his book Andrei said, "You're going to get diabetes if you keep that up."

"Thank you, doctor, I'll make a note of it."

Marcus came down a minute later rubbing his arm like he'd broken it in his sleep. "So can I go tomorrow or what?" he demanded. "You said you'd make up your mind by Saturday. It's Saturday."

He'd been nagging Lissa all week to let him take her car down to Milwaukee where the railroad museum was doing turntable demonstrations for the public. He didn't have a drivers' license, but this was no matter; Frida and Andrei and I had driven without one for years before it occurred to us to forge signatures on the driver education forms.

Lissa picked a nut out of her teeth. "Only if you take Jeff. I'm not going to babysit just so you can take a field trip."

Jeffrey came thumping down the stairs, looking browbeaten. He sank into one of the remaining chairs and rubbed at his temples. "I had another dream last night," he said to the room in general. "I was reading the story of Gondolin before bed, in my Tolkien book, and I dreamed I saw the city. I had to go through all these tunnels in the dark, and through these huge heavy gates, and then there was Gondolin with all the white towers. And I knew the city was going to be destroyed and I was so sad. But I could see a man standing in this high tower. The man had a crown with a mirror in it, and it was catching the light and flashing like a signal. Like a star. And then even though I knew the city was going to burn, I wasn't sad anymore."

Marcus looked helplessly at Andrei. "Can you come with and keep him busy? I can't study the turntable if I'm listening to this crap at the same time."

Andrei, who'd refused to look up during Jeffrey's monologue, turned a page. "As long as Abra comes, too."

Almost everyone slept late Sunday morning. But Jeffrey got up early and went into the dim kitchen, where he spotted on the linoleum a huge spider like the ones he sometimes saw in nightmares. Terrified, he picked up one of Lonnie's shoes and flung it at the monster, but when he turned on the light, he discovered that it was only a cricket he'd killed.

When Andrei and Marcus and I came in, we found Jeffrey stunned, inconsolable. "What can you *do*," he cried, holding the little crushed violin of the cricket on his palm. "What can you *do*?"

"Nothing, for God's sake," Frida said gruffly, padding into the kitchen in her nightshirt. "You think we want crickets keeping us up all night? You did us a favor for once."

Jeff went on crying. Marcus fumed beside the back door as Andrei and I played good cop/bad cop in an effort to pull Jeffrey together ("You're fine—it was just an insect. This is ridiculous"—me; "Look, he's in Heaven now, it's not that big a deal"—Andrei). Finally, seeing Marcus' agitation, Jeff tugged on his shoes and followed us out to Lissa's car. He buckled himself into his corner in the backseat and sat there white-faced and silent the whole trip down.

At the museum, Marcus parked on a stretch of gravel and went around to the trunk to retrieve his notebook and disposable camera. Jeff came close to him—why did he always do this?—and Marcus, either not noticing him or else seeing an opportunity, let the tailgate fall down on Jeff's right hand. I winced, waiting for the cry, but Jeff only stepped back, holding his hand to his chest. Marcus marched past us toward the museum, but I had cramps and went in search of a restroom.

I caught up to them just in time to board the train. As we settled onto green vinyl seats, an employee explained that we'd travel about twenty miles, then stop at the line's end where we'd disembark to watch the turnaround process. This was a restored 1911 steam engine locomotive, and it was taking us through a hundred-year-old tunnel built by hand . . . Andrei said, "Here, try this," and fished a mini spring clamp out of his pocket. He hooked it onto my left hand between my thumb and forefinger. "Acupressure," he explained. "I read about it." The pressure point throbbed for a few minutes and then my cramps abated. I dropped quickly to sleep, slumping against Andrei's shoulder.

At the other end of the line we filed out of the car and stood in a small crowd before the turntable. Turntables, the uniformed conductor said, were obsolete nowadays. But not quite. Wherever you found restored steam engines, you'd find turntables. It was a deceptively simple mechanism: a bowl carved into the ground, track laid at its base and a rail at its edge. There was a support span with wheels attached at either end. A little operator's shack moved in tandem with the engine, allowing a single worker to man the device, though this had not always been the case. Marcus moved to the front of the crowd and began snapping pictures.

"The old Armstrong models," the conductor continued, "were operated solely by human muscle. Men moved the steam engine on their own, pushed it through the turntable on a daily basis. It was an incredible exhibition of manpower. But they did it, and the train always came 'round."

I would have plopped down on the ground if the gravel hadn't been wet from the previous night's rain. But Andrei watched the demonstration with one hand at his mouth, as if privy to transmissions the rest of us couldn't hear, and Jeffrey wore a similar expression.

It was with a final, agonized breath that the steam engine completed its laborious circle and began chugging at a snail's pace along a track paralleling the one we'd come in on. Then it stopped, and the conductor directed us to re-board the train for the ride back. "The engine has moved to the opposite end of the train, though," he said, "So the first car is now the last, and the last car is now the first."

A young couple in front of us turned around when Jeffrey said, "That's it."

"That's *what*?" Andrei hissed. But Jeff wouldn't answer.

Marcus rejoined us. "I really wanted to get closer," he sighed. "But there are probably some parts in the museum."

I said, "Let's hope so. I mean we drove all this way for, what, a twenty-minute demonstration?"

Marcus ignored me. We reboarded the train, and now it was Andrei's turn to slump over and pass out. I found a spot across the aisle and settled down with my arms crossed over my abdomen, the mini clamp still hooked onto my palm. The train picked up speed. A few miles in, its clacking rhythm nearly lulled me to sleep again, but this time I was awake for the plunge into the inky darkness of the hand-built tunnel. The only light issued forth from tiny amber bulbs ensconced above our heads like lanterns. Just before the tunnel's terminus, this amber light played against the glossy black of my window, and half in a dream I swore I saw Jeffrey's face transposed over mine. In the next instant when we shot out into the harsh glare of the afternoon, I turned and realized Jeffrey was not on the train with us.

The attendant we spoke to back at the station looked at us with such obvious disapproval that even Marcus, outraged as he was, withered a little. "It's not our fault," he said twice. "*He* sneaked off." Alone with the same conductor who'd given the lecture, we rode the train back to the demo site, where we found Jeffrey crouched in the gravel. He was studying the site with his chin on his fist.

"What the hell, Jeff," Andrei cried as we approached him. "What'd you do that for?"

Jeff looked up, shocked. "Oh—"

"What is wrong with you?" Marcus demanded. "Did you not *notice* when we left?!"

Jeff turned toward him. "I'm sorry. I'm really sorry. But can I—can I please use your camera?"

Marcus took a step back. "What for?"

Andrei snapped, "I still don't understand how you missed the fact that the train was leaving."

"I don't understand how you missed the fact that he wasn't on it," the conductor muttered before herding us back onto the train.

Jeffrey was meditative on the ride back; there was neither shame nor reproach in his face. This needled me more than anything—that he'd either expected our negligence, or else didn't care what we did. I found myself taking Andrei's part and snapping at him any chance I could. And later that day when we got home to find our parents still in foul moods, and Rafe off missing, and Pablo and Frida not speaking to each other over some fresh offense, we added our own kindling to the fire. We told everyone how Jeffrey had wandered off, didn't even notice the train was leaving, and how the museum crew had to take us all the way back where we found him studying rocks like an idiot, embarrassing himself . . . how one of the parents in the crowd had asked if Jeffrey was "special" . . . Most of the details were lies, but we couldn't help ourselves.

Our parents enjoyed this story as much as we enjoyed telling it. For weeks after the turntable incident, all four of them made cracks about it: "Guess his gears aren't turning so fast after all." "Too bad he's not bright enough to *conduct* himself in public."

We were all liars that seventh year and it was in our own hearts that we nurtured the ultimate falsehood—that everything we hated about ourselves was Jeffrey's fault. And this is where we were the June we vacationed at the cabin in Ontonagon—the summer Rupert was born.

IV.

IT WAS ONE OF MY MOTHER'S sweat-lodge friends who offered her access to a log cabin four hours north of us near Ontonagon, Michigan, right on Lake Superior. She said the place could be ours rent-free for a week that June if we wanted it. There wasn't much to it—it had an outdoor privy, and a pair of loft bedrooms for the adults above a great-room where the rest of us would have to sleep—but we'd never taken a vacation before. My mother and aunt insisted we take up the offer. A retreat would be good for their art, they reasoned. They needed time to focus more on themselves. Lonnie didn't care either way, but my father grumbled about it, convinced that my mother had had a roll in the hay with someone in that cabin during one of her many retreats.

My cousins and I grumbled about the trip, too. We had no spirit for it. Maybe it was because Frida, who was now finished with high school and should have been the envy of us all, had become darker than ever. "I'm doing donuts, like in a car," she said to us, describing her life post-graduation. "Spinning and going nowhere. You guys are going to love it." It seemed a bad omen.

Only Jeffrey showed any enthusiasm for the trip. I remember a trio of plastic pool stones he brought along to the lakeside cabin—one green, one blue, one yellow. They were like stained glass, designed to catch and refract the light. The idea was to toss them into a pool or lake, then dive in after them. Jeffrey wasn't much of a swimmer, but he loved to throw the rocks into the shallows and then comb the silty floor for them. It was fitting. Like the biblical Joseph, he was heir to dazzling colors we would never wear, and like Joseph's enraged brothers, secretly we all clamored to put him in some hole.

That first night in the cabin, Jeffrey went to sleep with his three rocks lined up next to him and his head pillowed on a copy of Tolkien's *Silmarillion*. Most of us were cocooned in bedrolls on the floor. The fireplace was cold, clogged with last winter's ashes, and the breeze that seeped through the front door stirred them so that they kept flying up like tiny moths drawn to the dim overhead light. Trapped flies buzzed and banged around inside the bulb's dirty plastic casing. Pablo and Rafe lay next to each other near the door. Marcus was off to my left, isolated in a corner. Andrei was on my right, Frida on the sagging couch by the fireplace with her hands crossed over her chest like a dead woman. She'd been pale and wan all afternoon and I'd heard her throwing up in my parents' bathroom that morning just before we left for Michigan. Jeffrey was in the center of the circle like a bullseye. One or more of our parents had been smoking pot in the loft and the whole cabin was soaked in the burnt-armpit stench of it.

We were all in a sour mood. No one would say it, but it had everything to do with our bullseye—Jeffrey—and something that had happened that afternoon in downtown Ontonagon. The village was hosting a little fair, a low-budget carnival with food vendors and games, and we'd all trooped around bored and dispirited because we couldn't pay for anything there. Finally we found a free game: an old-fashioned duck tub where hundreds of rubber ducklings roved around in circles to the rhythm of a hidden current. You could choose just one from the water, and if you flipped it over to find a number, you'd get the prize that matched your number. It was a game for babies. Why did we care? Yet we each took a turn, and every single one of us came up numberless except for Jeffrey, whose duck had a number 12 painted on its bottom.

"Three choices," the barker cried, pointing: a blow-up bat, a pump-action squirt gun, a sorry-looking stuffed bear the color of cotton candy. Jeff took the bear. *Of course,* Pablo muttered. The same words were in all our mouths, and it had nothing to do with Jeff's selection, though it was certainly predictable. Pablo meant, *of course, Jeffrey would win.* Of course. Of course.

"I'm dying in here," Frida said into the musty room. "It's fucking hot."

"So go for a moonlight swim," Marcus said. "You didn't get in the water once today."

"Yeah, you know why? Because that fucking bathing suit Andrei bought for me was made for the Amish. Or for an octogenarian." She tossed a soda can at Andrei and it clattered off the wall behind his head. She had a point—the bathing suits he'd picked out for us at his resale haunt were big squares of flowery spandex that covered so much skin, we may as well have gone swimming in tee shirts and shorts.

Andrei turned over. "Go buy your own next time then."

"Trust me, I will. I just want to know what in hell made you pick those out."

"Maybe I don't want you two strutting the beaches looking like Taryn and Lissa, like all you need is a lamppost and a defense attorney to complete the look."

"What the hell's an octogenarian," Rafe wanted to know. "It's sounds like a fat octopus."

"And that's exactly what Abra and I look like in those shitty suits."

"Oh, *sick,*" Marcus said suddenly.

"What?" Pablo hissed around a cigarette.

"You can't hear that?"

We listened. One set of parents was having sex in the loft. You could just barely make out the heavy breathing and the creak of a floorboard.

"Whoever it is, at least they're doing it with each *other*," Andrei said. "Not some random third party."

Pablo laughed. "What do you care? Those aren't *your* parents up there." Rafe murmured in agreement.

"I wouldn't talk if I were you," Frida said. "I mean, the way your mothers get it on like rabbits with anyone who walks by? You're all probably as much bastards as Andrei and me."

Pablo blew a smoke ring. "Not everyone's a full-time whore like you."

"We do look just like them," I pointed out. It was true. Save Frida and Andrei, we were all sandy-haired and blue-eyed.

"Please," Frida scoffed. "Everyone in this room who can say he knows with total certainty who his biological father is, raise your hand."

Nobody moved.

"Thank you."

"So where'd Jeff come from, you think?" Rafe asked. "Mailman? Toilet-seat sperm?"

Frida shrugged. "Who the shit knows? I'm pretty sure those two were done with sex way before he showed up. Trust me, Jeffrey's got no father in this cabin."

Jeffrey shifted position in his sleeping bag.

Marcus said, "But they're up there screwing right now."

"No they aren't. That's Taryn and Jude. I can tell."

"Oh, gross," I said. "Come on, don't."

"I'm going to yak," Rafe moaned.

Frida said, "At least I don't have to put up with it much longer. I'm moving out, you know. Soon as my boyfriend has the money. We're getting a place in the city and I'm *gone*."

We'd been hearing this for months, so nobody really reacted. Pablo put out his cigarette in a plastic cup and lit another.

"Do you have to smoke in here?" Marcus asked.

"Shut up, dudmbass." Pablo chuffed out a big billow of smoke, then passed the cigarette to my brother. They'd both just turned fifteen but seemed far older and not in a good way.

"I have to piss," Frida said.

"Go in the bushes, or hold it," Andrei advised. "You don't even want to see that outhouse." Curled up beside him was Maximus, the big grey cat he'd adopted a few months earlier when it wandered into our yard injured. He'd nursed the cat until it was healed, and they'd been inseparable ever since.

"I saw it," Rafe said. "There's shit everywhere. Like something exploded, like a Chernobyl of shit."

I was struggling to get comfortable on the hardwood floor. "I'm not going to be able to sleep here," I said definitively.

Marcus' voice was faint: "Me neither."

"That's because we're like cats," Andrei said. "We're out of our territory and it feels all wrong. I miss the bagpipes."

"I don't," Frida said. "Fucking Scotsman. Dad says he's a washout."

At this point, we still hadn't figured out that Uncle Lonnie was pretty much a washout, too.

"Send Maxy over here," Rafe said.

"He's settled like a rock," Andrei said. "You still have that fish jerky? He might come over if he smells it."

"Fuck. I left it on the beach."

I addressed the group: "Want to play a game or something?"

"Are we five years old?" Pablo moaned, but Andrei said, "Like what?"

"Truth or Dare?"

Frida turned over in her sleeping bag. "I dare you all to shut the fuck up."

"I've got one," Andrei said, sitting up a little. Maximus woke up. He pushed his forehead into Andrei's proffered hand, then slid down to the floor and padded toward Marcus. Andrei continued, "I read it somewhere. It's called Last Words. You go around the room and each person has to answer this question and you get like a minute to think about it. The question is, if you were dying and had just enough breath for five words or less, what would you say?"

"Jesus Christ," I said.

"Is that your answer?" Pablo was laughing.

"It's so *dark*," I said.

"That would work, too."

"I'll do it," Frida said, flipping over again. "It's easy. *Life sucks and you die.*"

Pablo held up his cigarette in salute. "I can't top that. You're a dumb slut, Frida, but you have your moments."

"Slut? At least I'm not rubbing myself all over pictures of fake women every night. Do your friends know you can't get a real woman? Oh wait, you have no friends. Unless you count the occasional orphaned raccoon or fucking rat."

Pablo hissed something unintelligible in response.

"Excuse me?"

Loudly, Pablo said, "Your friends are all rats, too."

Rafe took the cigarette from Pablo again. He quipped, *"Don't let them change you."*

"That's my dad's phrase," Marcus said. "You cheated."

"Yeah? What's yours, dickwad?"

Marcus was quiet. He had the cat under his skinny arm. *"'The only real mistake is the one from which we learn nothing.'* Henry Ford."

"That's too long," I said. "Not fair." I was combing through my mental file of Van Gogh's letters, in search of something short and profound that would impress everyone.

My mother's head appeared from the edge of the loft. "I have one," she said gruffly. *"Don't apologize."* She withdrew herself, and we all looked at one another as if uncertain whether it really happened.

A beat later, Pablo said, "Are there points for the shortest one? Like if someone can get it down to two words?"

We all knew what was coming—*fuck this,* his phrase-for-all-seasons—but then Jeffrey sat straight up like a ghost reanimated.

"Love your crooked neighbor," he said.

A brief silence.

"With your crooked heart," Andrei finished, sounding a little stunned.

"What the hell is he talking about," Frida said.

"It's Auden," Andrei said. "I read it to him, a long time ago."

She talked over him: "Is that in your stupid Bible or something? You should move into that old monastery when we get home. Just bring a suitcase and knock on the damn door."

Through gritted teeth Andre said, "Don't think I haven't thought about it." Then, "I just told you, it's Auden. The poet. Do you ever listen?"

"Why would I? I live in the real world."

Ignoring them both, Rafe leaned forward. "You really want those to be your last words, Jeff?"

"Right now I do." Jeffrey was holding his blue stone to the glow of the overhead light, deep in thought.

"Why's the neighbor crooked? What'd he do?"

"I don't know," Jeffrey said calmly. "It doesn't matter."

Rafe said, "Why not?"

I was surprised at my brother's insistence.

Jeffrey thought about it. "Because I'm a pretzel."

"What?"

Rafe said, "I don't get it."

Frida said, "You don't need to get it. He's a freak."

"Little *genius*," Marcus mumbled. "So *gifted*."

"Somebody stuff a rag in his mouth." This was from Pablo. "Because you know there's more where that came from."

"I don't care who shuts him up," Uncle Lonnie shouted from overhead. "Just go the fuck to sleep already."

Startled, Jeffrey ducked back down. Frida switched off the overheard light and we listened as the panicked flies settled themselves inside the plastic casing. Rafe snickered: "Well, you're gonna like Fucktonagon, Jeff. We have a surplus of crooked people all in one house."

There was a late breakfast two or three days later, at which Lissa insisted on the mealtime prayer, the same one we'd revised to *bless us oh Lord, for our parents' gifts, which we'll never receive* when she was out of earshot. As we spooned up cereal, she carped about how there was no Catholic church up here and she'd have to miss Mass this week.

This complaint was insipid fare fished out of shallow waters, and no one had a taste for it. My father was scribbling on a napkin in an affected way, as if hoping one of us would ask about it. My mother was on the beach somewhere, doing yoga with the similar hope that someone would watch her, and my uncle was studying the back of a cereal box with the obvious goal of irritating Lissa with his indifference.

Pablo and Rafe were making a similar show of indifference, quiet save for the occasional assessment of the surrounding wilderness as "lame." Frida was glassy-eyed, Marcus still in bed. It was Andrei who responded to Lissa, but his remark rose frothing from a different sea entirely: "How's it any different from one of Aunt Taryn's random religions? Why does it have to be a Catholic service you go to, or any kind of service?"

"I have no idea what you're talking about," Lissa said flatly. Andrei pushed his bowl aside. On the floor, Maximus stopped eating and looked up from his dish as if in solidarity. Andrei said, "I'm talking about Christ not having anything to do with church, or vice versa."

"You do know the guy never existed, right?" Lonnie said. He was trying to pick a raisin out of his teeth. "Or even if he did, none of that miracle crap actually happened." He flicked the newly-liberated raisin across the table in an attempt to hit my aunt with it, but the raisin landed in the butter. It would remain there the rest of the week, blue-black like bird shit.

Lissa rolled her eyes. "Of course it didn't. I never said I believed in any of *that* nonsense . . . resurrections and walking on water and loaves and fishes—"

"That's not the point," Andrei said. He held his chin high as if attempting to balance something on it. "My problem isn't with whether he existed and it's not with the miracles. I mean, the miracles are their own problem, but that's not what we're talking about right now. My problem is with your church and what people do with it. I mean, so you do what they say, sit-stand-kneel, and that's supposed to be good enough. But you skip all the stuff your so-called leader said you were supposed to do—the trip up the hill with the load of wood on your back. Right? So why not worship the Greek gods, or the freaking sun? Or you could go the yoga route and call on your *energy fields* whenever you feel like it, like Taryn does. What's the difference?"

Jeffrey was listening to all this with open-mouthed fascination. Frida, who'd eaten three huge bowls of raisin bran in quick succession, got up suddenly and went outside. A second later, we heard her throwing up into the bushes.

"Bulimic," Uncle Lonnie said. "She's trying to get thin for that loser boyfriend of hers."

Rafe snorted. "Which one?"

"Saint Andrei," Lissa said, "when you try so hard to sound intelligent, it's depressing. Please, give it up."

"I'm not done." Andrei's lip curled. "I want to know, what's the difference between some crazy pagan religion, and a totalitarian regime like fucking Stalin or Hitler, and your church? Everyone in it gets to be a lazy piece of shit because someone else is telling you they know better, they know how the world's supposed to be, and that gives you an excuse not to think. And that's how people end up dead."

"Okay, what the hell have you been reading," my father wanted to know, finally giving up on the napkin charade.

Andrei hesitated. "Dostoevsky mostly. Some of Tolstoy's essays."

Lonnie let out a short laugh. "Where'd you get the books? Not in Jude's study. I thought he cleared out all that stuff after his big announcement." He puffed out his chest in imitation of my father: *"I am done with anyone's work but mine!"*

"He probably got them from that dopey couple, the ones who sell old clothes," Lissa put in.

Ignoring them both, my father said, "Dostoevsky? Let those dusty old bones lie, Andrei. You're not a writer, you're not a philosopher . . . read a beach novel and relax for once in your life." Then he got up and walked out, leaving his marked-up napkin on the table.

Jeffrey was still focused on Andrei. "The ten commandments came before Jesus," he said slowly. "Way before, in the Old Testament."

Andrei was wary. "Yeah? And?"

"You read me the Sermon on the Mountain."

"Mount."

"Mount. You said, it was a speech about what we were supposed to do, but it wasn't *rules*." He was working it out, ignoring the rest of us, even though we were all getting nervous. "It was like saying what we *could do*. If we wanted."

"Yeah?"

"So before the mountain speech, people only knew what *not* to do." Jeffrey's eyes narrowed in focus. "That was too easy. That's why he did the thing with the loaves and the fishes on the exact same spot. To show how hard it would be. It's like trying to feed a million people out of one basket." He stopped and his eyebrows shot up. "Or *wait*. Maybe it was to show that you could make the impossible happen, if you did all the things he was describing."

Lonnie snorted. "Lucky you, Andrei," he said. "I think he's making your point for you. And doing a better job as usual."

Jeffrey turned back to Andrei for approval, but Andrei wouldn't look at him. "Yeah," he said faintly. "He's a genius."

"You want a Ph. D in Russian lit," Lonnie continued, "send him to grad school as a proxy. At least we know he won't get his letters mixed up and come out with a Dh.P." He laughed at his own joke.

"I'll think about that." Andrei reached down and gathered Maximus into his arms, ignoring the cat's little yowl of protest. Then he walked out, leaving the screen door open behind him, and started down the beach. The diurnal moon above him looked like a crumpled ball of paper someone had tossed over his shoulder in disgust.

Lissa sat there coldly fuming.

Jeffrey asked, "What's 'bulimic'?"

"None of our business," Pablo muttered.

Jeffrey said, "Nobody cares if she pukes?"

Lissa came behind Jeffrey and lifted him out his chair. "Go play. Go." She gave him a hard shove toward the door, and he stumbled onto the porch and down the rickety steps. Once out there, he hesitated, clearly wishing to follow Andrei. But he veered toward the woods instead, leaving Andrei alone.

Down the road, Rupert would know to keep away from the maddening intricacies of theology, the temptation to arrogance. He had a comically disarming name for God—"Big Jesus"—and on the Christian holidays would point reverently to the sky. Watching *Ben-Hur* or *The Lord of the Rings* was a kind of sacrament, and sometimes we'd watch with him while pretending to be engaged with something else. I think we were drawn to the way he *felt* such stories, free of the irony that encased the rest of us like armor. Once, as a test, Rafe told Rupert he thought Big Jesus was bullshit and that Science had proved as much; what did Rupert think of that? In response, Rupert wrapped himself around Rafe's head in a wild hug. Watching this transpire, Andrei wore an expression not of resentment, but affection.

But that June at the cabin, Andrei never would have admitted that at the breakfast table, his envy had derailed his earnest passion. And I never would have admitted that I too sometimes wondered about *Big Jesus*, but never for very long, because anyone who might be up there was so obviously indifferent or else ranged against us. We were nobodies going nowhere after all, dismissed and ignored by our own parents, twice over in Andrei's case. Even if a caring God existed, how would a person approach such a being? It was easier to maintain the assumption that we were simply cursed.

As if to affirm this, Marcus came limping into the kitchen then, rubbing at his left arm. His face was all screwed up with pain. He wasn't faking it, not in gym class and not with us, but nobody seemed to recognize this.

"Stop that," Lissa snapped. "Stop that phony limping. You're not winning any pity with that crap."

Marcus said nothing, just slumped into Frida's seat and poured himself cornflakes. His elbow knocked her purse off the table—it was an ugly crocheted thing she'd stolen from some boutique—and a handful of colored cards spilled onto the floor. I leaned over to pick them up. They were paint samples on matte paper: *sea glass green, fresh orchid, sailor blue.*

"What the hell are these?" I asked when Frida came back in. "What, you want to be a painter now?"

She glared at Marcus. "You're in my seat." When he ignored her, she dropped into Jeffrey's chair, then turned to me. "What, now?"

I fanned out the cards. "They fell out of your purse."

"I never saw those in my life."

Marcus glanced sidelong at her. "Oh, so that was someone else who took them from that hardware store in town? Weird. She really looked like you. I even remember her saying, 'I have to piss, maybe there's a bathroom in here' and then coming out with her hand in her purse."

"I don't remember any hardware store." She sat there with her arms crossed. "All I remember was a stupid duck game, and wasting a lot of time."

I shrugged and tossed the cards into the kitchen trash behind me. "Weird."

Lonnie let out a belch, then shifted the subject to Frida's newest boyfriend. "What'd he get you for your birthday last week?" he wanted to know. We'd only seen the guy a few times, a tall scrawny twenty-year-old with tattooed forearms. He'd come by to pick up Frida in his low-riding sedan, laying on the horn until she came out. Then he'd bring her back after midnight, driving off before she'd let herself in. The one instance I'd glimpsed them together outside of that car, Frida had stood there with her face tilted up to his like a bowl waiting to be filled, while he appraised her as coolly as he might have some piece of merchandise he found alluring but felt no real urgency to buy.

Frida's chin came up exactly as Andrei's had. "It's forthcoming, she said. "He's working on something special."

Lonnie guffawed. "*Forthcoming*—that's good. I like that. I'm sure it is real special, Frida—a special gift for his special girl."

She was struggling to keep her cool. There was still some vomit at the corner of her mouth. "You don't know anything."

"I know if you're charging two bits, you shouldn't expect a candlelight dinner." Lonnie nodded toward Lissa, then toward the open front door to indicate my mother who was crossing the sand in her bikini. "Ask either one of them."

Lissa's chair screeched back.

Marcus and I got out of there before things got worse. Andrei was nowhere to be seen, and I didn't want to be alone, so I asked Marcus if I could come with him wherever he'd been going every day. He shrugged and said whatever. We passed my mother, who was performing a series of awkward yet intensely sexual yoga moves on the sand, her eyes constantly flickering sideways to determine whether the vacationers at the next cabin over were watching her.

"I have a theory," Marcus said under his breath. "Nobody who does that yoga-meditation shit would actually keep doing it if there was no one to watch them, or to hear about it."

His limp straightened itself out after a few minutes of walking through the maritime forest east of our little beach, and I wanted to come out finally and ask about it, but didn't. He led me to another cabin where a crinkly white-haired guy in neon swim trunks waved at us from the porch. "All yours, kiddo," he called. "Have fun." He picked up a tackle box and pole and started down a trail to the beach.

"Who was that?"

"His name's Wesley. I met him a couple days ago. He's got this old car—he says he doesn't care if I mess around with it. He's going to sell it for parts." Marcus pointed. There was a clementine-colored muscle car parked on a strip of gravel beside the cabin, a mess of peeling paint and dripping oil. "Isn't it great? Look, just don't tell anyone, all right?"

"Who would care?"

His mouth worked. "Maybe I don't want to watch Jeffrey learn the whole system in eight minutes. Okay? The old geezer would get all worked up and probably *give* him the fucking car. Because, you know, he's so cute and smart."

I said nothing, just plopped down on the grass to sunbathe while Marcus prowled around under the hood. He talked to himself, sometimes making little humming sounds. It was strangely soothing, and it wasn't long before I fell asleep on Wesley's grass. When I woke up, it was to the sound of a metal tool clanging against the gravel.

"Damn it," Marcus cried.

There was some frustration in his voice that went beyond the car or whatever he was doing to it. I said, "Marcus?"

He came around from behind the hood, rubbing at his eyes with shaking hands. "It's nothing. Sometimes I feel like my eyes just don't work right. *Nothing* works right. How can I ever be good at this if I can't even—?"

"You've been staring at that junk too long, is all."

He let out a strangled laugh.

"What's funny?"

"Nothing. Just, I was remembering something the priest said at Mom's church one time. He said, *God doesn't make junk.* But he definitely does. God definitely fucking makes junk. And no wonder he doesn't give a rat's ass about it. It's nothing like him. He doesn't even know what he's looking at."

Right then Jeffrey appeared at the edge of Wesley's property line. He was toting his sand pail and he looked happy to have found us. "I heard your voices," he said. "What are you guys doing?"

"Nothing." Marcus whipped out the word. "Nothing."

"I think I found some real agates," Jeffrey started, lifting the pail like an offering, but Marcus cut him off in a tone I'd never heard: "I said go the fuck back! Not everything is about you!"

Jeffrey set the pail down at Marcus' feet. Then he turned and ran.

It was just a few months after our time at the cabin that Rupert drew a picture of Marcus with arrows pointing to his limbs and eyes, followed by a note written in his silly crooked letters that said, "needs doctor!" My father, as conquered by Rupert as any of us, took Marcus to a specialist in Green Bay who diagnosed him with mild idiopathic juvenile arthritis and uveitis, both of which were complications of his untreated mononucleosis. That was when Marcus became as shyly affectionate as Andrei was with his stray cats. He'd pick up Rupert and head-butt him like a playful ram, sometimes even kiss him. He'd come home from school and call out, "Roooooo-pert!" until Rupert came thumping down the banister to meet him.

But that day in Ontonagon, before Rupert came to be, Marcus was so bitter that he carried Jeffrey's pail down to the beach and flung its contents into Lake Superior. The three colored pool stones were in there with the agates and other treasures Jeffrey had spotted with his keen eyes. Later, when Jeff discovered his loss and broke down, Marcus sat stony-faced and didn't offer a word of consolation.

Most of the week was like this. Lake Superior's quicksilver waters and Ontonagon's whispering woods were only stage pieces, a backdrop for a play rife with tension and sleeping discontent. But there was a singular, ethereal beauty to the night before we left, when Andrei and I walked the shoreline together in the gloaming. The maritime forest trembled in the Lake Superior winds, its foliage daubed with blue, and the sunset mirrored in the lake's nacreous waters was a double nebula of indigo and rose. It was the contrast of those two shades that made my heart close together. I wished I could paint that. I imagined how those colors would do battle on a canvas, not to overcome but to sustain each other. Wasn't it more difficult to love than it was to fight? Wasn't it even harder to love your perfect neighbor than it was to love your crooked one? I spoke the thought aloud, strange and unbidden as it was, trusting Andrei to understand. It was one of many truths I was destined to comprehend inside a solitary bright minute but forget shortly thereafter, the way you'd catch a firefly in your hands only to release it after it once flares green.

Andrei reached out and squeezed my arm. He'd taken off his wristwatch for a brief swim earlier, and its outline was a white specter on his skin in stark contrast with his tan. He said, "Sometimes, if I could wish for one thing, it'd just be that you'd talk with me more. Talk like this, I mean. It's safe with me, you know. It's safe when they're not around."

"I do talk with you."

"Not really. Sometimes, you get this look—"

"What look?"

"Nothing. Forget it. I think the problem is that I talk too *much*."

We sat down on the pebble-studded sand. Andrei had been whittling a wooden bird all week, and when he reached into his jacket pocket, I expected to see the little warbler fully-formed. But he removed a tight scroll of papers and just held it.

"Finish that," he said, nodding at the Coke I'd been sipping from as we walked. "Glass bottle is perfect."

"Perfect for what?"

"I've been doing some research." He spoke quickly, as though he'd rehearsed the speech. "The community college in Manitowoc is expensive, but I found an apprenticeship program I could start next summer, right after I graduate. For carpentry. When you're done, you're a journeyman and you can get good full-time work, with health insurance for your family even."

It sounded drab as dirt to me, but I tried to muster some enthusiasm: "That's good, Andrei. You're so talented with the wood—"

"It's not like that. Not creative at all. They teach you trim and cabinetry and stuff. Industrial stuff."

"Oh. Well, even so." I touched the bundle of paper. "I take it this is something . . . not industrial."

"It has to go. I'm not a writer. It takes me too long to . . . it doesn't matter. The point is, I don't want to end up acting like—like *them*. Someone's got to take care of us. Look how fucked up we are. Our parents depend on the state. Pablo and Rafe are going to get expelled one of these days for drugs or worse. My sister's going to end up pregnant. Your dad's the only one with a real job, and what happens when he drops it? Should we start a lemonade stand for Jeff's college fund?"

I said, "He'll get scholarships. He's not going to need our money."

It was a mistake. Andrei's tone's shifted: "Yeah, of course he won't. Well, that's one off the list. Thank God the rest of us are morons, huh? It's cheap to be stupid."

I tapped the papers again. "Are they poems?"

"They take me forever to write and they still turn out like trash. No surprise here of course." His mouth twisted in a smirk. "I'm sure our parents would agree that if you have to work that hard to make something good, you have official proof that you're completely fucking talentless. And it's a waste of time anyway. What's it going to get me?"

I took the bundle from him. "Let me look."

"Just put them in the bottle, will you? And since when do you want to read anything I—"

"Wait." I peeled open the first sheet, and my eyes fell upon a passage set apart toward the bottom of the page. *I have eyed these sad, tangled bits with rage, have kicked them back into the waves to punish them for what they are not. But you—you ask me to love them back to life, redress loss with the carving knife, sculpt the driftwood madness into birds, and words, that they might breathe and fly. But who am I? Oh, to wash up on shore myself, and be carpentered to life.*

All had gone quiet save the waves; we may as well have been marooned on an island. I read the passage a second time, moving my lips over the words. I could feel Andrei holding his breath beside me.

I said, "Andrei, *I'll* take care of them. I'll go to school—get the job. Just tell me what to do." Taken off-guard, I felt suddenly reckless with love, overcome with the need to make some impossible sacrifice for Andrei. The princess' bedroom and the artist's studio dissipated like fog rent by sunlight.

I said again, "Tell me what to do, Andrei." The firefly pulsed in my hands.

"You don't need to do anything." He snatched the papers and crammed them into the bottle. He shook me off when I reached for his arm, and a second later, he'd hauled the bottle far out into Lake Superior, where it made a tiny splash. "It's time for reality," he said. "No more poems . . . no more stories, either. They're a trick and I'm not falling for it."

I didn't ask him what he meant. We just sat there in silence watching the sun diminish into the mauve sky. At some point Andrei dug his watch out of his pocket and reclasped it around his wrist, and I was about to suggest returning to the cabin when Jeffrey came down to us.

"I fell asleep on the back porch after dinner," he announced as he dropped onto the sand. Frida's paint samples were sticking out of his shorts pocket. I was about to ask why he'd taken them from the garbage when he added, "I had a dream."

Andrei said, "Oh yeah? What about this time?"

I bristled. I was still savagely envious of Jeffrey's supercharged dreams, certain that their province should have been mine alone. But as Jeffrey narrated this one, I found myself forgetting all that. He said that in the dream, there was a wide blue lake with a pebbled shore. Andrei was crouching at the water's edge, and in the distance there was a rowboat making for the horizon. A person sat in it but Jeffrey couldn't tell who it was. There was a long rope knotted to the back of the boat, and Andrei was holding the other end of it. Then the light changed and Jeffrey saw that it was also Andrei in the faraway boat. The first Andrei wouldn't let the boat leave, but he wouldn't pull it in, either.

Andrei, Jeffrey told us, was so upset. And his hands gripping the rope looked like they were hurting.

Then I appeared in the dream. "Abra came," Jeffrey said, "and helped you let the boat go."

The sun flickered out at last. Jeffrey reached into his shorts pocket and produced a flashlight, and the three of us climbed to our feet.

Later, settled on the floor of the great room in our bedrolls, Andrei and I lay awake while everyone else snored and fussed in their sleep. I was finally beginning to drift off when he spoke softly, uncertainly, as though fearing I'd laugh: "Meet me at the lakeshore?"

"I'll be there," I promised.

The exodus from the cabin that Sunday morning was as chaotic as could be expected. Lonnie and Lissa's van was out of gas and my father had to use a siphon (packed in by Andrei, who'd seen this sort of crisis before) to transfer fuel from his car to theirs; somebody blew up a breakfast burrito in the microwave; Marcus went MIA. There was no patience for missing tee shirts or lost hairbrushes. Our mothers, full of fresh prowess after a week's worth of yoga and energy-tapping, were feverish with desire to get back to their canvases. "Hurry it up," they snapped at us. "It's time to move on." Lake Superior had already disappeared for them, though I doubted they'd seen it at all.

As we loaded up Lonnie's van and my parents' sedan, Lissa barked at Andrei, "Go find Marcus."

"I have to get Maximus," he said.

"I'll get him. He's already in his carrier, right? I saw him. Just go find your idiot brother."

Andrei went off in search of Marcus, who was probably over at Wesley's saying goodbye to the muscle car. But Marcus came back first, the two having missed each other in the woods. By the time Andrei returned, Lonnie and Lissa had left with Frida, Pablo, Marcus, Rafe, and my mother.

"Let's go," my father said irritably. "House is all sealed up."

"They took Maximus in the van?"

"Yes, yes. Come on."

We climbed into the sedan. Jeffrey squeezed into the backseat with Andrei and me even when we pointed out that he could have the front seat all to himself if he wanted.

"Let's try for some silence here, eh?" my father said as he backed onto the road. "I'm working on something in my head." So nobody spoke until about three hours later when we spotted Lonnie's van up ahead, parked at a small rest area.

"I have to go," Jeffrey said.

I said, "So do I."

"Ugh, fine." My father turned into the lot. "Just don't make this a production."

But it was a production, because sometime between my trip the bathroom and Lissa's return from the vending machine, it was discovered that they'd forgotten Maximus in the cabin.

"You said you'd get him," Andrei said in a daze, his eyes huge. "You said."

"He's fine." Lissa was red-faced beside the van, a Mellow Yellow sweating in her hand. My uncle was still in the bathroom. "It's an animal, Andrei."

"We have to go back." He turned frantically toward my father. "We have to go back. You said it, the house is sealed up, he'll starve to death in there—"

"He's an animal. He'll find his way out. He lived outdoors before, right? That's his natural territory anyway." My father rapped his knuckles against the driver's side door. "We're not driving three hours back the way we came. Uh-uh."

"I *asked* you if they'd gotten him," Andrei said. He was clutching at his head. "I *asked* you."

"We're not going back," my father repeated, but with less conviction.

"Of course not, Jude. That's ridiculous," my mother said firmly. Her voice was disembodied from within the van, her bare feet hanging out of a backseat window.

My cousins and brother listened to all this without a word. Jeffrey stole up behind me and said tearfully, "Maximus got left?"

"Shut *up*," Lissa snapped.

From the back of the van, Frida called out, "If we had to leave somebody behind, why couldn't it have been—"

"Jeffrey!" Pablo finished. "Yeah, what the hell. Is it too late to swap out?"

Andrei pushed past Lissa and vaulted into the driver's seat. Frantically he felt under the sun visor, dug into the console, checked the cupholders. A few seconds later my uncle appeared dangling the keys before the window. "Not gonna happen, pal," he said.

Andrei brought his fist down on the horn once, and then he was out of the van. His jaw was so tight I could see the veins bulging in his neck.

We piled into my father's car. On the road my father repeated his assurances that the cat would find a way out of the house, but Andrei only stared vacantly out his window. His hands trembled in his lap. Jeffrey, sitting between us, reached out once to touch him, but stopped when Andrei went rigid.

Ten miles out, Andrei started to cry silently. I sat there paralyzed, my hands locked together on my lap, as his jaw worked. I'd never seen anyone in the family weep. My father, careful to avoid our eyes in the rearview mirror, keyed up the radio to some news station. The miles slid past and Andrei went on crying, taking precisely-measured breaths as though this orderliness were the only solace available to him.

Meanwhile Jeffrey was doing something with his right hand, experimenting. He tried different arrangements of his fingers and walked little creatures across his own lap: an inchworm, an alligator, a crab. Nothing seemed to satisfy. Then he made a half-fist, tucking his thumb under his pinky and fourth finger, and raised his pointer and index finger like antennae. "Beetle," he said under his breath. He walked the beetle onto Andrei's lap.

I'm stunned even now at how quickly this creature took on a life of its own. It turned briefly, raised its eyes (Jeffrey's nails) to meet Andrei's, then stretched its antennae over Andrei's wrist in a kind of hug.

"Who's this?" Andrei asked faintly, struggling to smile. "A bug?"

"Rupert," Jeffrey said.

Rupert stayed where he was the whole ride home, and Andrei did not try to shake him off.

At the therapist's many years later, I started by trying to talk about what happened the night we got home. Andrei was in the woods somewhere with his grief, our parents were locked away in their studios, and the rest of them were scattered like jacks. I was alone with my dollhouse. That night, I dusted and adjusted all the furnishings and accessories. I changed the angle of the tiny easel and tapped into place the miniature leather books on the shelves. With a bit of spit I rubbed the tiny globe until it shone. I was like a queen appraising her domain, reassuring herself that the perimeter was secure and the gold ensconced in its cache.

I was so immersed in the story of myself at twenty-five, inhabiting these romantic rooms, that I didn't notice Jeffrey until he was right beside me. "Jesus," I snapped. "How long have you been up here?"

His wide eyes were taking in the dollhouse's meticulously-decorated rooms. "Can I play?"

"No. Go away."

There was a pause in which Jeffrey didn't move. I thought he'd just leave. Then his hand made Rupert again, and he walked Rupert over to the house's front door and had him knock politely. One of Rupert's eyes, like a periscope, peeked hopefully through the rectangular window above the door.

"How about Rupert?" Jeffrey asked timidly. "Can *he* come in? He's very small."

Why did I say yes? What overcame me?

Rupert walked into one of the bedrooms and climbed onto the bed. He explored the kitchen, knocking over a display of tiny wine bottles and a stack of faux-gold plates. In the gallery he studied the pictures one at a time. Then he scampered out of there and into the drawing room, where he overturned the tables. He went into the bathroom and tried to sit on the plastic commode. He studied his reflection in a mirror, then bumped into himself when he leaned in too far. I burst into laughter. Rupert was silly, guileless, sweet. He was making a mess of everything, but I was laughing, and on Jeffrey's face was a look of wonder—and revelation.

V.

OVER THE COURSE OF THAT SUMMER, Rupert van-
quished us all.

Even in the chaos of a conjoined household inhabited by
eleven people, we had never known joyful hilarity. Nor had
we known genuine warmth, the easy affection that was so
common in other families. Rupert delivered both. I doubt any
of us could have said exactly when it began, and yet I know
that we each had a moment, a timid introduction to him like
Andrei's in the car coming back from Ontonagon, or like
mine inside the dollhouse.

How did he "meet" Rafe, or Frida, or Marcus? How did
he first approach Pablo, the coldest of us? I can't even imagine how he presented himself to our parents. Yet it happened,
and each of these introductions was private, a secret kept on
both sides. It reminded me of an autumn many years back
when a solitary pumpkin bloomed in a patch of sunlight deep
in the state forest behind our house. Each of us believed the
pumpkin to be our own, a rune whose meaning we defined for
ourselves on our solitary walks. Then one Saturday morning
I crept out there to loosen it from its vine, knowing instinctively that it was time, only to find Andrei already there
with a carving knife, and Marcus not far behind. Back at the
house, Frida looked crushed when we sat the pumpkin on the
kitchen table for carving, and Rafe and Pablo demanded first
dibs on the design, since it was *their pumpkin.*

Nobody questioned the existence of Rupert, our little
pumpkin. Nobody ever said, "Jeffrey is crazy," or "he's too

old to be doing this." I believe we went through a simple pro-gression of stages—confoundment, curiosity, pleasure. In the final stage we simply gave in and accepted this twelfth member of our family as though he'd been there all along.

I could explain it from a distance and say something like, *my cousin's vivid imagination, his quirky sense of humor, made him a natural puppeteer.* I could begin every descrip-tion with the words *Jeffrey used to have Rupert do* or *Jeffrey used to have Rupert say.* But that's not how I think, and it's not how I remember. I remember Rupert as a complete being with a personality as definite as any of ours.

Who was he?

He was artless. Completely without ego. Goofy, grace-less, an absolute klutz. He fell into sinkfuls of soapy water. He walked into mirrors, toasters, windows. The first time I saw Rafe engaged with him that July was in our parents' kitchen, where Rupert had somehow gotten himself stuck in an upturned Mason jar.

"What the hell are you doing?" I said.

Rafe jumped a little. He'd been rubbing canola oil on Jeff's wrist. "Nothing. The bug is stuck. Look at him, he's so stupid."

Rupert banged his feelers against the glass in a panic.

"Hang on, Rupert," Rafe said. "Now slide. There you go."

"The bug," I repeated. Rafe didn't look at me, just patted Rupert's shell—the back of Jeff's hand—and went out the back door. I resisted the urge to call after him, to tease him. After all, my next move was to go to Rupert myself. "You okay?" I asked.

The feelers nodded.

Rupert couldn't speak, and when he wrote notes to us, they were in a comical shorthand and outlandishly mis-spelled. His handwriting was terrible, too; the letters were all tilted different ways, like his alphabet had gotten drunk at a party and tried to walk home without shoes. One morning he sat beside Andrei on my parents' couch while Andrei read some thick new text. His feelers scanned the page, then looked hopelessly up at Andrei and shook side to side.

Can he read? Andrei mouthed at me, stricken.

Again, I felt the impulse to tease: had he not heard Jeffrey read John Donne aloud? But I said, "I think so. But based on his spelling . . . not too well. What about picture books?"

In his excitement, Rupert shot his feelers straight up, so Andrei took him to the old couple's bookshop to make selections. It was all fairytale stuff he wanted, Norse myths and the like, and there was also an illustrated children's Bible with a ripped cover. "The older the better with him, apparently," Andrei said. "He's a myth-addict, he loves that goofy old stuff. He even found a *Beowulf* with pictures." I didn't point out that those "goofy" stories had been precious to Andrei just a few years earlier. After that trip to the bookstore, the two of them often read side-by-side, Andrei squint-eyed over his theological tomes and Rupert spellbound over his pictures of monsters and heroes.

When they weren't reading together, they were out back working a square vegetable garden Andrei had cleared and planted. At Rupert's insistence they grew mostly squash and sweet potatoes (he loved their chubby hardiness, their pocked and homely little bodies) and the plan was to set up a table by the roadside come autumn and sell whatever the family couldn't eat. Saturdays, I'd look out my window to find the two of them kneeling in the dark soil, so stark and reassuring against the weedy maelstrom of our backyard. Rupert would till the soil with his feelers as Andrei murmured instructions.

Rupert was also a master of slapstick comedy. Mornings when two or more of us gathered around our cereal, he'd walk across the table and jump on a spoon hanging out a bowl, sending milk and cornflakes flying halfway across the room. He'd climb into Lissa's paint and then walk across the tablecloth, leaving behind blue feeler-prints; he'd knock over boxes of brown sugar or plastic cans of drink mix, then gallop through the drifts like a tiny pony. If you heard a crash in a distant room, it was always Rupert knocking something over; when you got there, he'd be sitting like a shamed cat in the middle of the mess, waiting for his scolding.

These little accidents often timed themselves in the middle of an argument or otherwise tense situation. I recall a mosquito-infested night when my parents hissed at each other on the back porch as Andrei and I stood on the other side of the window, cleaning burned pork 'n beans off pans.

"You just *did* one," my father said tightly. He was talking about some three-day music festival my mother was about to leave for. "I know what they do out there. It's not like you're going to sit and breathe in eucalyptus steam, Taryn. This isn't good for you."

"And you're the one to decide what's good for me? You don't even know what's good for yourself." She piled her hair into a messy bun on top of her head, then let it drop so that most of it fell in her face. It was a habit of hers that he hated. "You don't know what I've seen, where I've been, when I'm out there. I go places—"

My father said, "Please, not this again. I have news for you, Taryn. You're not Confucius, you're not Rumi, and if you're Julian of Norwich, I'm the Easter bunny."

"I don't even know who that is—"

"I don't know what goes on in your little hallucinations. But you want to know what I do know? I know it's stupid to go on having these conversations, like you're a teenager and I'm—"

"Exactly, Jude. Like you're somebody's daddy. Which you aren't. Selling real estate every other week doesn't make you Mr. Responsibility. Do you even know where our kids are, ever?"

A hard laugh. "Do you?" Then, "Don't walk away from me—"

My mother opened the kitchen door and blinked into the light as mosquitoes and gnats streamed in behind her. She snatched her patchwork purse off its hook, then started for the front door.

"Where are you going," my father demanded, hot on her heels. He crushed a couple of fortune cookies underfoot as he crossed the living room; Lonnie had found a Chinese restaurant that kept a big trough of them by the front door, and my mother had been cracking them all week, using the little messages within as directives for her day.

"Does it matter? What am I, your chattel?" She slung the purse over her shoulder. "It's my life, Jude."

"I swear to God, Taryn."

"Why don't you do that. Look at your sister—goes to church every week and doesn't think two seconds about fucking whoever she wants. And you can't handle me going to a retreat. Why don't you go with her to Mass and start swearing to God? It might relax you a little."

"You know what, fine. The truth is I don't care either way whether you go, or what you do. At least I'll get some peace around here."

"Peace, yeah. You're all about peace with your fucking mood blowing up every eight seconds. You're a regular fountain of peace, Jude. A Buddha who can't get published."

Andrei and I just stood there drying pans, waiting to see how this would play out. I didn't even notice that Jeff had come down the stairs until Rupert opened the refrigerator with his usual difficulty and crawled into the shelves in search of something.

"Watch your feelers," I said sharply. "Don't land in jelly or something." Andrei had lined all the drawers with cut-up dollar store placemats to ward off mold, but it was my job to keep the shelves clean, and I hadn't been doing it. A moment later Rupert dragged out the sealed container of tomato-and-beet sauce Frida had recently concocted in the family blender. Convinced that our steady diet of grape soda, Ramen, and bologna was triggering her acne breakouts, she was in a whole-foods phase, though she continued to puke up a lot of what she made.

"That's probably still hot, bud," Andrei warned.

Observing none of this, my parents continued their progress toward the front door, both cursing.

I still don't know how it happened, but somehow, Rupert got the lid off the plastic cup. There was a loud pop. The pressure of the hot sauce within was such that the contents exploded, shooting red across the kitchen and into the living room, splattering the walls, firing bits of tomato and beet all over the sofas and the coffee table and the TV. Rupert let the cup drop and scuttled away in a panic, and my parents turned around with their jaws hanging open.

"Oh my God," my father said. "Holy, holy shit." There was a streak of red down his left arm, a little puddle on his shoe.

"What the actual fuck was that?!" Pablo shouted from upstairs. "Did somebody fire a gun?" We were all still standing there motionless, covered in tomato sauce, when he pounded down the steps and stopped at the threshold of the living room.

"Rupert did it," Andrei said when Pablo's mouth opened.

"You mean Jeff," my father said, though he knew perfectly well who Rupert was.

"Rupert," I said.

My mother dropped her purse, whose chaotic design was spattered with red. "For shit's sake, this is going to take all night to clean up," she said, her tone disgusted but the tiniest hint of a smile playing at her mouth. "This is ridiculous. Abra, get some paper towels."

"It's going to take more than paper towels," my father mumbled. He swiped at the sauce on his arm, then reached out to pick a piece of beet out of my mother's hair. "Jesus, we're both covered."

"I can get it, Jude," my mother snapped, but she didn't move her head when he leaned in again to retrieve a bit of pulp.

Andrei turned away to get the towels and laughed, the sound buried in his throat, as I came at Rupert with a dish sponge. "Get over here," I said sternly. "Look at you. Look what you did. Tomato Nagasaki."

We spent the rest of the night wiping up sauce. My mother stayed home. At some point my father made a comment about blaming imaginary creatures for our messes, but no one responded save Rupert, who simply scrubbed harder at the kitchen tiles with his little wad of paper towel. Perhaps it was the writer in my father, his natural imagination, that drove him to reach down and pat Rupert on the shell.

It was like this through much of the summer—most of us resisting, feigning annoyance with this strange little game Jeffrey was playing, but secretly loving it.

On a night not long after the tomato explosion, a handful of us lay sprawled around my parents' living room, the windows open while Marcus made adjustments to our handmade A/C unit. My mother was stretched out on the sofa, complaining about a headache, while the rest of us watched some movie on the VCR and tried to ignore her. She'd waxed for years about the healing power of crystals, but the lump of amethyst in her fist wasn't performing as she'd hoped. "That woman at Gaia's Truth doesn't know as much as she thinks she does," she told us. "I *told* her I was getting immune to this." At some point Rupert crawled onto the headrest of the couch behind my mother. Timidly, he tugged some of the hair on the right side of her head.

She swatted at him. "What are you doing," she said irritably.

A beat. "Rupert can help," Jeff said in a small voice. "With a headache."

"Freaking yanking at my hair isn't going to help." But she didn't complain as Rupert hooked another bit of hair between his feelers and gently pulled. He did this until my mother fell asleep.

He did something like this to me, too, now and again. I'd be reading or watching a movie on the VCR, and Rupert would sneak up behind me and pull a single hair on the right side of my head. I'd reach back to swat him, but he'd already be on my opposite shoulder, sitting all attentive to the television like he'd been there all along. There was something outrageously funny about this though I wouldn't have admitted it to anyone else. Playing his game, I'd return my attention to the TV and pretend not to feel him creeping across my back to my other shoulder. Then he'd pull a hair and start the whole routine over again.

He really seemed more bug than human. *Insectoid* was our word for it. He loved to run fast, his feelers tapping the tabletops so rapidly you could hardly see them. When amazed or struck dumb with admiration, he would extend his antennae straight out, and you felt rather than saw his eyes widen. When afraid or mortified, he'd pull in his feelers, shrinking back from some threat, or else he's shake violently. If hesitant, he'd tap one trembly antenna over an object until finally reaching for it. If he had to defend himself, he'd curl his antennae in and down, burying his eyes, then stick out his "emergency claw" (Jeffrey's pinky). In a fight, he'd spar for a few seconds, then hug the opposing beetle (one of our hands).

It was Pablo who brought this last quirk to light. Pablo, who like Marcus mostly pretended Rupert wasn't there, snapped at him one day and said, "Let's see you fight." He reached out and smacked Rupert's shell, knocking him sideways on the coffee table, and I heard Rafe take a breath. Rupert lay there stunned, then righted himself and put his feelers up like boxing gloves. He made tiny punches at Pablo's hand until Pablo grabbed him, trying to suffocate him in his fist, and pounded him onto the tabletop. When Pablo let go, Rupert curled in his eyes and shot out his claw as a last defense.

Rafe started to laugh. Pablo, whose eyes had lost their glint, made a few jabs at Rupert until Rupert climbed onto his hand and embraced it.

"That is *not* how you fight," Pablo said. "Fuckin' pussy, you're going to get annihilated at school."

"No one's going to know about him at school," Rafe said softly.

"How do you know?" I said. "Does he even understand that he can't—be around, in public?"

Rafe's eyes widened. "I don't know." He bit his lip, thinking. Then inspiration struck: "Rupert, look at me. Feelers on me. Listen. Science is looking for you. If Science finds you, they'll take you to a lab with white walls and do experiments on you because they won't understand what you are. Do you want that?"

Rupert shook his feelers side to side.

"OK. When you're not at home, you stay curled up. You don't come out, or Science might try to kill you. Understand?"

The policy made the rounds through both houses, and the term stuck. Science was out to get Rupert. We giggled over this, used it to keep him out of things. "Rupert, there's Science in the Cheetos bag—get out of there," we'd say. "Rupert, there's Science in the shower—better let me use the hot water first."

Rupert had picked up Jeff's old habit of studying our possessions when we weren't around, and one afternoon Pablo nabbed him in his room as I was coming out of the upstairs bathroom. He said, "What are you doing in my stuff? Don't look at that—" and I came to the doorway just in time to see Pablo tearing a porn magazine out from under Rupert. Unfazed, Rupert simply opened another magazine, then extended his feelers in horror when he was confronted with a huge pair of tits. I laughed. "He's worse than a dog," Pablo cried. "He gets into everything."

I know that Rafe caught Rupert going through his closet, that Frida found him rummaging through her jewelry box. I know that Marcus busted him in his room, too, over and over again. "What are you looking for," we'd ask, fighting to hide our pleasure. "What's so important in here?"

Andrei told us over microwaved pizza, "He steals, you know. Little things from all of us, mostly junk you'd never notice. He keeps the stuff in the bottom drawer in our room. That's Rupert's drawer."

"What the hell's in it?" Frida demanded.

Andrei counted off his fingers: "A bracelet of yours. One of Pablo's holey T-shirts. One of Rafe's marbles. One of Abra's headbands. And scraps from my woodworking projects, chunks of wood and stuff. Things like that. Oh, and when Mom's rosary broke and she threw it out? He got the cross out of the trash can and kept it."

"That's fucking weird," Pablo pronounced.

By August we knew all about Rupert's Christianity. He was devout, asking Andrei questions on paper about *Big Jesus,* and if God happened to be mentioned in a movie or in conversation among us (even as a curse), he bowed low, feelers extended and flat on the floor or tabletop.

"What's that all about," Lissa wanted to know one Sunday morning as she gathered herself together for Mass. "What is up with Rupert and his little Jesus crush." She never directly addressed Rupert, but she didn't exactly deny his existence, either. Lonnie was the same way.

"I don't know," I said, though Andrei theorized it had something to do with all that reading he'd done over Jeffrey's crib. This sort of thing happened a lot: we'd recall something Jeffrey had done as something Rupert had done, and in this fashion, Jeffrey's past began to disappear.

"Well, does he want to go to church?" Lissa asked, half-joking.

Andrei turned to him. "You want to go to church?"

Rupert looked from Lissa to Andrei, then shook his feelers *no.*

"Of course," Lissa said, rolling her eyes. "Naturally."

"He's coming with Frida and me to the mall today," I said. "He begged us to take him."

"Learning shoplifting skills early, eh? Have fun."

He was always following us around. If we resisted, he'd clamp onto the backs of our shirts exactly like a clinging beetle and would not be removed. "Oh Christ," we'd say, ornery and impatient. "Just come with, then, but stay down. Science is everywhere."

It turned out that Rupert wanted to scrutinize the optometry office at the Manitowoc mall. While Frida went into a boutique to lift some earrings she'd been eyeing for weeks, Rupert plastered himself to the window of the office and took in the details. I stood beside him, ignoring the curious looks of the patients inside who were awaiting their appointments.

Rupert had a simple aspiration: he loved eyes and wanted to be an eye doctor. He had conveyed this to us via several misspelled notes back in July. "Bugs can't go to medical school," Andrei pointed out, but this was no deterrent, and it was part of his appeal that he went on naively believing in something that could never be. We pitied him. By August we were submitting to regular eye exams during which Rupert would slowly hone in on our pupils, his periscope-eye coming within millimeters of our irises. He'd turn slowly, studying the eye from all angles, then gently pull down the lid so he could brush our lashes. We would have died before admitting how much we loved Rupert caressing our eyes, but we never said no to a checkup. He even had a vision chart, drawn in a notebook, that he made us read:

R

U P

E R T

T H E E Y E

D O C T O R

He'd point to each line with a feeler, then nod in approval when we got the letters right. You'd have thought we were all small children given the deep relaxation we derived from Rupert's careful attentions.

And careful attention was what we received. When school started back up again, he'd make us peanut-butter sand-wiches and then spear a little slip of paper with a tooth-pick, sticking it into the bread like a flag (*Made with Love in Rupert's Kichen*, it might read). I'd find notes in my backpack, too: *Hav a grate day Abra* or *I will Miss you*. Sometimes the note would reference something I'd told him the night before.

I recall him sitting beside me with his feelers curled in fascination over a picture of Van Gogh's almond trees as I talked to him about a dream I'd had in which the sky was the very same shade. "Only an artist could capture that," I said. In my lunch the next day was this note: *You can make the allmund sky if you werk hard.*

Once, when I was sitting around with Frida in her room, Rupert crawled under her bed and stumbled upon a stack of well-thumbed magazines. He dragged them out before Frida realized what was happening, and when I said, "Rupert's making a mess," she let out a squeak and shoved the pile back under the bed. It was exactly like what had happened in Pablo's room with the porn.

"What is all that?" I asked, scooting off the bed and onto the floor.

"Nothing. Rupert, God." Her face was pink. "You're such a busybody. It's obnoxious."

I laughed. "Don't tell me you've got porn, too."

"Gross!"

Rupert skittered back under the bed and tossed one of the magazines back into the open. It was *Better Homes & Gardens.* I glanced from the magazine to Frida.

"It was for some school project, or something. Ages ago," she snapped. The next time she went out for a night, I went back in there and found that the whole stack was comprised of such magazines. I flipped through a few and saw that she'd circled pictures of living rooms and bedrooms and kitchens with a Sharpie. This *was* her porn, I realized, shocked. Her most private fantasies involved not the dirty-haired boys she dated but these rooms with robin's-egg-blue walls and creamy carpeting and shining windows. There were even craft magazines teaching readers how to can vegetables or make candles in their kitchen, and these too had bookmarked pages and little notes: *Must do it exactly right or could make you sick; Very expensive hobby but maybe.* Strangest of all was a faded pink copy of *Pride and Prejudice* she must have stolen from my father's inherited library or from Andrei. I couldn't fathom any of it, and I never looked at her stash again. But Rupert did. I saw him in there with her sometime later, his feelers scanning the magazine photographs while Frida slowly turned pages. She didn't speak, but Rupert nodded approval at the pages she'd marked, and that seemed to be enough.

If Rafe vanished to Point Beach for one of his solo nights away from us, Rupert would be waiting by the back door in the morning. Rafe would stagger in and Rupert would point accusatorily as if to say, *I've been waiting all night.* Then Rupert would swat him with his feelers, sometimes right on the nose. "I'm sorry," Rafe would say. I'd never heard him use those words before. "Okay? I'm sorry."

Marcus, though warmer by nature than Frida or Pablo, maintained a frosty indifference to Rupert throughout that entire first summer. But Rupert had a gift for finding treasure-trash, and he'd drag in odd bits for Marcus to inspect, undaunted by my cousin's attitude. One night he hauled a battered wooden music box across the dining room table into Marcus' sight line and then sat there, feelers up, waiting for the reaction. Marcus rolled his eyes but opened it to find that the music box's complicated gold innards were paneled over with just a thin plate of glass. Ignoring our stares, he wound up the box and leaned forward, helplessly enchanted, to study the motions of all the tiny gears.

"Where'd you find this," he said guardedly.

Rupert wrote, *Garbidge. But is not garbidge.*

"Maybe," Marcus muttered. "We'll see." But he took the music box up to his room and spent the night tinkering with it.

Marcus wasn't the only recipient of Rupert's treasures. From a trash can or yard sale Rupert once scavenged a curious bracelet and gifted it to me. He did this in front of Andrei—he had some purpose in doing so—and it took us a few minutes to understand his two-feelered sign language. He pointed at the beaten aluminum that formed the bracelet's main band, then at me. He waited a beat, then tapped the undulating strip of warm copper that braided around the silver, and gestured at Andrei. A moment later, he reversed this pattern.

"You want us to separate the metals?" I asked. "You want us each to take one?" Frustrated, he thumped at the table-top, then repeated his series of motions until Andrei said, "I think I understand you, Rupert. I think so."

On a solo trek to the beach, I once came upon Rupert in the act of coming upon Pablo, who'd apparently been out for a hike of his own. I stayed out of sight. Pablo sat down in the sand beneath an aspen and lit a cigarette, and a second later Rupert settled beside him. Andrei had trained him well because he was careful to avoid the dune plants.

"What, did you come all the way out here looking for me? Don't you have anything else to do?" Pablo said irritably, flicking ash. Rupert shook his feeler-head side to side.

"Oh, you dumb shit. Want a smoke?"

Rupert took the cigarette between his feelers, then just sat there, stupefied.

"You have no lungs, idiot. That's why it's not working." Pablo took the cigarette back. "You're not the sharpest, are you. Look, I'm not coming back tonight. I'm staying out here. Okay? No one gives a shit anyway. Go home. Look, there's a bunch of people down there fucking around by the water. They could be Science."

Rupert drew something in the sand. Later, when they'd both started back to the house, I went over to the spot and saw a picture of Rupert on a bed, with a huge dialogue bubble emerging from his feelers. Inside the bubble was a stick-figure and a question mark. I translated it easily: If Pablo stayed at the beach, Rupert would be up all night, worrying.

I sometimes wanted to shake him. What did he care? Why was he wasting his time? But that's how he was with all of us. Later that same week, Frida came home after midnight from another of her disastrous dates, then dropped onto her parents' couch and sat there with her head wilted forward like a defeated sunflower. I was at Lonnie and Lissa's kitchen table with a book and Rupert was drawing pictures beside me. His doodles were as terrible as his writing—just totally random, patterns of circles inside squares and things like that.

I left my book and bent over her. "What happened."

"Nothing," she sighed. "Everything. Then nothing." Her right hand, clenched in a fist atop her thigh, opened slowly open like a clam to reveal a ring with a tiny diamond stud. There were red crescent moons pressed into her skin all around it. I said, "Holy shit—is that an engagement ring?"

She let out a hard laugh. "That is a piece of glass screwed into a piece of metal. And it's not like I didn't know it the second he showed it to me. I'm pretty sure I got one of these out of a gumball machine when I was eight. But he said, *it's for practice, like those plastic cars little kids drive around with their feet* and I went for it like a trout biting a worm."

We were all used to her post-date drama, so I returned to the kitchen, to my book. But Rupert forgot his drawings and sat there feelers-up, staring into the living room.

"He's worried about you now," I sighed, flipping a page. "Frida. He's going to be here all night if you don't talk to him."

"Who?"

"You know who."

"Oh, Christ." She straightened up on the couch. Her mascara had run down her cheeks. "What does anyone care."

Rupert crawled over to the kitchen phone and struggled to remove the receiver. He tapped it, then pointed at Frida, then at the second phone in the living room. Both phones were rotary-dial, old avocado-colored models that had been there since before the parents inherited the place. They'd been too lazy to purchase what we considered "real" phones.

"What? You want to call somebody?" Frida wiped at her face. "Huh?"

Rupert performed his series of gestures again. She said, "You want to talk on the phone?"

"He can't talk," I said.

"Fucking duh."

"He likes the phones. It's a new thing. Just humor him for God's sake. Pretend you're dialing his number."

With a great gusty sigh, Frida crossed the carpet and sat down beside the second phone. She twirled a few numbers, then looked at Rupert. He did a feeler-nod and tapped the earpiece on his receiver.

"This is ridiculous," Frida muttered.

I bent my head over my book, glad for the reprieve; she was Rupert's problem now. I expected her to let out a couple more sighs, then replace the receiver and disappear to her room. But she must have been tired, or a little drunk, or just incredibly sad, because the strangest thing happened a few seconds later: she started talking to Rupert. She held the phone up to her mouth and talked, not looking at him, telling him all about her horrible date and this boy who had left her in a pancake restaurant after she said no, she wasn't sleeping with him this time, she was tired of it all . . . The story went on and on, spiraling into older stories, a long and redundant history of romances gone sour. Rupert sat there nodding his feelers beside the phone, which lay on its side on the kitchen counter. If Frida's voice faltered, he tapped the plastic loudly to encourage her to begin again. This went on for nearly two hours. I fell asleep on top of my book, and when I jolted awake again, Frida was snoring peacefully on the living room floor, and Rupert was on the couch above her, curled up on the edge of a cushion.

I don't know how many times this scene replayed itself over the course of that first summer, but there were at least two other nights when I heard first the twist of the old rotary dial, then Frida's murmur in the living room. She would only do this with Rupert when the parents were either asleep or out somewhere. If I came down for water or a snack in the middle of such a one-way talk, Frida would clam up and wait for me to return upstairs before resuming her story.

We all began doing things for Rupert on the sneak. Marcus was the last person I would have expected to go out and buy Rupert a toy, but one Saturday he picked up a little corn popper cat on wheels from the Christian Center Thrift and left it on Jeff's bed. The cat's back was a clear plastic bubble filled with colored beads that rattled when the toy moved. Rupert was overjoyed, but it was just like when Rafe bought the plastic rattle for baby Jeffrey: Marcus vehemently denied having done it. Rupert didn't care. He rode the cat all over the furniture and nudged the toy into Marcus' arm anytime Marcus was close by. And he developed a way of interrupting a conversation by motoring across your field of vision astride that corn popper. You'd be in the middle of a sentence and then you'd lose it, unable to keep back laughter as Rupert rolled by all nonchalant.

If Rupert had something you wanted, he'd just give it to you. Everyone tested this. I recall Rafe saying, "Rupert, I want your corn popper, to keep." Rupert, after a mournful hesitation, nudged the beloved toy toward my brother, and Rafe stuck his lip out. "It's okay, buddy. Just kidding," he said. Rupert's generosity was so unbearable that we all started buying him gifts. By the end of September, he had a Barnum's Animal Crackers box filled with oddities we donated to him. We delivered these gifts in privacy and without comment. If Rupert spilled the contents of his cracker box across a kitchen table, we'd all pretend not to know where each piece had come from (the green rubber Rice Krispies toy from Frida, the mini Etch-a-Sketch from me, the McDonalds toy from Rafe—a little plastic ice cream cone that transformed into a dinosaur). I never did find out who gave him a coin bank shaped like a crayon, but Rupert loved it and he saved fastidiously, pulling dirty change out of the couches and tucking the coins through the slot with reverence. The thing must have weighed a pound by the time we returned to school. Only once did he spend some of his nickels, on a rusty harmonica from a junk shop in town. This was a pitiful purchase because poor Rupert would never be able to play it. It was not possible for him to push air through his feeler-tips.

"I can't stand it," Rafe moaned, clutching at his heart. "When he just sits there holding it, like he's pretending to make noises . . ."

Everything else Rupert owned fell into the category of Sad Things. This was how he explained it in his notes, the word Sad forever beginning with the capital S. He was always rescuing broken and abandoned objects. Initially we expressed disgust: "What the hell is that? Put that back in the trash!" Then we started to contribute to his little hospital. Andrei gave him a wooden bird he'd carved whose tailfeathers had broken off. Rafe drew a face on the tip of a cotton strip pulled from some pill bottle and told Rupert it was the Luck Dragon from *The Never-Ending Story*. "Look how easy he can rip apart," he warned Rupert, who immediately created a nest for it out of a folded sock.

The first time Rupert watched *Ben-Hur*—a tape Andrei had found years before at the used bookstore—he was mesmerized. I'd seen it once and only vaguely remembered it, but as the story began to unfold, I cast worried looks at Andrei.

"Yeah, it's going to get Sad," he warned quietly. "You don't see the crucifixion so much, but—"

I went to the VCR to hit *Eject*. But Rupert began thumping on the coffee table, hard enough to shake the glass top.

"Okay, okay," I said. "But you're not going to like this."

Rupert sat frozen in place through the final scenes—Christ climbing Golgotha, Simon briefly taking the cross from him when he fell, and then the crucifixion itself; the sky breaking into thunder and lightning as Christ gave up the ghost, the lepers emerging from their cave miraculously healed, the rain diminishing and Ben-Hur returning home to the dawn . . . When it was over, I glanced involuntarily at Jeffrey—his eyes were shining, wet—then looked quickly back down at Rupert.

I said, "Let's get him to bed. Come on, it's freaking late." I hit the power button on the VCR, then snapped off the TV. "It's just a story, Rupert. Okay? Come on. Don't be silly."

There were many moments like this, in which one of us snapped at him without understanding why. But Rupert went on being Rupert regardless of our moods. If you insulted him? Pushed him around, pointed out his stupidity or his clumsiness? He'd charge at you like a little bull, then hug your face or nuzzle your neck. Nobody pushed him off. Maybe it was because he was so unabashedly interested in us as individuals. If Marcus paused over his homework to stretch out an aching limb, Rupert would climb into the freezer for our raggedy ice pack. "I'm *fine*," Marcus would say. "Go away."

But he'd take the ice pack. If Andrei nicked himself working with his carpentry tools outside, Rupert swarmed him with gauze and Neosporin. If I lay on the sofa with a heating pad, wracked with cramps, Rupert would crawl over and shake a bottle of ibuprofen at me like a maraca. The tiny self-inflicted scars on Frida's arms troubled Rupert to distraction, and he'd touch them, then raise his feeler-eyes to her in agony. "Oh, leave me alone," she'd say, but come autumn, there were markedly fewer cuts on her arms.

When you were with Rupert, he was with only you.

Of course, we were far from being changed people by that first autumn. Like trains in the night, there were dark forces in our family that had been gathering momentum for years and could not be halted. But I remember that summer after Ontonagon as a kind of interlude in which the tone and tempo changed before the next act. I recall the inexplicable urge I felt to pick up Rupert, to pat and squeeze him. None of us had ever had a pet name, but we had a half-dozen of them for Rupert: Bert, Rupie, Roo, Beetlejuice, Bugsy, Beets.

Someone on the outside might wonder at the miracle of all this: how Rupert, or Jeffrey as Rupert, was so enameled, so safe from the scorn and the meanness and the resentment that had until then saturated our lives. But the truth was that Rupert was not the one in a chrysalis. We were, and he splintered the hard shell around us with his antics and his unconditional love.

"Let me get this straight," I have always imagined a spouse, friend or shrink saying, all agape. "Your entire extended family had this relationship with . . . *your cousin's right hand??*"

This would be followed by a beat of silence, and then, "Were you all completely insane?"

Finally, the most dreaded question of all: *"And what about Jeffrey?"*

What I cannot say even to Andrei is this: when I look back on those three years after Ontonagon, I hardly remember Jeffrey. He had cameos, his true self appearing only in snatches. What I remember in high resolution is Rupert, and therein lies my sin, my shame, and every truth I've fought to keep at bay for twenty years.

VI.

ANDREI AND I HAVE ALWAYS AVOIDED each other around Halloween. The reason is tacitly understood: it's too close to Jeffrey's birthday, too intimate for us both with its memories of a baby atop a dining room table bathed in lamplight. But eight years ago, Marcus inadvertently brought us together on October 31st when he asked me to come look at the engagement ring he'd chosen for his girlfriend. He'd just fixed the muffler on Andrei's truck, and Andrei was due to pick it up that same night. I didn't know this until it was too late. I was sitting with Marcus in the breakfast nook in his ground-level apartment, studying the tiny pear-shaped diamond, when somebody dropped off Andrei out front.

"Just tell me it's not too puny," Marcus said.

"Of course not. The shape is beautiful." I had just gotten engaged myself, albeit without much passion, and my left hand bore a similarly tiny ring.

"I know people sometimes go together to buy them," he continued, "but that seems sad. Like if the guy doesn't do it himself, it doesn't mean as much."

I didn't mention that Gary, my fiancée, had taken me into a jewelry store at the mall to pick out my ring. I said, "You're right. Really, Marc, she's going to love this." Then Andrei walked in.

He said, "Oh," and stood there on Marcus' kitchen mat, the door open behind him to let in the cold evening breeze.

"Hey. Truck's ready to go, doesn't sound like a Sherman tank anymore," Marcus said. He got up to fish Andrei's keys out of a jelly jar on the counter. "Here you go. Let me know if she causes trouble again."

The two of them had had their own problems in recent years, and their eye contact was cautious. "Thanks," Andrei said. "I really appreciate it."

"You guys, uh, want to get something to eat since you're here?" Marcus asked, his hand exploring the dark-blond stubble at his jawline. "Order a pizza?"

"No," we both responded. After a beat I added, "Gary's expecting me."

"Meri's at home, too," Andrei said. "I'm supposed to pick up Chinese."

"'K. Well, at least have a drink or something before you go. Take your coat off." Marcus opened his fridge and pulled out three glass bottles—two beers and a Coke. The Coke was for Andrei. He cracked the bottles open one by one and handed them to us.

"Here's to all three of us tying the knot," he said.

Andrei, who'd had an ugly flirtation with alcoholism a few years earlier, drank his soda in small sips as if the bottle itself were suspect. I choked a little on my beer. I suppose even then I knew my relationship was headed down a dead-end road. But it seemed different with Marcus. I said, "Congrats," meaning it, and toasted him.

We sat there a while, nobody drinking much. I don't remember what we talked about but I'm sure it was just like any other conversation we had when two or more of us gathered—mostly small talk, safe discussions of weather and local politics. Then the doorbell rang a second time, and Marcus slapped his forehead.

"It's freaking Halloween," he groaned. "I didn't buy anything. I've got nothing for those kids."

I pulled back his kitchen curtain and spotted rabbit ears and a sparkling princess gown.

Andrei said, "Just don't answer it."

"Wait. I've got one thing." Marcus dug in a cabinet and came back with a wan-looking bag of wintergreen Lifesavers. "Is this too lame?"

We didn't answer. He opened the door, bag in hand, and I glimpsed a third child on the porch—a little boy dressed like a beetle, antennae and all.

Andrei made a sound in his throat, then got up and left the room.

"Here you go . . . Sleeping Beauty. Mr. Rabbit." A pause, and then, with a hitch in his voice, "Mr. Beetle. Here you go. Sorry it's not Reese's or something."

Marcus closed the door. He sat down and took a swallow of beer. "The costumes look more elaborate every year," he said, very focused on his bottle. "Don't you think? Where's Andrei?"

"Bathroom." I could hear the tap running.

"Well, I'm sure you guys want to get home."

"Yeah." I tugged on my jacket. "She's going to love the ring. You did a great job."

"What? Oh, yeah. Thanks."

Andrei reentered the kitchen and reached for his coat when he saw me in mine. "Thanks for the beer, Marc," he said. "I owe you big on the truck."

"You know it."

Nobody was looking at anyone else. Andrei reached for the doorknob and I followed him into the night. The next little gaggle of children was coming up the road and I hurried to dig my car keys out of my purse.

Andrei swung himself up into his truck. "Drive safe," he called out faintly. But the driver's side door stayed open, and for a moment, I was afraid he'd climb back down and come to me. The kids were just two houses down now.

I said, "You too," and slammed my door shut. I put the car in reverse, and an instant later, Andrei's lights flared on. He turned right, I turned left, and we left Marcus standing alone on the porch, holding his bag of mints and trying to smile.

My recollection of that first Halloween after Ontonagon is colored more with Rupert than with anyone or anything else.

Lonnie was supine in the back bedroom and had made it clear that none of us were to bother him. He'd been moodier than usual lately, white-faced and shaky in the mornings, and we figured he was becoming disenchanted with pot and had decided to experiment with harder drugs. Lissa was for form's sake "taking a long, lonely walk" on the Mariners' Trail downtown, but we knew she was on a date with another of her lovers. My mother was in Madison for the weekend, learning Reiki from somebody. My father was in the kitchen with us, making himself the Cream-of-Wheat he always binged on when he claimed to hit writer's block. He'd load it up with so much brown sugar that you needed an excavator to find the cereal.

Frida was making lime Jell-O at the counter. Marcus and I sat at the table with our homework, sharing a plate of baked sweet potato soaked in butter we'd stolen in little packets from a diner in town. Andrei had dismantled his roadside vendor's table last week when the frosts came, and these potatoes were the last of his harvest. He and Rupert had pulled in about thirty dollars from meandering motorists who'd dropped cash in their coffee can, though Andrei insisted there should have been more and was vocal about his suspicion that Pablo or Rafe had broken into the can.

We had a good view of Andrei as he hovered over his backyard worktable, making a fresh attempt at mortise-and-tenon.

Every so often he shouted an expletive or threw something into the trees. It wasn't the first time we'd witnessed such a scene.

My father said, "What the hell is he doing now?"

I turned a page in my book. "Still trying to figure out mortise and tenon."

"I think he'd do better with a laxative."

"He needs Rupert," I said.

Frida looked up. "For what?"

"Have you seen his comics? 'Morris and Tendon'?" It was a comic strip Rupert had created on a yellow legal pad a couple of weeks earlier. It storied two badly drawn moose who wore toolbelts but, according to the hideously misspelled caption on the first comic, had been expelled from their union due to frequent accidents. They reacted to things like flies or rain and had no dialogue. For some reason Andrei found the pictures hilarious. Rupert would make a fresh drawing whenever Andrei got frustrated with his woodworking, then take it outside to show him.

Frida said, "Is that where he got those names? I never made the connection."

"They're stupid," Marcus said. "Nothing happens. It's just two stupid moose doing nothing. And he can't draw for shit."

"That's what makes it funny, Marc."

"What's it even for," my father muttered, smacking the back of the Domino sugar box to coax out the last few lumps.

"The comics?"

"No, this mortise and tenon business."

I leaned back in my chair to get a better view of Andrei, who was now talking heatedly to one of the large raccoons who regularly crept into our yard at twilight. "He just wants to learn the technique," I said. "I don't think it's for any specific piece of furniture or whatever."

My father said, "I still don't get it."

"It's just for practice."

Frida slid her Jell-O into the fridge. Rupert had started her on it, making her a big bowl of it after hearing her vomiting up dinner one night. Since then she'd been consuming it nonstop, but Andrei had told us in no uncertain terms not to harass her for it. "She's eating," he said. "Doesn't matter what it is." Frida closed the refrigerator door and said, "Practice? Doesn't he know which family he's in?" She shot a sly glance toward the front door to indicate her parents and my mother. "We don't practice. We just shit things out and call it brilliant. We're perfection right out of the gates."

My father's spoon fell against the lid of the pot.

"Not you, of course, Uncle Jude," she added, all saccharine-and-velvet. "Besides, he doesn't have the family blood. The Gift. He *has* to practice."

He resumed stirring. Marcus smirked, though he kept his head down. Outside, a crumple of yellow paper floated past the window like a birch leaf and landed on the lawn. Andrei picked it up, smoothed it out, and shook his head. But he was grinning when he returned to his worktable, the hard line of his jaw momentarily softened.

A minute later, Pablo and Rafe slammed into the house.

"Guess they're still alive," Marcus muttered. We hadn't seen them in a day or two.

"Oh, look," Pablo said from the kitchen threshold. "Family Time. Aren't we lucky?"

Rafe dropped into a chair. "Is there food?" His pupils were massively dilated, two big black pools of nothingness. He ran his hand luxuriously over the tabletop as though the texture of the wood bewitched him. His sweater, saggy in the shoulders because it had been Andrei's first, reeked of smoke and of missed showers.

"There's Jell-O," I said. "And sausage pizza from yesterday in the fridge. Andrei splurged and brought it home from Waverly's."

"Oh, Waverly's. That's the best. We never get that." He was on me like a monkey, his thin arms squeezing my ribcage. "God, what a great night. Abra, your hair is so soft. And I love this table. Have you ever really looked at it?"

A hug from Rafe was cometlike, an event for which you had to sit still because the next one might not come for years. I didn't move.

Pablo opened the fridge and stood there shoving cold pizza into his mouth. "He's all fucked on happiness tonight," he said, nodding like a proud papa. "You should've seen him stroking parked cars and trees coming back."

"Happiness," Marcus mumbled. "There's a new term for it."

Pablo narrowed his eyes at him. "You could use it. You've always got a stick up your ass. I'll hook you up. Trust me, it'll be worth your while. Results guaranteed."

"You always sound like someone trying to sell a car with a dead transmission, you know that? I think I'll pass."

"Where's Mother?" Rafe asked, still draped over me.

"Madison again."

His mouth turned down in a little pout. "I guess she forgot I asked to go."

"I thought you said she'd just leave you there if you went anywhere with her."

"I wanted to meet the hippies. Sort of an insurance policy. I was thinking maybe they'll take me in someday like a circus, if I'm homeless."

"I don't think it's a group, Rafe. It's just some lady who's going to teach her Reiki."

"Wish she'd stay here and Rakey the leaves for once," Marcus said.

I said, "That's Andrei's line."

"Is there a law against borrowing lines?"

"Yes," my father said from the stove. "If you're going to say anything, be original."

Following some new train of thought, Rafe disengaged himself from me and stood up straight. "It's Halloween, you guys. We saw little kids in costumes. Oh, they were great." His eyes filled up. "Did anybody make Rupert a costume?"

We all looked guiltily at one another like bad parents.

"ROO-PERT!" Rafe bellowed. Then to us, "Is he in his room?"

There was a scuffle somewhere above us, then a thump-thump-thump along the banister. A moment later Rupert appeared with the plastic pumpkin bucket Jeff had gotten from someone at school.

"You've got a pumpkin! That's good, Beetsie, that's good. Lemme see."

Rupert began dragging the pumpkin across the kitchen table like a chariot. Pieces of candy fell out when he did a U-turn and for some reason this was painfully funny to all of us, except Marcus who always fought laughter as though it would somehow betray him.

The pumpkin rolled over my homework, dropping a couple of caramels like a pair of turds, then progressed at breakneck pace to the table's edge.

"No, Rupert, dangerous!" Rafe lunged to catch him. "Nuh-uh, sir!"

My father spooned brown sugar into his mouth. "You've all lost your friggin' minds," he said. He seemed oblivious to the fact that Rafe was intoxicated or worse.

"I'm going upstairs," Marcus said, gathering up his home-work. "I have to finish this."

"Tough graders in the au-to-mo-tive department?" Pablo asked. He had deep disgust for Marcus' earnestness. It was, he'd said once, *bowing down to the Man.* Becoming a kiss-up, a slave to the system, a Shirt. *Mechanics wear overalls, usually,* I'd dared to point out once, and paid for it.

Marcus ignored him and went upstairs, while my father wandered off with his bowl. It was just understood that I'd wash the saucepan and put away the Cream of Wheat. Rafe locked himself into the half-bath off the kitchen where he lamented loudly that he had to pee but couldn't get it out.

"STD?" Frida suggested, twisting a lock of hair in one finger. Roo crawled across her free arm, studying it for scars. She looked down. "I haven't," she said, a private aside to Rupert.

Pablo said, "STD's are your territory."

"I can't fucking get it out!" Rafe yelled.

"That's what she said."

"That doesn't even make sense," Frida pointed out.

"It could."

Rupert turned toward the bathroom door, all concern.

"He's fine, Roo," I said.

Pablo, who was now scraping burnt brown sugar out of my father's saucepan, propped a leg on a chair. I hated that posture, recognized it from the star athletes at our high school who thought they were gods and loved to lord it over their friends in the cafeteria or in homeroom. There was a self-satisfied insouciance about it that made me want to punch them. As if hearing me, Pablo leaned in my direction and sneered.

"Don't you look at her like that," Frida snapped. "You phony little bully. You're scrawny as fuck and she could take you any day of the week and so could I. There's a reason you're not on the football team. They'd snap your chicken neck on the first play."

He turned slowly. I was positive that he'd hit her in the face. But there was a muffled cry overhead, and then Marcus came pounding down the stairs, wild-eyed.

To Pablo, he said, "Was it you?"

Pablo fluttered his eyelashes at him.

"Christ, Pablo, you took it all? How could you—" He was staggered, holding onto the doorframe for support. "Do you know how long? How hard it is to . . . what did you use it for, beer? Fucking drugs?"

Frida said, "Marcus, what are you talking about?"

He could hardly get his breath. "My money. Everything I had saved. I just checked the envelope, and it's gone."

"Oh please. You make it sound like it was ten grand. It was pitiful, Marc. A total joke." Pablo returned to the fridge, bent low in a show of indifference. "I can't believe you're changing lube for what they pay you."

Anyone else would have shoved Pablo's head into the bowels of the refrigerator. But Marcus, pale, trembling Marcus who always seemed to be in physical pain, just stood there with his arms limp at his sides.

Pablo closed the refrigerator door and called out to my brother, "Going outside, happy-ass." He cast us a smug grin and let himself out the back door.

There was no sound except for a sudden stream of piss behind the bathroom door. When Rafe came out, he looked at us in bewilderment. "What's wrong?"

Marcus sank into a chair and dropped his head into his hands.

Rupert sat frozen in front of his pumpkin chariot. Quietly Jeffrey said, "Rupert wants to know if Marcus' money is all gone."

"All gone," I said.

Inebriated as he was, Rafe had the good sense not to touch or try to talk to Marcus. Frida sat there watching her brother sidelong as she chewed a hangnail. I didn't even notice Jeffrey get up, didn't hear him on the stairs. When he came back, Rupert had his plastic crayon bank in tow.

Struggling with the weight of it, he pushed it into Marcus' sightline. When Marcus didn't move, he pushed it closer until it nudged against my cousin's arm. He tapped the crayon, then pointed one antenna at Marcus.

"Oh, Rupert," Rafe said softly. "Your savings."

Nobody else said a word. Rupert put his feeler-head down on the table as if to say, *I'll stay here all night with you.* We all just sat there unmoving, and that was the scene when Andrei came in covered in sawdust.

"Jesus, who died?" he asked.

Marcus pushed the crayon bank back toward Rupert. "I'm going to bed."

"It's like eight o'clock."

"So?" He got up heavily and went upstairs. Frida went to her room, too, leaving the three of us at the table.

I looked at Andrei. "Pablo took all Marc's money. Just stole the whole stash."

"Of course he did. I told you, I know he got into my coffee can and took some of our squash money. It's a reflex with him."

Rupert held up the crayon again.

"No, buddy," Rafe said. "But it was a good try."

"I could kill him for Marcus," Andrei offered. "It would take about five seconds."

Nobody responded to that. Rafe was coming down from his high but was still caressing the tabletop. After a beat he said, "Hey. We should go see the float. It's got to be going right now, right? All the little lights . . ."

The pumpkin float was a Halloween tradition in Two Rivers, in which volunteers carved dozens of big jack-o-lanterns, lit candles within, and sent the gourds floating downriver. Eventually, the pumpkins that didn't capsize spilled into Lake Michigan and drifted off into the night. We hadn't watched the ceremony in years and I had no idea what had made Rafe think of it.

"Rupert," Andrei said, "you want to go?"

An enthusiastic feeler-nod.

"Come on, before somebody hears us leaving. We can take Jude's car. Where should we watch from? Riverside Park like we used to?"

"No," I said. "The north pierhead. Nobody else will be there—no Science. It's too cold on the lakefront."

Pablo was smoking in the yard when we piled into the car. He drifted slowly toward us, feigning disinterest, but when Rafe told him where we were going, he shrugged and climbed into the backseat. So it was the five of us who drove out to a gravel parking lot near the North Pier, which was just a long concrete strip tarred over with seagull droppings and old feathers. The October wind was ferocious, fighting us as we trekked to the pier's end in our heavy sweaters and hand-me-down coats. There was no lighthouse to speak of at the tip, just a diminutive pillar painted white and red, but the waves were more insistent here where they shattered against the jumbled-rock island. Most of the homes and businesses near the river had obliged tradition by turning off their lights, and so even the coastline was dark, the silhouettes of distant buildings suggested only by the graze of streetlamps. An ashen moon attended by pallid stars winked through the haze of clouds that were the dregs of a midday rain.

"It's fucking freezing," Pablo yelled above the wind and waves.

"How did you think it would be?" Andrei shouted back. "Go sit in the car, pansy-ass."

Pablo tried unsuccessfully to light a fresh cigarette, then turned to Rafe. "We should've brought that old bow and arrow we used to have. I think it's in the garage somewhere. We could shoot them as they come out onto the lake."

Rafe glanced over at Rupert. "We don't shoot pumpkins," I thought I heard him say.

"What?"

"Look," Andrei called, pointing. Behind us and to the south, where the West Twin met the East Twin, were lights— tiny orbs of marmalade light constellated on the water. "Here they come."

We crowded around the rail, even Pablo who was rolling his eyes from beneath his beanie-hat. At this point I was annoyed with myself for having suggested the pier. My face stung and my throat was raw. But a curious thing happened when Rupert came and sat atop my hand. It was as though I saw the float through his tiny eyes, and when the pumpkins came bobbing downriver, my breath caught. The pale gourds slowed and separated when they reached the Lake, their lights still flickering, and in their ghostly migration I glimpsed covered wagons carrying families huddled around oil lamps, and Tolkien's elves passing from one world to the next, and apostles bearing sacrifices to some atavistic god. It seemed a miracle that the pumpkins were intact, that their lights had not been extinguished along the journey, and when they began to float past us and out into the velvety expanse of the water, I wanted to chase them down and hold them close. The strangest part of it all was that I felt suddenly implicated, as though their certain demise out there in the deep was somehow my own doing. Why was the vision of that slowly-fading constellation so ruinous? It dizzied me, this alien compunction. For years our parents had modeled how to spy oneself in such flashes of errant beauty, but it was always a glorious self they glimpsed, the mirrored soul swollen to twice its true size.

Rafe's voice was fissured either by the wind or by some peculiar upheaval of his own: "Maybe we shouldn't have let him see this."

We all looked at Rupert, who was rigid atop my wrist, motionless as the last of the gourds drifted by. Andrei said, "They're fine, Rupert, they're happy. They'll just explore the Lake and have an adventure." But as the moon's wan glow repossessed the sky, a mood settled over us. We returned to the car and drove back in silence. Only Pablo interrupted the quiet: "They're not fucking alive, people. In case you didn't know. They're vegetables."

We all went to bed in our clothes. Jeffrey—Rupert—was so tired that he collapsed in a pile of blankets on my parents' couch. When I got up for water a few hours later, I spotted Pablo fitting Rupert's plastic pumpkin into Jeffrey's arms as he slept. We briefly locked eyes before Pablo went back upstairs to Rafe's room as though he hadn't noticed me at all.

In the kitchen that evening, my father had said we'd all lost our minds, but by November he too had fully converted.

One Sunday night when my father was typing away in his study, Jeffrey wandered in there and I followed him. Rupert climbed onto my father's shoulder and gently tugged his earphones away, then tossed them onto the desk. It was the sort of thing the rest of us wouldn't have dreamed of doing.

"Rupert," my father said sternly. "I'm working."

Rupert peered down at the manuscript, feelers scanning back and forth.

"Is it good?"

Rupert gave an unimpressed little shrug—something else we'd never in a million years do.

"Well, that's nice. If you could read, you'd know it was at least original . . . Look, don't interrupt. My day's ruined tomorrow. I have to do an open house."

Rupert jumped down off my father's shoulder and skittled over to the open page of a notebook. He drew a house with Rupert inside of it, a big question mark accompanying his self-portrait.

"You want to go with? What do you care about some dinko house I'm selling?"

Rupert stretched out his feelers, the tips clasped together in his classic "begging" posture.

"Oh hell. Will you let me work on this manuscript if I say yes?"

Rupert jumped up and down in assent.

Surprising myself, I said, "I want to go, too."

"Huh?" He glanced up as if just then noticing me. "Since when are you interested?"

"I just want to. Can I?"

"Whatever. Yes. Just leave me in peace already."

He had yet to publish even a short story. The novel manuscripts he sent to the big houses were summarily declined, and I'd read a few rejection letters left crumpled up in the metal wastebasket behind his desk. In one of them, the editor decried my father's work as a *mess of abstractions for abstraction's sake, an unmitigated study in arrogance and self-delusion.* He caught me in the act of reading that one. "They're cowards," he said by way of explanation, snatching the paper from my hands. "Afraid of anything they can't recognize."

On the ride out the next morning, Rupert sat up front with the knapsack he'd taken to carrying everywhere. It was loaded with his trinkets and harmonica and big packets of the red Kool-Aid powder Jeffrey loved to eat straight. I sprawled out in the back as Rupert rolled around on a squat plastic bus somebody had given him.

My father played a mix of Eagles and Guess Who songs as we drove. He said, "You'll like this next song, Roo—it's called *Bus Driver.*" Rupert nodded his feelers but was staring out the window in deep appreciation for the scenery, which wasn't much. I peered into people's yards and found it all pathetically ordinary, the swing-sets and the garden tools and the recycling bins. Driving through a residential neighborhood like this always refreshed my appreciation for my parents' refusal to conform. The neat houses and painted fences depressed me, as did the sight of their drab little owners puttering about, tutoring their yards into submission. Teachers, nurses, factory workers, store owners . . . these were people who grew tomatoes in spiral-shaped cages and put plastic decals on their front windows during the holidays and bought mailboxes shaped like cows or lighthouses. It seemed to me that their lives were over before they'd begun.

My father's voice startled me out of my reflections: "I had a weird dream last night. Actually I've had it probably ten times. That's what makes it weird. It's always the same."

I said, "What happens?"

His face in the rearview mirror looked startled, and I realized he'd been talking to Rupert. "There's a beach," he said after a beat. "A beach with this big stone wall, old and covered in vines. And I'm sitting on that wall looking out at the ocean, and I'm getting impatient because nothing's happening and I can't *make* anything happen. It's just still and the tide's doing its thing and I can't change the picture. It's like I'm trying to conjure something out of the air in front of me to make it interesting, but nothing comes."

I was bored, but said, "Is it scary? Like a bad feeling?"

"Not really. I just don't understand why it keeps coming back." My father reached over and patted Rupert, who was fixated on the passing houses. "What do you think, Bert? Little pinhead, you probably don't even have dreams, do you? Do bugs dream?"

Had he really forgotten Jeffery's vivid dream-talk from just the previous year?

Rupert turned a little and shook his feelers side to side.

My father said, "Nah, didn't think so. You don't have to. Everything you love is already here, huh?"

He had a point. For all his obsession with fairy stories, Rupert loved the most stolid, mundane things—trashcans and scrub brushes and mail trucks. He was always hugging objects that meant nothing to the rest of us. I said, "He's kind of simple."

"You can say that again. Give him an old light bulb and he's happy for hours. Wish some of you had been that easy as babies."

I fought competing impulses to remind him that Jeffrey—Rupert—wasn't a baby, and to ask what the rest of us had been like when we were. There were no baby pictures in either house, no videos, and nobody had saved the things we made in preschool or kindergarten. The second impulse won out. I said, "Were we really that hard?"

"Nah. Only Andrei was a tough nut to crack. My sister thought it was going to be all fun and giggles taking in these babies and then she didn't know what to do when she realized it wasn't, so it ended up being me a lot of the time watching him. Poor kid was always crawling to the front door like he was waiting for someone, maybe for that floozy mother of his to show up, though as far as I know she never looked back. We never knew *where* she went. And before she gave him up, she told Lissa she didn't even know who the father was." A pause. "I remember that he would always try to grab pens out of my hand."

"But I was different." I had too much pride to pump him for specifics, but I was hoping for something revelatory, a snippet of proof of my latent talent.

"You had your weirdness. Mirrors made you cry." He turned left and slowed down. "We're here."

The house was a pink bungalow near the river with a sagging backyard. "Built in 1918," he said as we climbed out of the car. "A geezer if you ever saw one. All it needs is a cane and an I.V., don't you think? And a cup of slurpy peaches or something."

He expected us to be as put-out as he was, but I'd never walked through an empty home before, and the sensation was similar to what I felt with my dollhouse—the pure possibility of possession. I moved slowly through the bare rooms mentally furnishing them, brightening the walls, suffusing the grey spaces with myself until they shimmered. I did this sort of thing on my babysitting gigs, too, delegating childcare to the television so that I could meander through the house dreaming, only in those rooms it was harder, for I had to root out the resting furniture, strip the staid shades and photographs from the walls before my mind could renovate them in accordance with my own refractory tastes.

Rupert followed me around, caressing windowpanes and doorframes, lingering over anything faded or damaged as if pondering the history of each scar. "It's fine," I kept telling him. "Not Sad. Relax." In the background my father complained that he wouldn't be able to sell the place even if he liquored up his potential buyers blind. When I came back to the kitchen to help him set out cheap cookies and brownies on trays, he mumbled something about the whole business being beneath him. "How," he moaned, "did I get stuck doing this for a living?" He slapped down a stack of clear plastic cups.

"Isn't there pop or something?" I asked, glancing around for it.

"Oh shit, I forgot it."

"People are here," Jeffrey called from upstairs.

More expletives from my father.

"There's tap water," I suggested.

"Yeah, Abra, let's pour the buyers tap water from the rusty sink." He shook his head and went to the front door. "This house is going nowhere."

He greeted the buyers so spiritlessly that I was embarrassed for them. A couple of them were elderly, and when they looked at me with pleasant interest, I had to explain who I was because it didn't occur to my father to introduce me. As he led the group through the living room, he was like a tour guide who'd given the same speech so many times that the words were just noises.

I don't know when Jeffrey went into the kitchen, but when we rounded the corner, Rupert was mixing bright red Kool-Aid into a glass pitcher he must have dug out of the cabinets. He'd found ice in the freezer and the cubes bobbed noisily in the ruby liquid as he stirred.

The clients were utterly charmed by this little boy with his tufted hair, mixing juice at the countertop. Of course no one knew that it was Rupert holding the stirring spoon. At one point I sidled up to him and whispered, "Rupert, *Science*," but he went on with his task as if I weren't there.

"What a sweetum," one of the women said, accepting a plastic cup of juice. "Lucky you to have a helper like this."

Everyone took a cup. People started to ask questions about the house. The showing went on, my father becoming more energetic. A second wave of viewers arrived later that

morning. Rupert used up all his Kool-Aid. Toward the end
there, a woman with wide, sympathetic eyes took my father
aside and said, "He must have a tough time at school, with
the way kids are. How did it happen?"

My father looked blank. "How did what happen?"

She nodded to indicate Jeffrey. Rupert was now rinsing
the pitcher under a stream of tap water. "Was it an accident,
or a birth defect kind of thing? I'm only asking because my
brother's a surgeon, and . . ."

She thought Jeffrey's hand was deformed, that he was
missing fingers. I caught my father's eye, saw him struggle to
keep back incredulous laughter. "Oh," he said, "we've done all
we could. It's just who he is now, though, and it's okay, really."

"Well, he's a brave boy," the woman said. "He's adapted
wonderfully."

When at last it was time to lock down the house, my father
picked up Rupert and gave him a sound pat on the shell.
"We're going to get an offer," he said. "Maybe more than one.
And I think it was all because of your magic beetle-juice."

Rupert climbed out of my father's hand and went to the
legal pad lying on the counter. He wrote, *good for the howse.*

"How's that, Roo?"

The shaky letters came quickly: *Sad. Needs love.*

"That's not really my concern, buddy."

Rupert shook his feeler-head vigorously. Lower on the
page, he wrote, *YOUR JOB,* then tapped hard on the words.

My father laughed at this. It was just a house. But a month
later, he landed his first publication in a literary journal—
the story of a home inspector who made up defects about an
old house he loved, because he couldn't bear to see it fall into
the wrong hands. At the story's conclusion, the narrator realized that he'd been lying to himself, too, but inversely: he was

always pretending to be clean and up to standards, but on the inside, he was all faulty wiring.

It was around this time that I began to tackle my schoolwork in earnest. Believing I'd caught his fever for gainful employment, Andrei brought home a community college catalogue for me and highlighted programs that guaranteed immediate placement upon completion. "If we're both working decent jobs, we could really turn things around," he said to me. *What things?* I wanted to ask. *Our siblings and parents? Are you crazy? What can we do anyway—and why is it* our *responsibility?* But I feigned interest in the catalogue and didn't mention to Andrei that only one of its glossy pages incited me: a leaflet toward the back that described classes in graphic design. Was this the road to my atelier? It wasn't as romantic as paint, but the catalogue boasted of "endless possibilities" with such a degree, which to me was synonymous with *escape.* There was also a line about "embracing your talent" that flattered me.

While I attended to my geometry and Spanish, Andrei worked an after-school job cleaning spilled soda and sticky pretzels off the bleachers in the high school gymnasium. On the weekends, he was outdoors or in the garage for hours at a time, getting to know the miter box and table saw he'd bought used from a yard sale. He hoped to enroll in a pre-apprenticeship program come summer, and he was resolute, sticking to his vow to leave poetry behind though I knew he went on reading his theologians at night, grappling with his inchoate apologetics as he had even over Jeffrey's crib. He still came to me with the ideas that troubled him, but now he was hyperalert to any shadow of boredom or frustration on my face. "Sorry, you're probably not in the mood for this," he'd say, saving me the trouble of checking him before his outpourings taxed my patience. I sometimes feigned interest, but all those labyrinthine deliberations seemed futile to me, silly, as if he were running a maze that had no exit and no reward. The answer, I wanted to tell him, was simple: there was no answer. Once he accepted that the maze's senseless switch-backing chaos was just life, and that such a world wasn't so terrible after all, he could relax. But I held my peace, partly because I didn't want to argue and partly because I felt sorry for him.

Back then, I had no idea of his exceptional intelligence, no sense that he was different from other eighteen-year-old boys. I lived so much inside my own head and was so isolated from my peers that I simply didn't see it. And there was an arrogance festering in me, composted by all that insulation. My cousins and brother seemed well-matched to simple, mechanical employments, but I had begun to nurse a sly suspicion that I was the one budding talent among us, the star waiting to break through the clouds. I suppose I had a great deal of my mother in me, for I lusted after the sort of lazy-but-glittering transformative experiences she spoke of when she returned from her retreats. I was certain that if there was anyone in the family who could act as a conduit for such power, it was me.

These illusions were only possible because Jeffrey's cynosure was over. His budding brilliance had snuffed itself out the moment Rupert appeared; his teachers' formerly laudative remarks ceased to accompany his homework, and he seemed, like the rest of us, to be doing only what was necessary to get through unnoticed. In the meantime, Marcus, who was still a year behind me at the high school, worked at an oil-change shop. Frida, Pablo and Rafe were always stumbling home drunk or high and no one dared ask where they'd been. It was obvious they were going nowhere.

One night as I worked resentfully on my math homework at the kitchen table, Marcus came back from work and fell into the chair across from me. He took off his glasses and let his head drop onto his forearm.

"You smell like a diesel truck that ran over a pile of movie-theater nachos," I said.

"One of the guys gave me this cheese pocket thing at lunch. It was disgusting." His shoulders twitched. "God, everything hurts."

"You're working too much, Marc."

"That's not it."

The overhead light flickered twice, then fizzled out.

"Andrei picked up bulbs from the dollar store like yesterday," Marcus said without lifting his head. "How does he always know when to buy them?"

"Maybe his watch tells him when to do it. He always knows when to replace the furnace filter, too. I wouldn't go near that thing with a ten-foot pole, even if we were all freezing to death."

"You and our parents both. It's beneath you, right?"

Ignoring this, I went and grabbed a table lamp from the living room and plugged it in. The sudden glare illuminated the wild cicatrix of silvery slug-trails that often marked our kitchen floors. The creatures got in through cracks or holes somewhere beneath the sinks and sometimes went topside, doing recon across the countertops before retreating to their unknown headquarters. As children we'd loved to extend our fingertips to the slugs to allow them to suck on our skin with their tiny mouths. Slug kisses, Rafe called them when he was a toddler. Even Andrei, who'd read somewhere that you could get meningitis from slugs and wanted us all to get vaccinated, loved it.

"Looks like the slugs are back in droves," I said. "You should see the tracks."

"I know. I came down here at like five in the morning the other day and they were all out for a war council or something. There were so many of them, I felt like Braveheart at Falkirk."

"Please. You adore them."

"Whatever."

I moved on to the next pointless little equation and worked in silence for several minutes, Marcus sleeping or spacing out beside me.

"Who else is here?" he said suddenly, head still down.

"Just my mom, somewhere."

"Who's she talking to?"

I cocked my head. "I don't know."

Marcus went back to sleep. I put down my pencil and tiptoed up the carpeted stairs to the landing. In an attempt to combat the musk-and-incense smell in both houses, Andrei had set up a cheap humidifier at the head of each set of stairs, then added eucalyptus oil and mouthwash to the water. The plastic tank sat chuffing its antiseptic sweat on a cleared-off square of carpet over in the corner, but this area was otherwise purgatorial in both houses, home to a farrago of unfinished projects and half-eaten snacks. I had to kick aside quite a bit of refuse on my way to my mother's door.

When I peered into the bedroom, I found her sprawled across her bed with her hair dangling over one side. Jeffrey was standing beside her, and Rupert was playing with her hair, combing his feelers through it as she talked. There were clothes everywhere and the air was thick with stale pot and musk oil, Andrei's efforts notwithstanding. Parti-colored light was confettied all over the room, filtered through the dreamcatchers and glass-shard chimes that covered her windows.

My mother had her hands folded on her belly. "There were three of them," she said, continuing some story. "Three little boys I watched. God, I was so young, like fifteen. The youngest one was just a baby. My first night working for them, the parents told me the baby wouldn't go to sleep unless I lay down with him in their bed. I was like, really? The last thing I wanted to do was climb into these people's bed with a drooling baby."

Rupert went on combing her hair. I couldn't get over her voice—so tentative, a far cry from its usual commandeering gruffness.

"So that night, I put the older two to bed and then lay down with the baby. I guess I fell asleep. When I woke up, this is the thing, he was touching my face with those tiny fingers. I mean just going over every line, like he was learning what a face was. Like he wanted to draw it after I was gone. I had goosebumps over my whole body." A small laugh. "It tickled so bad but I wouldn't let myself move. I didn't want it to stop. I felt so—it was like being—"

Patient, Rupert scratched at her scalp. I stood there transfixed. My mother had never spoken of her girlhood here in Wisconsin. All we'd ever heard about was her life in the communes, after she turned eighteen.

She said, "That's what I've been thinking about lately and I don't know why. Know what I realized, Rupert?"

Rupert came around the side of her head to look her directly in the eye.

"I can't draw faces. I never learned. I didn't think it was important." Then, her tone shifting back to its familiar abruptness, "This is stupid. I don't know why I'm talking about this. Go play, Rupert. You can be done with Hair Salon now."

In response, Rupert began to trace the features of her face: brow, nose, cheek. My mother went still. I took a silent step back, then another, until I was halfway down the stairs. I returned to my seat at the kitchen table and resumed my homework. Marcus went on snoring. But the numbers in my textbook blurred together. It had come to me in a rush that our parents required kindness and attention just like anyone else—the occasional 'good helper' Rupert had been at my father's open house. We'd spent our childhoods resenting them for what they would not give us, but it never occurred to me that we could have, as Andrei said, *turned things around* by offering them the very thing we'd been denied. Would it have been so hard? Were we all so starved and parsimonious that we couldn't lend a nickel's worth of affection without promise of its immediate return?

The revelation was fragile, a dandelion's skeleton. When the front door banged open a minute later and Lonnie came in all slit-eyed and bellicose, it was easy to let the wind shatter it. Feral cats were better parents than ours, and they deserved nothing.

"Where is that tramp?" Lonnie demanded.

I assumed he meant Frida. "I don't know."

"One of her boy-toys is at our house, looking for her. Running his mouth like it's my fault I don't know where she is. He was just waiting inside when I got back from town. Want to know how? He has a key! The dumb bitch gave him a *key to our house.*"

Marcus lifted his head a little. "Since when do we even lock doors?"

Jeffrey came down the stairs, Rupert thumping his way along the banister. He went straight to Marcus, who ignored him when he pressed his feeler-head into his upper arm.

Lonnie said, "I can't write music when she's letting these creeps in and out of my house whenever they damn please. That's my space. Does she own the house? If she wants to pass out house keys, she should at least get a job and start pulling her weight, all sixty pounds of it. For Christ's sake, I need some fucking *quiet*."

The timing of this remark couldn't have been worse. Andrei must have just gotten home, because outside the miter box came to life with a screech, and two seconds later, the Scotsman launched into his nightly practice session, practically shaking our windows with his opening notes. In another house the ensuing cacophony as chanter competed with miter saw might have been hysterically funny.

We all looked wide-eyed at Lonnie, Rupert included. His feelers swung up and around, and then his whole body began to shake.

"It's okay, Roo," I began. It was automatic.

My uncle lifted his hand. For a split second I thought he was going to hit Jeffrey. Instead he gave Rupert a couple of rough thumps on the back of his shell. "It's been louder," was all he said before turning away and exiting the house.

Marcus shook his head in disbelief, then limped over to the fridge to look for dinner. Even with his back turned to us, he must have been able to feel Rupert watching his movements, because he stopped rummaging and snapped, "I'm fine. Go find something to do already."

Not too long after this, Rupert wrote his note insisting that my father take Marcus to a doctor. When my father and Marcus returned from Green Bay with the diagnosis, Marcus went straight to Rupert and lifted him to his face. Andrei and I watched, breathless, as Marcus pressed his forehead to Rupert's antennae. "Not going to be like this forever," he mumbled. "Thank you, Roo."

My father watched also. Then he cleared his throat and explained to us about mild juvenile arthritis, how it would resolve itself on its own in a few years, how in the meantime there were painkillers Marcus could experiment with, but I wasn't listening.

Rupert had eased Marcus' glasses halfway down his nose. He moved the tip of one feeler over my cousin's lashes, then over his closed lids. Marcus stood there as if receiving a blessing. The moment only broke when the phone rang. We all jumped, but Rupert ran down Marcus' arm and across the counter to the phone. He got the receiver out of the cradle, peered into the mouthpiece, then turned to look at us as if to say, *oh no! I forgot I can't talk!* Then he slumped forward on the countertop, eyes down, in comical despair.

Everyone laughed. Andrei picked up the phone and fielded the sales call. Most of us ate around the same table that night—Lissa and Lonnie's—and after dinner, my father startled us all by saying he might try writing at the table for a change, just to see. When I fell asleep on the living room floor, it was to the sound of keys tapping, their music ascending from the most unlikely point in the house: its center.

What did he write that time? Not a story. It was a formal letter addressed to Rupert B. Bug, from a fictional optometry school, offering him a full ride. My father printed it, folded it into a plain white envelope, and stuck it in the mailbox. Rupert loved mail and it was a given that he'd see it first.

I had no memory of my parents playing with me when I was a child. Certainly no one made up such an elaborate game as this just to make me laugh. And yet I felt no resentment; I wanted in on the fun. With my babysitting money, I bought Rupert one of those glasses-repair kits, the kind that came with a tiny magnifying glass, so that he could class up his practice. For his part, Andrei wood-burned him a small sign: *Rupert B. Bug, Dr. of Optometry.*

I recall the way we all froze when another of Frida's boyfriends, passing through the house with her, saw Andrei's sign and said, "What the fuck is that?"

He wasn't the only one to ask. It happened every time a stranger came onto our property. *Why are there bugs drawn everywhere? What's up with that?* On a junior-year field trip to a lapidary museum later that year, I spotted a glowing nugget of opalite and blurted out, "God, Rupert would love this."

Maybe we were all crazy. But Rupert, our family secret, had begun to bond us together, and it was his name my dying father was destined to cry out before everything went dark.

VII.

MOST YEARS, WE WERE TOO DISORGANIZED for holidays. Christmas was a slapdash affair—Lonnie might pick up an alcohol-soaked fruitcake from Two Rivers, my aunt might force a few of us to Mass (her one concession to the silly trappings of Christmas "conventions"), my cousins might build a lewd snowman in the front yard. New Year's Eve was a forgotten entity and passed each January like a comet for which no one bothered to watch.

But I do remember New Year's Eve of that first year after Ontonagon. It was a Friday night and snow creaked on the roof while a motley crew of us sprawled in my parents' living room. Lonnie and my mother had escaped south to crash with some old commune friends, as they often did when the forecast called for the kind of snow that trapped people in their homes. Frida had told everyone she had a date, but the two of us were on the outs and I figured she was just trying to avoid me. Rafe was out, too, and even Pablo didn't know where he was. So it was my father, Lissa, Andrei, Marcus, Pablo and me, with Rupert sitting under the ridiculous Christmas tree he'd made back in December when no one was willing to bring home a real one. It was a wooden tennis racquet standing upright in a plastic stand, both items dug out of a bin at the Goodwill. Rupert had strung colored lights and tin ornaments along the racquet strings before plugging the mess into the wall outlet.

"So lame," Pablo mumbled from his place face down on the sofa. He was nursing an epic hangover-headache and had flung to the floor the amethyst necklace Lissa had dropped on his head as an anodyne.

"At least he tried," my father said. He had a newspaper on his lap.

"What should we do?" Lissa paced around, biting her nails. She was always like this when Lonnie left—so was my father, when my mother went on her trips—though none of us understood it. What did they care? My aunt said, "We should do something."

"Die," Pablo offered.

"Snow hike?" Andrei suggested.

Marcus, who'd been tinkering with our forever-malfunctioning grandfather clock, crossed the room and resettled himself on the floor near the space heater. He was always cold, and it didn't help that the heating systems in both houses were defective. He said, "That's a great idea, Andrei. How about we just open the door and invite Pneumonia in for a party? And her sexy friend, Bronchitis?"

"We need television," I said. "Normal people watch television on a night like this. It fills the space." When no one answered, I said, "What's with the newspaper, Dad?" We never read them in either house. There was no delivery route where we lived, and if any of us bought one from a supermarket or gas station, it was to kindle a beach fire or stuff a rat hole.

"I was looking for story triggers."

Andrei rolled his eyes, and he wasn't subtle about it.

"Is there a problem, Andrei?"

"Why would there be a problem."

My father shook his head, then snapped the newspaper back open. "Seems it's been kind of a violent month in northern Wisconsin. You know somebody drowned himself right in Two Rivers? Young guy, weighed himself down with a pack of dumbbells from his home gym and jumped right in. Picked the East Twin, for whatever reason."

"Sounds pretty half-baked to me," Marcus said. "If you want to end it, Lake Michigan is the gold standard. You go in far enough and that current is as bad as the ocean."

"Like you've ever been to the ocean," I said.

"I don't have to. Our waves can reach twenty feet high when the weather is right."

"Thank you, Encyclopedia Eeyore."

"So why'd the guy do it?" Lissa asked idly, twisting a lock of hair around and around her wrist.

"Who knows." My father turned a page. "There was a backyard murder, too, in Milwaukee. Some teenager tracks down his dad after the guy leaves them and moves in with a new family. Finds his father out back at the girlfriend's house, chopping wood, and just shoots him."

"With what?"

"Uh—it says a twenty-two rifle."

"You can barely drop a snake with one of those," Marcus said.

"Well, it says he killed him." My father closed the paper. "Brutal."

Lissa said, "Never underestimate the petulance of a kid who didn't get picked for Daddy's Team. I met a few of those in the communes. You could always tell. They just couldn't get over it. I never understood it. I mean, move on already."

There was a minute explosion to my right. Andrei, who'd been examining a broken light on Rupert's racquet-tree, had cracked the red glass between his fingertips.

"We'll get you better lights next year, Roo," Marcus said. "Those are from like the eighties."

My father was staring at his sister. "Who, exactly, is *petulant*, Lissa?"

"Maybe *pathetic* is the better word," she responded. "You know, the type to do the same thing over and over again, even when he's getting the same results, because he's still trying to impress Dad."

"I just published a story in a fucking journal. A pretty big one, too. But you probably didn't notice. You were too busy blowing your nose onto a canvas."

"As if you'd know the first thing about art—"

"Must be nice," Andrei interrupted. "Having all the time in the world to write stories and get published and hunt down *story triggers.*"

My father rocked forward in his chair. "Okay, Andrei, that's it. If you've got something on your mind, let's hear it. Because you've been a passive-aggressive little shit for like two weeks. Did I take something from you or what?"

Andrei's eyes on my father were cold. "What could you take? What is there to take?"

Rupert wrote something on his legal pad. He tapped it loudly and I bent to look. *New Year's Rezolooshuns!*

"He wants us to make New Year's resolutions," I said.

"Please," Lissa said. "No one keeps them anyway." In a mincing voice she parroted, *"I'm going to lose weight. I'm going to take better care of my teeth."*

"They don't have to be that lame," Marcus pointed out. "Sky's the limit. Besides, don't most people just put down something they want? Rather than some chore?"

Rupert started tearing out little pieces of paper for us.

"What do you think they're doing tonight?" my father asked Lissa out of the side of his mouth.

Andrei said calmly, "Frida's screwing someone in an icy truckbed and Rafe's getting stoned."

My father's eyes narrowed. "I wasn't talking to you. And I meant Lonnie and my wife."

"Also screwing someone in an icy truckbed, and getting stoned," Marcus muttered.

Both Lissa and my father pretended not to hear. Marcus rolled over and dug something out of his pants pocket—one of the big gingerbread cookies Frida always stole around Christmastime. He peeled back the cellophane and took a huge bite.

"Where's you get that?" I demanded.

"It was lying on the driveway."

"You know that's Frida's. It probably fell out of her purse or something."

"What, you want me to put it back in there for her?" Marcus snorted and took another bite, almost taking off the head of the St. Nicholas decal that was sugar-glued to the dough. "Kinda late for that."

"At least give the decal to Rupert to give back to her. She's obsessed with those."

Lissa said, "With the stupid Santa stickers? Why?"

I didn't answer. Meanwhile Rupert handed out our slips of paper. My father went into his study and came back with a metal cup full of ballpoint pens. "What the hell," he said, passing the cup around.

Rupert switched the tennis racquet lights off and on again as a signal. We rolled our eyes but bent over our papers, all of us save Pablo who dug his thumbs into his temples. A few seconds later, the Scotsman started up next door playing "The Little Drummer Boy" on his bagpipes. It was loud enough that some of the icicles fell off our roof and crashed to the porch.

"It's like a bad dream," Pablo moaned. "My God."

"This *is* almost comically depressing," my father admitted, pretzeled in his armchair. "Look at us. Not even a candy cane in the house. Other people are . . . well, they're not doing this." He bit his pen, then scrawled something across his bit of paper.

I sat there watching the rest of them write. What did I want? Finally I put down, *paint THE picture*. It was just a blur in my mind's eye, but I had an idea of it, this painting that would jumpstart my escape. I sat back, satisfied. It didn't occur to me that I would be asked to read my resolution aloud.

"Who's first," Andrei said once the rustling of paper had died down.

Pablo turned his face to say, "Mine's easy. I'm going to *get* those pricks who buy pot from me and then act like they don't know me the next day at school."

Lissa folded her arms. "You need some ibuprofen, Pablo, if you won't use the stones. Or get a good night's sleep for once."

"Why don't you give the porn a rest," I suggested.

"Why don't you leave my shit alone."

"I never touch it." This wasn't exactly true. Regular trash-duty involved my going through all the rooms with a yard waste bag to snatch up the old food and soda cans that might otherwise attract rats. A week earlier, I'd noticed a Picasso book stashed in Pablo's room with his porn mags. I had a good laugh over it—could there be anything more ridiculous?—then yanked the book from the pile, adding it to my own collection of pilfered volumes.

Pablo muttered into the couch, "You do worse than touch. You steal. And not just from me."

I bristled. "Whatever Frida told you was total bullshit."

He picked up his head and gave me a sly smile. "I don't think so." To the rest of the room, he continued, "Rumor has it Abra nabbed some shit out of Frida's closet. And then she was dumb enough to think she wouldn't notice. Hello, you can't steal from a thief and get away with it."

Reflexively I reached back to touch my hair, which I'd been keeping coiled in a messy bun to hide the zigzag pattern Frida had shorn into it as I sat on the edge of her bed, clueless. "I don't know what you're talking about," I said.

Pablo laughed, then made a sound like he might throw up.

"Not on the couch, Pablo," my father said. "Not this time."

Marcus said, "What'd you steal?"

"Nothing. I didn't touch her stuff. Her room is such a mess, she doesn't need anybody's help losing things." But I was careful to avoid eye contact with Andrei. The truth was that I'd gone into Frida's closet in search of a missing sweater and had stumbled upon a little stash of art supplies she'd obviously swiped from a store somewhere—two miniature canvases and a pouch of paints, everything small enough to have fit under her waistband. I stood there for a few seconds, beads of sweat breaking out on my forehead. What was she doing with this stuff? If it was meant to be a gift to me, she would have given it to me already . . . and Frida didn't buy people gifts. I felt so unaccountably threatened that I snatched up the bundle and rushed from the room in a blind haze. I'd almost forgotten about it a week later when Frida told me my hair was looking straggly at the ends and could use a trim.

"Liar," Pablo sang out.

"Please," I said. "Marcus has a *safe* in his room because of you."

"Is that why you dragged that thing upstairs?" Lissa asked. "For some reason I thought it was a mini refrigerator. Where'd you get it, anyway?"

"Junkyard," Marcus said. "I know a guy at the junkyard. And yeah. I have it because otherwise Pablo would take my money *and* my fucking painkillers."

Pablo had either fallen asleep or couldn't be bothered to defend himself.

Marcus shifted position on the floor. "Speaking of the junkyard guy. My resolution is to get him to let me look stuff over before anyone else does. There's some jackass from Manitowoc who crawls in there first thing in the morning and he always gets the best stuff from the day before."

"Bribe him," I suggested.

"I'm going to. I know how these things work."

"I'm going to look around for an agent," my father cut in.

Lissa snorted, "Like a movie star? Please . . . I'm going to revolutionize my collages. Start using organic material in ways no one's thought of before." She glanced around at us, then added primly, "And I'm going to recite the rosary once a month."

Andrei let out a bark of a laugh. "Well, that's all you need to do. Just say that rosary."

"My sister, the schizo," my father sighed. "The only hippie Catholic in America. Though maybe that's not fair . . . you're neither hippie nor Catholic. More like a half-baked streak of each. You know, you could play with any old necklace, and it won't make a difference."

"You sound like Andrei. Mr. Bible, our little Protestant."

"That's TBD," my father said, tenting his fingers. "I've seen some Kierkegaard lying around, but I've also seen him knee-deep in Saint Augustine. Very Catholic. Not to mention a whole bunch of other bigshots from every clique you can think of." Then, like a game show host, "What denomination is behind door number four, ladies and gents?"

"Nothing," Andrei said. "I'm not anything. Maybe I *will* be when someone explains things well enough. I liked Luther tearing into all the Catholic bullshit, bribing your way into Heaven and all this pope garbage, things they made up but passed off as being old as dirt—"

Lissa let out a loud, exaggerated yawn.

"—But once you read him, you have to wonder, what else is made up that people just treat like a given?" Almost to himself, he added, "I don't know about Augustine, either. I don't get it, these guys who say God is only good and only ever was good. It seems too easy. I mean at first you'd think, of course he's all good. He's freaking God. But something's off."

I said, "Off?"

Andrei turned toward me. "If God's only goodness, and he's supposed to be the creator or the designer of everything, whatever, then where does all the evil come from? I mean did God wake up one day and jump out of his skin and say, 'wait, what's that sinister-looking thing in the corner over there? I didn't make that! How did that get there!?' If that's true, that means he's not much of a God at all, right? But if it isn't true—if he's got the, you know, the Dark Side in him, then—then the same question, right? What kind of God is he then?"

"I'm officially exhausted," Lissa interjected.

Marcus said, "How did we get on this subject, anyway?"

"Resolutions."

Lissa said, "How about you tell us your little resolution, Andrei, instead of playing Professor?"

"Fine. My resolution is to teach the rest of you, minus Abra, how to wash a fucking dish. We'll go real slow, take the lessons in five-minute increments so there's no confusion. And don't worry, we'll be sure to set aside enough time in the schedule for Jude to write his amazing stories, and for you to make your snot-paintings, and for everyone else to do whatever they feel like, whenever they feel like—"

"Oh, get over it. I'm sick of this martyr complex. You don't have to do any of it if you don't want to," my aunt snapped.

"Oh really?" He straightened up. "Do you know what happened last week? The only reason you didn't take a shower in vomit was because I cleaned up after Rafe sprayed the whole bathroom. And how about Taryn's experiment with that bread machine she brought home from Goodwill?"

My father said, "What about it?"

"Did no one notice that there was never any bread? I was in your kitchen, like ten days after she said she was going to make sourdough, and I swore I saw the machine *moving*. It wasn't even plugged in. I went over and pulled off the lid and it was swarming with maggots. She got halfway through and just forgot it. There were so many worms, the thing was—"

"Okay," Marcus said. "You can stop right there."

"Good thing I didn't though, right? Or there'd be worms crawling all over the kitchen, breeding in the goddamn drawers. I threw the whole machine out and I don't even think she noticed *that*."

Mouth twisting, my father said, "Probably she was saving the maggots for her *art*. Organic material and such."

"Okay, let's hear Abra's resolution," Lissa said hastily.

Andrei turned to me. "Please, do something to elevate this stupid game."

I curled my slip of paper into my fist. "Mine's just to help out more," I said. In the moment, I meant it.

Pablo called out, "Boo," then winced.

"Hey," my father said, pointing at the floor. "We forgot one. What do you have there, bud?"

Rupert held up his paper and we all leaned forward to see. It was a self-portrait with a big thought-bubble above the feelers. Inside the bubble he'd drawn ten stick figures. He tapped the figures, then pointed with one curled-in feeler to the pad just below Jeffrey's pointer finger—Rupert's heart.

"Oh," my father said. Another icicle hit the porch and shattered.

"How about Swiss Miss," Lissa said, going into the kitchen. "I think we have the kind with the dried marshmallows already in the packets."

Nobody bothered to respond. The bagpipes finally went silent, and my father pulled the newspaper over him like a blanket and closed his eyes. Marcus lay back as if to sleep. I glanced at Rupert, whose feeler-eyes met mine. "Take a nap, bud," I said. "I promise I'll wake you up to see midnight." But I was tired, and I knew I wouldn't do it.

When everyone else had passed out, Andrei beckoned me upstairs where he sat me down on the edge of the bathtub and cut my jagged hair straight with a pair of Fiskars. He didn't ask about Frida or explain how he knew what she'd done; he only said, "Come on, I know this is impossible to do yourself," and I submitted, watching the hard line of his jaw in the mirror as he snipped away.

At one point he said, "Feel like talking? I've got things nagging at me."

I closed my eyes. "There's no such thing as a free haircut, huh?"

"Never mind." He brushed out my hair to check his handiwork. "All done. No fee."

Eventually we returned to the living room and fell asleep on the floor. Deep into the night, I thought I heard my father on the phone with my mother—I caught the words *alone* and *home,* along with my name and Rafe's—but when I woke up, I was certain I'd dreamed it. In the blue glow of the early morning Andrei turned over, battling a nightmare, and Marcus reached for a blanket that wasn't there. I was too lazy to get up, but Rupert read my mind and used his feelers to tug down an old quilt we kept folded on the sofa. With difficulty he covered Marcus. Then he patted Andrei's hand. Lastly he rubbed Pablo's forehead as my cousin slept, his feeler-tips moving in gentle circles until Pablo's knotted muscles relaxed.

On a wet afternoon a few weeks later, I slogged through the door in my soaked boots to find my mother and Lissa in our kitchen, passing the telephone receiver back and forth.

"Is there video? How do you know he's not making it all up?" my mother asked.

"Give me back the phone," Lissa hissed. "This is total bullshit."

I dropped my backpack on the table. "What's going on?"

My mother waved me off. "If there's no video, there's no proof," she went on.

"Damn right," Lissa said. She snatched the phone from my mother. "This is just some spoiled brat looking for attention. He's making it all up," she informed whoever was on the other end. "Nobody got hurt, right?"

I said, "Mom."

She piled her hair onto her head, then let it fall into her face. "Some athlete is saying your brother and Pablo cornered him in a bathroom at the school, with a knife. Threatened to kill him, or something. They want to suspend them both. They say we're lucky they're not expelling them."

It didn't even occur to me to doubt the story. I said, "Did they cut the guy?"

"No," Lissa practically shouted at me, phone still in hand. "Nobody got hurt. And there's no proof anything even *happened.*"

My mother took back the receiver and listened for a few minutes before hanging up. She turned back to us. "They did find the knife on Pablo," she said, her tone expressionless. "A big knife. And she said there are other students who've come forward and mentioned threats, things they've said in the hallways."

"Kids," Lissa said flatly. "It's how boys are."

I let out a short laugh. "Not normal boys. Those boys take it out on the field. They don't trap people in bathrooms like sociopaths."

My mother looked stunned. Lissa also stared at me.

"Let me guess," I sighed. "They missed the bus because they're in some office, and you want me or Andrei to go pick them up."

Lissa recovered first. "I'm not going out there." She addressed the kitchen appliances, the table and chairs, as though they'd criticized her. "I'm not playing into this crap. They've been harassing us since you kids were in grammar school." She was referring to the truancy offi-cer who used to hang on the doorbell when we missed too much school. "They won't be happy until we're working bake sales and fundraising for Kiwanis Club. Which is probably what the brain-dead mother of this little whiner does all day long."

"I'll go." My mother lifted her purse from its hook by the stairs. She was wearing one of her Lookaway dresses despite the cold, but she at least had the sense to tug a sweater over it before exiting the house.

I tugged my boots back on and followed her outside to the car. "Mom," I said. "Be careful. They can be . . . if they're angry, just be careful."

She was halfway into the driver's seat, but she stopped and looked at me. "What?"

"Maybe you should take Andrei with you. If you wait a few minutes, he'll be home. I think he was picking up Rupert and stopping at the hardware place."

I watched her pale features struggle to arrange themselves into an expression of disdain. "What are they going to do? They're kids. Don't be so melodramatic."

I shrugged and stepped back. I watched her pull out through the dirty snow and then I turned to find Lissa fuming on the front porch.

"Don't tell me you believe all this," she said.

"I don't know."

Forty minutes later, Andrei pulled in in Lissa's car. Rupert was holding a small plastic bag from Ace Hardware—Andrei had bought him a tiny measuring tape and pair of mini-pliers—and he got busy measuring my arm at the kitchen table while Lissa explained to Andrei what had happened.

"So they, what, one of them held this kid down and the other put the knife on him?" Andrei demanded.

"You're not listening. I'm telling you, it wasn't even real. God, you're as bad as her." Lissa indicated me with a flick of her wrist.

Rupert stopped playing with the tape and sat there on the tabletop listening.

"The stupid little basketball player is making it up," Lissa went on. "He's just a brat looking for favors. I wouldn't be surprised if he was the one putting a knife on *them*. You should have heard the principal on the phone—'*one of our star athletes! He said he was afraid for his life!*'" She clutched dramatically at her heart. "Oh, the poor baby!"

"Why would he make it up?" Andrei moved to the sink where a stack of filthy dishes waited and started the tap. "Six-foot-something athlete admits Pablo and Rafe scared the shit out of him like that? Don't you think that'd be kind of humiliating? Especially because it's *them*."

The back door had opened and Pablo stood there with his mouth working. "What's that supposed to mean, Andrei?"

Andrei didn't turn around. He didn't even stop scrubbing.

Rafe came in on Pablo's heels. Behind him I glimpsed my mother in the backyard, pacing around in the snow with a cigarette.

"Really, Andrei, I'd love to know," Pablo went on.

"What I mean," Andrei said calmly, stacking a dish, "is that it's twice as embarrassing for someone like this guy you assaulted, when it's somebody like you doing it. What I mean is that you're the school losers. It's like admitting to being scared shitless by couple of rooting possums."

For a second, no one moved. Then Pablo approached Andrei. Very delicately he ran his fingertips over a huge pair of scissors lying on the drying board, the scissors we used to cut up frozen pizzas. Andrei watched this but continued washing dishes. Their eyes met.

"Go ahead," Andrei said softly, unblinking. "Improvise. I'm sure they confiscated your knife."

I held my breath. I was so wonted to Andrei's dutifulness that I sometimes forgot about his raw courage—and his capacity for violence. It was like glimpsing heat lightning from a tremendous distance.

"Stop it," Lissa cried. "Both of you, shut up. There was no knife."

Cigarette smoke billowed into the kitchen; my mother was now in the doorway. "Yeah, there was. They showed it to me in the office." She let her purse drop to the tile floor. "They're both suspended for a week."

Lissa smacked the countertop with the flat of her hand. "That's ridiculous."

"Rupert is shaking," Rafe said quietly.

We all turned to look. Rupert had crawled into the plastic sack from the hardware store and the whole bag trembled.

Andrei shut off the tap and came over to the table. He fished Rupert out of the bag and picked him up, holding him clam-shelled between his hands. "What'd you get out if it?

I mean, scaring this kid. Did you feel like big, bad boys or what? How'd he piss you off—bullying you around or just being who he was?"

"He had it coming," Rafe said, his chest puffing out. "He was a dick to us, him and his friends, all the time—" But he broke off. He was still watching Rupert.

I swung around toward Pablo. "You were really born in the wrong time, you know that? Or the wrong country. You'd fit in great in some Neanderthal tribe, you know, the kind with an eye-for-an-eye system, and a ten-word vocabulary."

He only grinned at me, like he knew me better than I did. I wanted to leap up from the table and shove him backwards into the counter.

Rafe sat down gingerly beside me and picked up Rupert's tape measure. "What's this, bud? Is this yours?"

Rupert peered out of Andrei's hands, then darted back in like a frightened turtle. Rafe put the tape measure down. He looked like he might cry. "No Science, bud," he said. "Just me. C'mon."

Pablo turned and left for the other house. After a beat Lissa followed him, shaking her head at us as though we were the offenders. My mother made herself a cup of instant coffee, pouring in way too much powder, and dropped into the chair across from me.

"Rafe," she said. "Are you drunk?"

"What do you care," he said lifelessly. His head was down on his forearm.

My mother pushed the coffee cup toward my brother. "I'm sure it was just a misunderstanding," she said, as if to herself. "I'm sure."

"Pablo told them it was our camping knife," Rafe went on in that dull tone. "We use it to get kindling down by the lake. He said we forgot we had it."

"They're both failing most of their classes," Andrei said gently, as though Rafe weren't there. He set Rupert down on the table. "Not that we can talk—Abra and I have screwed up plenty. But if they don't turn it around a little, like we are, they won't graduate, or they'll graduate in such bad shape no one will ever give them a job. Like Frida."

My mother's look was faraway.

"*Aunt Taryn.*"

She snapped to attention.

"They're not artists. None of us are artists. We need reality, and we need it because we have to make it in the real world. Some of us might want to take charge of our lives . . . and maybe be able to take care of other people, too, not just ourselves."

My mother's face hardened, the way Rafe's or Pablo's did when they were insulted, but this only lasted a moment. For my part, I wondered who he meant besides himself. I had no intention of "taking care" of anyone. I was still focused only on escape, a way to live as freely as our parents did but in some place more romantic than this.

Rafe tried to hand Rupert the tiny pliers. "Are you learning skills, Beets?" he asked. "With Andrei?"

Cautiously Rupert nodded.

"Who do you want to take care of? A bug family?"

Rupert shook his feeler-head. He pointed to me, to Andrei, to my mother, and then to Rafe.

"We weren't actually going to cut him," Rafe said suddenly to my mother.

"Who held the knife?"

"Pablo."

"Whose idea was it to—scare him?"

He hesitated. "Mine."

My mother got up from the table and went upstairs without another word. The four of us sat at the table beneath the ticking clock for an eternity before Rupert made sleeping motions to indicate he was tired.

How easy it was to swell up with righteous indignation that night in the kitchen. And how easy to forget it less than a month later when I found myself alone in the high school art lab, a room I'd refused to enter all three years of my tenure there.

It was the first time I'd entered such a classroom. I'd absorbed my parents' contempt for formal schooling in art, their assertion that such training decimated raw talent and conscripted one's work into the endless ranks of copycats. It was fine to read a bit, to eye the paintings of the greats, but to have someone grip your wrist and show you how to move the brush? To have a writing instructor review your work and tell you what must be cut or redone? This was a betrayal of self. And so I had never enrolled in the school's watercolor or printmaking classes, never considered the big posters proclaiming upcoming student exhibitions in the gym.

But earlier that day in homeroom, a clique of girls had gathered around one of their queens, Margaret Peters, who'd apparently just won some contest. She waxed forever about some arts program out of state that found students apprenticeships with real painters and sculptors. Flushed and breathless, she confided to her little crowd of supplicants that she thought she had a chance at a scholarship now that she'd won this contest two semesters in a row.

I knew Margaret. She was spoiled, her father a doctor. Probably she didn't remember it, but I'd gone to her house once, when we were just third-graders, for a birthday party. I'd never been invited, of course. It was an accident, an invitation meant for an *Abbie* left in *Abra's* locker, but I went to the party anyway like a fool. I got there late because it took forever to track down a parent to drive me over. Margaret's mother told me to head on through the house to the back deck. Then she left me, trusting me to do as I was told. I wandered in the direction she'd indicated but stopped at the sight of a huge aquarium running half the length of the living room wall. The softly rippling water, the blue-green glow of scales and fins, drew me nearer until I stood with my nose to the glass. In the pellucid depths were fairy castles with drawbridges, billowing ferns with rosy lights nestled around them, colored stones tracing paths through pink anemone gardens. There must have been thirty kinds of fish moving in their placid circles. Occasionally one of them paused to nibble at the food-flakes someone had sprinkled over the surface. To the side, small devices worked to regulate the temperature and keep the water clean. The tank hummed gently. When I tapped the glass, a yellow fish streaked with blue darted away to the shelter of a gazebo, then turned back to study me, treading water.

Instinctively I knew that the care of something like this was completely beyond my family. The water would go untreated; the fish would die. The house would reek for months and no one would ever admit to having been at fault. "Pet store lied," someone would say, or, "That tank was broken when we bought it." Andrei would have to flush the slick little bodies down a toilet and drag the tank out to the curb.

Staring into that aquarium, I was struck dumb with admiration—and yearning. And then Margaret Peters walked in and gaped at me like I was a raccoon or squirrel who'd crept in through a broken screen. "What are you doing here?" she asked in perfect bewilderment. Her voice shattered the awe I'd felt, and as she coolly explained that there must have been some mistake, she'd never sent me an invitation, I eyed the aquarium and decided there was nothing beautiful about it after all. It was just another thing rich people had, and what was the point? What could you do with pet fish anyway?

At seventeen, Margaret was as maddeningly sure of herself as she'd been in the third grade. She was the kind of girl to roll her eyes and mutter something into a friend's ear if she saw me in line in the cafeteria or changing out of my ill-fitting clothes in the PE locker room. Spoiled as ever, she'd been taking private painting lessons since freshman year, and now she thought she was God's gift to the art world. She was no doubt picturing herself gilt-framed on a wall in the Art Institute of Chicago before turning twenty-one.

I had to see this so-called prizewinning painting of hers, so I missed my bus, waiting in the library until the halls had emptied out, and crept upstairs to the art lab.

The walls were crammed with ugly portraits, cheesy watercolors, and predictable still lifes of apples and pears. It was the visual equivalent of walking into the bath and cosmetics shop at the Manitowoc mall where Frida sometimes employed me to divert clerks while she pocketed lip gloss: a thousand competing smells and an instant headache rising in protest of the dissonance. But when my eyes adjusted, it wasn't hard to pick out Margaret's piece, because the frame had a huge blue ribbon pinned to it.

"Like a winning dairy cow," I muttered as I made my way over to it. I expected it to be a picture of her own face. But it was a wintry scene done all in violet, walnut, ice-blue, and cream with streaks of ochre. There was a low house in the foreground—a simple structure with a thatched roof, encircled by rough fencing—and a lone tree with stripped limbs. Between them stretched a wide path that terminated in either a distant sea or a mauve mountain range. The fence's blue shadow was etched like a musical staff with faint notes of mica climbing the bars, and a man and his dog trod the path, their figures suggested by just a few brushstrokes. The light in the scene was spectral. She'd captured either the pre-dawn or the gloaming, those inceptive times between day and night, sound and silence, minutes I both loved and feared because in that narrow purgatorial space you were drawn with equal insistence toward memory and anticipation, to the point where you felt you might split in two. These were the sorts of colors you felt on the back of your neck.

Despite the picture's cold tones, there was nothing frigid about the scene. Maybe it was the ochre braided into the snow that made it seem as though this winter were incipient or else finally dwindling at the first touch of spring. I found myself appreciating the ambiguity of it all. Had the man emerged from his thatched house so that he might savor one last bearable afternoon before the blizzards came? Or was he ecstatic to be out and about at the tail-end of a brutal winter? The longer I stared at the scene, the more convinced I became that an apricot sun was soon to rise and burn the blue from the snow. It was an hour of resurgence, and the lone man was a man of faith, certain of a certain returning.

I shook myself. The wall clock told me I'd been hovering there for nearly half an hour. What was I doing? This was Margaret Peters' work. The work of a spoiled, silly, stuck-up girl who'd slapped some oils together and gotten lucky. The big blue ribbon pinned to the frame looked ridiculous. That this girl should get a free ride to a good school and be paired with some artist struck me as a vile injustice. Who was she?

There was a plastic bin of permanent markers on a shelf below the painting. I fished out a thick black one, uncapped it, and drew a long streak of ink diagonally across the canvas. Then I walked out, the marker still in my hand.

Back home, I found Marcus in the driveway hovering over the propped-up hood of Lissa's car. He had Rupert inside an upturned baseball cap, antennae peeking over the rim, and was raising and lowering him to give him a view of various parts. "Under a car, and under the hood, it's like a solar system, Beets," he told him as I walked by. "All these parts work together, and if one is out of orbit, the whole system tips. Don't touch that cap! If the car is still hot, do *not* open that cap. Bugs can get burned this way, even in winter. You hear me?"

Marcus had never tried to teach me or anyone else for that matter about cars. I was in such a foul mood that I almost stopped to point this out to him. But then my own irritation struck me as absurd (when had any of us expressed any interest in what he loved? When had any of us shown a willingness to learn?), and I moved on.

I found Andrei at his worktable in the garage. He was chiseling away at a burl, one of those knobs of tumored wood that sometimes broke loose from dead trees like overripe apples. "This thing is impossible," Andrei muttered through his scarf. "It fights me from every angle."

"It looks petrified. What are you trying to do with it?"

"Get it open, carve it out. Rupert found it along the trail and he kept jumping on it like there'd be a diamond inside. But it's not a freaking geode. I tried to explain this to him but he wouldn't take no for an answer. I guess it's a Sad thing, since it was just lying on the ground or whatever."

"It's diseased. Did you tell him these things form because of fungus?"

"I told him it would be all rotten inside, or just an ice ball, but he doesn't care. Even if there's hard wood in there, I'm betting anything the grain's going to send my tools flying right back out. It'll turn a power tool in circles."

"You should just toss it."

"I know. But Rupert."

"Yeah."

I wished him luck and went into the house to find myself some dinner.

An hour later, I lay on my bedroom floor beside my dollhouse, ill at ease. Rupert was in the dollhouse with his tape measure. Across the hall, my parents were engaged in a terse conversation that kept turning like a lazy Susan.

"You've never skipped this retreat," my father said. "I don't get it."

"Are you trying to get rid of me? You want me to go? Is that it?"

"What, no. I didn't say that. I'm just confused. This isn't like you."

My mother's voice rose a little: "So you don't have an opinion either way."

A pause. "No, I'd, I'd like it if you stayed."

"Before, you said you didn't care anymore if I went or not."

"I don't. I mean, I wouldn't stop you. You have your own life." He was fumbling. "But it wouldn't be so terrible if you were—here. We're always different people even after a week, you can't watch somebody change just like you can't sit in front of a plant and watch it pop out of the dirt. But it's your life," he finished hastily. "I want you to do what you want to do, be with the people you want to be with."

I knew that tone. It was carefully nonchalant, a tone that made no eye contact. It was the tone we all took when we were afraid to admit how much we wanted or needed someone. We'd taken it all through our childhoods and we were still taking it, except with Rupert. Reflexively I reached out to give his shell a little shake.

My mother said, "Well, if it's all right with you, if it's not going to disrupt *your* life, I'd like to skip this retreat." Careful, tapping at the space between them as a blind man's cane taps the ground for obstacles and holes. "But if I'm in your way, you should say so."

"And if you're feeling boxed in, and you change your mind, you should say so," my father finished.

"I will. Yes."

"Okay then."

There was an awkward silence. I could picture them standing on opposite ends of the room, my mother suddenly interested in her nails, my father suddenly concerned with the unfolded laundry.

Rupert was busy measuring the length of my artist's studio when my father appeared in the bedroom doorway. "Want to go for a twilight walk on the Ice Age trail?" he asked. He looked different somehow, more relaxed, hands in his pockets. A hint of a smile played at this mouth.

Startled, I said, "Me? or Jeff?"

"You and Rupert. Want to go, Bert?"

Rupert banged into a wall in his excitement and my father laughed. "Okay then. Tell you what, we'll even stop at the Penguin Drive-In for a late-night burger afterwards. Get your warmies on."

You would have thought I'd been asked on a first date. I was like Rupert, bumping into walls as I rushed to tug on my boots and coat.

The sun was already beginning to drop through the sieve of the trees when we began our trek toward the beach. Rupert sat on the platform of my father's hand and listened, feelers high, as he taught him the names of trees: red oak, white pine, hemlock, cedar. He was wearing a mitten, but Marcus had cut holes out of the first two fingers so that Rupert could still see.

"Birch is best," my father told Rupert. "Especially when there's a whole family of them together. They look like ghosts.

And if there's a good wind, you can hear all the paper fluttering like birds' wings." He peeled away a bit of the creamy paper and handed it to Rupert. "Isn't that nice? You could write on this if you had nothing else to write on. I mean say all the paper disappeared, and you had to start the world over with stories, you could write on birch bark when there was nothing else."

After a while he forgot I was there. He went on talking animatedly to Rupert: "I used to walk in Point Beach Forest with my father, weekends when we'd drive up. Before he left. I was so young I barely remember but I do remember a few things. He taught me some practical stuff, animal tracks and all that. Deer have two parentheses above two periods, foxes have five pad imprints, voles leave this design like a little crab. But it wasn't always textbook wilderness stuff. I remember he said that a tree was honest, and if you started to see things through a dirty lens, you should go back to the trees to get straightened out."

In response, Rupert sat up very straight.

"Yes, like that, Bert." A pause. "You know, I know he was a genius and all, but when I read some of the last things he published before he died, I got the feeling he wasn't looking at trees anymore."

I glanced sidelong at his profile. Rupert pointed at the tree line, then back to my father, then back to the trees.

"I'm trying," my father said. "But trees have a way of making you feel guilty, so it's hard to keep looking."

I was startled. I hadn't realized it until he said it, but this was what I'd always felt looking at Van Gogh's cypresses and olive trees. It wasn't that the trees were perfect, or even beautiful. It was that they'd been willing to show themselves fully to the painter—their shadows and shoots, their spalted skins and mangled roots, their worm-trails and nubs of gall.

They never asked to be painted in a more forgiving pose. I wanted to say, *I know just what you mean*. But I didn't want my father to stop talking. The moment seemed so frangible, like the light.

We emerged from the pines onto snow-locked sand. The dune-junipers glimmered wetly, and the little flood-pools tucked into the swales between the ridges were iced over, mirroring a sky mottled with cirrostratus clouds. In the frigid wind, the dark tendrils of surviving dune plants rippled across the snow in parallel lines like calligraphy on a white page. Only a thin belt of tamped-down sand at the water's edge had remained snowless, and down there discs of ice the size of dinner plates lay scattered, refracting the purpling light. The water was a hard teal darkening to lapis near the horizon line. We stood there taking this in and then my father said, "Bert, you remember when I yelled at you because I thought you deleted my story? Remember that time?"

It was Jeffrey he'd accused, but Rupert nodded his feelers.

"Well, I just thought I'd tell you, I know you never did that. I'm sorry I yelled at you. It was Taryn that time. And now it's Andrei. He doesn't know I know, but it's him now."

I said, "What? What's he doing?"

"Oh, he goes into my files, whatever I'm working on, and he deletes random paragraphs. The kind of thing to make you feel crazy. He goes in there and makes Swiss cheese out of it. What he doesn't know is that I save every copy in a separate folder, every time I work, so I just go back to the saved draft the next day."

Rupert looked as shocked as he could look. I said, "It's probably Pablo or Rafe doing it. Andrei doesn't care, he's not trying to be a writer anymore."

My father shook his head. "It's funny, I don't remember ever having bad blood between us except maybe after

Ontonagon, when we left his cat out there. But after I published that one story . . . well, he never cared what I was doing as long as I wasn't doing anything, you know what I mean? Then that story came out, and he was different."

"Bet you anything Rafe did it. He goes after Lonnie's instruments, you know."

He shrugged, then turned back to Rupert. "You want to play in the sand? There's a little bit there for us. Can you handle the cold, buddy? C'mon, there won't be a soul down there. No Science, I promise."

A search through a pile of icy driftwood and other detritus at the waterline produced a cracked plastic shovel and an assortment of décor, including a barrette, a sun-bleached bobber, and a couple of silver soda tabs. My father used the shovel to soften up the cold sand near the waterline, yelping when a little stray rill splashed his hands. "We can work with this," he breathed. "And oh yeah, I brought these." He produced a little heap of waterproof handwarmers from his pocket and tucked them into our mittens. "Play with the sand, heat it up, it'll work."

We did as we were told. We patted together little mounds and sculpted turrets and bridges. My father used the plastic shovel to scoop up Rupert now and again just to laugh at how frazzled he got when he was pulled away from his project. It became more of a sand-city than a castle, with small houses encircling the bigger buildings and a stick-fence forming the perimeter. Rupert etched a cross into the side of the tallest building, then bowed reverently before it. "The anointing of Wintertown," my father said.

Our faces were raw from the cold and we had to keep stopping to re-wind our scarves around our necks. We'd be walking back in the dark if we stayed much longer, but my father in his strange new mood hardly seemed to notice. Watching

Rupert reshape the window-holes in a tower, he said softly, "You're a good bug, Roo. Loyal. You carry things through."

His voice was suddenly as complex as an iris. Competing fibrils of color pulsed there, nebulae whose intricacies you could not fully appreciate without standing close. He was trying to tell us that he knew he wasn't much of a father, and I was so surprised by it that I said, "Dad, I ruined something today. Somebody's painting at school."

He looked askance at me. "You what?"

"I was jealous." I felt sick. "There was a painting that won a prize, and I drew a line through it with a marker. I just did it, without even thinking."

Rupert was looking at me, too, antennae up.

My father said, "Oh." He made an unnecessary adjustment to one of the towers. "Why did you?"

"Because it's easier to destroy something than try to make it yourself." The words flew out of me, landed on the sand between us where they became something I now had to look at. "Because that's all we know to do, Dad. We see something we want, and we take a knife to it."

His posture sagged. He looked down at Rupert, covered him with his hand as if to keep him from hearing. "Oh, Abra."

I said, "I want to know what my name means. She's not even an artist. She's just some character in a book, right? You said she wasn't even the main character."

"She's in Steinbeck's *East of Eden*." He was watching the horizon now, the darkening line above the water's lethal blue. "I skipped around in it. There's a pair of twins, and the dark one gets the light one killed, I think, because he's jealous of him or something. I didn't read the ending. I got the feeling it wasn't something I could take. But when you came, Abra was the name that was in my head. That's how it was naming all of you really."

"But who was she?"

"Ask Andrei." He looked tired now. He climbed to his feet with Rupert gripped in one hand, like he couldn't stand up without him. "I'm sure he's read it all the way to the end. Come on, the wind is picking up. We're all going to get sick if we stay out here much longer."

The garage light was burning when we got home and I thought Andrei would be in there, still working the burl. But the room was empty, the burl resting on a stack of folded shop towels directly beneath the glow of the single bulb. It was a bowl now, a half-moon. I turned it in the light. In the fine lines and dark inclusions of that wild, turbinate grain I saw constellations, even words; it was as though Van Gogh's *Starry Night* had been etched into wood by nature's convulsions. Unnerved, I turned the burl bowl upside-down and hurried into the house.

It makes sense, since it's not like I have anything going on, you know, for myself. It's not like I'm getting anywhere with woodworking. And you guys need to make your *art*." Lonnie nodded. He was a little high. He said, "Marcus is too sick to bring in much, he still misses too many days. And we all know how useless Abra here is."

"I babysit," I started, but he laughed and waved me off. "'Preciate it, Andrei." He meandered back downstairs.

"One day he'll ask me for a kidney," Andrei mumbled before he rose and went downstairs as well. I followed, leaving Rupert alone on the landing with the open copy of *East of Eden*.

Lissa was standing at the kitchen sink, chain-smoking as she sometimes did when anxious. For some reason Easter weekend had always unnerved her; she stayed away from church and paced around both houses with her nails in her mouth like she was waiting for a doctor to call her with a terrifying diagnosis. She barely acknowledged us when we entered the room. She paid no attention to Marcus, either, who sat at the table shoveling macaroni into his mouth like it was the best thing he'd ever tasted. Rupert was always harping on him via notes and pictures to eat more, and he was starting to get some color in his face. He glanced up and said, "It's Easter this weekend."

I said, "So?"

"I was thinking we should get Bert one of those cartons of candy eggs. He'll go nuts."

Lissa went into the living room with her cigarette, trailing a grey haze in her wake.

I said, "Not sure about candy eggs, Marc. He'll probably build them a nest or something."

"I know. He's not brilliant. But that shit makes him so happy."

Andrei went to the back door and stood there looking out.

"What's his problem," Marcus wanted to know.

"I guess your dad got fired. He wants him to work more hours to make up for it." I squinted at Andrei. "Why are you so mad? Just don't do it."

Without turning, Andrei said, "Oh, right. It's that simple. God, you people can be so clueless sometimes."

"Don't take it out on us," I snapped. "Look, you're the one who decides to do all this stuff for us. But it's not much of a gift if you begrudge it all."

Marcus let out a harsh barking laugh I'd never heard before, and Andrei and I both turned toward him in surprise. He wiped cheese from the corner of his mouth and shook his head. "Abra, that's hilarious, what you just said. You're a real comic genius."

"What the hell is that supposed to mean?"

"As if *you're* the Giving Tree of this family," Marcus went on. "As if you can talk."

I was furious: "Who washes every fucking dish in the house? In *both houses*?"

"I stand corrected." He scooted back his chair and took his macaroni bowl to the sink. "Don't worry, I'll wash this one myself."

I found my coat and hat, stalked out of the house, and wandered the trails for hours as I seethed. Eventually I got hungry and cold. My hope was to slip into bed without having to see anyone, but just as I reentered the backyard, I glimpsed Andrei slinking out of Lonnie and Lissa's house dressed in dark pants and a black hooded coat. I froze at the tree line. He had his duffel bag, the one he'd been filling and refilling with supplies for years. There was a long beat after he'd closed the back door before he turned and hurried down the strip of lawn between the houses. He carried the bag oddly, like a suitcase, instead of fitting the straps over his back.

I followed in a panic, pausing only to snatch a flashlight from Marcus' toolkit in the garage. What was he doing? He bypassed the family cars, turned right down our backcountry road, and started down one of the wooded trails that led to the ranger's station northwest. I kept as far back as I could without losing sight of him, and if he slowed or stopped, I kept back until he resumed his brisk pace. An hour into the hike Andrei veered right onto a spur trail I didn't recognize.

We were at the foot of the old monastery before I realized where we were. Its pallid domes shocked me where they loomed out of the darkness like low-hanging moons; it seemed impossible that we'd walked so far. But Andrei didn't pause. He curved around the building as if he knew exactly where he was going. As I stood panting behind a hemlock, he climbed atop a dumpster, and there was a soft click followed by the rush of a window sash gliding up. Two seconds later, Andrei had vanished into a room on the second floor.

I stood there listening to the surf beyond the broad black dune that stood between the monastery and the Lake, trying to remember what I knew about the place. There were no more monks housed here—the place was unmanned just like the expired lighthouse whose pale tower hovered to my right—but caretakers tended it, and it was still open for tours, or so Andrei had told us. I recalled him going to a craft sale there a year or two before Rupert was born. He came home with a set of Russian nesting dolls painted bright red and yellow, and Pablo and Rafe made a game out of stealing one little head at a time until only the outmost shell was left. Maybe, like the nesting dolls, the monastery was just an empty casing now, a shelter for squatters; maybe Andrei had been sneaking out here for years, sleeping in a cold chapel to get away from us. My panic returned, and a minute later I had hauled myself onto the dumpster and was scrabbling my way through the window he'd left halfway open.

The room I dropped into was inky dark and smelled of must and old books. I could just make out shelves and bindings, but I hardly gave the walls a glance as I groped my way into the hall. Only weak red emergency lights illuminated the corridor, and the hall seemed impossibly long, door after door after door. I stood there and listened. Nothing. It was as though Andrei had melded himself into the walls. After a hesitation I switched on my flashlight and started testing doors. Most were locked but some swung open to reveal stark rooms furnished like jail cells, just spindly tables and naked beds without headboards. Monk bedrooms, I decided. The whole place was as staid and ugly as I'd imagined a monastery to be. Andrei had to be downstairs in the actual church where there was stained glass or a painted ceiling, something worth seeing. I could just make out the crimson glow of a sign—*STAIRS*—at the end of the hall.

It was halfway there when the contents of one of the larger rooms arrested my flashlight beam. I stepped into the cool dark space and moved the light slowly over wide tabletops, revealing what must have been the stock for the next craft sale: nesting dolls, woven blankets folded into triangles, painted icons, wooden statuettes, white candles. Calligraphy printed on slips of paper noted each piece's origin and maker. I slid the beam over the furthermost table, and something flashed like a diamond.

It was a purse or clutch made of deep blue velvet, and into the velvet was embroidered a reindeer dancing amid swirling snow. Curls of white thread formed the snow and from them wisped hair-thin tinsel that fluttered beneath the wind of my breath. The reindeer's body was a mosaic of white and silver beads, its hoofs made of crystal, its eye onyx. It was poised to leap into the star-studded sky above, and in the firmament lay the true wonder of the scene: the aurora borealis woven into the velvet in undulating strands of pink, blue, and green. I felt my skin pebbling. I'd seen the Northern Lights only once, during an unseasonably cold October when I was a small child, but I remembered them well and the artist had captured the miracle exactly. Here were skid marks from some cosmic near-accident, proof for the belated witness of an eleventh-hour grace. Someone or something had been permitted against all odds to thrive. My fingers flexed to hold Rupert—I felt his appreciation, felt him there with me as surely as if he'd crawled into my hand—and I was startled to find myself alone.

The card beside it claimed the purse had been made in the northernmost monastery in Russia, near to the Arctic Circle. I picked up the clutch and held its rich soft sky between my hands, thinking of that impossibly faraway place. I easily could have stolen it then. Or I could have escaped through the portal of that image, forgetting everything to weave some new fantasy of myself in a foreign, glittering world where all was sparkling glass. But the truth was that for a few minutes there, Andrei and I had switched places. It was not fantasy that held me in thrall as I stood there, but a hard, raw reality: I imagined monks slaving away on their arctic homestead thousands of my miles from my comfortable world. I saw them hacking at ice to unfetter their walkways, and baking dense bread in deep ovens, and tending to sick men and women whose eyes implored them for mercy and understanding, and then, at night, picking up slender needles and stringing thread with minute silver beads . . . I was awestruck by what it must have taken to create this thing of beauty I held. But down the hallway, Andrei was the one neck-deep in fantasy.

He was so focused that he neither heard nor saw me when I crept behind him. He stood inside the last cell before the stairs, just looking at the narrow bed and the blank window, rigid with the duffel bag still grasped in his right hand like a suitcase. I didn't move. I could almost hear him thinking. He wanted to stay. He wanted to root down in that little cell, tuck his bag into the corner beside the bed, and close the door against all of us, against the whole world. He'd sit there and read and think and master every question that had stalked him since he was ten years old, until he could sleep undisturbed like a body entombed. His yearning was palpable to me, not as heat but as a cold wind. I opened my mouth to speak, then took a silent step back. I withdrew into an open room just across the hall and stood there shrouded in shadow while he carried on his silent debate. So much time passed that my muscles cramped and I began to tremble. Then suddenly he hoisted the duffel onto his shoulders like a backpack, turned right, and retreated down the hall toward his entry point.

I waited until I heard the faint thump of his shoes on the dumpster outside before I pulled back the musty curtain of the room's single window. There was nothing to see until a heavy cloud drifted west, suddenly unclothing the moon so that white light lanced down through the dead lighthouse's glassed tower and refracted along the grass below. Andrei's form passed over the lawn, briefly limned by that refracted light, then vanished into the woods.

I wasn't sure I could make the jump as well as he had, and so after a few minutes' wait I went to the head of the stairs, thinking to let myself out through an actual door somewhere on the first floor. I was exhausted and wanted only to be home in my bed. But when I switched my flashlight back on, I gasped. The staircase that unspooled before me was something out of a queen's castle, utterly incongruous with the drabness of the second floor; it was carved of a deep rich wood, and it swirled its way down to a carpeted landing before continuing its helical course into unseen depths. I was afraid of the pure darkness at the bottom—it was like looking down a well—but the majesty of that first sweeping curve stopped my breath, and I saw myself moving regally down those steps, running my hand over the banister . . . There was no need to go all the way down. I wanted only to reach the halfway point, where the stairs were their most glamorous and enticing. It was pure compulsion that moved me. With my head held high I floated down to the last step of the first spiral, imagining myself in another country, another world. I closed my eyes. Then when my foot touched down on the landing, there was a flash of white light, followed by a piercing siren that braided itself with my own shocked cry.

"Oh, Christ," I cried as I spun around and started back up the stairs at a dead run, realizing that I'd set off a motion sensor on the landing, a spot marking some implicit boundary in the house. I couldn't remember where the open window was, and I went in and out of rooms with my hands over my ears, the flashlight abandoned somewhere on the stairs behind me, until at last I found the window overlooking the dumpsters. Andrei had closed it behind him and I had to throw all my weight under the sash to force it open. The alarm pealed on behind me as I lowered myself from the dumpster to the grass and bolted into the woods. I ran until I had to stop to catch my breath, and I swore I could hear sirens competing with that muted wail behind me. Andrei would never forgive me if he found out. The police would start watching the grounds now, and it would be impossible for Andrei to return to his little refuge ever again. "Shit," I said softly, hands on my knees. It was four in the morning when I finally reached home.

I stayed in bed until noon that Saturday, dreaming of pale stags dancing in snow. When I woke up, daylight chased away the more elusive feelings of the night before, and I felt brisk and alert as I showered. It was silly, that business with the reindeer clutch. It was just a purse. And Andrei was a child if he thought he could live in some monk's cell undetected. How long could that have gone on before some caretaker discovered him like a mouse living in a pantry, nibbling on crumbs? I wanted to knock on his door and have a laugh about it. And yet I spent the rest of the day alone in my room, avoiding everyone.

Late that night, when everyone was either out somewhere or lounging around downstairs, I crept out of my room and caught Jeffrey standing at my parents' bedroom door with a grocery bag. When he noticed me, he transferred the bag into Rupert's grip.

"What are you doing?" I said. "What's in the bag, Bert?"

"Rupert just has to hide some eggs."

"He's making an egg hunt for us?"

A hesitation. "No. Just one for each."

"Oh." I peeked into the bag. It was bright with dollar-store Easter eggs. "Can I look inside them?"

Rupert pulled the bag back.

"Okay, okay. Go ahead, I'll keep watch."

I followed him from bedroom to bedroom in both houses, standing in the doorways as he nestled his eggs under the pillows. I figured he'd used his quarters to buy jellybeans or something, but a few hours later when I climbed into bed, I shook my egg and found that it contained a miniature magnifying glass. On the little handle was Rupert's shaky script in black marker: *Tim.*

It took me a minute to get it—*tim,* in an eggshell. Timshel. But what was the magnifying glass all about? I sat up in bed and listened. I imagined that I could hear mattresses creaking and bedside lamps clicking on as the others cracked open their plastic eggs. The urge to jump up and knock on doors, to ask what lay inside the others' shells, was electric. But I willed myself to lie back down and sleep. I'd ask tomorrow, I thought. And anyway I was overthinking it. It was just Rupert.

When I asked Andrei that Sunday, he simply handed me his blue egg and left the room. Inside was a plastic soldier figurine, drab green and weightless, the kind that came in packs of a hundred. As children we'd played War in the grass with such soldiers for hours at a time. I recognized the mold as the one we always discarded: a man bent beneath a massive pack, his head down and knees high as if he were frozen midway up a steep hill-climb. You couldn't kill anyone with this guy, was our reasoning. Even the one carrying a flag at least had some purpose, but the backpack one was a junker. We preferred to line up the ones sporting rifles and machine guns and grenades. While the backpack soldier languished in the dirt somewhere, we'd pulverize one another with bombs and artillery fire.

Later, I found Andrei scouring the toilet in the upstairs bathroom. I held up the magnifying glass. "Why do you think he put this in my egg?"

He dug in deep with the scrub-brush. "Don't overthink it," he said flatly, surprising me. "It's just Rupert."

Pablo, who was passing through the hall, paused to lean into the bathroom doorway. "Such a good little housewife," he said to Andrei. " While you're at it, can you snake the drain? I'm taking showers in a lake."

"You could do it," Andrei suggested. "Or you could go fuck yourself."

I said, "What was in your egg, Pablo?"

Pablo ignored me and returned his focus to Andrei: "I should buy you an apron."

Andrei stood up, and this sent Pablo loping down the hall, laughing.

"He's probably high," I said.

"No. He's pissed because I went through his shit and found something I wasn't supposed to find. I was looking for some cash I was missing, but—"

"What'd you find? The egg thing?"

"Pictures. Like, developed from a disposable camera, in with his smut rags. He must get them developed in town. You can get a whole roll done for dirt cheap. They were all taken down at the shore or in weird places in Two Rivers."

I snorted. "What, does he think he's some artsy photographer now?"

"He's got this fishing boat moving downriver past the pelicans, with this old guy trying to keep the sun off his eyes, and there's a scene where purple light is sort of climbing up the brick wall of Schroeder's . . ."

"Oh, come on!"

He shrugged and went to the sink to wash his hands. Over the tap he said, "He took the whole pile out to the trash after I found them."

"Trust me, the only photos Pablo is interested in are of tits and blow-job lips."

Through the floor vent, we could hear my father's voice: "Come on guys, just tell me what was in yours." Then my aunt: "Don't you have anything to do, Jude?", and a beat later, Marcus' voice: "Is a little privacy so much to ask around here?"

The next time Pablo and Rafe disappeared for the night, I crept into their room to hunt for the photographs. I found none, but I did come across a red plastic egg buried deep in Pablo's middle drawer. Folded into the tiny space was a coupon cut out of a magazine: 20% off film development at the Two Rivers Walgreens. I rolled my eyes and let the paper fall to the floor where it vanished into a mess of food wrappers and dirty clothes.

As far as I knew, there were no more late-night escapades that spring. Andrei stayed put, spending his weekend mornings on the lawn with his tools and his afternoons doing odd jobs around Two Rivers.

Sometimes I'd come down early to wash the previous night's dishes while Andrei labored in the yard and the rest of the family slept in. I had a long-term contract going with the kitchen work: I got to resent everyone for leaving it to me, but I also got to revel in my status as the house slave, downtrodden and abused. By the time the family got up, I'd be so swollen with self-righteousness that I'd feel perfectly justified in ignoring them all.

One Sunday morning, I heard a thud and paused midscrub. Uncle Lonnie had fallen off the couch and was moaning like he'd broken his back. "Get Andrei," he managed. "Go outside, get Andrei."

In the living room, Andrei knelt on the carpet and hoisted Lonnie partway onto his shoulder. I grabbed Lonnie's left arm and together we got him back on the couch in a sitting position.

"Trash can," Lonnie said, and I got it in front of him just in time for the splash of vomit.

"Beautiful," Andrei said. "What did you use last night?"

"Nothing. I don't know what the fuck's going on. Get me Taryn's ginger oil, will you?"

"Something tells me that's not going to do the trick."

I took the trash can outside to rinse it out, leaving them to their debate. Of course, the hose had ten bulging knots in it, so by the time I got back my uncle was in his bedroom and Andrei was just standing in the living room with his chin in his hand.

"What was that all about?" I asked.

"I don't know." His voice was flat. "He said it happens sometimes when he rolls out of bed. He gets dizzy, like vertigo, and it's there for hours. Poor baby."

There was a soft step behind us and we turned to find Rupert peeking around the wall. "Rupert wants to know what's wrong with Dad," the disembodied voice said.

"He's fine," I said. "He just gets dizzy sometimes. Go back to bed, Beets."

He went back upstairs. Andrei followed me into the kitchen to help finish the dishes, then to perform his monthly hunt for the utility bill in our massive pile of mail. He stood there dropping envelopes and magazines into the trash, stopping every so often to set aside something addressed to Rupert (none of us had a clue how this had happened, but Rupert was starting to get real mail, postcards from local dentists and pleas from charities and coupons for oil changes).

"Has anyone in either house ever been to a dentist?" Andrei murmured as he slapped another postcard onto the Rupert pile. I went on scrubbing plates, cursing Lonnie under my breath. I had no intention of adding vomit-mop-up-duty to my routine.

The following Monday, my father tasked me with picking up Rafe from detention, an almost weekly routine at this point. Pablo was such a natural snake-charmer that he usually managed to wriggle out of punishment even after the suspension, but Rafe couldn't stop himself from telling his teachers off. He'd been more foul-tempered than ever since the knife incident, unless of course he was high. I was surprised that he showed up for his detention sessions until he told me he had friends in there, kids with older siblings who paid for the beer and pot at the parties he crashed.

I was about to leave the house when my father realized Jeffrey hadn't come home on the bus. "Where's Rupert?" he asked, peering out the front window. "I swear I heard the Beetsie Bus earlier."

"I don't know. Am I his babysitter?"

"He might've missed it. You'd better drop by the school."

Disgusted, I said, "Don't worry, I didn't have anything I was planning on doing tonight." Lissa and my mother were out for the night, and I'd been hoping to steal some of their paints and play around a bit out back behind the garage where nobody ever looked. Since vandalizing Margaret Peters' picture in the art lab, I'd been experimenting with our mothers' paint-slinging in secret. I liked the feeling of savage power that came over me as I made those canvases. I liked that there were no rules, just pure movement and emotion exploding against the white. How, I wondered, had the old-school painters like my brother's namesake had the patience for their intricate portraits? It all seemed fussy and dour to me now, hopelessly constrained. Even Van Gogh had dropped in the ranks for me. After all, his painstaking labors had only landed him in the loony bin. Had he ever had crowds of people milling about his paintings while he was alive? And if I hoped to be truly original, I needed to sever myself from anyone who came before—especially someone like him.

"You should go now," my father said, snapping me out of my reverie.

When I found him, Rafe was in a mood as sour as my own. He was always on one extreme end of the spectrum or the other, either effusively happy or coldly enraged. He threw his backpack onto the floor and climbed into the passenger seat smelling of cigarettes and stale deodorant. "Great job," he said. "I love sitting on the concrete doing nothing."

I said, "I'm not the one who got detention."

"Shut up and drive. And stop at Al's. I need you to buy me some more cigarettes."

"They won't sell to me, Rafe. I'm underage."

"They will at Al's." His face hardened. "You going to do it or not?"

I was tired. "Whatever. But we have to stop to get Rupert. He didn't come home today."

A pause. "He never came home?"

"He just missed his bus."

We drove in silence to Jeffrey's school. There was no one milling about outside, so I parked the car and suggested that Rafe wait. He shrugged and made like he was going to take a nap.

When I did spot Jeffrey, he was coming out of the school's little library. He said, "Oh," and then Rupert popped up, waving.

"Where were you," I said sternly, giving Rupert a shake. "Bad bug."

"Rupert was reading. He lost track of time." Beets reached up to tug a lock of my hair. Then in my peripheral vision I noticed a teacher watching curiously from a doorway. I said, "C'mon, Rafe's waiting in the car and he's not in a good mood."

We were halfway home, Rupert sleeping in a little ball on the console between Rafe and me, when Rafe reached into his backpack and pulled out what looked like a test tube. Following this was another glass flask, and a long rubber cord.

"What the hell is all that?" I asked.

"Shit we stole from the science lab. I know someone who can make a bong out of it."

For a second, I thought he said "bomb," not "bong," and the memory of Rafe and Pablo in that clearing in Ontonagon socked me in the gut. I said, "Rafe, bring it back."

"They owe it to me, all those dick teachers."

"You're going to get suspended again. Or worse. You think they won't know you took it?"

He held up one of the flasks so that it caught sunlight. "What's your idea of something worse than suspension?"

"Oh, I don't know, juvie?"

"What difference does it make? I can just get a GED in jail if I really want one."

I reached out for the flask. "Rafe, come on. We can turn around right now—" My sentence ended in a scream. He'd grabbed the steering wheel and veered us into the oncoming traffic lane, a wild grin on his face.

"Rafe, let go," I shrieked, trying to shove him away. "Rafe!" There was no one in the oncoming lane—not yet—but I could see the glimmer of cars in the distance.

"Say you're done," he said calmly. His left arm was steel. "Say you're done, and I'll let go."

It was deja-vu, a flash of something I'd heard the older boys say to him on the playground back in middle school. *Say you're done and we'll let you go.* But what I felt was rage, not pity. I screamed at him: "You crazy fuck, let go before you kill us! What are you on?"

I released one hand from the wheel long enough to slap the side of his face, but this didn't faze him. He just laughed. The line of cars was still coming at us. For a few seconds there, I believed we were going to be hit head-on. We were going to die for the sake of my brother's stolen bong-tubes.

"You pathetic piece of shit," I cried. "You've lost it, you know that?"

Something moved under my arm. It was Rupert, tugging urgently at Rafe's sleeve. Rafe and I looked down and saw a quivering shell, a pair of feelers clasped together as in prayer. It was pitiful. I said, "You're scaring Rupert."

And Rafe let go. He sagged back into his seat, letting the glassware fall to the floor, and didn't speak the rest of the way home. Back at the house, he vanished into his room and I collapsed on the sofa. But when Frida wandered in, Rupert picked up the kitchen phone, and listened to Frida talk for an hour while I pretended to be asleep.

I was shaken all week and took pains to avoid my brother, which was easy because he and Pablo lived mostly in their room now, holed up with their porn or whatever else they did.

Sunday morning, Lonnie fell off the sofa again. But when Andrei and I entered the living room, Rupert was already there. "Rupert can help," Jeffrey said. "He's just a dumb bug, but he knows a trick that might work for dizzies."

"Move it, Roo," Andrei said. "I've got to get him upright."

Rupert shook his feeler-head. "Dad needs to go on the bed. Rupert can show you."

"Yeah, I'm taking him there." As Andrei hoisted Lonnie up, Rupert scrambled to draw on his notepad. It was a picture of Lonnie on his bed, belly-up, with his head hanging over one side.

"That's not a good idea, Beets," I said. "You want him hurling on you?"

Another vigorous *no,* as in, *you don't understand.*

I sighed and followed my uncle and cousin into the bedroom. Rupert was right behind me, and he was so insistent with that drawing that finally Lonnie said, "Oh Christ, whatever he wants! It can't get any worse!" His face was ashen.

Rupert got my uncle to lie down as the picture demonstrated (though Lonnie swore he was going to die if he did this). As he coaxed Lonnie down, he tilted my uncle's head dramatically to the right. He kept it in this position, supporting it, as it fell below the level of the mattress. Lonnie's eyes darted back and forth in a frantic nystagmus. "Oh my God, the whole world's spinning—" But Rupert was calm, feelers tapping out an unhurried rhythm which I realized was a counting out of seconds. A minute passed before he rotated Lonnie's head straight up, then to the left. Lonnie went on complaining but his voice softened. About a minute after this, Rupert got behind Lonnie's right shoulder and feeler-nudged him forward. He looked at us and pointed at the ceiling.

"I think he means you can get up now," I said to Lonnie, mesmerized. The color was already back in his face. He sat up slowly and took a long breath. "It's—it's almost gone," my uncle murmured. He turned a little to look down at Rupert, but Rupert shook his feelers and again pointed up.

"Keep your head up," Andrei said.

Obediently, Lonnie kept his chin up and his eyes forward. He reached down blindly to pat Rupert. "What was that? How did he know to do that?"

We discovered later that Jeffrey had gotten help from the school librarian and learned about *benign paroxysmal vertigo*—dislodged crystals in the ear that could be put right again with a series of careful movements. There were plenty of other conditions that caused vertigo, but Rupert had made an intuitive diagnosis and gotten it right. Lonnie didn't have another episode until a month later. Andrei, who'd memorized the moves, performed the treatment flawlessly with the help of his wristwatch, but once Lonnie was sitting up, he asked for Rupert.

Andrei sent Rupert into the bedroom and closed the door behind him. We sat on the floor and listened. Without preamble my uncle started telling Roo about his father, who'd been a cop in Manitowoc. " He had a bad ear sickness," Lonnie said. "He lost the hearing in one ear and he had this tinnitus he said was so loud, he couldn't believe we couldn't hear it. I was always scared I'd get it one day, and never be able to play guitar or piano because my hearing'd be ruined. So I asked him how he got it." His father, he explained, was a new cop, second year on the force. He wasn't even on duty. He was out walking one morning when he smelled smoke. Around the corner, a two-story house was going up in flames. He got hold of the fire department and they told him to stay away from the building, give them three minutes. But Rupert's grandfather heard screaming somewhere on the second floor, so he bashed open the front door and plunged in.

He had to go up and down the smoke-choked stairs three times—for a woman, a toddler, and a dog. During that final descent, he felt something happen in his ear, so deep and intrusive that it was like a hammer had broken through to his brain. There was a shrill ringing, loud as a fire alarm except it was all trapped in his head. Vertigo sucker-punched him. He tumbled down the rest of the stairs and the dog bolted out of the house on its own. When the firemen arrived, they dragged him out and gave him oxygen.

"Pressure in the building or something," Lonnie said. "Something broke for good, and he was sick his whole life. And all I ever worried about was that it would be me next."

Rupert must have written or drawn something, because a moment later Lonnie said, "Yes, he's gone now. Yes, to Big Jesus. My sister and I don't even go to the grave. And I was thinking, he got his sickness saving strangers in a burning house. And I got mine rolling over in bed after too much pot."

A weak laugh. "If only you'd been around to help him out. That's how it goes, though. Hero vomits up his whole life, and someone like me gets a miracle treatment from a—a beetle. The family clown."

Andrei eased the door open a crack and we saw that my uncle was fast asleep, Rupert on a pillow watching over him. "Well, good for him," Andre muttered before closing the door again.

I doubt Aunt Lissa ever knew about any of this. She was in her own world most afternoons after she'd gotten up from her melatonin-sleep, and she was still having her short-lived affairs. One morning she approached my mother, whose beauty she'd always envied, and asked her how to revive her looks. I was in the garage with Andrei and Rupert and we overheard the whole thing.

My mother had dragged an easel onto the lawn and was just standing there thinking, something I'd never seen her do. Even if she thought she was alone, she was always performing, doing tribal dances or twisting her body into theatrical meditation poses.

She studied Lissa. "I could make you a matcha honey mask. But honestly, you could just start by losing some weight. You and Lonnie are both looking kind of—"

"Easy for you to say. You and Jude inherited your skinniness. You're cheaters." Lissa noticed my mother's canvas. "What're you doing—astral projection?"

"Is this face thing really for you, Lissa, or is this just to please some new fling?"

"Oh, look who's talking."

"I haven't. Not in a while." My mother rolled her hair into a bun and wrapped it in the leather bands she always wore on her wrist. "So who is it this time?"

Lissa took another tack: "Why are you out here instead of upstairs?"

"Because the attic smells like a cannery, that's why."

Lissa had taken to making collages using the eyes and gills of dead fish she scavenged from Point Beach. It was, she said, a new direction for her. "At least I'm doing something original," she snapped before marching back into the house. A few minutes later, she yelled out the back door, "Abra! Are you out here?"

I winced. "Y-yeah."

"Hike down to the beach with a bucket and get me some fresh material. I won't ask twice."

That week, Lake Michigan's beaches were smothered with dead perch, a freak thing that happened every so often. I looked at Andrei. "You're coming with," I said. "I don't deserve this."

We hiked the two miles with Rupert and his corn popper in tow. When we came out of the pines and over the dunes, the flat expanse of beach was smothered with silver fish, thousands upon thousands of them, stacked and layered in a mass grave. Their frying skins glistened like spilled gasoline and the hum of flies was like the din in a crowded restaurant. The smell was atrocious. Rupert hid his eyes in my neck.

"Is that Pablo up there?" Andrei pointed. Sure enough, there was Pablo high on a sandy hillock at the edge of the tree line. When we approached, he was sprawled on his back like a shipwrecked pirate, a bottle of Lonnie's vodka tucked under one arm.

"What're you guys doing here, a fishing exhibition?" Pablo slurred. He had a sprig of beach pea tucked behind his ear, another in his shirt pocket like a corsage.

I said, "You mean expedition? Your mother wants some *material*. For a collage."

"How can you stand to just hang out here?" Andrei demanded. "The smell—" He noticed the beach pea. "Did you rip those flowers out of the ground? How many times have I told you, those plants are what's holding the dunes in place—"

"Relax. One missing weed isn't going to start an avalanche. And up here you don't notice the stink so much." Pablo offered us the bottle. "Come on. What else are you doing?" Then he spotted Rupert, who came out from behind Andrei. "Oh."

"Where's Rafe?" I asked.

"No idea. I'm not his mommy." Pablo took another swallow before handing the bottle to Andrei, who just looked at it.

There was a rustle in the bushes behind us, and Marcus came out, zipping his fly. He stumbled a little before he sat down. "Whoops," he said.

Andrei said, "Is today some kind of Wisconsin holiday I wasn't aware of? Since when do you two hang out? And since when do you *drink*, Marcus?"

"Marc here had a bad date last night," Pablo said, eyes closed. "Bitch liked him all right until she asked him *what do your parents do, Markie?*"

"First they don't like me because I'm skinny and gimpy. Then they don't like me because I come from losers. I'm going to die old and alone with cats on my lap," Marcus said. "A nice big kitty-blankie with a zesty urine scent. It will be *the fabric of my life.* That's how the commercial goes, right?" He took off his glasses and started cleaning them with the hem of his shirt. *"The touch, the feel, of kittens..."*

Andrei reached down to grab Marcus' wrist. "Stop it," he said. "The sand grains will scratch the hell out of your lenses."

Rupert seemed torn between concern for the fish graveyard behind us and for his drunken brothers. "It's okay, bud," I said. "They're just having some fun." At least they weren't trying to kill us on the open road, I thought. At least they were speaking to each other. A glance at Andrei's face confirmed that he was thinking along the same lines: Pablo was in a rarefied pleasant mood, and Marcus' dejection was almost comical, so that he seemed like a normal teenager for once instead of a frail old man.

"You can have fun, too. Come on, Saint Andrei." Pablo tapped the bottle. "One shot."

"Abra too. Let's play a game or something. Something they do at colleges, where we'll never go." Marcus flopped over on his stomach, made a face like he might vomit, then recovered. "Yeah."

"What's the nastiest thing you've ever seen? Winner takes all," Pablo said.

I pointed back down the beach at the fish-heap. "That."

"Drink," Marcus urged. "This is borderline pathetic if you don't do it with us."

Andrei sipped, looked at the bottle again, and surprised me by taking another long drink. We all watched his Adam's apple bobbing until finally he brought the bottle down and passed it to me. I took a shot and almost immediately felt woozy. Meanwhile Jeffrey stretched out on his stomach like Marcus, and Rupert sat on his corn popper watching the proceedings with extreme interest. The vodka skipped him as it moved around the circle.

"Change it to the most beautiful," Andrei suggested, taking back the bottle from Marcus. "Say the most beautiful thing you've ever seen."

"Oh God," Pablo moaned.

"Quit whining. Best thing, go." Andrei took another big swallow. "Someone."

Marcus smiled dreamily. "I like when you're driving on a highway, and you see two cars changing lanes up ahead of you, two at the same time, changing places. They look like swans on water. I see it, and I can understand how the planets do what they do, all the orbits and nobody ever getting knocked out of the ring. You know? Something's *working* there."

"Nothing's working," I said. "It's luck."

"Oh really? I can do you guys even better." He dug a folded sheet of paper out of his pocket and spread it open on the sand. It was a high-resolution photograph of frost crystals, intricate and dendritic. *Fractals,* the caption explained. *Within each small figure is repeated the greater character of the whole.*

"I ripped it out of a textbook," Marcus admitted. "Sorry Abra, but there is something going on there. Something big-picture. It almost makes you think, for a minute . . . it almost makes you crazy enough to wonder, if something as small and stupid as snow is this intricate—"

"Is this really what people do in college?" Pablo interrupted, taking the bottle from Andrei. "It's pretty fuckin' overrated. But I do have something." He sat halfway up and the sprig of beach pea fell out of his hair. "I was out walking, like really far, one of the farm roads. And there was this guy who was doing carpentry shit on his lawn like you do, and he said hey and waved me over. He was old as fuck and you know how geezers love to talk. Anyway he was telling me about this donkey he had for years and how it died, and he buried it on his property under these old Swedish trees. I mean cedar trees. Then one of the cedars died and he decided to use the wood to make a bookshelf."

Marcus exhaled through his nose like a horse. "Did you steal something from him?"

"No, dumbass. Anyway he says to me, you wouldn't believe what happened when I started to plane the wood. And he goes into his shed and comes out with this big cedar slab"—He struggled briefly with the two words—"Ce-dar slab, and there's a donkey's face in the wood, like perfect, the nose and eyes and the ears and the whole ship, the whole shape of it exactly like a donkey."

"You mean he carved it there," I said.

"I mean it was already there in the wood. It was the colors and the, you know, the swirls and stuff in the cedar. The face was already there. Like it worked its way up from the grave into the tree. And the donkey came back."

Rupert was mesmerized. Marcus said, "You're pulling our leg. Or he was pulling yours."

"I got a fuckin' picture of it. I took a picture right there."

"Oh, your mysterious pictures," I said mockingly, but I was calm, pleasantly numbed.

"What's yours then, huh?" Marcus asked me.

"I need a nap. Ask Rupert."

"Rupert'll just point to us. We're his beautiful," Marcus responded, before letting his head drop back onto his arm.

"Andrei then," Pablo said. "Also, courtesy warning: I might yak at any time."

Andrei leaned back against a rock, and his eyes were green pools, reflecting the twist and flutter of tree branches above us. He smiled faintly and said, "Mine's a pitcher."

"A pitcher of what? Kool-Aid?"

"A baseball pitcher, shithead. Have you ever watched a really good pitcher do his thing?"

Marcus opened one eye. "You have a crush on a pitcher? Is this a coming-out party?" He giggled.

"You morons." But Andrei must have been very drunk, because he was more relaxed than I'd ever seen him. "No. I mean any good pitcher, the way he moves. How his arm comes all the way back, his whole body, and there's the spin, and then the ball goes flying forward . . . one day I was standing by the fence at this field, and I realized it was like looking at a T.S. Eliot poem incarnate." He paused. *"The end of all our exploring will be to arrive where we started, and know the place for the first time."*

The thought came to me unbidden that it was exactly the sort of thing Jeffrey might have said back in the years before Rupert. Even more disconcerting, I suddenly realized that *everything* the boys had described was something Jeffrey would have loved—and been punished for loving. Reflexively I turned toward my cousin, but the blinding afternoon sun was right behind him. When I turned back to Andrei there were only phosphenes, lingering swirls and spots behind my eyelids in place of Jeffrey himself, and it was a kind of mercy.

I said to Andrei, "I thought you were done with poetry and all that."

"Some things just stay in your head all on their own."

"Unfortunately," Marcus muttered.

"I know how stupid it is. You don't have to tell me." Andrei fell back on the sand.

Pablo got up to puke in the bushes. When he came back, we settled into silence, and I dozed off. I dreamed a scene in which donkeys and swans drank from a rippling blue pool in the middle of a field. Something bobbed in the water. I edged closer and saw that it was a baseball, and I had the thought that I should get it for Andrei, but the water looked deeper than I'd first gauged. Shafts of sunlight were swallowed whole as they journeyed downward; far below, dark shapes shifted in some archaic dance. I backed away.

The boys were still fast asleep when I sat up from my dream. Andrei's eyelashes were wet tags as though he'd fallen asleep after a good cry, but the muscles of his face were slack, his hands turned palm-up at his sides as if to catch rain.

He looked so defenseless that I impulsively leaned over and kissed his forehead. Then I turned to dig a water bottle out of Rupert's knapsack—he could always be counted upon to have water—and realized with a start that Jeffrey was gone.

I stood up to scan the beach, and for a moment could have sworn I saw Jeffrey crossing the lake as he would a busy street. Then I realized he'd pulled up his shorts and was just wading in the shallows. "Not safe for Rupert," I called out as I started down the dune ridge on unsteady legs. He was bent low, reaching for something in the water. I waded out to him and saw that he was moving one of the perch back and forth, trying to revive it.

"It's dead, Beets," I said. "What're you going to do, try to save five million of them?" The vodka had left a headache in its wake, and I was impatient. "Look, it's just natural, Roo. It's something that happens in Nature." Saying this, I had a flash of Rupert watching *The Snowman* one Christmas. He'd broken down when the boy got up one morning to find only a puddle of snow in the backyard where his friend had been. Rupert went to sleep curled around a cheap snow globe, and in the morning, broke the glass over the kitchen sink so he could take out the plastic snowman and hold him.

It hit me a beat later that Jeffrey was four years old the year he watched that movie. There was no Rupert that Christmas. A little shaken, I said, "Let it go, bud. This is silly."

"What's the matter?" someone called out. I spun around. It was Aunt Lissa, emerging from the Ice Age trail with a bucket thumping against her leg. Furious, she waded in behind us. "I've been waiting hours. Did you just forget? And what's he so upset about?"

"He thinks he can bring them back to life," I said tiredly.

"Oh, Lord. Come on. You'll change your mind when you see my collage." Then, echoing me, "What're you planning to do anyway, dunk the whole gazillion of them back in the water?"

"No," Jeffrey said faintly. "Just the one." Rupert, his antennae wrapped around the fish's middle, gave the creature one last push. The back fin flicked once. A tremor rolled through the silver body and then the perch was swimming away into deeper waters, making tiny ripples in his wake.

We all just stood there for a few seconds, unmoving. Then Lissa said, "Did you see—"

"It wasn't dead," I said firmly. "Look, where'd you find that one, Bert? Was he right by the water, like still in it?"

Rupert, now sitting on my arm, nodded.

"It probably just washed up a minute ago. It wasn't dead yet."

Lissa looked down at Rupert. "You know," she said, "I don't think I want to do that collage after all. Taryn's right, it's too smelly. Plus, all the flies."

I said, "Great. Let's get out of here." I left the boys sleeping where they were, choosing to hike home with Lissa and Rupert. The sooner I got to an aspirin, the better, and I figured if Pablo or Marcus couldn't walk, Andrei would haul them home on his back one at a time.

On the trek back, Lissa was light-years away, sometimes drifting off-trail into the weeds before catching herself and returning to the gravel. Later that night, her new fling called at the house looking for her, and she told him she wouldn't be able to meet him this weekend. Something had come up.

I fell asleep on my bedroom floor and dreamed that Rupert was giving me an eye exam at the kitchen table. He was getting worried because I couldn't read his chart. I kept failing and failing.

IX.

FIVE YEARS AGO, AFTER a brassy Thanksgiving dinner at Frida's house characterized by our usual directionless chatter, Andrei and I took a long walk through the streets of Green Bay. We were at cross purposes that night. I had a headache and wanted only to clear it before driving back to Milwaukee where my husband waited. Andrei wanted to talk. He was auditing a course in ancient literature and he practically quivered as he tried to tell me about it.

"It was a hell of a lecture she gave the other night," he said, his breath making silver clouds. "It was all about myth and how it isn't like history, where you can just lock it down on a timeline somewhere and say, 'there, that's done, we've mastered it.' She said myth gets reincarnated over and over again. You can access it whenever you want to, because it never stops happening."

I rubbed at my temples. "When you say access, you mean like we can still read about it."

"No. I mean yeah, sometimes, but . . . the thing never dies because it walks around inside *us*. It has all this power, even if it's not real like this is real." He rapped on a mailbox. "And after class I started thinking, that's the Christ story, isn't it? I mean, what it was meant to be. Before all the stupid wars between Catholics and Protestants, and the Inquisition, and the Crusades—all that projection, all those people saying *we're the angels and you're the demons*—and then all the philosophers and scientists trying to own it with their clever little arguments, when really, the second you start trying to talk about it like that, the second you start dissecting it like it's some dead animal in a lab, you lose it."

Andrei was always like this when we were alone together: there'd be an effort to cram everything he'd been thinking for weeks into a couple of hours, and no matter how I resisted, the torque of his talk would propel me into territory best left untrod. He never apologized, for it was understood that there was no one else with whom he could speak so baldly. But I had no patience for it tonight. At dinner, Pablo's baby (the first in the family) had reached over and put his soft little fist on top of mine, his pointer and index fingers stretched out like antennae. I stood up quickly, startling everyone, but covered myself by suggesting we were due for a wine refill.

Andrei was oblivious to my crossed arms, my quickened pace. He went on: "People like that, they love all the power they get from telling people they know best, right? They're all little pharaohs and popes and dictators saying look no further, the answers are here with me, and once you're in lockstep, you're all set, there's nothing more you need to do. They're the types pumping out garbage ideology that says, 'if we just follow this little system we made, we'll be perfect, even if we have to kill a million people to make it happen.' I don't think it's a coincidence that they always want people to forget all the stories that came before them. I think they're afraid, I think they've always been afraid, that if they'd just let the myth breathe, we'd be able to take everything we need from it, and we wouldn't need anyone to do it for us. Because this myth just happens to be true, and if you believe in it . . . you can copy the model. You can tunnel through all the hell you've made, and come out on the other side, and relume." He lingered over the word as if he'd just then discovered it. "You can do the most creative thing in the world."

He burned with such energy that I thought he might take off running. But he rambled on, "The crazy thing is, I already *knew* this. It's like I knew it all along, even as a kid. But there's a difference between knowing something with your brain, and having it drop on you like a storm. Sometimes I think, you can't find a truth; it has to find you."

I came close to saying something horrible: *Sometimes I wish you were still drinking and living in your truck.* Instead I said, "I don't get it. Are you talking about art?"

"What? No, I—"

"Then what's the most creative thing in the world?"

A pause. It was beginning to snow, the falling flakes spaced cleanly apart like the boles of the pine grove we'd known all our lives.

"*Timshel*," he said at last. "Being accountable."

I was so self-absorbed, I believed he was deliberately goading me, trying to force me to remember what we'd all fought so hard to forget.

"Great," I said bitterly. "That sounds great. So how do I pull that off, Andrei? How do I do that? Let me just go ahead and build a time-machine so that Rupert never—so that Jeffrey doesn't—"

It was the first time in years I'd spoken Jeffrey's name, and to my horror, my voice broke. I turned away from Andrei and tried to lose myself in the vision of fresh snowflakes affixing themselves to the hood of a parked car. As I stood there I had a flash of the photograph from Marcus' textbook—the frost crystals, the fractals, each tiny dendrite an echo of its archetype.

"Abra, that's not . . . hey, look at me." He turned me around. "That's not the point. There's more than just guilt, something past that." Did his eyes fill, or was he just blinking through the snow? "You know what I figured out? I want what's on the other side, so bad. I'm just not strong enough to get there by myself." He pulled me in closer. "I wish you'd help me."

Shakily I said, "Not that long ago you were raving to me, on and on, about the individual as the *makeweight of everything*." I was pleased with myself for having remembered, so that I could fling it back at him. "Now you need my help to find your God? It's one fad after another, Andrei. I can't keep up."

"They're not fads. Everything builds on what came before. You learn." He wouldn't let go of me. A couple of passersby glanced our way. Andrei said, "It's complicated. It's not about giving people an easy out. It's about being the one who . . . who picks up the cross when it gets to be too much, and carries it for a little while before passing it back. I mean, some random person even did it for Christ himself, didn't he, for a few minutes there when he was climbing the hill. I think that's what love is."

I succeeded in extracting myself from his embrace. I couldn't take his eyes anymore. "I just wanted to take a walk," I said. "I have a splitting headache, and all I wanted was to walk. Is that too much to ask? Can we never just talk like normal people?"

"We did that all night." He jerked his head in the direction of Frida's house. "It's all we ever do with them."

But the conversation was over. We walked back. We got in our separate cars, drove back to waiting spouses in separate homes. I had a dream that night in which I asked Andrei what was on the other side of the guilt. In response he skipped a rock into Lake Michigan, and it skittered all the way to the horizon where I could just make out a rowboat with a lone paddler.

I was halfway through my senior year, coming up on Thanksgiving break, when Frida told me she was pregnant.

I was sitting on her bed, which was layered over with discarded clothes. For a moment I just stared at her. "Are you serious?"

She turned to one side and pulled up her dress. The swelling wasn't much, but after two years' worth of throwing up her meals, Frida was rail-thin, and I was amazed that none of us had seen it.

"I need money," she said. Her voice was brittle. Her hair, which had thinned severely with the bulimia, was twisted in an ugly knot at the back of her neck. She said, "I have to get this taken care of, now."

I stalled by turning to study her windowsill where she'd always kept mementos from boyfriends and dates. There were Styrofoam soda cups, cigarette cartons, keychains, rubber coasters stolen from restaurants. Dried-up flowers treading brown water in a plastic vase. A folded-up undershirt, glow sticks that no longer glowed, a little glass jar of fool's gold. Cobwebs stretched between some of the souvenirs like tensile byways for insects. The only clean, bright thing was her red jewelry box, which she had long forbidden any of us to touch.

Finally I turned back to her and said, "Whose is it?"

"I think Sean's. Honestly, I don't know for sure. Does it matter? Even if it's his fault, it's *my* problem."

I didn't argue, but she pressed on, becoming more incensed: "I'm not having a baby. I'm twenty-one years old. I don't even have a job. How can I get one? Remember when I tried, in Manitowoc? And that woman said I was *unhireable.* The bitch. Like you need a 4.0 GPA to hang clothes on a rack."

The objection had been more about Frida's appearance in her fishnet stockings, not to mention her reputation at that mall for shoplifting, but I wasn't about to point this out. I said, "What *about* Sean? Can he help?"

"That's a laugh. Sean's got enough on his plate with his video games and his porn. God, the porn. He's got a thing for the same shit Pablo and Rafe do—all these women with tits so huge, they make you think of lady brontosauruses feeding their dino-babies on the jungle floor. Don't laugh— I'm serious. Big swinging tits made for giant milk-sucking babies. You know only a certain type of guy likes that kind of thing—guys who want mommies. You're safer with an ass man whose instinct is more to make a baby than to be one. It means they're more inclined to take on a little responsibility, whether they know it or not."

"Where did you read that, one of your magazines?"

She flopped down on the bed and a makeup case fell to the floor. "Does it matter? Look, I have this baby and I'll never get out of here." Then, "They've all let me down, every single guy. 'Oh, we'll get a place soon as I have money.' 'Oh, I'd love to live together someday, Frida, I could see that, a little house just you and me. We'll put up Christmas lights at Christmas and have birthday parties for the kids on the back deck.' Like they're going to be some Mr. Darcy if I just wait it out. But all they wanted was to screw, and they said what they had to say, because I'm just fucking dumb enough to pretend like I'm the kind of girl who gets the house and the princely guy, all that bullshit . . . so here we are. If I could afford my own car, I'd live in it."

She was horribly pale. I said, "Look, we'll figure this out. Have you told Andrei?"

"Saint Andrei? Mr. Responsibility? Christ, he'd tell me to keep it. He'd go out and buy a damn stroller and a onesie for it."

"But he has money."

It was true. His apprenticeship training ran for a week every three months, and in between, he was working full-time doing site cleanup, pulling nails out of bracing materials and being, as Pablo joked, "a carpenter's bitch."

I said, "He never spends anything, except on those tools. Where else are you going to get it?"

The pragmatism of this had snared her interest. "Huh. Well, abortions aren't cheap. You think he can pay for the whole thing?"

"There's no one else to ask except Marcus and he's not giving away jack with Pablo stealing from him half the time." I didn't mention the babysitting money I'd been hoarding since freshman year. Surely it wasn't enough, anyway. I added, "We don't have to tell him what it's for, you know. I'll tell him I want to apply early admission to a bunch of community colleges. They have big application fees. I'm pretty sure they take applications in winter."

"Holy shit. You're not stupid, Abra, you know that?" She got up again to study herself in her floor-length mirror, which was stippled with little smudges of mascara like squashed flies. "You think he'll go for it?"

"Yeah. I do."

She moved one painted fingernail over her lips, then down her sternum and over her abdomen. She met my gaze in the mirror. "You haven't had sex yet, have you."

"No."

"Lesbian?"

I rolled my eyes. "No."

"Don't rule it out. I heard your mom say once she used to experiment a little." Her mouth turned down. "Look, the point is, you're not missing anything. You know what sex is? If there's a God, it's just a way for him to play around with women like they're game pieces. Men get to walk away from the board whenever they want to, but we're screwed right into it. We just move around in a maze until checkmate, and then what do you think happens after that?"

I waited.

"Even God leaves the board."

Her eyes scared me. To divert her, I said, "I didn't know you believed in God."

"I don't. It could be Nature, or the fucking moon. It's all the same." She came back to the bed. Shoving her hand between the mattress and the wall, she produced a nubby pink diary that was vaguely familiar. "Know what this is?"

"Didn't you have that—"

"When we were little, yeah. Look at this." She held it in front of my face and began flipping pages. There were no words, only endless vertical lines, like number 1's, marching across the paper. Thousands upon thousands of them, page after page.

I said, "I don't get it."

"These are tally marks, Abra. Tallies of prayers. When I was little, I believed those fucking priests at Mom's church and I thought, if I prayed a prayer enough times, I could get what I want. So I'd lie here at night and mark off forty, fifty, a hundred damn *Hail Mary's* or *Glory Be's* and then I'd wait for things to get better. But in the morning, everything would be the same in this house, and it would be the same at school, because His Holy Fatherliness wasn't ever listening." She tossed the diary aside. "So much for fathers in general."

"I think Andrei would agree with you on that at least."

"Nobody knows what Andrei really thinks about anything. Which is interesting since all he does is read. I mean who does that unless it's homework? Or even if it *is* homework?" A pause. "But I'll give him one thing, he doesn't live in a fantasy world like some of us. Not anymore."

"What the hell's that supposed to mean?"

"I'm talking about me. Not just the stupid journals. I mean the dumb dreams I make up about these guys, and other things I know aren't going to happen for me."

"Did you want to be a painter?" I blurted out. "I wondered—"

Frida let out a snort. "You mean when you found my stuff and stole it? Don't worry your pretty little self, Abra. You want to be the artist, the title's all yours, whatever that even means around here. But if you really want to know, there was just something in a magazine and I loved it so much I wanted to try and paint it. It was a picture of a room. It was fucking stupid. You wouldn't understand." She looked away. "It's probably a good thing you took that crap out of here."

Downstairs, there was a commotion as Rafe and Pablo came in from wherever they'd been. Their voices boomed in that "we hope someone's listening to us being outrageous" way that had become tiresome.

"Drunk again," I said.

"No. They've been messing with MDMA, off and on. Ecstasy. I never tried it, but I guess it's total euphoria, a one-way ticket to fantasy-land. Your mom would be proud."

I looked blankly at her.

"Don't worry, it's not like it's heroin or coke. They could never afford it anyway. Everything they get, they're bumming off somebody else. It's all they know how to do."

I crossed my arms. "Rafe wouldn't do that shit if Pablo weren't doing it."

Flatly Frida said, "He doesn't have a choice. Pablo is his only friend."

Loud, forced laughter downstairs. I heard Rafe say Rupert's name.

"They're almost schizophrenic," I said. "Especially Rafe. He's so different when Rupert's around—so sweet."

Frida's face softened. "I know," she said. "We all are. I guess Pabs isn't Rafe's only friend, is he?"

I almost asked if she wanted Rupert to come with her when the time came. But I checked that impulse, remembering that Jeffrey was attached. I couldn't see abortion clinic doctors letting a nine-year-old into the room.

Frida said, "Look, when are you going to talk to Andrei?"

"Tomorrow morning. When he's outside, working on his stuff. Nobody else'll be up."

Early the next morning I found Andrei outside with Rupert. His work-area was normally spread out on the lawn between our two houses, on a patch of grass he regularly trimmed using the borrowed push-mower from the Scotsman. But now that the snows had come, he'd set up shop in the garage where his collection of used tools rested on two big tables he'd put together himself. He now had a router, grinder, hand drill, palm sander, and a full set of small carving chisels, and he was proud of what he'd amassed with his earnings. From the threshold, I said, "It's looking like a bona fide carpenter's shop in here."

Andrei nodded. "Took me long enough to move all their crap out of the way." He gestured to take in the remnants of our parents' many fads dating back to our babyhood—fishing gear, aerobics mats, gardening tools, craft supplies in plastic drawers. He was straddling a stool, sanding something while Rupert watched. A Goodwill space heater Marcus had repaired for him buzzed quietly at his feet.

I came close. "What are you two working on?"

"Something Bert wants," Andrei said, leaning in. "You know how he gets when he has an idea. I figured better do it for him now than have twenty notes show up in my pockets."

It was a simple cross he was sanding, but the wood was a startling color, somewhere between lilac and wine. I looked at Rupert. "For Big Jesus?"

The antennae nodded.

I said, "Hard to believe there are trees that look like this on the inside."

"Yeah. Purpleheart's a strange one." He kept sanding. "So what's up?"

Above and behind him, there was a flutter of movement; Frida had pulled aside her bedroom curtain and was watching us.

I'd never outright lied to Andrei. Still, I wasn't expecting to feel as sick as I did when I said, "I was wondering if I could borrow some money, for early applications. I think I want to try some of those community colleges."

He didn't look up. "Oh yeah?"

"I just want to see if I can get in. Like you said, there's good job training. But it's expensive." I swallowed, waiting for him to say, *come on, what's really going on?* When he didn't, I had no choice but to push on: "I'd really like to try."

Rupert had climbed into the pocket of Andrei's coat. He crawled back out holding a dusty quarter between his feelers. He offered it to me, in that cheery way that always broke us all down. "Oh, thanks, bud," I said. "That helps a lot." Now I really felt sick.

Andrei, still not meeting my eyes, said, "The Idiot."

"Who?"

"It's the title of a book. Dostoevsky. It's the book I keep my money in so Rafe and Pablo don't find it. It's a big book on the bottom shelf in my room, black and white cover. Just take what you need."

"You don't even want to know how much?"

"Take what you need."

I hovered there for a minute, bewildered. Then I went to Andrei's room and found the money.

I skipped school and in my mother's car drove my cousin to and from her appointment in Milwaukee. It was a Friday, and our parents were down in Madison meeting old commune friends who had meandered east to rekindle their connections. When we got back in the early afternoon, the house was deadly silent.

Frida didn't want me anywhere near her. She let me help her up the stairs to her bed, then told me to leave her be. If anyone asked about her—not that they would—tell them she had a stomachache. Her voice was empty, totally without rancor. She looked half-dead.

"How about a Chaos Cake?" I offered. "I think there's flour and stuff at my parents'. I could make it for you in like ten minutes." It was a crazy dessert I made for myself now and then, something Andrei found revolting. I'd toss dollar-store chocolate and peanuts and even gummy bears in with the flour and eggs, then swirl in strawberry sauce from a plastic bottle. The final product would be dense with candy shrapnel, indigestible, but all those mismatched flavors thrilled me. To Frida, I said, "It might make you feel better. You taste so much at once, you can't focus on anything at all."

"Oh, God." Frida's face was pinched. "I'm going to throw up just thinking about it."

I left her and for some reason detoured into our mothers' studio in the attic. Lissa's newest paintings were the usual fare, big splotches of color flung at the canvas from three feet away, but tucked into the corner on my mother's side was something new: a portrait. It was foggy, grey, as though a cloud had lodged between the face and the painter.

I couldn't even tell if it was a man or a woman. But the eyes were unnervingly alive, and I hurried out of there.

Downstairs, I dug under the bathroom sink for the heating pad Andrei had bought Frida back when she first started getting menstrual cramps, then hunted through the kitchen cabinets for aspirin. I found the latter behind a small army of jam and syrup bottles Andrei had left turned upside-down to drain the remains, but in my shakiness I dropped the aspirin into the grimy crack between the fridge and the counter. I had to hip-check the fridge sideways to salvage the bottle. This exposed a small landfill of sticky remains—pills, chunks of charcoal from burnt meals, curls of raw Ramen, foil gum wrappers, raisins—that had been gathering for years. We all had a habit of kicking fallen trash under the nearest appliance instead of leaning down to pick it up, so the mess shouldn't have startled me, but it did. I leaned in and glimpsed a party of black ants roving through the filth before I shoved the fridge back into place.

I washed my hands, then got out bowls and started making the lime Jell-O that was Frida's all-season favorite. I couldn't think what else to do. Stirring the green liquid, I had a flash of her at ten or so, chubby and big-haired, wearing an emerald dress she'd found at a consignment store. It was somebody's reject prom dress, practically made of plastic and covered in sequins that kept popping off and pasting themselves to furniture all over the house. She wore it day and night for a week despite our parents' derision. Christmas that year, she walked into Two Rivers and came back with the ingredients for cookies she'd seen in a magazine somewhere. They were wreaths made of cornflakes and marshmallows and green dye, with little red candies stuck into them like holly berries. They were so exquisite on that baking tray, so unwontedly meticulous, that even little Pablo and Rafe were afraid to eat them. Our parents called Frida Betty Crocker, Mrs. Cleaver, all sorts of names until she took the cookies into her bedroom and ate the whole batch on her own. Even after puking it all up in the bathroom a few hours later, she'd had a regal coolness about her, spurning both affection and pity.

I put the gelatin in the fridge to set, then sat down at the table under the ticking kitchen clock.

I fell asleep in my chair. My dreams were bloody, accomplices to my own dread. I saw a thresher moving over a slumbering white-tailed deer in a winter field, a pair of robins' eggs cracking apart on ice, a spray of incarnadine leaves staining the snow. In the final dream, I was with Rupert, driving around in my father's car. A pale green inchworm worked his way across the dashboard while we drove, and Rupert followed him with his eyes, fascinated. "We'll put him outside as soon as we park, bud," I promised. The dream skipped ahead to nightfall. I lay on my bed, drowsy and content, until Rupert pounded at my door in a panic. He tugged me downstairs and outside to the car and pointed frantically at the windows. Filled with foreboding, I unlocked the car and switched on the dome light. We searched every crevice for the inchworm but there was so sign of him, and I knew that he'd dried up and died while we were in the house. "Rupert," I said, preparing the words. Then he began to hop up and down in excitement. He pointed into the little cup where my father kept spare change, where I could just make out the slow progress of the inchworm across the pennies. With my fingertip I lifted him out of his well and brought him outside. We watched him crawl through a shaft of moonlight into the leaf-strewn grass, and then Rupert fell forward, collapsing from relief.

I jolted upright when the school bus—what my father called the Beetsie Bus—rumbled by. It meant Rupert was about to wander in. I got busy and was spritzing the Jell-O with canned whipped cream when Jeffrey swung through the back door carrying his knapsack. His gaze was faraway, keenly focused on something, but when he saw me, Rupert jumped onto the counter to wave hello.

"I'm making Jell-O treats," I said in answer to his silent question. He dunked his antennae in the whipped cream and came up looking ridiculous, two big dollops hanging over his eyes.

"Rupert, look at you, you look like George Washington." I cleaned off his feelers. "This isn't for you, anyway, it's for Frida."

Rupert looked at the ceiling.

"She's not feeling well," I said. "So don't bother her."

Of course, Rupert went thundering up the banister before I could grab him. I followed him, calling out to Frida that I was sorry, I'd told him to leave her alone . . .

"He can come in," she said faintly from behind her door. "It's okay."

Rupert went straight to the bed where Frida lay on her side with her hands curved over her belly. I wasn't sure which of us she addressed when she said, "They tell you it's no big deal, but it is."

She was crying. I backed away, sat down on the hallway floor. There was no sound for a long time. Then I heard a scuffle of paper and a small laugh from Frida. "Not sick," she said. "Sad. Can you stay, Beetsie?"

I knew Rupert was nodding, ever-faithful.

"Beetsie. You remember that day you killed the cricket? Because you thought it was a bad spider?"

This had happened the day we went to the turntable demonstration, long before Rupert appeared. I moved closer to the door and saw that Rupert was nodding his feelers anyway.

"And you cried all morning about it?" Frida continued. "I killed a cricket, too."

Rupert scribbled something else and held up the paper.

"Axe-i-dent? No. I knew."

Rupert didn't move.

"I don't know why I'm like this," she went on brokenly. "I don't know. You should go away. I'm not good. You don't want to be near me."

Rupert inched his way up her forearm and shoulder. Sitting on her neck, he reached down and hugged her face, wrapping his antennae over her eye, her cheek.

"I'm sorry I smashed your paper hummingbird, Rupert," she went on. "That day. Do you remember?"

Another feeler-nod.

Frida reached up to hold him. She didn't seem to notice that Jeffrey was on the bed with her, his head resting on the same pillow. I was still standing there motionless when Marcus came down the hall. He glanced into Frida's room and did a double take, but I shook my head and indicated that he should keep walking.

I followed him into his room and leaned against his dresser as he heeled off his boots. As if expecting some horror, he said in a low voice, "What is wrong with Frida."

"Wrong with her? Just cramps. She's in that cranky-cat mode she gets into. You would've gotten clawed if you'd gone in there. I was just trying to save you from that."

"She's not pregnant, is she?"

I reeled back a little. "Why would you say that?"

Marcus shrugged and threw his coat on his bed. The whole room smelled of the auto shop. "Just a weird feeling," he said.

"It's just cramps. Rupert's on top of it."

"Thank God. Could you imagine another—" He stopped and made a little frown. "I almost said, another Jeffrey. But that didn't turn out so bad. I mean, we got Rupert out of it, didn't we?"

I stood there in his doorway trying to think how to respond, until he dismissed me: "Look, I'm wiped," he said. "Can a guy get some sleep?"

"Sure, Marc." I closed his door behind me and went back to the other house.

I wouldn't have admitted it then, but it was out of a vague, nameless guilt that I enrolled in a night class at the community college that December. It was a just short-term course that would finish in January, something called *Intro to Drawing Fundamentals*. I found the title redundant, not to mention insulting (who needed an *intro* to the *fundamentals*?), but it was the best I could get. The graphic design classes didn't start up again until the New Year, and they wouldn't let non-degree students take them anyway. I saw no point in bothering with the application process when I knew I'd never stay there for two full years. "How wonderful," the admissions counselor gushed over the phone when I called to sign up. "How wonderful that you're embracing what you love!"

I wasn't impressed with my classmates, those other people "embracing what they loved." The group was a mix of doddering senior citizens with too much time on their hands (wealthy, I figured, and taking birding or basket-weaving classes somewhere too), and twenty-somethings who thought they were wildly gifted. One of these women showed me a tracing she'd done of an Audubon illustration and said proudly, "It takes a steady hand to do this."

I'd decided I disliked her even before she spoke. She always came to class dressed to the nines, delicate silver bangles clicking on her wrists, and I'd heard her mention to the instructor that she'd been to several museums in Europe on a backpacking trip after high school.

I said to her, "It takes Audubon, and first-grade tracing skills."

She pulled back like I'd stung her.

The instructor spoke of vantage points and depth and dimension. She took us through agonizingly dull practice sessions that made me think of assembly lines—each of us making the same small, insignificant part on repeat with no concept of how it fit into a whole—or else sophomore-year geometry, the long strings of meaningless formulas memorized only for the sake of the exam. I wanted to scream. My arm pulsed with the need for sudden, unconstrained movement; I trembled with impatience as I twitched my charcoal pencil. When would we be free to *draw*?

By the halfway point, I knew I'd never stick with it. I had no patience for this snail's pace, this laborious study of composition and technique. The *fundamentals* were stultifying. And there was no vibrance, no verve, to any of it; I had the sense of being trapped on the back side of a canvas, where the staples stuck out and the naked wood showed itself dull brown. How long could an artist be expected to live there? I took my frustration as a good sign, affirmation that I had in spades the inborn talent that the others only pretended to have. I returned my pencils to the instructor and politely told her that my work schedule had interfered with class and so I could no longer attend. She eyed me in a way I didn't like but said she was sorry and hoped I would try again someday.

Just as Andrei had never told anyone about the tutoring sessions he underwent for his dyslexia, so I never told anyone about the drawing class. Who save Andrei would even notice I was gone for those three hours a week? But while Andrei had concealed his labors to anneal himself against scorn, I hid mine because I knew on some level that I wouldn't see the thing through.

I needn't have worried; not even Andrei asked me where I'd been. Rupert was the only one who figured it out. He came into my room the Saturday after I quit and laid a charcoal pencil in my hand.

"Why are you giving me this," I said, though the pencil was unquestionably a straggler from the loaner-set I'd gotten at the college. "It's not mine."

He only pressed the pencil deeper into my palms.

"I'm not in the class anymore, Rupert," I said at last. "It was boring. It was stupid."

The feelers wilted over the pencil.

"What do you care? Go play, bud. Go play." I picked him up and deposited him on the roof of my dollhouse. Then I found my coat and boots and left the house for a long walk.

We'd had a break between snows and the trail was manageable, though Molash Creek was glass. I was halfway to the beach before I realized I still had the charcoal pencil in my fist. When I flung it into the trees, something in a trailside maple caught my eye. One of Jeffrey's acorn-faces from years earlier was tucked into a little squirrel grotto. Shaking my head, I wrapped my arms around myself and kept walking.

It was desolate out there even at midday, the water slate-grey and the dune plants iced in place. I pulled up my hood and kept close to the tree line, ultimately settling down into the snowless room beneath a thick conifer. Its lower branches were so laden with ice that they tilted down umbrella-like, creating a frosted glass window that encircled the room and refracted prisms of light onto the cold floor. As a little girl I'd often crept into hideouts like this. In better weather I'd stash snacks in the branches, and until Andrei caught me and chewed me out, I'd rip up stairstep moss and layer it on the floor like carpet. I'd stay there for hours, imagining that all manner of storms and fires and wild animals ravaged the coast but miraculously passed me by. Sometimes I'd fall asleep. Now, though, I wasn't sure why I was here, why I needed this. But the urge to curl up under the evergreen roof and sleep like some hibernating creature was powerful.

It was not the piercing cold that jarred me from my brief nap, but a faint voice the wind carried southward. I sat up, hitting my head on a branch, and cursed. Then I sat there listening. Somebody was humming or singing down by the water. Slowly I crawled out of my shelter, careful not to sink my knees into the snow, and hoisted myself up. I crunched my way to an opening in the woods and peered down the beach. A small figure layered up in faded winter gear followed the waterline. When the figure drew closer, I recognized his coat as Rafe's.

I stayed where I was. Rafe went on singing—I couldn't make out the words—and occasionally he stooped for a rock or piece of debris. I remembered that when he was small, he pestered me constantly in wintertime about the animals and fish, wanting to know how they survived the bad weather. *Where do the salamanders go, where do the turtles go* and so on. He used to build little shelters out here like he was preparing real estate for them. In my post-nap haze, I wondered briefly if I might be remembering this wrong (wasn't it the sort of thing Rupert would do? And how could the Rafe who'd tried to kill us over a glass beaker be the same person who'd once built emergency housing for wild animals?), but a moment later Rafe came inland and began scraping together dead branches to make a "beach nest" as he had many years before.

"Hey," I called out.

He kicked aside the wood scraps. "What are you doing out here? It's fucking cold."

I came close. "You got here first. What are you doing?"

"Nothing." His face was red from windburn. "Just didn't want to be at home."

"Why, are Mom and Dad fighting?"

"No. It's weird though. I feel like there's something going on inside the other house. I've had bad dreams all week."

I studied him. He wasn't high or drunk, but he looked exhausted. I said, "There's nothing weird going on. It's business as usual, Rafe."

"I guess. But I don't know." He shrugged and looked away.

To jolt him out of his funk, I said, "Remember that one winter when we all came down here and made Tunnel City?"

"You hated Tunnel City. You said it was ugly."

In truth I'd found our snow-tunnels terrifying and had refused to crawl into them, spending that Saturday pouting by the trees while the boys clambered through their maze and popped out of secret windows like jack-in-the-boxes. I said, "Yeah, but as Marcus would say, the thing had a good infrastructure."

I was hoping he'd laugh, but he only squinted at the water, which was now an ominous midnight-blue beneath the worsted texture of the winter sky. "I had a horrible dream last night," he said. "There was a blizzard or something, and we all came down here and there was this huge snowy dune going all the way to the water. We were all standing on top of it talking or fighting or something, and Rupert was down at the bottom making a little snowman. I think we were so heavy that we started an avalanche. Anyway I looked down one minute, and Rupert was there, then I looked down a second later and there was just a mountain of snow and sand, and nothing. I was screaming *the baby, the baby* and then I woke up." He made a sound that wasn't quite a laugh, then dug into his coat pocket for a cigarette. "I don't fucking know."

I watched as he fumbled to light it with gloved hands. "That shit will kill you," I said.

"That's the point," he responded. The cold glint had returned to his red-mapped eyes. "It speeds up the process."

"And you would want to do that because—?"

When he didn't answer, I said, "Rupert hates it, you know."

The glint petered out. "That's why I only do it when he's not around."

"Come on, let's go back. It's death out here."

We hiked back. Rafe worked his way through two more cigarettes along the trail, then snuffed out his third when we saw Rupert waiting in the kitchen window.

Not so long after this, the night of the heaviest snowfall of that winter, I came upstairs in search of Andrei and found Rupert with Frida again. They were in her room, engaged in what seemed like a simple chore but on closer inspection was some kind of ceremony or rite. Rupert crawled across the bureau, picking up makeup and tossing one clamshell after another into a plastic trash bag Frida held open for him. He pointed at the closet next, then tugged clothes off hangers, adding midriffs and skirts to the trash bag. Then he feeler-kicked off her windowsill the long line of mementos she'd kept from boyfriends who'd dumped her.

"It's all junk anyway," Frida said. She didn't notice me hovering in the doorway. "You're right, Roo, it's just junk."

He tapped her red jewelry box with a feeler.

"Not that," she said, her voice tightening. "That's mine."

He tapped it again, insistent, pointing at the latch as if he understood that he was not allowed to open it himself. Frida stepped over and opened the box, revealing her jumble of bracelets and earrings. As she stood there shaking her head, he dug out first the jewelry and then a sheaf of old ginger-bread cookie decals. The box emptied, he pointed again.

"Christ. How did you know?" She lifted what I now saw to be the box's false bottom. "Okay, happy now? Is this what you wanted to get at?"

Rupert nodded and reached back into the hollows of the box.

"No. Not safe. I'll do it myself, okay? If that will make you happy." Frida took out a stack of razors and after a brief hesitation let them drop into the trash bag. "There. Okay? But I get to keep the box, and the cookie stickers. Look at the windowsill, it's all bare and ugly now."

Rupert solved this problem by dragging over his knapsack and delicately removing the contents one tiny piece at a time. On the sill he laid out a line of origami birds, each one unique. Teal, lilac, coral, pink. They were only paper, but they caught up the light of Frida's bedside lamp like glass. The whole lot of them trembled as if alive.

"Oh," Frida said softly.

I backed away. Forgetting why I'd come upstairs in the first place, I found my coat and wandered outside into the twilight. The snow had already begun to cling, delicate as eyelet lace. I started to hike beachward again but was soon put off. The checkered light beneath the canopy was eerie, ash-grey where it struck the snow as if diluted through a dirty lens, and in the near-dark the firs were swiftly merging into a black wall.

When I came back, I found Andrei alone at my parents' kitchen table—an odd place for him to be. He was sitting there under the lamplight with a loaf of Wonderbread, a bowl of blueberries, a glass jar of turmeric and a ball of string. I recognized the marble pestle my mother had purchased back when she was in her herbal medicine phase. Andrei was so focused that he jumped when I said, "What's all this?"

He shrugged and went back to what he was doing—rolling bits of bread into little balls. The snow was blowing in sideways, pelting the living room windows.

I decided to sit down without waiting for an invitation. He'd been avoiding me and I was tired of it. "Where've you been all the time, on the trails?"

"Some."

"Are you making a necklace or something?" For some reason I had a flash of the amber heart necklace I'd taken off my classmate's doll back before Rupert was born, and I felt a little sick.

Andrei said, "Something like that."

"What's the spice for? And the blueberries?"

"Dye. I'm going to color them yellow and blue. It's an approximation."

"Of what?"

"Something this labor camp survivor I was reading about did. He was in a Russian gulag forever, and he ran into some Lithuanians who taught him how to make rosaries out of old bread. They'd use tooth powder and burnt rubber to dye the beads."

I was still uneasy, only now I was thinking of Frida's tallybook. "Rosaries are a Catholic thing."

"It's not what you've got in mind. He used the beads to keep track of things he wanted to write later, if he ever got out. It was the only way he could think to do it." He was smashing up the berries now, creating a dark juice. "A lot of it was stuff he figured he'd otherwise not be willing to think about, once he was back to normal life. Like when he realized he was just as bad as the camp guards, because before he came there, he did horrible things to people back when he was a soldier."

"Did he ever get to write anything down?"

"He memorized twelve thousand lines." He rolled some of the beads in a little heap of turmeric, staining his fingertips yellow. "I know what I'd do, if it were me. All I'd be thinking about is escape. I'd be slick as a rat. I'd probably murder my own friends to get out of a prison like that. And then I'd dodge my way into some safe zone, and huddle up there, and stay angry forever."

"Andrei, what are you talking about?"

He began stringing the beads, head down. "Is she all right? I can't ask her."

A little firework show of nerves started up in my solar plexus. "Is who all right?"

"You know. She hardly leaves her room."

I swallowed. "You knew?"

"She didn't have to tell me. She's my sister, Abra."

"Why didn't you say something when I—when I asked you for the money? What the hell, Andrei?"

He strung another bead. "You really want to know? I was hoping she'd do it." He stopped, looked directly at me. His eyes were mapped with red. "I wasn't up to raising another kid. I did it once already, why should I have to do it again? I even told myself it wasn't fair to you. You'd end up carrying the other half of the load, just like with Jeff. I thought, fuck this, like Pablo would say. Fuck this, I'm not doing it."

"Andrei—"

He cut me off: "I thought I could weasel out all that *and* her decision to get rid of it. Nobody asked me, right? You said you wanted application money, so I gave it to you, and no one can say I asked Frida to do it or even that I wanted her to." A twisted grin. "Except me, of course. Unfortunately, I can't seem to stop myself from knowing. Not sure how to work with that little problem." He pinched a bit of bread between his fingertips.

"Andrei, it was her decision. And she was the one who got herself pregnant to begin with." I was getting heated. "Why should you feel guilty? You helped her." What, I wanted to add, was he implying about *me*? Was I supposed to feel guilty, too?

He said, "I didn't do anything for her." He pummeled some more blueberries with my mother's pestle. "You know who *has* taken care of her? You know who's been there? Dopey little Rupert. He's with her all the time. He told me in a note, he's going to go with her to Schroeder's when she's feeling good again."

"What the hell for?"

"It's a secret she has. Or I thought it was a secret but Rupert knows somehow. She goes there sometimes and she talks to some old lady at the alterations counter about clothes. And then she goes to the top floor where they have all the yarn and the quilting stuff, and she just looks at things. It's the one place she never steals anything. I know because I've followed her up there a couple of times. These assholes she dates, they wouldn't believe it that the girl screwing them in their car likes to look at yarn and batting needles because it makes her feel safe, like maybe she's destined for something more . . . *stable* than all this. And dopey little Rupert gets it. He's dumb as rocks, but he gets it."

I stood up to leave. I couldn't have said why I was so angry. Almost pleadingly Andrei said, "You could stay up with me."

"I'm tired," I said. "I'm going to bed." I left him there at the table.

That night, I dreamed that I made one of those bread-bead necklaces, too, and that I carried it through all manner of strange and chaotic scenes. Somewhere along the way, though, I lost it. The dream's final image was of the rosary languishing in a puddle in the driveway. In the water's reflection, clouds traveled and leaves fell, then snow; four seasons elapsed. Yet the beads remained intact, still yellow and blue. In the dream I hated them for this, for waiting there like saints long after my passion had been subdued.

I jolted awake with the thought that *this* was something a real artist would try to paint. Oh, it would hurt to do so. It would wound. But it would tell the truth. I nursed this understanding for a full minute. Then I shook myself loose of the dream, released the firefly into the night, and went back to sleep.

X.

IT'S BEEN RAINING STEADILY for hours now, the night beyond Rafe's bedroom window inky dark. A flash of pink lightning illuminates a mountain range of clouds over Lake Michigan, and I know there will be a monstrous thunderstorm along the coast before morning breaks.

I didn't want to come in here and think of my brother as he was when he rocked in front of this window with my old baby doll in his arms. I didn't want to think about the night we almost lost him.

I've always known it was Rupert who tipped the scales, who kept both Rafe and Pablo from total self-destruction. But I have never asked myself just how or why he did it. I don't dare unearth the writhing worms beneath the surface of those years. My cousins and I have worked too hard to layer dirt, grass, and concrete over it all. And this of course is part of why I cannot imagine moving into this house, nor even transplanting pieces of its furniture into the white rooms of my faraway apartment. I am not a glutton for punishment. I am not Andrei.

Spring of that second year after Ontonagon, I was more in my own world than I'd ever been. Andrei kept pressuring me to decide on a program at the community college, and I sidestepped these conversations because I didn't want to tell him that I had no intention of learning some drab little trade. I was still painting in secret behind the garage, convinced of my latent talent.

Sometime in March, I completed the painting I thought would make me. For once it was not a random splattering of color on canvas. It was a scene from a dream, something vaguely familiar and yet inexplicable, like a misted-over memory from a previous life. The background was a pale yellow sky faintly stained with apricot. In the foreground was a stand of tattered pines like the ones near the beach, their limbs blue-grey and wind-gnarled, their attitude that of old men determined to stand tall despite their exhaustion and pain. Bouquets of muted green needles at the tips of those stripped limbs curved upward like hands cupping the sun. An empty grass-fringed lane passed beneath the trees. When I first finished the picture, it was spare, disciplined even, the sort of thing my mother and Lissa would disdain. I had a sense that some other hand had commandeered mine as I painted. I could not remember touching the brush to certain points on the canvas, nor could I explain how the trees had come to be so alive and willful.

I like to think there was some honesty and humility in my initial reaction to that picture. But within a week, the awe gave way to euphoria. *Brilliant,* I imagined people saying. *God, so brilliant, at just eighteen years old. Where did this come from?!* This was far superior to that ribbon-winning painting I'd marked up in the school art lab a year earlier. This was the real thing.

In a fever, I started adding to the picture, layering the paint. I kept at this all through April. At first the sky became yellower, stark and bright as if captured in its noonday refulgence. Then, as I swirled in stray shades of violet and fuchsia and pink, the sun's locus obscured itself; it could have been sunrise and sundown together, or an obliteration of both. I clad the boles of the trees in unnatural blues, then added nosegay after nosegay of greenery to the pines' branches until the interstices closed. They had no need now of those daz-zling rays overhead; they were their own light. These were young princes and princesses strutting peacock-like down the grassy corridors of their castles, about the sort of busi-ness ordinary souls could only guess at. The canvas became so front-heavy that I constantly had to adjust its angle to keep it from toppling forward.

I stored it in my parents' musty basement where nobody ever went. Down there was the furnace and water heater, those dully functional machines only hired men tinkered with if something went wrong. I kept the piece covered with tarp and went down there every day to tug on the light chain and admire my work afresh. It grew bolder by the day, more audacious with each touchup, and I'd ascend the stairs smil-ing to myself the way our mothers did when they had lovers. I was nurturing a glorious secret now. Andrei, watching me brush out my hair in front of my bedroom mirror, even asked me once if I had a crush on someone.

"Not exactly," I said.

As far as I knew, he still did not write. That spring, though, his studies reached fever-pitch, and changed tone, too. In place of the self-flagellating, night-prowling theologians and dead saints of old were smug philosophers and triple-degreed social scientists whose author photos captured expressions of patient superiority. Andrei seemed surprised by the shift, as if it had happened to him while he slept, but to me it was as natural as three following two. When had he been satisfied with God or faith, since the days of mock-confession at Lis-sa's church? When save in childhood had the spirit-world, the world of stories and strange dreams and all their attendant mystifying symbols, sufficed as a laboratory in which to for-mulate his beliefs? Now, depending on the night, God was so superior to us that we couldn't possibly connect with him or even capture his interest, so what was the point in trying to mimic that perfection? . . . or God was just a word standing in for what was really Nature's intelligence . . . or he was a story humanity had concocted purely for its own comfort, or else to employ as a tool of domination. Some of those ideas yielded strange fruit, errant thoughts he relayed to me shorn of all context: "Did you ever think about the fact that the pyramids are still there, still honoring the pharaohs who were freaking horrible people, but when Moses died, this person who was supposed to be so holy, who did everything God wanted even though it basically killed him, they say that God buried him someplace no one even knew about. Like a pet dog in a back-yard or something. What does that say about God?" One book's bibliography would launch him into the arms of the next, and his face sometimes mirrored what I'd seen in Pablo's or Rafe's when they ached for a cigarette or new high—or in Frida's when lust and desperation sent her prowling for a new lover.

Sometimes he forgot that these people's ideas were not actually his, and he played the part of the mad scientist who'd been up all night amidst beakers and violet smoke, concocting hypotheses inaccessible to us laymen. One Satur-day morning, Rupert was in the living room watching *Ben-Hur* for the millionth time when Andrei wandered in with a wine-colored book and sat down on the edge of the sofa. I hadn't been watching the film—I'd been floating in a kind of lucid dream, like the ones my mother chased with the help of her drugs—and at the sound of his voice I came parachut-ing back down, feeling my fantasy go limp around me like the sheets of the childhood blanket-forts Andrei used to tear away when he decided I'd been holed up too long.

Incensed, I said, "You shouldn't interrupt. Rupert's had to wait a week to get time with the TV." Technically, it was the truth. Pablo and Rafe had gotten a pile of action movies somewhere and had been watching them nonstop. They'd played *Total Recall, Predator,* and the *Terminator* movies enough that I was starting to hear heavy artillery in my sleep. Andrei was undeterred. "Rupert can focus fine," he said. "It's one of his few talents. Just listen. I bought this without knowing what it was, it was like an accident, and now I'm just—I don't know. Just listen."

Turning pages, Andrei tried to explain the man's thesis. It was all about desire as *triangular,* one man yearning for something another man has, only to realize he can't have what he wants without eliminating his competition. The resulting cycle of violence had entrapped mankind from the beginning of time. "It's a zero-sum game," Andrei said. "And the worst part is that people start thinking that whole shit situation is *life* and there's nothing else. So when they can't get what they want, all this frustration builds up. It's like they know that they're empty, but they don't know how to fix things, so the frustration keeps building into a charge that has to go off somewhere."

I picked at a loose thread on a throw pillow. I wanted to take Andrei downstairs and show him my canvas. He wasn't the only one with a vibrant mind.

"In comes the scapegoat," Andrei continued. "Society zeroes in on one person and basically says, 'it's all his fault that we feel this way', and then they annihilate him."

He was so intent that I felt myself coming over to him against my will. I said, "How do they pick the person?"

Rupert was now right up on the television, tapping the screen. It was one of his favorite scenes, when the arrested and enslaved Ben-Hur passes through Nazareth in a chain gang and encounters the young Christ.

Andrei said, "It's someone who's pointed out that they're living wrong. People want to think that it's somebody else's fault that they feel all this frustration, but the truth-teller says, 'No, that's a lie, it's what's on the inside that's a problem, that's what you have to fix,' and they hate him for it, so they burn him down. It's like destroying evidence. Out of sight, out of mind."

"Okay . . ."

"But after they burn down the scapegoat, the whole process just starts over again. Nobody feels better for very long." He shook his head. "I haven't finished the book yet, but the obvious question is how do you break the cycle."

Rupert was insistent now, banging on the TV with his feelers. We both glanced over. Christ, his back to us, was bent low over Ben-Hur, bringing a ladle of water to his chapped lips. His hand passed over Ben-Hur's head, combing cool water through his matted hair.

"Yes, we know, it's your favorite, Rupert," Andrei said impatiently. He turned to back to me. "I mean, how would it even be possible? People are what they are."

"No clue," I said, shifting position on the sofa. I knew it would exasperate him, but I said, "I'm stiff. I feel like I need a walk or something."

To my surprise, he tossed the book aside. "I'll come with you. Honestly, I don't think I'm going to read any more of this one. For some reason I just don't—"

At that moment, the front door swung open and Pablo and Rafe stumbled in, reeking of alcohol. "It's too bright in here," Pablo said loudly.

"Where were you guys this time?"

"What's in that weird box on the porch?" Rafe wanted to know. Innocent question aside, he was glinty-eyed, unquestionably on the black end of the mood spectrum.

"Rupert's caterpillar hotel," I said. "It's too easy to step on them in the driveway so he made them a box." He'd found a big clear plastic case somewhere and filed it with dirt and grass and bits of fruit, then propped it open with a long twig so they'd have oxygen. The caterpillars had been squirming around in there, living their lives, for two days. Very few of them had crawled out, though when they did, Rupert respected their choice and did not put them back in.

Pablo rolled his eyes. "We need beer," he said. "Hangover medication. Where's Frida?"

"You can't get one of your loser friends to buy it?" Andrei studied them. "God, what have you two been doing? You look like hell."

I said, "Frida went for a hike down to the lake. Leave her alone."

Rafe came over to the couch and sat on the arm. Up close, he smelled like vomit. "At least get us some fucking cigarettes."

"You could get a job," Andrei volunteered. "You could actually contribute, instead of mooching off everyone under the sun or stealing from Marcus every chance you get. You're a couple of fucking turkey vultures, you know that?"

"We wouldn't have to steal from Marc so much if you'd leave your shit lying around once in a while. But nobody hides his money as good as Andrei does," Pablo said, addressing the room as though speaking to a crowd from behind a podium. "He's such a genius little hider."

"He's not *that* good," I said. "He doesn't have to be. Criminals tend not to be bright, lucky for everyone else, huh? For the functioning half of the planet, I mean."

At first I thought it was Pablo who'd struck the side of my head. But it was Rafe, and a second later, Andrei crossed my sight line and knocked him to the carpet. "You little piece of shit, I swear to God—"

Pablo leaped on him and started clawing. Andrei flung him off and tried to pull my brother to his feet. When Pablo came back for more, he was smiling that same snakelike smile I'd seen back in the clearing in Ontonagon, and one hand slid into his pants pocket. Dazed as I was, I had the distinct impression that he was about to knife his brother. But Andrei pivoted and swung hard, sending Pablo staggering backwards into the armchair.

"Are we done?" Andrei was panting, still holding Rafe by the upper arm. Rafe stood there lifeless as a dummy, grinning faintly. I turned away.

Andrei let Rafe go. My brother followed Pablo back out the front door. A second later, Jeffrey rose from his crouch beside the TV.

"No, Roo," Andrei said firmly. "Do *not* go after them."

But Rupert was afraid they'd kicked over his caterpillar hotel. He pointed frantically toward the porch.

"All right, let's go look," I said. My head was beginning to pound.

We trooped out to the crumbling front steps. Rupert peered over the ledge of the caterpillar box and affirmed that all his guests were okay. Andrei, standing behind me, gently pulled my hair back and felt the side of my head for a bump.

"I'm fine," I said, but in truth I was livid. The flat of Rafe's hand against my head had taken me back to the humiliations of junior high, girls mocking me, kids shoving my face against bus windows, the enraged powerlessness of it all. I wanted to bruise my brother back, do him one worse than he'd done me. Who did he think he was?

"Rupert," Andrei said, "if they'd smashed up your caterpillars, what would you have done?"

Rupert crawled over to study Andrei's scraped-up knuckles, then wrapped his feelers around Andrei's hand.

Our fathers were in Milwaukee that weekend. Lonnie had finally landed a good gig and my father had decided to go with him, expressing the surprising sentiment that someone should be there in case Lonnie had another dizzy spell. Our mothers spent Saturday in their attic studio, oblivious to the rest of us. Frida and Marcus came home and went to bed. Rupert was unsettled all night, constantly checking his caterpillars and peering up and down the street for Pablo and Rafe. At some point Andrei and I coaxed him into the living room and put on another movie. We were used to the boys' noctivagance and thought nothing of their still being out at two in the morning. I passed out and dreamed of naked pines beneath a dark grey sky. *No,* I insisted in the dream, *wrong sky. It should be bright yellow, and pink, and purple . . . And bring the green branches back!*

Liar, a voice responded from somewhere down the grassy lane. *Coward.*

I jolted awake, blinking into the blue dark of three in the morning, and found that I had fallen asleep on Andrei's chest. He was awake, too, his arms locked around me. It was a strange thing. We were still a family that rarely touched, unless of course we were holding or patting Rupert. The little compass on Andrei's wristwatch no longer glowed, but I could hear the faint ticking of the hands. It was a man's watch—too big for him when he first bought it—and now it was tight around his wrist. The fact that it still pumped away unsettled me. He must have replaced the battery ten times to keep it in service.

"Do you think it's true?" Andrei said softly, dispersing my thoughts.

I lifted my head a little and looked around. Jeffrey was asleep on the floor, Rupert curled up in a little ball atop a pillow. I said, "Do I think what's true?"

"That we're just moving around in triangles. Trapped."

Always he compelled me to honesty. "Yes," I said. "Almost all the time."

"When's it not like that?"

Instinctively I glanced back down at Rupert.

"Yeah." His voice was strangled. "That's what I've been lying here thinking."

I let out a little sigh. "Why are you thinking about this."

"I don't *want* to think about it, but it comes anyway. I think truth is like water . . . you can build all kinds of dams to hold it back but it'll always try to fill whatever space is around. And if you can't talk to the people around you about the truth, you start to feel like you might drown in it." He turned his head and coughed as if actually choking on water. "But maybe that's what I deserve."

He hadn't named me, but I felt myself implicated. How many times had he surged toward me like an eddy, only to be checked by my resistance, driven back upon himself to flood the recesses of his own doubt? The firefly pulsed somewhere in the room with us; I felt as I had that night on Lake Superior when Andrei told me he'd never write poetry again. "Andrei," I said. "You're too hard on yourself. You always are."

"Ha. If you only knew. I'm just like him, you know—I mean Andrei in *War and Peace*. He can hold a grudge longer than anyone in history. He stays angry and hateful until he's all blown apart and it's too late."

I sat partway up, which was difficult because he would not loosen his hold on me. "What grudge are you holding?"

"Are you kidding? Where do you want me to start? I'm out there cleaning up work sites and thinking the whole time, I'm doing this for a bunch of slobs who don't even notice I'm paying the bills. I used to read to Jeff in his crib and think, I can already tell this kid is smarter than I'll ever be, why am I making it worse by teaching him words? Now he comes with me to the dollar store, and the cashier lady looks at him like he's disabled, because he doesn't speak and because Rupert's putting things on the conveyor belt. And I'm happy about it. I pretend to be annoyed that he keeps coming out in public even when I tell him *don't, Rupert, there's Science around here . . .* but at the grocery store, moments like that, I'm happy because I look at Rupert and I almost believe it that my brother is retarded and not a genius after all like I was afraid of. And I feel good, like I'm finally getting the payout that's coming to me for doing everything all these years, for taking care of everyone, all this shit nobody deserves from me to begin with . . . I think I'm winning, because he's retarded, and I'm the one going places. I actually think that. What the fuck is that, Abra?" His voice shook. "I wanted to kill Rafe today, and Pablo. But it almost didn't matter who it was. I just wanted to destroy something. I think I always do, and I don't even know why."

"Andrei," I said quietly, "breathe."

He went on as if I hadn't spoken: "I've been having this same nightmare for years now, literally years. There's a crisis coming, like an apocalypse or something, and Ru—Jeffrey and I are on our own and we have to go into the wild to survive. And I'm furious at him because I've got this duffel bag full of clothes and first aid stuff, and books on the things we'll need to know how to do once we're out there in the wild, and all he'll carry is this wooden bowl. I'm telling him, this is stupid, what can you do with a bowl? Pull your goddamn weight! Then later in the dream, we're in this grey desert, and we're dying of thirst, and I have to dump all the books because they weigh so much and they're useless in this place, and then I have to drop the rest of it too because I'm too weak to carry it. And then when it finally rains, Jeff uses his bowl to catch the water, and we live. And even though he's saved my life, I want to kill him. I want to kill him because he had it right from the start, and it's not fucking fair when I'm the one who, I'm the one who –" He was practically gasping for air. "I wake up, and I'm out of the dream but I'm still ready to put a knife in someone."

I touched his lips, as he had touched mine the night Jeffrey was born. "Stop it, Andrei. That's not who you are." I almost added, *that's who I am.* Instead I said, "Whatever is ugly in you, won't win in the end. I know it." And I believed it.

Andrei said, "How do you know?"

I opened my mouth to answer and then his hand was on my cheek and he was kissing me deeply. I didn't think; I just returned it. When he rolled me beneath him, I wrapped my arms around him and felt a tremor course through his back. There was a bright light, like a camera's flash bulb, somewhere behind my eyes and in a rush I saw Andrei leaving the confession box at the church after having told the priest that he wanted to find his real father. There was no one to tell him what to do, he'd said. I understood it. There had never been anyone to tell us what to do, or what we should, or *could,* do. Even if God existed, he spoke directly to no one. But I had the thought that with Andrei, I could learn. All my artifice could be pared down by love as a piece of driftwood was made clean by water, wind, and sun.

It was a truth I couldn't bear to warm in my hands for more than a few seconds. Was I grateful when a crash in the kitchen startled us out of each other's arms? I only know that I leaped up before Andrei did, and nearly stepped on Rupert in my rush out of the room.

"What the hell—"

At first I saw only Pablo. He'd flipped on the overheard light and the scene was a filmy yellow, lurid as a nightmare. A chair had been knocked over and I saw shoes. Pablo turned to me, frantic. "He's fucked up, fucked up bad," he said. He was clinging to the countertop, struggling to stay upright. "Get Andrei. I think he's having a s-seizure."

I came around the table and dropped to the floor. Rafe was writhing on the tile, his muscles jerking unnaturally. His eyes caught mine and there was a wild terror there, like that of a trapped animal, and I struggled to get him into my arms but he was out of control, spasming against me. His jaw snapped and I thought he was going to break his own teeth apart. I reached up for a dishtowel, managed to get part of it in his mouth, and when I put my hands on his face his skin was hot to the touch. His pulse fluttered visibly, frantically in his throat. A second later, he was unconscious, his head lolling against my arm.

"Andrei," I screamed.

He was right behind me, reaching down for Rafe. "What fucking happened, Pablo? What was it?" he spat out as he lifted my brother. "What was it, huh?"

My mother appeared at the bottom of the stairs, hair in her face. "What is going on?!" Her eyes widened when Andrei moved into her sight line with Rafe in his arms.

"We need to call 911," I said, and my mother, still dazed, started toward the phone.

"911's not fast enough," Andrei said. "We have to take him in ourselves. He's overdosed on something, Taryn. Get dressed." He was already moving for the front door. "Abra, get Rupert and the others and follow us. Pablo, you're coming with me, and if you don't move fast I'll put your fucking head through a wall."

I rushed next door and did as he asked. Everyone threw on clothes and shoes. Nobody spoke en route to the hospital. My mother kept her eyes on the road, while Lissa kept one hand on her door handle as though hoping to launch herself out of the car before we reached our destination.

In the emergency room waiting area we found Andrei pacing along a row of chairs. "The doctors took Pablo in with them to find out what happened," he told us. "He told me in the car it was Ecstasy that Rafe was taking. He said he took more than he usually did, and that maybe it wasn't pure or something—"

"And he wasn't taking any himself?" I cut in shrilly. "It was just Rafe?"

"He's pretty drunk, but he said he didn't use anything tonight."

"So he just sat there and watched Rafe overdose."

"I don't know exactly what happened. There wasn't time—"

"Oh, Christ," Lissa cried. "This is insane. Where'd they get it, anyway? I thought it was just pot they were into—"

"Oh please," Frida snapped. "Don't play innocent. It's a little late to pretend now, don't you think?"

Lissa took a step back. "What are you, parent of the year? Where were *you* when this happened?"

"Am I supposed to follow them to their fucking parties?"

My mother said softly, "Shut up. I think this is the doctor."

A doctor approached us, his expression neutral. My mother confirmed who she was and he told us they were doing everything they could for Rafe but that it was too early to tell. "We're trying to bring his blood pressure and temperature down," he explained. "This particular drug causes serious dehydration and can cause organ failure if the problems aren't addressed immediately." He looked at Andrei. "We had a difficult time getting complete answers from your brother. Can you tell me about how long ago the overdose happened?"

"We don't know," Andrei said. "We found Rafe like this a half hour ago."

I said, "Organ failure?"

A small voice said, "Is he going to die?"

We all turned around. It was Jeffrey, strapped into his knapsack. To anyone else it would have looked like he had his hands folded in front of his stomach, but really his left hand was holding up Rupert.

"We're going to do everything we can," the doctor repeated. I fell into a chair. There was more talk but I didn't hear it. Overdose, organ failure, death. Rafe. When Pablo reappeared and sat down in one of the chairs across from me, I refused to look at him. If my brother died in this hospital, and Pablo went on being Pablo outside these walls . . .

The doctor disappeared. My mother and aunt sat down, keeping a chair between them. Marcus and Frida did the same while Andrei went on pacing. For a moment Jeffrey stood there like the last one left in a game of musical chairs. Then he sat down beside me and perched Rupert on my chair arm. Strangers moved around us; sodas rumbled out of the vending machines at the opposite end of the room. There were people slumped apathetically in their seats like they'd been there all night.

"I hate hospitals," Lissa muttered.

My mother shifted position. "Go home, then, if it's stressing you out. God forbid."

Pablo got up suddenly and let himself into the restroom beside the vending machines.

"How'd he get the black eye?" Frida asked.

Andrei said tiredly, "Me."

"What?"

"He's still drunk," Marcus said with disgust. "Puking up his guts."

"He'll be perfectly fine come morning," I said. "Isn't that nice? Because that's fair. He has a hangover and Rafe might have organ failure."

Marcus said, "That's how it always goes."

"That's how what goes?" Lissa demanded, leaning forward.

"The worst ones always get the easiest pass." Marcus said this with surprising passion, his eyes flashing behind his glasses. "The shit-faces like Pablo get away with everything, no payback."

Lissa said, "Oh, and Rafe's a perfect angel, huh?"

My mother closed her eyes at this. I said, "Everything's always Pablo's idea. Everything. Rafe wouldn't be using if Pablo weren't dragging him out every night."

"What did he do to you, anyway, Marcus?" Lissa wanted to know.

"What'd he do? You mean besides stealing from me, making my job totally pointless? Besides that? You know, one time he was so pissed at me for not giving him everything I had that he let himself into the auto shop at school and trashed a bunch of our equipment. I mean it wasn't just me that had to deal with that. A bunch of other guys were using that lab. And when I tell administration I know who it was, they roll their eyes because this family is a joke. So they don't check the cameras and they let it all slide. To them that's better than dealing with losers like us."

Andrei gaped at Marcus. "He did what?"

"It doesn't matter. That's the point." Marcus took off his glasses and rubbed furiously at them with the hem of his shirt.

"What do you mean, this family is a joke." My mother stared at him, her neck flushing. She looked dazed, as though she didn't quite believe any of this was real. "What is that supposed to mean?"

"I wonder," Frida said, tapping her chin with a manicured nail and staring at the ceiling. "Gosh, that's a hard one! Maybe it has something to do with our parents being losers who barely work. The kinds of parents you don't even bother calling when their kids are flunking out or trashing a school, because you either can't get a hold of them or they barely know their kids' fucking names. Could that be it?"

I wanted to launch myself across the aisle and wrap my arms around her. *Keep going,* I silently begged her. *Say it all. Burn them down.*

"Our art is our work," Lissa said. Like my mother, she was coloring up. "Just because we're not slaves to tradition, to these ridiculous conventions, doesn't mean—"

"Oh, tradition! Oh, convention!" Frida drew the back of her hand across her forehead like a fainting belle. "There are worse things, don't you think?" When there was no answer, she went on, "You do know the seventies are way behind us, right? Like, you're not in a hippie commune anymore, eating weed for breakfast? You do know that you're just a big fucking blur in America's rearview mirror?"

Andrei said, "They're not hippies—don't give them too much credit. They can't even follow through with *those* conventions."

Lissa ignored him. Lip curling, she turned back to Frida: "And what are you doing with your life that's so impressive? What are you, twenty-two now? I don't see you with a job. Unless you consider boyfriends to be jobs. There's a name for that sort of career."

"You'd know it," Marcus said under his breath.

Frida said dully, "I don't have a boyfriend. I haven't in a long time."

Pablo reappeared, looking wan and nauseous.

"Did you have a nice puke?" I asked.

He sat down slowly.

"How did you pay for the Ecstasy, Pablo?" Andrei came around and sat down on the other side of me so he could face his brother. "When you ran out of Marc's money, how'd you do it?"

Pablo shrugged. "We know people."

"You see," Lissa broke in, "it's not his fault. He's met bad people. And the school—shouldn't they be responsible for this on some level? I mean what are *they* even doing?"

My mother flicked her wrist in Lissa's direction. "Shut up."

To Pablo I said, "You understand that he might die. You get that, right?"

Pablo dropped his face into his hands.

"Oh, you don't want to hear about it," I went on. "Well, sure. I'd hate to distress you. Everyone, let's be sure to pretend that everything's all good, so that Pablo can get some beauty sleep in the ER waiting room."

Andrei reached over and touched my arm. I shook him off. "If he dies," I said softly, "I'll kill you in your sleep, Pablo. That's a promise."

"Stop it," Andrei said. "Stop it, Abra."

"Oh, big peacemaker," Pablo snapped, lifting his head. "Didn't you just punch me in the face like ten hours ago? Piece of shit hypocrite. Saint fuckin' Andrei."

Andrei's patience broke. "Are we going to pretend not to know how *that* started? Maybe if Rafe weren't so pathetic that he was willing to hit a girl—"

My mother said, "Rafe hit a girl?"

"Abra."

I touched the side of my head. "He was drunk. Or hungover."

"He's *jealous*," Frida snapped. Then, turning to Pablo, "You're both jealous. Of everyone. Marcus because he's not a total fuckup. Andrei because he's good at something, and because he's not an ugly little wiener like you. I mean Christ, he looks just like the guy in that Terminator movie you're

so obsessed with. Kyle Reese. And you're like a goddamn fla-
mingo, you're so scrawny and stupid-looking—"

Marcus said, "They're both assholes."

Lissa had folded her hands in her lap and was now mumbling a *Hail Mary.*

"Oh, my God!" Frida roared. "Do *not!*"

The mumbling stopped. We all went quiet. People were
staring at us, and I made deliberate eye contact with a few
of them, trying to message them telepathically: *I don't care
what you think. Go ahead, complain, see what happens next.*

"Has anyone called Jude," Andrei asked quietly.

My mother started, as if just remembering that she had
a husband. Lissa looked equally surprised to recall that she
had a brother.

Andrei said, "I didn't think so. Taryn, do you want me to
call him for you?"

"He's over an hour away," she said, still sounding dazed.
"I don't know."

I said, "Rafe might *die*, Mom." Then, "They can't fix this
with an amethyst, you know?"

She flinched as though I'd struck her but said nothing.

Andrei stood up. "I'll call him. I'll be back."

A few beats later, the doctor returned. "He's coming in
and out of consciousness," he reported. "He keeps asking for
someone named Rupert. Is that one of you?"

Jeffrey stood up. I'd almost forgotten he was there.

"I'm Rupert," he said.

The doctor held out his hand like a crossing guard. "You
can't come in there, not yet, son. But I'll tell him you're here.
When we get him stabilized, we'll see." He glanced at the rest
of us. "It might be a long night. If you like, we can move you
to a private family waiting room, and you can sleep a little if
you want to."

"That might be a good idea," my mother said.

"All right. A nurse will show you where to go in a minute here."

The private room was somehow worse. It was a square windowless space with a single TV suspended above two faux-leather couches and a cluster of chairs upholstered in faded pink. Old magazines were stacked on a plastic coffee table. Pablo immediately stretched out on one of the couches, and my mother and aunt took the other. Marcus shook his head. "Of course," he mouthed at me.

"I'm starving," Frida admitted. "I feel bad saying it, but I am."

Rupert dove into his pack and resurfaced with little bags of cheese crackers, pretzels, peanuts. He went around the circle handing out the packages until the room filled with the sound of crinkling paper. Everyone but Pablo had taken something. For once we opened the bags like normal people, instead of stabbing them with pens or pocketknives the way everyone did at home.

We slept in snatches. I kept waking up to the shock of the room's white light and the too-cheerful voices of newscasters. At some point Andrei changed the channel to a documentary about severe weather, and then my dreams were rampant with hurricanes and tornadoes.

"Sorry," Pablo called out once in his sleep, jolting me awake again. "I didn't—I wasn't."

Rupert crawled onto Pablo's head and patted him until he went quiet.

A few minutes later, the doctor appeared in the doorway. "Rupert?" he said softly.

Jeffrey gathered his knapsack and started toward him.

No one else was awake. I whispered, "Please, let me come too. I'm his sister."

The doctor hesitated. "All right. Come on, just for a few minutes."

In the dimly-lit room, machines beeped, IV's dripped, and my brother lay white-faced with his head turned to one side. He had asked for Rupert. I wanted to take his hand and make him talk to me, but it was Rupert he wanted, so I forced myself to sit down in the chair beside the bed and just listen.

Rafe turned his head. "This is brave of you, Rupert," he said softly. "This is a hospital. There's Science everywhere." Then, noticing the knapsack, "What'd you bring, buddy? Did you bring your Sadhouse?"

Rupert dove into the bag and dragged his Barnum's Animals box out onto the bed. He pointed to the box, then at my brother. *For you.* Then he started unloading it. These were his Sad Toys, all of them rescues made over the last two years or even earlier when none of us paid attention. There was the tiny Etch-a-Sketch I'd given him, now broken, that permanently framed a shaky illustration of a turtle. A tiny rubber cow with a missing ear. A mini fire engine with no wheels. A broken pumpkin eraser. Finally, the old harmonica. Rafe's hand, limited in its movements because of the IV, moved reverently over each object as Rupert brought it out.

"Where's Stumpy," he wanted to know. His voice was a faint rasp.

Rupert dug out the fat little wooden bird that was his treasure—the one Andrei had whittled, but whose tailfeathers had broken off. He lowered it into the cup of Rafe's fingers.

Rafe started to cry weakly. "I'm sorry, Roo. I'm so sorry."

I sat there frozen. Rupert climbed up Rafe's shoulder, then face-hugged my brother.

"I don't—take care of things like you do," Rafe continued. "But I want to."

He went quiet for a minute, maybe to sleep. Then he stirred and said, "Eye exam?"

Rupert was only too happy. He brought one eye close to Rafe's and began his routine of turning side to side, upside down, studying from all angles. Rafe let out a tiny laugh. Rupert did the other eye and then coaxed Rafe's lids down. Finally he returned his toys to the cracker box, everything save the harmonica, which he tucked beneath the edge of Rafe's pillow.

"Let him sleep now," the doctor said from behind us. "All right?"

He led us back to the family waiting room, where everyone still slept soundly. I sat down beside Jeffrey and asked him what else he had in the knapsack, just to distract myself. Rupert unzipped it and held it open for me. I spotted a few more packages of snacks and some books. Rupert picked up a packet of oyster crackers between his feelers and offered it to me. I peeled open the plastic. The plain crackers were so soothing, I could have broken down.

I wanted to tell Rupert a story about something I'd done long before he was born. Rafe was five years old. He'd had his eye on a toy at Walgreens, a cheap action figure that was a knockoff of what the other kids had. He tried to snare our parents' attention long enough to convince them how much he wanted it, how he'd play with it forever and not get bored, but they weren't interested and the request didn't stick. I'd been hoarding spare change for months, anything I could dig up out of couch cushions or the car (the same way Rupert later would, in his crayon bank), and I got the idea to walk all the way into downtown Two Rivers and buy the toy for Rafe, then leave it under his pillow. It would be a terrific surprise.

I stuffed a backpack with snacks and hiked out to that Walgreens the next morning. There was the action figure in the toy aisle: a plastic man in military garb with a cloth parachute trailing from his fist. He cost three seventy-five. I double-checked my grubby change purse and found that I had just enough.

But there were other things in the toy aisle, things that caught my eye. The gem was a paint set that shimmered like Frida's eye shadow palettes. It came with three different brushes and the case had a clear cover embedded with glitter. It was the same price as the GI guy.

It was my money, I told myself. Why shouldn't I have something? No one was buying *me* any surprises. So I bought the paint set instead, and walked all the way home with it in my fist. Later that night I found that the paint was so cheap that it left almost no color on my paper, just faint watery streaks of pale blue and even paler yellow. It was junk. Furious, I marched out of my room to dispose of the set in the bathroom trash. I passed by Rafe's door and saw that he'd strung guy lines between his bed and dresser and was playing with a pitiful action figure he'd made for himself—a clothespin with pipe-cleaner legs.

"Rupert," I said into the silence of the waiting room.

He climbed into my hand.

"You never would have bought the paint set."

He just listened.

"I don't even see him. Most of the time, I don't see any of them." I could barely get the words out. "I need eye treatments, Rupert."

Andrei stirred awake in the chair beside me. "What?"

A few minutes later, my father appeared in the waiting room doorway. "Where is he?"

Pablo and Jeffrey were missing come morning, and Andrei sent me to prowl the hospital in search of them while he kept watch over the others. I found Jeffrey first, in the hospital's little one-room chapel where he sat in a pew by himself.

The light in there was rosy and warm where it refracted from a circular stained-glass window. A simple cross stood in one corner at the head of three carpeted stairs, and there were Bibles stacked on a table by the wall.

"Roo," I said. "How long have you been in here?"

The feelers popped up and made a little shrug.

I slid into the pew. "You came to see Big Jesus?"

A nod.

"Rafe's going to be okay, though. You know that, right?"

Rupert's feelers clasped each other in prayer anyway. Then, from behind us, someone said, "Is this private?"

We turned around to find my father standing in the chapel doorway, looking haggard.

"No," I said. "Rupert just wanted some Big Jesus time I guess."

"Yeah." He came in and sat down with us. "He's not as stupid as he looks, huh?"

I didn't know what to say to that. My father looked at the cross. "There's a phrase. No atheists on the battlefield," he said. "Death cozies up next to you, and what do you do? You go straight here, even though nobody has a clue if God gives a damn, or if he's even there."

I sat there, waiting.

He was handling a Bible he'd picked up from the table near the door. "Rupert," he said. "You've heard Andrei's little speeches. He wants to know, how's this book all about the same God . . . that's what put me off when I was his age, too, stuck going to church with my strung-out mother listening to all the gobbledygook. Because for the first thousand pages or so, God is pretty much a jealous vengeful OCD egomaniac. He's not exactly a lighthouse. No offense, Bert."

Rupert scrambled for his notepad. He wrote carefully, then slid the pad toward my father. I leaned forward to read it: *All same God. God fix God. Practiss makes perfict.*

"Oh Rupert. I don't get it, buddy. But I'm sure it all makes sense in that tiny head of yours. And that's okay. At least somebody's comforted." He put his head down on the edge of the pew in front of us and went quiet.

I started digging around in Rupert's knapsack just to make some noise. I found one of his Norse mythology books, loaded with pictures, and the illustrated *Silmarillion* he'd dragged around for months. A shred of looseleaf in the latter marked an illustration in which two spirits stood opposite each other, the luminous one with his eyes and palms tilted skyward and the dark one hunched over an orb of murky light he held captive between his hands. I stuffed both books back into the bag. To my surprise, the third volume in Rupert's pack was mine—an anthology of Van Gogh's paintings and letters I'd once pored over for hours at a time. As I flipped through it, my father stirred a little but didn't look up.

I was about to return the book to Rupert's knapsack when something caught my eye. I flipped back a few pages and stared in disbelief. It was my painting, the first draft of my basement painting. The naked blue-grey pines and the pale yellow sky were unmistakable. I'd plagiarized without even realizing it, and then I'd smothered it with layer after layer of extra paint until the bones of the picture disappeared entirely.

I snapped the book closed. "I need to go outside," I said. "I can't breathe in here."

"Go with her, Bert," my father murmured, head still down. "Keep her company."

So I left the hospital with Rupert in tow, and we'd only been walking a few minutes when we stumbled upon Pablo sitting on a bench, an unlit cigarette dangling from his hand. The eye Andrei had blacked was swollen and watering.

"Hey," he said hoarsely.

"Hey." I hesitated. "We needed some air. You want to walk around with us?"

"Sure." Out of habit he crushed the cigarette with his sneaker before standing up. He looked like he'd lost ten pounds overnight.

We meandered three or four blocks past the hospital, nobody speaking. There wasn't room for three of us to walk comfortably astride so I was in front. I turned around once, just to make sure they were still with me, and saw that Rupert was holding onto Pablo's sleeve.

Eventually we found ourselves on a fishing pier that jutted into the West Twin River amidst pale reeds and floating litter. Exhausted, we sat down on the sun-bleached boards and tilted our faces to the sky. We might have fallen asleep had we been alone, but a father and his two small sons were floating close by in a metal rowboat, and their voices turned our heads.

"Beautiful," the father said, holding up a brown trout the younger boy had just reeled in. "That's three now!" The little boy beamed, but the older son sat rigid in the stern, arms crossed, silently seething. His gaze on that newly-caught fish—and on his brother—was murderous. He hissed something, and the father said, "Oh, you will," and then the older son said in a louder voice, "But I don't, I never do, it's always him. Don't tell me, use this pole, use this bait, I'm sick of it, I never catch *anything*—" A second later he had the fish in his hands and had torn the hook out of the creature's mouth with a soft wet rip that made me wince. The father grabbed his wrist; the younger boy wailed, "We're supposed to put them back, now he'll die," and the older son snapped, "Good. What's the point if you put them back in anyway? What're we even out here for if we're not going to eat them?" The father started grappling with him for the writhing fish that was now bleeding a pinkish fluid from the mouth. "Stop it, stop it—"

I turned away, thinking to pick up Rupert and cover him, but Pablo had already done it.

"Fucked up," he said softly.

"Let's go somewhere else," I said, and he nodded, but nobody moved.

Finally Rupert crawled out of Pablo's hands and swung his feelers toward the rowboat, which had moved on so that the continued argument was out of earshot.

"The fish is okay, Roo," I said, ignoring Pablo's look. "It's fine."

Rupert touched his feelers to my forehead as if testing for fever. And in fact I did feel ill, because for some reason the image of my trumped-up painting in the basement had risen before me again in all its dizzying garishness. I vowed right there to smash it. I would put my foot through it and fold it into a trash can the second we got home. I couldn't bear to see those gaudy colors ever again.

I said, "We should get back." Then I held out my hand again to help Pablo down. I went on holding it, trying not to care about how strange it felt, on the walk back to the hospital. Rupert held the other, so that we stumbled a little trying to stay on the sidewalk together.

While we were all away, the twig holding open Rupert's caterpillar box broke. The lid snapped shut and the caterpillars all suffocated, so that when Rupert finally found them, they were just limp bodies scattered in the dirt.

I burned my painting in the backyard. Andrei, watching me do this, confessed to me that he'd lost his bread-bead rosary a long time ago; he'd dropped it on one of his walks to the lake, and for weeks didn't even notice it was missing. But Rupert kept his empty caterpillar box beside his bed. He forced himself to look at it every morning and every night, long after Rafe was home and well, and butterflies had filled the backyard.

XI.

THE LAMP IN ANDREI'S BEDROOM flares to life like a lighthouse beam lancing through fog. His window is directly across from Rafe's, and I remember how as small children we once strung a tin-can telephone between the two houses so that we could talk to each other through the night. If only it were that easy now.

The storm hovering over Two Rivers has sulked quietly long enough and is now working itself into a rage. Like Marcus, I can smell its drama through the windows—upturned soil, rent leaves, writhing worms. Thunder reverberates through the Cape Cod, the acoustics from the Lake magnifying its voice so that it seems as though huge trees are being felled in the woods out back: first there is the creak of dry wood leaning, bending, contending, then a pause, followed by the snap of the tree's spine and finally the boom as the trunk crashes to the ground where the heartwood is split open to reveal the dark circles of its long history. I can't see Lake Michigan from here but I know its waters are churning beneath the clouds with an ocean's ferocity, and that come morning the beaches will be dense with thickets of washed-up debris.

When I moved to Chicago after my divorce, I thought I could escape all memory of home inside the walls of a tiny high-rise apartment. I lived far from downtown and never visited the Magnificent Mile where memories of my family lingered. Irving Park's hot-dog cafes and busy laundromats and graffitied overpasses were all soothingly foreign to me. At first it seemed that Lake Michigan, too, was a stranger there, where the so-called beach was just a long strip of concrete. But I soon realized that the Lake was tenaciously itself from any shoreline, its mercurial moods and shifting blues only affirming its singularity, as the persistent inconsistences do in the people one loves. I should have known there would be no escape.

Andrei's figure moves past the window and disappears. The last time he and I were alone in that house was three years ago, the autumn after we both got divorced. I still couldn't quite believe in Andrei's decision to take the house after his parents had died; none of us could. Oh, how quickly we'd all moved away after that final summer . . . how swiftly we'd found excuses never to see home again. We couldn't bear to walk the old trail to the water, any more than we could bear the sight of the little pen-drawn Ruperts on the walls. We couldn't afford to go far, but we did our best.

Except Andrei, who moved only to Manitowoc. And when Meri left him, he stopped renting out Lissa and Lonnie's house to vacationers and moved in. He repaired the old appliances, repainted the walls, made new furniture to replace what had broken down. He'd even landscaped the property. In the woods out back, he'd secured glass Mason jars to every other tree until he reached the official border with public land. The jars housed tea lights he switched on at night and regularly replaced. *Who's it for,* I asked when I first saw them, bewildered. He didn't answer.

"You want to have Christmas, *here*?" I said to Andrei that autumn night we were there together. We were hovering awkwardly in the middle of the living room because I refused to sit down. The rare times I stepped inside that house, I moved as though the walls and furniture were wrapped in electric fencing. Everything was hot the touch, lethal with memory. I said, "You're out of your mind. No one's going to come."

"You're here, aren't you?"

"I only followed you in here because I wanted to finish this conversation," I said.

"You mean, because you wanted to make sure you'd win it."

I shrugged.

"The house needs some life, some voices," he said. "It's wrong, treating it the way we have. And what about your dad? You've been there, what, once? One time since we all left?"

There was a twist of compunction in my gut. Mostly he was the one to drive down to Milwaukee, then Chicago, to see me. I said, "One time, yes. Okay? One time. You know why I didn't go back? When I was there, he told me a story about something he did a few weeks after . . . a few weeks after we all left. He was trying to get over things, and so he took all of Ru—he took all the old storybooks in your old room to that buy-and-trade place in Manitowoc, and he sold them. And then he went back twenty-four hours later and was at the store until the place closed, trying to find the books again. He said he was frantic. He said he bought them all back from the store, every last one. He could barely tell me about it. Andrei, just being in that house, either house, is a trigger—"

"You could try again, for his sake."

"He's got you next door now."

"You know what I mean, Abra."

"I know it sounds like you want to push everybody into territory we'd be better off forgetting."

His eyes met mine. "Maybe I do."

"If you're not careful," I said, "they'll divorce you, too."

Silence.

"Damn," he said softly.

"I'm sorry—"

"It's not like you've done so well either," he said. "You and I can't keep a marriage intact for the same reason, and we both know it."

"Oh? And what reason is that?"

"We do everything in our power to make them think that we're complete, that we don't need anything. And then we're crushed when they believe us." He turned and flicked on the stairway light, then started up to the bedrooms.

"Andrei." I followed him, keeping my hand off the rail. "Where does all this end? I mean, so you get everyone over here for some family dinner, and then what? All you're going to do is cause pain."

Over his shoulder, he said, "There's got to be something on the other side of that. I wouldn't be in this miserable house if I didn't hope there was."

"I can't take it tonight. I can't take this . . . saintliness, Andrei."

"Saintliness. God, what a word. What a fucking word." He went into his room in the near-darkness and opened a bureau drawer. I hovered in the doorway with my arms crossed. When he turned back, he had Rupert's caterpillar box cradled in his hands.

"Don't," I said, stepping back and almost falling down the stairs.

He unlatched the box and removed a little spiral of driftwood from the jumble of objects within. "You remember that morning? When you found me down at the beach?" His voice faltered on 'beach.'

Holding myself tightly, I nodded even as I scrambled to think of something else. I had no strength for a memory so terrible.

"This was what I came home with that day. This." He sat down on his bed, let the bit of driftwood fall to the floor. "I'm still trying to pull . . ." He stopped, passed his rough hands over his face. "I'm still trying, because nothing I do ever makes it, nothing ever changes it . . ."

I knelt on the floor in front of him and reached up to touch his jaw, that eternally locked jaw that even now was hard as stone against my fingertips. "Throw it all away," I begged him. "The box, the house. Everything. Pretend it never existed, never happened."

"Has that worked for you? Is anything about your life working for you?"

Suddenly deflated, I let my hand drop. "No."

He pulled me up off the floor. "Come with me. Help me."

I knew what he meant. I knew it wasn't something I could survive. But when he lifted my face to his, all I could think was that there were no other eyes that knew what lay behind mine, there was no other voice that spoke the truth as his did, and then we were clinging to each other, falling back on the bed. As we kissed he reached out to switch on a lamp. He didn't have to say why. It was critical that what happened here be different from how it was with others. We would meet each other's gaze unflinchingly, suffer no dishonesty even in the movements of our hands. I was, for that hour, one of the blue-grey trees in the Van Gogh painting, wind-stripped and true.

And then after, when I told Andrei that while we might not be blood, we were still family, that no one would under-stand this, that there were a million reasons we should keep our distance except for when the family got together or just for a phone call now and then . . .

I blighted the trees with lies, and painted in a false sky.

We had a birthday party for Rupert that summer after Rafe recovered. What a thing to explain to a stranger: a photograph of Jeffrey's right hand sitting on a cupcake. Little toys and oddities wrapped up in dollar-store paper, a blue bow stuck to Rupert's shell like a hat. Murmurs of "oh, Rupert, that's all yours, bud," when he tried to cut his cupcake into ten pieces for us all to share. The best gift was a shiny piston-head from Marcus, which he explained would make great protective headgear for Rupert since he was always banging into things. Rupert immediately tried it on over his feelers and crashed sideways, weighted down. Everyone laughed.

That fall, we would forget Jeffrey's October birthday entirely, as we had for years. But that was something we were destined not to think about for a while yet. It was the beginning of the happiest year of our lives.

Andrei, who was so quick on the uptake that he'd been allowed to bypass a good chunk of his union training, was due to earn a journeyman card in two years. He spoke contemptuously of the other guys in his program, pegging them as lazy and unimaginative. "All they want is to lay trim for a decent wage and health insurance," he said, forgetting that this had been his original reason for entering the program. He was more industrious than ever in the backyard, his productions ranging from a picnic table for our use to a floating shelf carved from aromatic cedar that looked like two enormous maple leaves caught on a breeze. When I complimented that shelf, he lifted his chin and said, "This is something *I* can do." The emphasis on the *I* was a decoder ring for that sentence; what he'd meant was, *this is a talent nobody else here has ever had.*

Rupert flattered him by watching his every move while working as his miniature helper. As compensation for his labors, Andrei built a secret into the picnic table—a little trundle that pulled out of the tabletop for Rupert to sit on. If we were outside eating at that table, Rupert would be perched on his trundle with a shot-glass of juice, nodding along with our conversation, and Rafe might absent-mindedly hand him a potato chip, or Frida might dab a bit of sunscreen on his shell before applying it to her own skin.

Frida stayed away from boys and started to gain a little weight. In July a new diner in Two Rivers posted a Help Wanted sign, and a week later they took her on as a waitress. Marcus was researching scholarships for tech programs. While Rafe and Pablo still chain-smoked and came home drunk now and again, they'd left the drugs behind. As for me, I'd stopped babysitting and gotten a job at the community college of all places. I was just a mail-sorter, helping to put together packets for prospective students, but it felt better to me than putting kids in front of a television while I daydreamed. There were no more paint sessions behind the garage, either.

The changes in our parents were subtler. If Lissa's affairs continued, we didn't know about them. Lonnie started taking on odd jobs to earn money in place of working scams on storeowners and waitresses. My father was working on a manuscript. "It's probably crap," he'd say. "But just in case it isn't, I don't want to gum it up by talking about it." There were no more invectives against critical editors. My mother surprised us by taking on a commissioned painting from a woman in Manitowoc who wanted a portrait of her daughter before the girl went away to college. It was exactly the sort of pedestrian project she and Lissa had always scorned. But she approached the task earnestly, and the resulting portrait was affecting, the girl's deep-pool eyes reflecting an unknown future.

I recall the seven of us camping on the beach on a still-warm September weekend. In all our years of hiking through the pines to the water, we'd never hauled out tents and firewood, the things normal families brought to state parks on weekend getaways. We found most of what we needed buried in the garage and made the long hike with all manner of gear slung over our backs, calling out to each other as we kicked up dirt and gravel on the trail. We laughed at the skittishness of black and yellow garter snakes who shot into the weeds at our approach, but we let them be.

The Scotsman's bagpipes trailed us into the woods, and Rupert sat on my shoulder swaying with the chanter's rhythm. Someone had found him a tiny first aid kit in a miniature red backpack, which he wore with pride even though its contents were expired.

"The first aid kit suits you, bud," Rafe told him, patting the backpack.

"I could see him rocking it playing Dr. Dodgeball," I said.

Andrei said, "Oh my God, Dr. Dodgeball. The only good part of gym class."

Marcus gave a shudder. "Don't bring up gym class. I get 'Nam flashbacks."

"We should fry a fish," Pablo suggested. "Like on a spit."

"Do you even know how to do that?" Andrei asked. He had two tents strapped across his shoulders.

"Roo-pert!" Marcus yelled. "Sad Alert up here!" He bent to show Rupert a snail creeping along a rock. "He could be crushed."

Rupert lifted the snail by its shell and deposited him off-trail in a patch of moss.

It was Andrei's idea to take a spur trail out to a more isolated beach, the place where Molash Creek emptied into Lake Michigan. Sometimes the channel was bottomless, a forbidding brown, but in drier seasons the crossing was shin-deep and silvery blue, serving as a shortcut to the northern stretch of state forest. One the south side of the passage we hurried to pitch our four tents and to furnish the orange and blue rooms with our sleeping bags and flashlights. Pablo and Rafe built a fire while Frida explored the waterline, kicking aside chunks of driftwood. Rupert rode his corn popper cat over the sand mounds while Marcus meandered along behind him with his hands in his pockets. His arthritis had been abating steadily and he now walked without a limp.

Andrei began unpacking books. I glimpsed Dostoevsky's name and said, "Still at him? I thought you weren't reading fiction anymore."

"For some reason he won't let go of me. He's worse than a deer tick."

I sat down beside him. "I feel that way about Vincent. I can't get rid of him even when I want to."

"You're on a first-name basis with Van Gogh now, huh?"

I laughed. "Jealous?"

"Yes."

We broke eye contact. At no point had we talked about that kiss the night Rafe overdosed, but these moments kept finding us anyway. After a beat Andrei said, "Reading him, it's like . . . it's like driving with one hand on the wheel and the other one lying open on your lap. You're the one turning pages, but then things are sort of falling down on you that you didn't ask for and you can't totally understand. The way it is in a dream. And mostly I want both hands on the wheel so he can't do that thing to me. Reading these other guys, reading what I've been reading lately, it's a two-hands-on-the-wheel thing. You know? I'm in control, I feel like I'm mastering something. But then I get this funny feeling like I'm going to crash if *don't* keep one hand off the wheel. So I end up going back to Dostoevsky in the middle of the night . . . It makes no sense."

Pablo yelled, "We got rain coming." He pointed to the horizon with a roasting stick. Low, blue-black clouds had gathered there while we hiked through the dense woods.

"We're okay," I said. "It's a long way off still."

A few minutes later Pablo and Rafe had the fire blazing, and we drifted to it like moths to lamplight. Frida opened a box of graham crackers and a pillow-sized bag of marshmallows while Marcus peeled the foil off three huge chocolate bars. Rafe showed Rupert how to hold the end of his miniature roasting-stick and signaled him when it was time to pull the smore out of the fire. "Good bug," he said. "You did it perfectly."

Rupert promptly sat down on the sandwich, and marshmallow came shooting out in globs.

"Oh, Beets," Rafe groaned. "Not brilliant."

Rupert could not smile, but you felt it when he did.

Rafe cleaned him up. "Secret handshake," he commanded. It was a dance they'd perfected: Rupert's antennae tapping two of Rafe's fingertips, then Rupert's claw touching Rafe's pinky, followed by a gentle bump of Rafe's fist against Rupert's feeler-head.

Marcus held out his fingers. "Do me next."

Pablo grinned. "That's what she said."

"Hey, did you tell them yet?" Frida asked Andrei.

Andrei looked askance at her. "What are you talking about? Tell them what?" But a tiny grin was playing at his mouth.

"Oh, come on." She addressed the rest of us: "You know that leaf shelf thing? He took a picture and sent it in to one of his woodworking magazines. And they wrote back they wanted to show the photo in the next issue. They have this thing where anyone can send in their stuff—"

"They don't publish just anything, though," Andrei said quickly.

"Holy shit," Marcus said. "Andrei."

"That's crazy, man," Pablo murmured.

Rupert tapped the tips of his feelers together in applause.

I already knew about this—he'd burst into my room a few nights earlier to tell me—but I reached over and squeezed his arm. "That shelf is a work of art, Andrei," I said, though in my arrogance I couldn't quite think of woodworking as an art form. "You did a great job with it."

"That's what the guy at the magazine said," Frida yelped. "He's an artist. Nobody tell our parents!"

Everyone laughed. Andrei said, "They didn't call me an artist. They said the shelf was artist-*ic*. But, I mean, it's a start. It could mean . . . I don't know." He lifted his chin a little. "I guess they're not blind. I mean, they have been running this magazine for like twenty years. I guess they'd know originality when they saw it."

"You think I could do union training someday?" Rafe wanted to know. "I mean how hard is it? Can a moron do it?" He glanced down at Rupert. "Could Beets? He could be my partner. Carpenter's helper."

"There're different kinds," Pablo said before Andrei could reply. "You can do plumbing, or electrician work. There's different trades you can learn."

"You interested, Pabs?" Andrei asked, surprised.

"I've read a little about it." Pablo looked embarrassed. "Not much."

"I think I'd be good with carpentry," Rafe said. "Beets, what do you think? You still got that little measuring tape? You want to be my assistant?"

In response, Beets drew a sand-picture of Rafe carrying a toolbox with Rupert hanging out of it.

Rafe nodded. "Business partners. It's a deal, then."

It was after midnight when we finally crawled into our tents—Andrei and Rupert in one, Pablo and Rafe in another,

Frida and me in a third. Marcus had his own but he'd pitched it right beside ours to make a kind of duplex.

Flashlights clicked on and off; tent zippers sang. Disembodied voices rose from our little village. Somebody called out, "I just heard a raindrop," and somebody answered, "So go home, pansy-ass."

"Pablo farted," Rafe shouted. "Oh, God, there's no ventilation. Marcus, can I sleep with you?"

"*You're* the family methane factory. Your ass could power every stove in Two Rivers."

"Is that a no?" Rafe demanded.

"It's a pretty solid Fuck No."

Pablo's voice floated up: "You should all know that Rafe brought salami just for himself and he's eating it in secret right now."

Frida said, "*You* took the salami out of the fridge? Son of a bitch!"

Rafe laughed. "How does that Caesar thing go? 'Weenie, weekend, eatie?'"

"Veni, vidi, vici," Andrei moaned.

This continued for few minutes and then there was a sylvan rustling beneath the tent roofs as everyone settled down. I lay back, breathing in Frida's scent of vanilla and lilac, and drifted off a little. Through my half-sleep I swore I heard the opening note of a harmonica.

"That's Rafe playing," Frida mumbled into the crook of her arm.

I said, "Is it?"

"I've heard him, in the woods."

More notes, the beginnings of a recognizable tune. I lay there listening until the notes blended into a dream where I saw a line of white candles lighting up one after another.

"Does anyone have Rupert's cat," Andrei whisper-yelled, jolting me awake again.

The harmonica went silent. Rafe said, "Not me." Then, "This keeping you guys awake?"

"No," Marcus murmured. "It's actually not bad enough to make me want to off myself."

"The corn popper's in here," I said.

Andrei said, "He doesn't like to sleep without it," as if I didn't know that.

"Hang on." I unzipped our tent flap and crawled onto the cool sand. "He's coming, Roo."

Andrei lifted his tent door. I climbed in and nestled the plastic cat into Jeffrey's sleeping bag. "There you go, buddy," I said. Contented, Rupert curled himself into a ball beside his toy. Within seconds Jeffrey was snoring softly.

Maybe it was the light, the way the swollen moon over the beach bored its way through the tent's blue roof to illuminate the contours of Jeffrey's face. Maybe it was the touch of Andrei's hand at the small of my back. But I found myself flashing back to the night Jeffrey was born, and I heard the first eight notes of "Hallelujah" as clearly as though the now-drowned singer were strumming his guitar on the sand.

"Who is he," Andrei said quietly from just behind me. "Does anybody know?"

I swallowed. "He's Rupert."

"Yeah."

I was afraid to turn around. I think he knew it, because he said, "Let's go for a walk."

"Okay."

We walked along the foremost ridgeline, then descended toward the creek crossing. The clouds were heavier now, rolling like surf toward the full moon as if intending to submerge it, and the carpets of bearberry around us were wine-dark. Every now and then a raindrop exploded on my arm. A loon called out—a ghostly, mournful cry that always made me think of ships lost in fog—and Andrei froze, putting his hand on my arm. "Wait," he breathed, and a beat later a second loon answered, three smoky notes to match its mate's, but higher on the scale.

"Good, she's there with him," he said. "Come on, let's cross." Shoes in hand, we forded the channel and started north.

To my relief, he didn't mention Rupert again. Instead he resumed our talk of Dostoevsky and Van Gogh. "I think they were connected somehow," he mused, "even if they never talked to each other. I think their beliefs kind of mirrored each other's. You can see it if you look close enough."

"They died pretty close together, right?"

"Like ten years apart. I read somewhere that when Van Gogh had to move, he went racing back to his apartment to grab one of his Dostoevsky books. The guy was seriously imploding but he still knew himself well enough to know that he needed his Dostoevsky. And it's not like it's pleasure reading, you know? It's not a blankie you wrap around your-self at night." He stooped low to gather a handful of sand and stones. Finding a flat disc in the moonlit jumble, he cleaned it off in the water, then skipped it hard across the lake's shim-mering surface. It jumped several times before it drowned in a wave.

I was thinking of the monastery when I said, "Is it because he's Russian? Is that why you're still on him?"

He laughed. "Because he's Russian? No."

"You know, Frida once said to me, nobody ever knows what you really think about anything. You tell me everything you read, but the one thing you never say is what you actually believe." I had a flash of Rupert watching his movies, and an elusive ache flowered open in my chest. "Do you actually, really believe in any of it?" I didn't have to clarify what *it* was. "Did you ever? I mean, if you don't, why are these guys still under your skin?"

I waited as he selected a couple more stones from the waterline.

He said, "Every idea those two had about God was something I didn't want to hear. That was a big clue, you know, that they might be onto something. But a novel is still just fiction, right? A painting is just one person's interpretation of what the world is. Look at our mothers. We both know everything they make is bullshit." He let the second rock fly, watched it sink. "And religion is just like mythology, it's just like Rupert's dumb storybooks. The stories are all miracles and visions and crazy heroics. And I always think, no sane person would make these choices. They'd run like hell is what they'd do, because when it comes down to it, what God's always asking for is a kind of suicide. Everyone has to die before they die, and who would do that? So these stories, they can't ever be real." He paused for a breath. "But I read something once in this biography, something Dostoevsky said when he came out of Siberian prison . . . It's bagpipes, Abra. It blasts everything else out of my head when I hear it."

"What was it?"

"He said, 'If someone proved to me that Christ was outside the truth, and the truth was really outside Christ, then I would prefer to remain with Christ than with the truth.'" He skipped the third stone. It vaulted the wave-wall and sailed out of sight.

It took me a moment to respond. "That sounds like . . . Rupert."

"I know."

"I don't even understand how, but it does."

"I know."

The elusive ache in my chest was keen now, hollowing me out. I tilted my head back to search out the last slip of the moon and just then it began to rain in earnest.

"Come on." Andrei gestured back down the beach. "Time to head back to Tent Village."

We veered right to find tree cover. Just before we recrossed the creek, I said over the rising wind, "You didn't answer my question."

"I think I want to. I'm just afraid."

"You're afraid to answer it?"

"To believe."

We crawled into our tents. Frida was still sound asleep, her hair tangled on her pillow. I leaned over and gently combed it out before zipping myself into my sleeping bag. "Me too," I said to the orange walls.

That November, a story of my father's took second place in a literary magazine contest, securing a two-thousand-dollar prize. It was the first time anyone in the family had had such a windfall. I watched Andrei for signs of the spitefulness my father had assigned to him back when his first story was printed, but all he said was, "We could use the cash. We need someone to come out and look at the water heater again. And they're not even publishing the story, you know. They only put the first prize one in print. He told me."

My father paced around with the check for a week before announcing that we were all going to Chicago at Christmas. "One night at the Palmer House Hilton," he said. "We can get five rooms, and with the parking fees, gas, and meals, it'll be just enough." He did the math on an index card, which he showed to each of us as though fearing we'd doubt his accounting. "A day and a night in the city. We can go to the Art Institute, free admission on Christmas Eve, and we can see the new Bean sculpture thing."

We'd not been on a family trip since that miserable week in Ontonagon, and I think we were all a little stunned by the proposal. But even Andrei, who'd had more practical applications in mind for the money, was interested. My father made more notations, this time charting out the room arrangements, then called for the reservation. Two single-queen-bed rooms for the parents. Three double-queen rooms, for Frida and me, Pablo and Rafe, and Andrei, Marcus, and Rupert. The third room, he assured us, came with a pull-out sofa for Rupert.

And so on Christmas Eve of 2004 we traipsed through snow and slush along the Magnificent Mile, craning our necks to take in the skyscrapers and jumping back onto curbs when plucky taxis turned the corners at impossible speeds. The splendor at the Palmer House had left us all a little dazed; its soaring ceilings and twinkling chandeliers in the lobby were almost too much to take in. We were all a bit cross-eyed and eager to get outdoors, even if it meant walking against the vicious lake-effect wind.

We took our time getting to Millennium Park, stopping in shops whenever someone in our party showed an interest in something. Andrei noted a skyscraper under renovation and Rafe held Rupert high so he could see. "When you're my carpenter's helper, you can be up there with me," he said.

I was in the market for a snow globe. In the souvenir shop where I found my prize, Rupert spotted a small stuffed bear with a missing eye and held it up.

"Of course we'll get him for you, Beets," my father said.

When the saleslady went to ring up the bear, she glanced at my father and said, "Oh, sir, it looks like this one's damaged. Do you want to switch it out?"

My father looked appalled. *"No,"* he said, so emphatically that the saleswoman took a step back. We all stifled laughter.

Back on the sidewalk, our parents instructed us to steer clear of panhandlers and the "robed weirdos" who sometimes circled pedestrians, trying to sell them cheap jewelry or candy in the name of charity. "Scammers," Lonnie told us. "Don't make eye contact." A bold one followed us for several yards, focusing his energies on Aunt Lissa who remained resolutely indifferent. "Just one meal tonight," he said, or something like that. "One meal on a freezing night. You probably got a few dollars to spare."

Rafe grabbed Rupert and covered him up with his hat. "He won't understand," he murmured. "He'll try to give his crayon money away."

The giant Bean looked like a spacecraft when we first came upon Michigan Avenue. We circled it, inspected our stretched and oblong reflections in its seamless surface. Rafe held Rupert up to the mirrored panel where he was magnified to many times his size, a force to be reckoned with in contrast to the tiny-faced crowd behind us. Rupert studied himself. We studied Rupert.

"Bert," Marcus said, "give the Bean an eye exam."

Rupert zeroed in on the reflection of Rafe's eye, and we all laughed again. I noticed that my parents were arm-in-arm, and that Lissa and Lonnie were sharing a coffee.

"Art Institute," my father urged. "Before we all freeze. Don't worry, Roo, not the Museum of Science and Industry! This is the good one. You'll be safe in there."

We climbed the vast stone steps and stood in the foyer unfolding maps. Frida, Pablo, and Rafe feigned total indifference. Marcus immediately located an exhibit on antiquated machinery and said, "See ya," starting for an elevator. Andrei was so awed he looked almost grave. As for me, I was scared out of my wits. All that brilliance together in one house had a pulsating power, like that of a cathedral. Even the air tasted different.

Seeing my distress, my father said, "A good place to start is the Impressionists. You'll get lost fast in all the medieval galleries, and the colonial American stuff is a snooze." Then, "There are Van Gogh pieces up there, you know. Three or four, and one's a self-portrait I think."

"What?"

"Go on, go." He gave me a little push. "Let's all agree to meet back here in two hours. If you run into Marcus, tell him where to go when he's done."

Lonnie, Lissa and my mother appraised the modern art. Sometime during that first hour I caught sight of my father standing motionless before the long line of Monet's wheat stack paintings, but I moved on, safeguarding his privacy. Beets stayed with Andrei and I heard Jeff's small voice requesting "the oldest paintings" on Rupert's behalf. Pablo and Rafe went into the café for a sandwich. Ignoring my father's advice, I ambled through the American galleries first, then spent a desultory half-hour drifting past Greek and Roman artifacts.

It was a stalling tactic. After the ancients, I stumbled upon a dark, U-shaped exhibit featuring intricate dollhouse scenes in recessed glass boxes. There was familiarity here. Whoever designed these scenes with their elaborate detail had immersed herself in other times and other lives with the same passion I had when tending to my old dollhouse. With a little imagination you were right there in the fireside libraries, the white tearooms and Victorian bedrooms. I lost myself in those miniature worlds until I noticed Frida in the gallery too, peering into one of the dioramas with such naked yearning on her face that I instinctively stepped back out of sight. I watched her for a few minutes before slipping out of the gallery to consult my brochure's list of must-see pieces. Picasso's *The Old Guitarist* was listed there, and I weaved my way through crowds to find it, feeling Van Gogh's eyes somewhere behind me all along.

When I found the painting, Pablo was there with Rupert. There were a dozen people in a semicircle around the work, taking frantic photos, but Pablo was utterly still, almost statuesque in his dignity as people pushed and murmured around him. I had never seen him so focused. Rupert was hooked around his left arm, feelers up and out but in a way only someone in the family would notice. They were simply studying the painting together, natural as brothers or best friends.

I came a bit closer. Pablo said, "You don't like him, do you. Picasso."

Roo shook his feelers.

"I thought so. But this one's different. This painting's not Cream of Wheat, you know what I mean?" From his jacket pocket he took a disposable camera, then snapped several pictures. After a beat he said, "It says on the plaque, the painter's friend committed suicide."

Rupert's antennae drooped in sorrow.

"A lot of artists died that way, all over the world. Not this one, but a lot of people like him, and writers too. It's Sad, Rupert." Any bystander would have assumed that he was talking to Jeffrey. But I knew that he would never say such things to anyone other than Rupert, and as I had in the dollhouse exhibit, I slipped quietly away.

The museum was now sardine-packed with people. I kept my head down as I traversed the throng, mumbling *sorry* and *excuse me* and becoming a little heated. Finally I stumbled right into Andrei. Without a word he took my shoulders

and turned me in another direction. "He's in there," was all
he said. "If you don't go now, you'll regret it forever." Then he
vanished into the crowd like an apparition.

During the brief sojourn from that spot to Van Gogh's
self-portrait, I moved of my own volition even as I felt snared
in an undertow, a living will ferried by a momentum not its
own. The tension in my bones was familiar. My wish always
was to retreat into the vapid sunshine of day or else to curl up
and sleep inside the cocoon of night—never to linger in that
field that lay between, where aqueous light made ghosts of
trees and a diurnal moon spoke of impossible resurrections.
I wished for some accident to knock me backward or forward. But a moment later I stood miraculously alone before
those piercing green eyes, and a single line from one of his
letters boomeranged back to me unbidden: *My plan is not to
save myself.*

How many of his self-portraits had I studied in my books
as a small child? Before entering the museum, I would have
said that I knew them all. Yet what did it mean to know a
face? 1887, the plaque stated. Andrei's Dostoevsky was dead.
Vincent had just three years left to live. I took a step closer.
How densely, how intently, the million daubs of paint were
laid. Fiery orange, blue, green, red. They comprised backdrop and body alike so that the man seemed both integral
and separate. In the mosaic was a forest floor thick with
autumn leaves, a night sky teeming with stars, a river rippling over a bed of stones. There was just the faintest sug-
gestion of rotation, as though a kaleidoscope had been frozen
mid-turn. From the dizzying fray it was the orange that
leaped out at me most vividly. Did its spark originate in the
celestial sky—did Vincent take it into himself, accepting
the agony with the rapture as was the artist's duty—or did
its genesis lay in him? Perhaps he'd exhaled those stars at

dusk, after a long afternoon's labor in the field. I blinked, and swore the whole picture revolved. Maybe it all happened at the same time.

I was unsettled all night. At dinner I kept wringing my napkin beneath the table as if to choke the memory of that portrait into submission. It was ridiculous, I told myself. It was just a painting. And yet I felt as if I'd gone to meet a lover who'd found me disappointing enough to turn out before we could touch hands.

But there were plenty of diversions on the seventh floor of the Palmer House. Our five rooms were clustered together in a dead-end hallway, and for that night, we owned our own wing of the hotel.

"This is a serious matter, babe," I overheard my father saying to my mother as I passed their open door. "International relations have collapsed over things like this."

"Things like what?" I asked, popping my head in.

They were standing in their bathroom. "This," my father said, pointing to the roll of toilet paper affixed to the wall. "Toilet-paper orientation. They've got it in the over-position. I prefer the under-position. I'm telling you, there are psychological studies on this."

My mother was laughing. "Oh my God, Jude. Who cares which way?"

"I care," I said. "The over-position looks stupid. Like the toilet paper is tripping over itself."

"Yes! Thank you!" He grappled with the wall-mount. "I'm changing it right now. Do you think Marcus brought a screwdriver? My God, this thing is *bolted* in place! That's it, I'm filing a complaint—"

I continued down the hall and two seconds later it hit me: my father believed he was writing something of value.

When asked about it, he referred to it as a "mushrooming dung heap," but his eyes sparkled. His face and posture had changed the same way Marcus' had after he found out his illness would pass: *Not going to be like this forever.*

Frida came out of our room in the high-necked sweater-dress she'd found at a consignment shop specifically for this trip. Her hair was braided, her eye makeup understated. "I'm going to go sit in the lobby and watch people," she announced.

"Get hit on, you mean," Pablo called from his and Rafe's open doorway.

Frida shrugged and tapped an elevator button with an almost regnant dignity.

I knocked on Andrei's door and found only Marcus in there, propped up with pillows on one of the queen beds. Next to him was the 1950's radio he'd been trying to restore. He'd fixed one from the forties back in autumn, and music and news issued nightly from his room.

"You packed that?" I said.

"I lose continuity if I walk away from something for more than a day. I was getting somewhere." He was sipping at a coffee he'd purchased downstairs. "I have to look at it every so often so I don't lose my place."

"Is this one harder to fix than the last one?"

"Kind of." He put down his coffee, then leaned over to wrap his hands around the radio's curves, as if covering its ears. "The first one was my favorite," he admitted in a low voice. "It had more character."

I laughed. "Marcus, I don't think you can hurt a radio's feelings. Only Rupert would worry about that."

He shrugged and picked up the TV remote. "All yours if you want to watch something with me," he said, gesturing at the other bed. "They get so many movie channels, it's making me dizzy."

I flopped down. "Where're Andrei and Rupert?"

"Out walking. Don't worry, Andrei can take care of them both if some wacko bothers them." He paused on *Braveheart*. "Oh, now my night is complete," he murmured. "I think they even have room service here."

"You ate like a pig at dinner."

"So?"

We watched for about twenty minutes before Rafe and Pablo burst in. "We're ordering a pizza," Pablo announced. "You can go right into the lobby to get it."

"Bring it in here," Marcus said. "Get the biggest one they have. No onions though."

Rafe nodded at the TV. "Fuck yeah, *Braveheart*. We'll be back. Or you guys can come over to our place."

"'Our place'?" I laughed.

"Well, you know."

They departed to order their food. I glanced over at Marcus. "Friends with them now?" I asked lightly.

A commercial started up and he muted the television, then settled on his back. "You know, for the longest time, every time I shut my eyes I'd just think about all the ways I was going to get revenge on them. Especially Pablo." He stared at the ceiling. "I did some horrible things, in my head. If Rupert knew, he'd be so scared of me. You know what I mean?"

I turned on my side to face him. "What about now? Now what do you see?"

He closed his eyes, smiled faintly. "Oily stars," he said. "Oily stars in the galaxy beneath a car."

I lay back on the bed. The movie returned and Marcus pumped up the volume. Who were they, I wondered with a sudden shock. Who were these silent poets I'd lived with all my life? I could feel Vincent's eyes on me and I thought with humiliation of my youthful arrogance, my secret belief that

I was the one true talent among my sublunary siblings. Convinced of my own gravity, I'd forgotten that even satellites could lay claim to stellular revolutions all their own.

"You okay?" Marcus asked suddenly. "You don't look so good."

I wanted to shatter the revelation as quickly as it had come. "I think I ate too much," I said. "I might try a walk or something."

"Wear layers. It's fucking cold."

I went to my room and tugged on a second sweater and my coat. Snow fell thickly past the window and clumped on the sills of the building opposite ours. At the last minute I grabbed an extra mitten from my duffel bag, thinking of Rupert.

Downstairs, I spotted both Lonnie and Frida in the grand lobby, but they seemed unaware of each other. Lonnie sat at a piano in one of the far corners of the room. A small crowd had gathered around him, sipping cocktails. It took me a few seconds to realize that he was playing someone else's music. Normally he resented requests to play anything other than his own zany compositions. Stranger still was the fact that he seemed pleasantly detached, not so much performing as just playing. I'd seen him do a few gigs over the years and he was always the type to flirt with his audience between sets and give bombastic accounts of his musical journey.

Frida reclined in a huge upholstered chair nearer the doors. One leg was slung over the other, and she had a glass of white wine, still full. She was more beautiful than ever now that her hair was growing back and her hips had begun to fill out. I watched as a man approached and spoke to her. Frida smiled politely, said something, and he moved on. I caught her eye. She held up her glass and nodded. She was in control, and she was trusting me to let her go on enjoying it. I nodded back and felt a tingling along my spine. What else had I missed? What else had slipped past me in all my years of dollhouse-play and airless fantasy? I wanted to drop everything and paint my beautiful cousin just as she was in that gilded chair.

The frigid wind assaulted me the moment I stepped out of the hotel. A porter rushed by to help a young couple unload their bags from a taxicab; a gaggle of businessmen smoked on the sidewalk and erupted into raucous laughter in response to some joke. I understood why Frida had wanted to "watch people." Suddenly, it was all I wanted to do—watch. Pay attention. I hovered there until the cold became unbearable and then I began to walk at a hard clip toward Michigan Avenue. I willed myself to peer into every face that passed mine. The streetlights were all ablaze now and the shopfronts glittered with Christmas lights so that the orange sparks from Van Gogh's painting seemed to flicker in every corner. Not a single face was colorless, and inside another firefly moment, it occurred to me that those flecks of orange fire might be everywhere save within me. If I wanted them, I would have to earn them—and take their burn when they came.

This second unlooked-for revelation was still smarting like a slap when I spotted Jeffrey half a block away. He was engaged with one of the "robed weirdos" our parents had cautioned us about. Jeff nodded as the man spoke. I saw hands, an exchange. Something went into the pocket of his coat, which was two sizes too big for him because it had once been Andrei's.

"Rupert," I shouted, glad for the distraction. A few heads turned my way. Jeffrey looked up, too, then back at the robed man. He said something else before taking his leave of the man. It was disconcerting, watching him walk toward me beneath the glow of the streetlamps. I so rarely saw Jeffrey head-on this way. He was always somewhere in my periphery while Rupert was just before me.

"Beets," I said sternly, grabbing him. "You're not even in a mitten. This is terrible." I found the spare one in my pocket and hurried to tug it over him. His antennae were red and cold to the touch. "What did you give that man, Bert? You shouldn't go near those people. They're scammers, remember?"

Rupert, now blind within the mitten, shrugged.

"Where's Andrei?"

Rupert pointed toward Michigan Avenue. "He told Rupert he was going back to walk by the lake," Jeffrey said softly.

"He left you alone?"

"He took Rupert back to the hotel but Rupert sneaked out."

I gave Rupert a shake. "Come on, let's try to find him. And let's get you a hot chocolate to warm you up."

The wind was becoming ferocious when we sighted Andrei making his way back to the hotel. "You left him," I snapped the second he was within earshot.

His eyes widened. "I didn't. I took him back to the Palmer House."

"You should have brought him all the way in. He went out on his own once your back was turned."

Andrei picked up Rupert. "Don't ever do that," he scolded him, pressing his lips to the mittened antennae. "You could have gotten lost, or hit by a car, or—"

"Come on," I said. "I can't take it out here anymore, my face is numb. What the hell were you doing, anyway, Andrei?"

"I don't know. I just wanted to walk, and look at people." He wrapped his arms around us and propelled us forward.

We were at the Palmer House doors when Jeffrey said, "Rupert wants to know why so many artists killed themselves."

We stopped. Beneath the golden spangle of the entryway lights, Andrei's face was stricken. A little tremor coursed through me; I was taken immediately back to the two of us at ten and nine, playing the role of young parents.

Andrei crouched on the slushy sidewalk and held Rupert right in front of his eyes. "They did it because they felt very alone. Sometimes artists give everything they have to the world, but the people around them don't see that, or they just see the art and not the person. But the artist is a person just like anyone else and he doesn't want to be alone without love."

"So he goes to be with God, where he knows there is love." It was unquestionably Jeffrey asking this question, but Andrei and I would not look at him. Instead we held Rupert, soothed Rupert, made a lullaby of our assurance that he need not think about these things, ever.

And in a way, we were right. Rupert had become the heart and hearth of our family. That night he went up and down our hallway knocking on each door with a Christmas gift—a bracelet purchased from the robed street peddler with his precious crayon-bank money. The bracelets were strung with cheap wooden beads and a rough crucifix where the string knotted together, but each of us accepted the gift with effusive thanks. "Love you, buddy," we said. "Love you." Rafe and my father wore theirs to breakfast in the morning. I've never asked, but I know they all have those bracelets still.

That final spring was a period of quiet industry in both our houses. My father went on working on his manuscript. My mother earned two more commissions painting portraits for strangers. Marcus was accepted to a tech program downstate, while Rafe and Pablo were on track to graduate. Frida was saving money. I was still working. And Andrei spent every spare minute on his patch of sawdusty lawn between our houses, perfecting his craft. In April, he began a second floating shelf. This one would feature big ginkgo leaves, he told me, carved out of yellowheart to mimic their actual color in autumn. It was an ambitious project. He figured it would take him all summer to finish the shelf as he imagined it, but he was intent, flushing with pleasure and pride as he chipped away. "If the magazine liked my first one, they're going to want this one on the cover," he told me.

Even Rupert had a project. It was a secret, he told us in one of his silly notes. We were not to go in the garage until he said so. He drew ten shaky lines and demanded that we each sign our name in agreement, which we did, delighted by his fastidiousness. We joked about what little Beets was doing out there. A huge family portrait drawn in finger-paint? A collage of Sad things glued to cardboard? A hotel for lost chipmunks or baby mice? We were supportive when he asked for little oddities like a special kind of glue or some of Andrei's old books. "Whatever you need, Roo," we said, grinning. "Go play, buddy."

It was all a joke to us then, before we knew what it was. But what came slowly together inside that garage over the course of the spring wasn't funny, and our discovery of it was the lynchpin falling out of place, the beginning of our inevitable unraveling.

He revealed it to us on a windy night in late May. His note demanded that we all come outside at the same time to see it. *Prezent for You*, it proclaimed. *Werked very hard.* Giggling and conjecturing, all ten of us followed him down the driveway and waited as he stepped through the garage's side-door to put the final touches on the big mystery.

There was a scuffling, and then the garage door rose slowly, opening from the inside.

I have no other memory of the whole family together that way—silent and unmoving. We stood like that for perhaps a full minute. And as adept as I've become over the years at evading certain memories, I cannot, will not, escape that singular minute nor what I felt within it.

Centered in the dark garage was a tree standing upright from a base of stone. It was a sapling pine whittled down to golden-white and its naked branches curled and twisted skyward like reaching hands. Three of the hands held up flagstone shelves like offerings, and on the shelves were heavy marbled candles, their bright flickering flames creating haloes. Taken as a single entity, the tree's shape was that of a lightning bolt turned upside-down as if striving to return to its origins. The wondrous glow of the whole of it, the breath and the language of it . . . it was *alive*. It was newborn and ageless, jubilant and melancholy all at once. Impossible and yet standing right there before us. Many years later, fumbling with words as I tried to tell Andrei what I'd felt in the moment of first setting eyes on that tree, he told me that what I had seen reached back farther than my own memory. I had the word *holy* in my mouth, I sensed the living spirit in the room, because the tree made extant some long-forgotten metaphor, like a fossil-den yielding up in the flesh the same fabled creature that had expired within its walls centuries before. In Jeffrey's art was something instantly recognizable even to the most clouded eye.

And it was Jeffrey's, and it was art. He beckoned us into the cool space of the garage so we could take in the nuances of his design. The cut of the flagstones spoke of birds' wings. Onto the stones he'd lacquered leaves—some real, some silk, so that there were autumnal reds and browns but also deep blues and tulip-pinks—and words. The words were lines of poetry scissored out of vintage books, and the yellowed paper had been fitted into the stones' furrows in such a way that the letters seemed to have been there always, like inclusions.

"It's all T.S. Eliot," Andrei said in response to my question. "From *Marina, Journey of the Magi, East Coker . . .*" His tone was empty, unreadable.

Meanwhile Jeffrey explained how he'd made the tree, though no one had asked. He'd gotten the flagstone from a landscaping supplier, drilled a hole through the bottom rock and the tree itself and inserted a metal rod through both to create a support system. The real leaves, he'd dried last autumn, and the silk ones he found at an antique shop in Two Rivers he'd walked to . . . but the thing was, he said, there was more to it. He'd used his mind, his hands and eyes, but something *else* was there with him, and he'd never be able to explain exactly how everything had come together. It wasn't totally his, he said. He wasn't sure that it was his at all.

Rupert was nowhere to be found. Jeffrey was gesturing freely with both hands, breathlessly animated, his owl-eyes bright with passion. It was the first time we'd seen the other fingers of his right hand in three years. He didn't start his sentences with, "Rupert said" or "Rupert wanted," but with the alien *I*: "I thought, I made, I felt."

Oh, the look on his face. It was pure hope, reckless faith. Jeffrey believed in us. He knew we had come to love Rupert, and he trusted us finally to love *him*—Jeffrey—too. The reveal of the tree was the reveal of himself, a little boy dawning into existence nearly eleven years late.

But the silence in the garage shifted from awestruck to ominous. I could feel that wariness as palpably as the May wind that picked up when we took our collective step back. The truth was only beginning to sink in.

Dopey little Rupert had betrayed us. Jeffrey, the true star in the turbid sky of our family, had been rising in our periphery all along.

XII.

IT'S THREE O'CLOCK IN THE MORNING and the storm is still seething, only now I can no longer picture the thunderheads gathered over the Lake, can't imagine this as a system broad and impersonal. The power has flickered out, the sound of the wind in the trees is that of rags being torn apart, and with each roll of thunder it's as though a giant is crouched on the roof, fist-pummeling the shingles. I can almost hear the beast pausing for breath between assaults. Shaken, I feel my way downstairs in the dark and go to the kitchen window facing the patch of lawn where Andrei still does all his woodworking. Rain eddies down the glass in sheets so that I see the backyard as if through splintered crystal. I blink and squint, fighting a headache. A moment later a twist of wind lifts a black tarp on the lawn and sends it whirling across the yard like a demon taking flight. The thing careens straight for me. "Christ," I cry out, jumping back from the glass, but the wind shifts hands and sweeps it past the window at the last possible second. When the next flash of lightning illumes the other house, Andrei's silhouette is nowhere to be seen.

He has spent twenty years believing himself to be both Cain and Judas, murderer of brother and friend, the ultimate traitor. He couldn't have known, because none of us ever would have voiced it, what collective relief we felt at this. He gave us all a story to tell ourselves at night: *it was not my fault.* In working the wood, in taking back the old house, in pacing the floors and beaches on which the rest of us would not set foot again, he lifted the cup, or so we told ourselves.

I drop my head against the glass. Lies, all lies. Where does the cruelty end? I want to cross the lawn in the throbbing dark and go to him. I want to pull him into my arms and tell him that the blame is to be shared, that we can face it together. But I can't, and I don't.

The consternation, the soundless unease in both our houses that summer after the tree reveal, was terrible. We would go to talk to Rupert or pick him up, then stop as if remembering something. At the breakfast table or in the backyard we would turn to hand him some object, then pause with our hands frozen in midair. We began to walk around Jeffrey the way Frida, Pablo and Rafe had years ago, like he was a piece of furniture or a dog in the way. Conversations were stilted and strange. Each of us began to spend more time alone in our rooms or taking solo walks. There was no birthday party for Rupert that June.

If my youngest cousin stood in a room with me, with whom was I speaking? I think we all flailed to answer that question, and in our confusion and fear, simply avoided him as best we could.

In the backyard, Jeffrey continued to work wood at Andrei's side, but Andrei was coldly detached, responding to his questions in monosyllables. The ornate gingko shelf project vanished. When Jeff asked about it, Andrei said curtly, "Don't worry about it." Yet Jeffrey seemed not to notice his tone. He talked happily as they worked, words surging around the ancient dam. I caught the tail end of one of these outpourings: "I've thought about learning to work things like silver and copper, too. I want to make something like Aragorn's ring. You know? In the story it's thousands of years old, and you know the design means something, but Tolkien never really explained it. He just said, '*Their heads met beneath a crown of golden flowers, that the one upheld and the other devoured.*' But I had a dream about it and I think it means that even the king has to bite the dust once in a while. If he only wears the crown, he thinks he knows everything, so he turns into a monster. If he only eats the crown, he's so weak he can't do anything for anybody else or even take care of himself. So I think it helped knock Aragorn back to the middle if he started drifting too far one way. I mean that ring was riding on the hands of all these ancestors of his who ended up losing the path. All the way back to Numenor, to those kings who got really full of themselves and tried to go to war with the gods. And then the line got weak and everything crumbled apart and there wasn't even a king anymore. So it must have scared him to death, just looking at it. But the ring *survived,* which was crazy if you think about it, I mean how did it make it through thousands of years and all those wars without getting lost? Just the thing being *there* was a sign. I mean, it was proof that it was still possible for somebody to get it right. Whatever I make, or whatever I write, I want it to be like that. Something that makes me sit up straighter when I look at it."

It was so disconcerting to hear Jeffrey in all his articulate passion that he may as well have been a green alien teleported onto our lawn from another planet. Andrei stood there white-faced for a few beats before he said, "You're writing things? You mean stories and poems and stuff?"

"I have for a long—" Jeffrey stopped, peering at Andrei. He amended, "I might try someday, yeah."

Andrei dropped his handsaw with a clatter. "You're talking like it's actual history, like these were real people. There's a reason I don't read that stuff anymore. You know it's for babies, right? You shouldn't waste your time with it either."

Rupert would have gone limp in surrender, acknowledging his own foolishness. But Jeffrey said quietly, "Not this."

"I've got a headache. You can do cleanup here, yeah?" Andrei turned his back before Jeff could answer.

Meanwhile Marcus explored the family cars alone, waving Jeffrey away when he approached: "No time to teach today," he said, face averted. "Too busy." If Jeffrey waited for him when he came home from work, asking in his own voice how his day was, Marcus would get busy hunting down a snack in the fridge or cabinets. "Fine, good," he'd mumble before hurrying back out.

Rafe quit making his friendly jokes about going into the trades with Beets as his partner. When Jeffrey asked him if he wanted to walk with him to the hardware store to look at some tools, Rafe said, "That's not really my thing," and turned away.

Jeffrey was surprised. "Oh. I thought you said—"

"Not to you," Rafe muttered before stepping out the back door. Like Andrei's ginkgo shelf, his harmonica had disappeared.

Jeffrey followed Rafe with his eyes. "It's okay," he called after him. "Maybe later."

I was no better. Every time I saw Jeffrey, I saw that tree, and I wished he would dismantle it (though none of us had set foot in the garage since the grand reveal). Once, Jeffrey put his hands into the sinkful of soapy water where I was washing dishes, and I jumped aside as though he'd stung me. "I've got it," I snapped. "I don't need help." The large blue eyes met mine—patient, warm—and Jeffrey said, "Okay, Abra. But I can do tomorrow's. You shouldn't always be the one doing this." Then he was gone.

Our parents were beginning to snap at each other or else retreat into cool silences. Lonnie delivered a non sequitur one night: "I don't want people—anyone—using my piano. Okay?" No one in either house save Rupert had touched it in years, but we all understood: he was afraid that Jeffrey, creator of the fire-tree, would sit down at the keys. He was afraid of what haunting melodies might supplant those comically atonal disasters that were once Rupert's compositions.

Lissa decided the house was too cluttered and that she needed more mental space to work on her art. The solution to this was to ask everyone to clean out their rooms of anything they didn't need. She took the liberty of sacking Andrei and Jeffrey's room herself and managed to remove most of Jeffrey's books.

One afternoon a week later, my father snapped at Jeffrey from his writing-desk just as I had done from the sink: "Did you need something? I'm fine in here." And my mother, lying full-length on the couch with a headache one night, jumped when Jeffrey moved behind her to play with her hair. "I took an aspirin," she said shortly, sitting up. "It's fine." We all watched him from the corners of our eyes, expecting a sudden and threatening movement.

Jeffrey became quieter with each passing week of this, but the light I'd seen in his face the night of the tree reveal remained. It was for this reason that we became colder still, taking advantage of any small chance to slight or ignore him. We were employing what tactics we could to negotiate a kind of hostage exchange—Jeffrey for Rupert—and we were patient only because we were desperate. Nobody talked about any of this. But it was as though we'd taken in one big collective breath and were determined to hold it until Rupert returned intact.

One night in early July I feel asleep with my window open and dreamed that needle-thin rays of light pierced a tree canopy dark as onyx. Notes chimed out of the earth with each touch of light as if hidden scales lay beneath the grass waiting to be played. When I woke around two in the morning, it was to the same sound I'd heard in the dream. It was coming from somewhere in the woods, floating up through the trees like smoke. I slid out of bed and went to the window. "What the hell," I said softly. Sometimes campers or hikers passed through the woods at night on their way into the state park, and I'd see the dart and bob of a distant flashlight. But there was only that strange faint voice like wind combing a seashell. I tugged on my shoes and moved silently downstairs and through the backyard to the Ice Age Trail as if siren-called.

The moon had waxed enough that I could fumble my way past Molash Creek without trouble, but three times I stopped and dithered, thinking to turn back. Who wanted to hike into the wilderness in the dead of night? And for what? I only pressed forward through the red pine grove when I realized there were words. Someone was singing in the middle of the maritime forest.

In the darkness, the old cluster of massive conifers at the outskirts of the grove was suddenly unfamiliar, towering like an assemblage of giants or monsters. I had a flash of the Argonath—colossal statues of ancient kings guarding the Anduin River in a picture Andrei had shown me when we were children—and I almost turned back. But Jeffrey was there among them.

I froze in place, my skin pebbling. I'd never heard a voice so lambent and clear, like a bell pealing through some mythical city to awaken long-slumbering souls in stone towers. I recognized the song as something he'd loved long before Rupert appeared. It was a song everyone save Andrei had made fun of: *Who said that every wish would be heard and answered, when wished on the morning star? Somebody thought of that and someone believed it, and look what it's done so far. What's so amazing that keeps us stargazing, and what do we think we might see?*

I could almost hear the piano chords he'd learned or written long ago, before Lonnie banished him from the piano, to accompany the words. But he didn't need them. He was singing at the top of his lungs, head tilted back, hands open at his sides. There was urgency to it now, as though he sang to some doubting Thomas who needed to be convinced of the miraculous and could not be delivered any other way. The night around him was crystalline, the owls and crickets asleep or listening. I stood there bracing myself against a birch as he began a new verse. Then I happened to glance left.

Andrei was there, too. Like me he stood supporting his weight against the ghostly pallor of a birch. He was transfixed, seeing only Jeffrey. I stepped back into deeper shadow. Jeffrey took a huge breath and sang on: *Someday we'll find it, the rainbow connection . . . the lovers, the dreamers, and me.* As that last word lengthened into a verse of its own, strange images fluttered through me, kaleidoscopic, until I recognized their patterns first from stories Andrei had spoken into the darkness when we were children and then from the dreams Jeffrey had shared before Rupert was born. I could hear the dragons and the mountain passes, the wizards and the warriors, the lamps in the sky and the treacherous waters, all that he loved and feared and revered, and in a flash I understood that sickness came when we let our symbols degrade. Sometimes we inflated them and so ourselves, seeing kings and queens in mirrors, jewels piled in our hands . . . and sometimes we demoted them to the rank of reverie, a child's fancy, so that we might sidestep their demands. Hadn't we all, save Jeffrey, done one or the other? It was no wonder that he sang alone.

I had never felt so shoddy or deficient in my life as I did when the bell-call of my cousin's voice finally deliquesced into the night. There was a long pause before Jeffrey, looking spent, moved slowly back to the trail and began the hike homeward. I remained in shadow. Andrei waited ten minutes before starting down the trail, and I waited ten minutes more, so that the three of us reached our beds one after another like staggered solitary stars destined never to touch.

My feeling the remainder of that month was that an intruder inhabited both houses. I'd tried to quash the firefly underfoot, to chase out the memory of what I'd seen in the garage and in the woods, but Andrei's haunted look kept foiling the attempt. The beach was no refuge; neither were the trails. Even my sleep was minatory, dogged by nightmares. In those dreams I saw Jeffrey seated at a piano or before an easel, sometimes singing behind a microphone up on stage somewhere. As he painted, he addressed an invisible audience: "They're all stupid—you wouldn't believe how stupid. Don't tell them I know." Or, hands crossing over the keys, "Pick any one of them, and ask them what they wish they could do more than anything in the world . . . I do it better, and I hardly have to try." Then I'd see him returning down the gravel road to our house, fixing his face into an expression of blandness as he lifted Rupert to his hip. Once I woke not from a dream, but a memory: an otherwise ordinary night a year earlier when I was out walking and the notes of some ethereal composition came hang-gliding downwind like a heron. Surely it had been Jeffrey at Mrs. Hambly's piano, and yet I still could not quite believe it. Over the last three years Jeffrey had become first a shadow and then a penumbra, so vague and ash-colored in his marginality that it was beyond my imagination to accept him as a body of his own. There had to have been some mistake, a misunderstanding of titanic proportions. Perhaps we'd dreamed the fire-tree, and if we went back into that garage, we'd find only a Sad Thing—a Goodwill tennis racket strung with broken Christmas lights.

Andrei slept poorly, too. From the upstairs windows I often spotted him leaving in the blue hour before dawn, not to hike the Ice Age Trail but to drive Lissa's car God knew where. He'd come back in time to shower before work, and if I saw him downstairs over breakfast, he'd avert his gaze. At first I thought he was sleeping at the old monastery, but where would he have parked the car, and how could he have gone undetected?

One Sunday I decided I couldn't take the mystery anymore. I climbed into the backseat of Lissa's car at four-thirty in the morning and lay huddled there, waiting. Twenty minutes later Andrei lowered himself into the driver's seat and turned the ignition. He didn't even glance in the rearview mirror before backing out of the driveway and onto our gravel road.

"I'm coming with," I announced once he'd turned down the county highway toward Two Rivers.

"Jesus Christ," he cried.

"Sorry." I leaned forward. "What are you doing, Andrei? It's five o'clock in the morning."

"I'm having a heart attack, that's what I'm doing."

"Did you pick up another job or something?" It was the first time I'd thought of it, and my chest tightened in panic: "Are you saving up to leave? Sooner than you'd planned?"

"No, I don't have another job. As if I'd have the energy for that." He flicked on the brights. "There're deer everywhere this time of day," he muttered.

"It's not day. It's not a time any normal person should be out. Where do you go?"

"Nowhere. Just to the preserve, the wetlands."

I frowned. "You mean that little place with the old barn? And the walking trails?" I'd only been there once, on some grammar-school field trip to study frogs and birds. "Why?"

"I don't know. I just walk there sometimes. Is that okay with you? Or do you have more questions?"

His voice was brittle, on the verge of breaking. I should have left him alone. Instead I said, "What happened to the gingko shelf?"

"It was crap," he said shortly. "It was trash."

I sat back. Outside all was blue-black save for the occasional distant porch or barn light someone had left burning through the night. I exhaled hard through my nose.

"What."

"I don't sleep, either, you know," I told him. "I don't think anybody does. I hear Rafe pacing around, and if I'm sleeping in your parents' living room, I watch Marcus come down for water about ten times, and I hear Frida's floor creaking . . ." Then, "My father's not writing anymore. I never hear the keys."

No response. He turned again, slowed down as the little visitors' center materialized as a dark hillock against the horizon.

"Is it even open?" I said.

"The trails are, and they don't care if people park. I guess they trust people. Pretty naïve. This place'll be vandalized by the end of the summer."

I found myself scrutinizing this statement without really knowing why.

He parked the car and we got out. Wordless, I followed him into the wetlands, first down a muddy path and then along a little walkway made of wood planks. The swamp grasses were hugely overgrown and they whispered and brushed up against us as we walked. All the vegetation was still silver-netted with dew. Strange birds, different birds than what we knew in our woods and on our beach, cried out in alarm as we approached.

"We're scaring them," I muttered.

"Sun's coming up. Funny how they always sound horrified at that. At least, now they do. When I was little I thought the birds were all excited. Like, 'look, it's a new day, isn't that great'!"

There wasn't room for us to walk astride. I was behind him, trying to read the back of his neck. I said, "Horrified?"

A turtle fell off a log somewhere to my right and landed in the stagnant waters with a plop. The air was still cool but humid, the wetness clinging to my skin. Andrei just kept walking, leading me through the jungle, until we reached a kind of overlook where a plaque was nailed into a wooden bench.

Andrei ignored the bench, and the plaque with its picture of an osprey. He said, "You know what Lake Nippissing is?"

I repressed a sigh and moved up next to him, reaching out to clasp the wooden rail. Sprawled before us was an endless swamp, misty in the predawn and dun-colored save for the occasional yellow flare of marsh marigold. "It sounds familiar," I said. "Is that what this is?"

"It's Lake Michigan, what it used to be. Way back when, it was way higher than it is now, and the glaciers held it back like a dam. Then they melted, and the water spread out, and these huge waves made the sand dunes like the ones on our beach. They used to be underwater. Then the lake levels fell and left them behind."

"I didn't come here for a history lesson." I wrapped my hand around his arm. "Andrei. Talk to me."

"Since when do you *want* to talk?"

"What?"

"I try, I always try, and you get that look." He shook his head. "That look. Do you know how isolating that is? You're supposed to be the one person—" He stopped.

I pulled my hand back and stared resolutely out at the wetlands, where a huge bird, a crane or falcon, took off from a distant tree with a sound like a shutter opening. The old elusive ache ballooned again behind my ribs.

Andrei said, "I'm sorry. I'm taking it out on you." With an obvious effort, he turned sideways to face me. His eyes were grey-green in the smoky light and his olive skin was shadowed with a three-day stubble. "You tried, in the car. In a way. Look, let's just head back. We both have work in a few hours . . ."

"You're here because he's never been here," I said suddenly. "You're here because this place is a blank canvas."

He stiffened.

"You want me to talk? You want truth? You love them *so* much, your uncomfortable truths." I was inexplicably angry, close to tears. "You're here because Rupert's never been."

"Go ahead," he said softly. "Keep going."

I said, "You think I don't get it? I feel like there's a burglar in the house. I feel like . . ."

"Say it."

"I feel like my heart's racing all the time and I don't even know why."

"Yes you do." He spun me toward him, gripped my arms. "Yes, you do."

He was hurting me, wrangling the words from me, and I almost hated him for this power he had to induce me to honesty: "You were right, in the tent that night. We didn't know him. We don't."

"And?"

"He's a liar," I cried, hardly knowing what I said. "He tricked us all. He's—false."

"Who is? Jeffrey, or Rupert?"

I didn't answer.

"Both wrong," Andrei said. He pressed me backward, against the overlook rail. "Say it, say who's *false*, Abra."

How could I have known then that he wanted me to say his own name? That I could have helped him, changed the course of the future even, just by flinging the word into the swampy air, and opening the door to whatever confession he longed to pour out to me?

I said, "Let go of me. I want to go home."

He dropped his arms. We stood there for a few seconds as birds and amphibians began to stir themselves awake around us, and then Andrei turned and started back toward the car.

Back at the house, we went our separate ways. I fell asleep for an hour or so on my parents' couch, and when I woke up, I found my father alone at our breakfast table with a stack of burnt toast. He glanced up at me with red-rimmed eyes when I reached for the refrigerator door. Scanning the shelves, I said, "How is your manuscript going, Dad?"

"It was crap," he said hoarsely. "Trash."

I let out a sound that wasn't quite a laugh. I took an apple from the fridge, saw that it was rotten, and tossed it into the kitchen trash. In with the other garbage were a couple of Pablo's disposable cameras, the rolls still full.

Upstairs, Rafe was rearranging the meager furniture in his room, making track marks across his carpet. I asked him what he was doing.

"I just don't like it in here," he huffed, shoving his bed into the opposite corner. I noticed that he'd cleared away the little mess of Rupert's toys he usually kept atop his dresser.

"How different can you really get it?" I said.

"Not a whole fucking lot," he responded, and his tone was ugly, sharp and too bright like a sudden slap to the face. "Not a whole lot, Abra!"

I backed out of his doorway, then retreated to the bathroom where I locked the door and avoided the mirror above the sink. I went to the window and rested my head against the glass. Below, Marcus was pacing around in the backyard. He was smoking a cigarette—something I'd never in my life seen him do—and Pablo was sitting slumped against a tree with his arms at his sides. He looked like he'd slept out there.

There was a knock on the door. "Abra?"

I opened it. Frida stood there in her pink bathrobe.

"My dad's hogging our bathroom," she said shortly, as if I'd challenged her. Yesterday's eye makeup was smudged around her lids. "I think he's hurling up his guts or something. You about to shower or what?"

I almost said, "Get Rupert for him," then stopped.

"You can have the shower," I told her. I moved out of her way, and as she reached to close the door, I thought I glimpsed a fresh, tiny scar on her left arm.

I told myself I'd only imagined it. Then I went to my room, changed clothes, and left for work. I didn't know I was two hours early until I tugged at the office door at the community college and found it locked.

Jeffrey finally understood. He reversed course in mid-July, his voice vanishing overnight. Rupert returned full-force and began to climb into our hands and knock over boxes of Kool-Aid mix again. The first time he did this, on a night when several of us congregated in one kitchen, my mother let out a relieved laugh and went to find some watercolor paint to egg Rupert on.

He drew his self-portrait afresh in all the mirrors. He left notes on the tables, addressed to no one in particular: *evryone have a grate day today!*, or *can sum-one pleeze bring home Darey Kween?*

On a Saturday afternoon, the ice-cream truck trundled down our back road, and Rupert got so excited that he ran across the top of the couch and straight into the living-room window. After the blow he slid down the glass, dazed.

"Oh, no," I said, reflexively jumping up to grab him.

"We can get him something," my father said, pulling back the curtain. "Here comes the truck. Marcus, run out there."

Marcus took the two dollars my father held out to him and hurried outside. He came back with a mitt-shaped ice cream bar with a candy baseball stuck into it. Rupert pointed excitedly to the baseball and Marcus obliged him by prying it out of the ice cream. He glanced around at us—Frida and Pablo were there, too—then said, "You want me to pitch to you?" The tiniest hesitation: "Rupert?"

Soon we were all involved in a ridiculous miniature nine-inning game on the coffee table. Rafe came in and arranged some cork coasters to form bases, and my father even dug up a pen shaped like a bat that he'd gotten from the real estate office years before. I was catcher. Frida and Pablo played outfield, sitting on opposite sides of the coffee table, and Marcus was the top batter for the opposing team. Rafe took turns with my father pitching the gumball. When Andrei came home, he stood in the doorway watching Rupert strike out with his pen-bat, and the muscles of his jaw relaxed.

Rupert kept up his antics through the remainder of July and then August.

Frida stepped into a doll shop in downtown Manitowoc after work one day and came back with a tiny plastic fireman's hat. We sat on the back porch and fit it over Rupert's feeler-head, then fell over ourselves laughing when he made a mad scramble for the hose. "He takes on his duties so fast," Marcus commented, watching this from the open kitchen window. "We should make a little fire for him to put out. Pabs, give me your lighter."

Can bugs be fire-men, Rupert asked us in a note.

"Of course," we told him, then shared pitying looks. "Of course they can. You just get strong, Beets, and then you can apply."

He fell into the goldfish bowl Rafe and Pablo had been keeping in their room and splashed like a maniac until Rafe pulled him out. "No sir," my brother shouted. "We don't drown in bowls!" At dinner one night, Rupert walked across a freshly-delivered pizza, slipped, and fell feeler-down in the grease. I picked up two slices of pepperoni and stuck them to Rupert's eyes and we dissolved into laughter. A few days later, Rupert got stuck in a plastic Baggie and writhed frantically around, knocking over everything on the counter until we came to his rescue.

"Oh, Beets," we moaned. "Poor pea-head, got lost in a plastic bag."

There were moments in which we were still guarded, half-expecting Jeffrey to suddenly reappear and laugh at us. But he was making progress, winning us back.

He was careful never to mention the fire-tree or to be seen near it. At some point he even draped a tarp over it. In the meantime Andrei allowed him to shadow his woodworking once more, though he would not let him touch any tools. Frida left him a miniature bowl of Jell-O in the fridge with his picture taped to it, and Marcus gave him a dollar-store paddleball set. It was a riot watching him try to use it, his feelers wrapped around the paddle's handle and the pink ball flying everywhere, often smacking him in the eyes. He took this one-bug comedy routine into my father's study, the living rooms, our bedrooms. I think we all gave a collective sigh of relief. Maybe we really had only imagined the tree's artistry, and under the tarp stood a joke that had taken on specious gravitas with the help of romantic lighting . . .

Somebody bought a faded Parcheesi game from a thrift store and we took turns playing in groups of four. It had complicated rules and at first no one wanted Rupert to play—the fear was still there—but when we finally let him in, he drove us to hilarity by playing as the ultimate pacifist, misusing all his rolls, refusing to "eat" other players when he had the chance, staying so far back on the board that by the time we got our wooden pawns onto the Home square, all four of his little men were miles behind, like stragglers in a marathon who wouldn't cross the finish line until after all the cheering spectators had gone home.

My father took part in these games and he kept moaning and slapping his forehead: "Beets, no," he'd say. "You're doing it all wrong, pal. You should have *eaten* Abra's guy. You don't get it," and then, "Oh hell, Beets, you play how you want . . . our little pinhead." So Rupert would roll a fourteen, and he'd divide up his numbers so that none of his guys got anywhere, while the rest of us consumed one another in our race to the prize.

By late September, Jeffrey had effectively vanished again, and we were all beginning to relax.

But then one morning, he slipped. Jeffrey—not Rupert—asked Andrei to help him with a new project when he came home from work. It required use of the table saw to make some intricate cuts. He showed Andrei a geometric design he'd sketched in a notebook, stars within stars comprised of scalene shards of purpleheart and cedar.

Jeffrey explained to Andrei that he'd need to make thirty-three precisely-angled cuts, some of the pieces razor-thin. He said that he wasn't comfortable yet around the table saw but that this was the only tool that would serve his purpose. Andrei's secondhand saw was rusted-over and dangerous to begin with, malfunctioning so often that he either avoided it, or asked me to spot him while he worked just in case he got hurt. Andrei said curtly, "Yeah, fine. I'll help you when I get home today."

Jeffrey seemed not to hear his tone: "Thanks. I know, it's a lot. But I really want to do this while the fire is going."

Frida, Andrei, and Marcus went to work. So did my father. Lissa and Lonnie decided to take a day down in Madison and my mother asked to tag along. Pablo and Rafe went to school. Jeffrey, fussing with his designs on the back porch, missed his bus and asked me if I would take him to school on my way to the community college. I was irritated. Was I the family chauffeur? I hurried him into Lissa's car. When I pulled up in front of his school, I said, "Be good, Ru—" and stopped.

Jeffrey was already out of the car, but he turned around and looked at me.

"Go, you'll be late," I said, putting the car in drive. "Go."

His right hand made Rupert, and Rupert gave me a little wave. I was suddenly choked up and could hardly manage a wave back. I sped out of the lot.

Was it coincidence that we all found reasons to come home late that evening? I offered to take on a few extra hours for a girl who called in sick. Pablo and Rafe walked to a fast-food restaurant after school let out. Our parents had all manner of excuses for not coming home at dinnertime. But Andrei was the one who'd promised to be there, and no one ever found out where he went after his workday was over. He simply didn't come home, and when Jeffrey's bus let him off down the road from our house, he found himself alone. He waited a couple of hours but was so eager to begin his new project that he decided to work the table saw on his own.

I came home at around seven o'clock to screaming. Frida was in the backyard where a massive quantity of blood stained the worktable, the saw, the driveway. Pablo and Rafe were just coming up the street as I burst out the back door. The phone in Lonnie and Lissa's house rang and rang and rang. "Somebody get it," Frida cried. "What the fuck happened here?!"

I was frozen, sickened by the sight of all that blood. Rafe bolted into the house to get the phone. My father's car pulled into the driveway and a minute later he'd gone inside, too, and we could hear his panicked voice as he spoke to whomever was on the other end.

"Hospital, now," he cried when he came back out. "Jesus, oh God. Get in the car."

We piled in. I think I pulled Rafe halfway onto my lap. I just remember holding him and feeling his breath coming fast like a terrified bird's.

At the hospital we discovered Mrs. Hambly pacing the waiting area like one possessed, and in a trembling voice she told us what had happened. The table saw had malfunctioned horribly and mangled Jeffrey's right hand. He was so dazed and delirious from blood loss that instead of trying to dial 911 he dragged himself over to the Scotsman's. When no one answered there, he hobbled down to Mrs. Hambly's house. She heard a thump on her back porch and discovered Jeffrey passed out there in his own blood. She'd been trying to get hold of us all afternoon, but no one had answered at either house.

At the end of her story, her red-rimmed eyes met mine with open reproach. I took a step back.

"Thank you," my father said hoarsely. "Thank you for helping him. But please—you should go."

"Where was everyone," she murmured. Her violet blouse was spattered with wine-colored stains. "Where?"

When no one responded, she again looked at me. "I want to know if he's all right," she said. "I'm asking you to please call me when you find out."

I nodded and was surprised at the anger that frothed up in me as I did so. What business of hers was it? Who was she—some woman whose piano he'd played? She didn't know him. She'd never held Rupert in her hands or played a game with him on a countertop or read one of his absurd love-notes tucked into a lunchbox or under a pillow. *Go,* I pleaded silently.

Mrs. Hambly turned and left, shaking her head. We paced the worn carpet, waiting to know what we didn't want to know.

It was an interminable wait before the doctor came out to tell us, "He's going to make it." But his hand was mangled beyond recognition. He'd lost his first finger and most of the second, and there was severe damage to the tendons. He wouldn't be able to use that hand normally again.

None of this registered at first. My father kept asking about the blood loss, were they sure he'd make it, what were they doing for him exactly? Rafe just stood there white-faced and silent. Frida grabbed my hand and Pablo grabbed hers.

"Call home," Pablo whispered. "Marcus should be back by now."

"He has to make it," my father said loudly, as though someone had contradicted him. "He's only three years old, for God's sake—only three—"

The doctor peered at him. "Eleven," he said gently. "Going on eleven years old, sir. You should sit down. Can you help us contact your sister? Where did you say she—"

I lowered myself into a chair and stared dazedly at the carpet. I forgot anyone else was there until a second doctor appeared and said, "He keeps asking if someone named Rupert is okay. Was someone with him? Is it possible someone else was hurt?" When we failed to respond, his voice took on an edge: "This is important. Could there have been someone else on your property when this accident happened?"

"No," I managed. "I don't know who that is."

My father shook his head. "I don't know, either."

"There's no Rupert we know of," Frida said softly.

No one spoke again until Marcus came, and then we had to tell him the full extent of what had happened. We took turns, speaking in strange monotones as we explained the blood loss, the injuries, the permanent damage.

Marcus stood there listening, his expression blank. His arms hung limp at his sides. For a minute I thought he simply didn't believe us or didn't understand. Yet he was the one to say it first: "Rupert's gone?"

Rafe jumped out of his chair and walked away.

I nodded.

"Where is Andrei," my father wanted to know. He wouldn't make eye contact with any of us.

"He got home right after I did," Marcus said. "He was there when I answered the phone. He wouldn't come with me." He glanced at me. "He was in the backyard throwing up when I left."

"I'll go home," I said, rising.

Marcus put out a hand. "Trust me, that's not a good idea."

But I had to get up and move, had to do something other than sit there and think about what it all meant, and so I chased after Rafe. He'd gone into the men's bathroom and I opened the door not caring who else was in there. I found him standing in front of the mirror, holding his own right hand cradled against his chest like a baby. He was rocking back and forth, weeping.

"Get out of here," he cried when he saw me. "Just get the fuck out!"

I stumbled backward and let the door swing closed.

Over the course of the next hour, the rest of the family save Andrei arrived at the hospital. It was an unbearable vigil, the nine of us sitting there in silence. In time I left them and found the little chapel where Rupert had once prayed over Rafe, and I sat down in the back pew and folded my shaking hands.

But I could only withstand that place for a few minutes. The stained-glass window blinked cobalt and yellow like an eye, and I could not meet its gaze.

When Jeffrey finally came home from the hospital, his mutilated hand wrapped in a thick bandage, it was only on a kind of furlough, for he was scheduled to return almost immediately for continued treatment. The doctors had said it would be good for his morale to be home a little. That evening, the entire family ate together at Lonnie and Lissa's enormous dining room table. It was something we'd never done before and would never do again, and so the occasion had an aura of finality even before we fully understood what had happened to us.

Jeffrey sat dead-center at the table between Andrei and me. My father and Rafe were across from us, the rest of them crowded in on desk-chairs and the piano bench, whatever they could find. Our mothers were making an obvious and painful effort to be cheery: "Who needs fresh fruit for fruit salad when DelMonte is this good?"; "Frida put double cheese in the mac!" We passed around bowls of macaroni, hot dogs cut up with beans, bread rolls. Jeffrey was still hazy from the painkillers and did not react when we heaped food onto his plate.

At some unspoken signal, we began to talk. Frida complained about a waitress at work who was always skipping out. Pablo mentioned a teacher who'd quit suddenly; Marcus described the innerworkings of a vintage car he'd seen in a magazine. Lonnie was garrulous on the topic of this generation's lack of musical taste and Rafe fought back by defending some contemporary groups who were in vogue. We didn't know it, but it was a rehearsal for the conversation we'd be having for the next twenty years: frivolous and floating, white noise flailing to fill a desperate emptiness.

No one would look directly at Jeffrey, much less speak to him. Andrei was a stone beside me, as pale and silent as he'd been since the day after the accident when I found him passed out in the woods behind the house, drunk on Lonnie's vodka to the point of illness. I'd been walking around in a daze of my own, unable to talk to anyone. I was grateful that no one spoke Rupert's name or asked Jeffrey any questions. I prayed that we'd all have the good sense to keep this up forever.

But it was my father who broke the bubble. In the middle of that dinner, he reached over, natural as anything, to pet Rupert.

His hand stopped and hovered an inch above the bandage. Then it dropped. Jeffrey turned to look at him, then at me . . . and finally, at Andrei. Until that moment I had not registered that his eyes were precisely the same shade of blue as my own.

What did he see in our faces? Did he know what we knew— that he was not loved, for we had not changed? That all we wanted was Rupert, that we were at a loss now that we were left with Jeffrey? That not a one of us had the humility to love him for the strange, luminous being that he was, but forever preferred the fantasy to the real, the imaginary friend to the living soul, the known entity to the complex and uncontainable? Did he understand that, consciously or not, we refused to love or even acknowledge him unless he established himself as our inferior? He was gifted, special, chosen. He was *good*. Did he realize that we hated him anew not just for this, but because his very presence forced us to confront the reverse in ourselves? For what sort of father, mother, sister, or brother would despise a child for his magnanimity? What sort of monsters were these people passing around bowls of fruit and bread? For three years we'd walked with him on our shoulders and in our pockets, and it was true that he'd worked on us. Like timid apostles, we'd glimpsed the miraculous and begun to believe. But the dream was over now and in its wake was just Jeffrey to show us what we were not. Oh, it was even harder to love our perfect neighbor than it was to love our crooked one. It was a saint who sat at the center of our table, but we could not look at him, because we could not look at ourselves.

Jeffrey knew. He moved his bandaged stump onto his lap and did not speak for the rest of the meal.

Three days later, in the predawn, he got up before any of us were awake and put on his heaviest boots. In the garage he used his good hand to remove the flagstones from his tree. He made the long hike through the pines to the beach with the stones loaded in his backpack. I imagine that he stood at the waterline for a long time as he waited for the first spark of sunrise. Then he triple-tied the straps of his backpack around his chest, knotted his shoelaces so his boots wouldn't fall off, and walked into Lake Michigan. He kept walking until the current caught him, and he drowned.

It was the Lake Michigan Sector Coast Guard who discovered his body, many miles down the coast. But I found Andrei down at our beach the day after, hauling refuse out of the shallows. He was soaked, sobbing, hysterical when I tried to pull him back.

"They have him," I cried, clinging to his sodden clothes. "Stop it, Andrei. They have him. It's over."

He shook me off with a violent jerk and crawled back into the water. He scraped at buried stones and tried to haul out huge driftwood branches as if these objects could be resuscitated with his own breath. His hands were bleeding. I stayed, pleading with him, until I couldn't take it anymore. Then I left him there.

XIII.

I FALL BRIEFLY ASLEEP at the kitchen table, head pillowed on my forearm, and am taken into a dream. It is the peak of springtime along the coast and I am walking through the maritime forest that fringes Point Beach. The air is heavy with the scent of flowers and the woods are opulent in their greenness. In the distance I glimpse a solitary, exotic tree whose thick leaves glisten wetly and speak to me of sugar, of plump fruit fitting neatly into my hand. I am hungry and so I make straight for this tree. But when I reach the bole and peer into its lush canopy, I can find no fruit. It's a deception, I think, and so is the flowering jungle behind me. All may be blossoming, but there is nothing of substance ripening on the branches. I stand there pondering this and then some unseen force swoops around me from behind, ruffling the fabric of my clothes before it levigates the barren tree to dust. Like a dry flood the dust travels outward to overtake the forest behind me, from the low-lying shrubs to the towering pines, and then suddenly the land is a desert. In place of the lake is a deep crater, its walls pocked and striated. I turn in circles, eyes straining against the hard light. Wind kicks up scorched grey sand and the sun bakes bare stone to smoking. There are no bird calls. Everything is dead, everything is in ruins. Even the driftwood looks as though it will disintegrate at the touch of a fingertip. There is dust in my mouth and in place of hunger I feel a desperate thirst. Once again I glimpse a solitary tree in the distance—this time, a lone birch, bone-pale and desiccated—and I make for it.

Its peeling bark has dried to the finest paper and the sheets curl away from the trunk as if asking to be plucked. Gently I loosen a piece, expecting it to dissolve in my hand, but it remains intact. On some instinct I guide it to my lips. The bark becomes water in my mouth, pure and sweet. Surprise shivers through me. It's impossible, I think. How can there be sustenance in this?

I jolt awake to the sound of a door opening. With the taste of that water still on my tongue, I go to the kitchen window. Andrei has stepped out his back door into the slackening rain and is just hovering there like a ghost. He hasn't even bothered with a raincoat or umbrella. I know he can't see me— the kitchen behind me is pitch dark—but still, I take a step back as he crosses the lawn between the houses. He heads for the tree line and vanishes down the path through the woods. Very slowly, the first stretch of the trail glimmers to life; he's switching on the tea lights in his Mason jars one at a time.

I know he's headed for the beach to wait for the sunrise, to comb for fresh driftwood washed up by the storm. The right thing to do is to open the door and follow him. But I don't. Instead I turn back to take in my parents' kitchen, then the little rectangular living room with its faded sofas and bruised end tables. My father stayed here out of loyalty to Rupert, or Jeffrey, or both. He was the only one who could bear it. As for the rest of us, our unacknowledged guilt entered the world as violence over the course of those first ten years after Jeffrey's death. Most of the violence was toward ourselves.

We started by abandoning first our parents, then one another. Andrei and Marcus pooled their money to rent a duplex in Manitowoc, near Marcus' tech school; Frida and I did the same, choosing a one-bedroom apartment in Milwaukee and picking up new jobs. We left Pablo and Rafe with our parents, whose marriages quickly began to disintegrate. We heard that Lonnie hit Lissa in the mouth after she confessed to an affair with one of his friends, and that my mother began disappearing again for her month-long retreats, leaving my father alone in the Cape Cod. The boys were drinking heavily and graduated high school by a hair's breadth.

Frida began bringing men back to our apartment, losers with tattoos and beer breath who were rough with her in bed and made obscene comments to me when she was out of earshot. Some of them hit her and she'd hit back, not to defend herself but to egg them on. She never broke up with these men, only waited for them to leave her.

After about a year, I was tired of watching this. With only a high-school education I couldn't possibly support myself alone in the city, and so I copied my mother's pattern: I had no money to ship myself out West, but I found a kind of communal hobby farm northwest of Manitowoc County where a group of hippie-types owned twenty-five acres of woods. Most of the members were like me, on the run from something or someone, though of course no one spoke of their circumstances in those terms. We tended vegetable gardens, milked goats, and built bonfires at night. Living on next to nothing was an art form, they told me. It was singular and ennobling, a way to converse with Nature and with the earth in its innocence. At night people spoke dreamily of the personalities of plants, of electromagnetic hot spots around the globe, and of the energy fields my mother had once pursued on beaches and yoga mats.

While I was hidden away in this godless monastery, Andrei and Marcus fell out. Marcus was still struggling to get through his tech program but Andrei had dropped his journeyman training altogether and had begun to drink. One night Marcus called Frida to tell her that there'd been a barfight, and to ask if whiskey was all right to pour over a deep cut if he had nothing else on hand. She assumed it was Pablo who'd gotten himself beaten up, but it turned out it was Andrei. Off the grid as I was, I didn't know about any of this for months.

"I can't help him," Marcus said to Frida over the phone that night. "I can barely take care of myself."

Pablo enlisted with the Army, thinking he'd be fed and clothed for free for a few years, but was summarily kicked out of boot camp for drug abuse. Rafe followed him around for a while the way he always had before joining me at the hobby farm where he sank with me into narcotic forgetfulness. We never spoke of our family. In fact, we hardly ever spent time together alone. There was always the distraction of some chore to do, or else we were absorbed into the loud, impassioned conversations around the fires at night. In that smoky haze we were strangers to each other, just two people who'd willfully emptied themselves of identity and become merely goat-milkers and sweet-potato-pickers, children of the earth. We were full to our ears with soil and grass and we liked it that way. There was no time or place to think of anything else. Relationships, especially sexual ones, were easy there; I recall waking from post-sex sleep tasting not the man, but dirt, and feeling as impersonal as a stalk of corn or a carrot in the ground. What we'd done was natural. What we'd done was part of an earthly cycle. I would never have to battle the complexities of love, as Frida had, nor be responsible for someone else's happiness, as our parents had so miserably failed to be in their marriages. I didn't care if the man got up and left me in the middle of the night. Most of the time, I preferred it.

And there was a bonus to life on those twenty-five acres: a door to the glitzy mystical power our mother had always coveted. In this setting we could convene with forces that made us seem romantic to ourselves, but that never inconvenienced us by asking for anything in return, save that we respect Nature in all her grandeur. This task was so deliciously undemanding that Rafe and I shouldered it with an enthusiasm that impressed our fellow-woodsmen.

In the meantime, Lissa moved in with a lover somewhere in Minnesota while Lonnie went to New York in a fit of delusion, thinking he might have a belated break there. He rented out the old house to vacationers to Two Rivers so that he'd have something to live on. My mother left my father for good, sending him a postcard from a retreat in Oregon: *This time I'm staying. I'm sorry.* And my father, like Andrei, began to drink.

Every so often, I'd hitch a ride out of the commune and travel southeast to Manitowoc County to see Andrei. But he and I could not be together even for a cup of coffee without one of us breaking down before the night was over. These breakdowns alternated from angry outbursts to uncontrolled weeping and at some point they became unbearable. I could not look in his eyes. He could not look in mine. We would admit to the horrible choices we were making but neither of us dared to say to the other, *You can do better. You must.* So he drank, and lost one employment after another until he was doing odd jobs around Manitowoc County and practically living in the truck Marcus had helped him buy from a friend at the tech school.

One night, he didn't show up to the pancake house near his apartment where we'd planned to meet. I waited an hour before walking to his place ten blocks down and pounding on the door. No answer. I let myself in and found him on his couch, tossing in his sleep and reeking of alcohol. When I woke him, he made a sound like a wounded animal. "This horrible dream," he gasped, reaching blindly for me. "God, this dream—"

"I don't want to hear about it," I said, but he told me anyway. He'd been fishing in some pond in the woods and had left his pole lying on the ground. When he came back to retrieve the pole, a large frog had swallowed the hook at the end of the line and was choking. Andrei picked it up and tried to hold it still in one hand while gently removing the hook with the other, and the frog was panicking, breathing fast, its huge eyes fastened on Andrei's . . . finally Andrei thought he had it, and he tugged, but he pulled too hard and the frog unzipped like a bag, viscera unspooling into an oily puddle, and when he jumped back the frog's eyes were still open and staring at him where they floated in the mess . . .

"Don't go," Andrei cried when I stood up. His hand was steel on my wrist. "I can't stand it."

"Stop it, Andrei. Come on, let's take a walk, get some air—"

"He was trying to make himself believe, that night," he moaned. He wrapped his arms around my waist and sank his head against my belly. "In the woods—that song he was singing in the woods—"

For a moment I let my hand rest in his hair. Then I said, "I don't know what you're talking about. Come on, Andrei. Get up."

Even Marcus, the steadiest of us, began to spiral the drain. He got involved with a girl who used him and stole from him, and when she left him, he crashed his car—the first he'd purchased and built up himself—into a tree. Pablo was then living with a couple of other guys in Green Bay and when he went to pick up Marcus from the hospital, he was so shaky from alcohol or drugs that he couldn't drive them back. I happened to be in the area then with a couple of my fellow kibbutzers, buying the provisions our camp could not supply itself, and I had to go the hospital to retrieve my cousins.

I said nothing during that car ride. Who was I to ask questions, or to criticize? What was I doing with my life?

The doctors were concerned that Marcus might have a concussion, so I followed him into his duplex to make sure he went to bed with his head propped up. He was asleep within minutes after I'd gotten him settled. Pablo was waiting in the car for me, but I stopped to take in Marcus' bedroom—miserably ascetic, just the bed and a cheap pine nightstand and some clothes hanging on a portable wire rack on wheels. On some instinct I opened the top drawer of the nightstand, and from within the pile of boxers and tee shirts came the familiar plastic clamor of Rupert's corn popper cat. I quickly closed the drawer and exited the duplex.

Back in the car I said to Pablo, "I don't have a way to get back to the commune. My ride left after they dropped me at the hospital. I might have to stay with you a night until someone can come for me in the morning."

He dug his thumbs into the pressure-points below his eyebrows. "Can you drive? Monster headache."

"Geez, you too? Fine. Get out."

We drove in silence awhile, Pablo watching the windshield as if some bleak movie played there. At intermission he shifted in the passenger's seat and said, "So how is—how's Rafe doing out there?"

"Fine. Though I don't see him as much as you'd think." I hesitated. "You could come out, you know. They wouldn't turn you away. It's nice there. Calming."

"Yeah, I'm sure it is."

We never returned to the topic. I spent that night on the yard sale sofa that was normally Pablo's bed while he lay on the hardwood floor beneath. His housemates played violent video games all through the night, their laughter intermittently startling me awake. Lurid blue light from the big-screen television flickered and flashed through the crack in the bedroom door like deranged lightning. Around three in the morning I finally turned toward Pablo, who was lying there staring at the ceiling with his hands folded over his chest.

"Do you ever sleep?" I said.

His eyes floated to mine. "No."

I would love to assign the whole lot of us a certain nobility of spirit and say that we were punishing ourselves. But what we were really trying to do was escape. We lost ourselves in drugs and alcohol, in meaningless relationships, in meandering late-night walks and in commune bonfire-talk and in jobs that asked nothing of us. In that first panicked exodus from home after Jeffrey's death, I think we imagined that we'd eluded some violent accident of our own, only to realize belatedly that we'd been just as cut and battered in flight as we would have been had we stayed put. No one was unscathed. In an effort to numb those wounds, we became first fugitives and then somnambulists, going through the motions of life with as little consciousness as could be spared.

At the end of that ten-year period, we'd all hit rock bottom. No one was in any position to help anyone else. If Andrei had not woken from this nightmarish sleep first, it's likely none of us would have. He came to the commune one Sunday, asked for me, and walked me down a dirt path away from the camp. He made no criticism of the place or anything I was doing there.

All he said was, "I'm finished with it, Abra. I'm starting by apologizing to Marcus, because I failed him when we lived together. I'm starting there and then I'm going to talk to the others. If you want to help me, it would mean a lot."

I returned to the camp but was unable to sleep near or with anyone else that night. I found a quiet corner and curled up against the wall. My dreams since I'd moved to the commune had become gauzy abstractions, empty of memorable narrative, but that night I dreamed that Andrei and my father and I were sheltering in a farmhouse in the middle of a field after some apocalypse had befallen the world. We never spoke, as though we believed silence would shield us from further harm. We simply survived. Hours in dream-time felt like months and as the seasons passed in peace I began to feel safe. But then I started noticing strange things around the house, like a host of carpenter ants biting hieroglyphs into the floorboards of the wraparound porch. My father dropped a carton of blueberries on the kitchen floor and the berries started moving around of their own accord, forming ciphers along the tile. From an upstairs window we saw the tall grass in the field twisting in the wind to form letters, and at night, even the lamps would blink out code. Finally Andrei broke the silence, announcing that he had to leave. There was no paper here, he said. No pens. My father agreed with him. I followed them into their rooms as they packed. It was dangerous, I insisted. They couldn't go. How could they leave me here alone? "Come with us, then," Andrei said. But I wouldn't. When they'd gone, I went back into Andrei's room, where the pattern of triangles on the quilt on his bed started to rearrange themselves into a word. On his dresser was the velvet reindeer clutch I'd found in the monastery. As I stood there, the swirls of snow and studded stars floated up to the borealis like notes finding their stave, and these too began to spell out a word. I turned away before I could read it. Then I woke up.

"What did you smoke?" Rafe asked, his expression carefully disinterested, when I tried to tell him about the dream the next morning. It was the first time we'd attempted a serious, private conversation since he arrived at the camp.

I said, "Nothing. I don't know."

I started thinking I'd dreamed Andrei's visit, too. But Andrei made good on his promise to apologize to Marcus, after which he began seeking out the others one by one. Whatever annoyance we expressed at his interference was a thin veneer for our gratitude that once again, he'd become a still point on the horizon amidst our whirligig lives, our one shot at curing ourselves of a motion sickness that had almost knocked us flat.

About a year after his visit to the commune, Andrei introduced Frida to someone he'd worked for, a man named Daniel who had a reclaimed-wood business in Green Bay. It was through him that Frida learned about the market for old barnwood shutters. Daniel invited her up to his property to show her how to paint and refinish them, and she went expecting him to ask for sex and then send her packing. He didn't. He taught her all about the shutters and then took her downtown for dinner.

She told me all about it, fumbling for the words: "It's such a nice idea. You see these sad old barns everywhere, no one's using them, but the wood's still good. Dan takes all the sad wood and rescues it, and next thing you know, it's up on somebody's windows."

Her inflection on the word *sad* brought back the crooked letters in Rupert's notes as clearly as though he'd drawn them across my kitchen wall. I had to take a deep breath before responding, "That's great, Frida."

"Yeah. I mean, I don't know where this is going, I don't want to assume anything or get my hopes up, but if he can care that much about some old wood . . ." She didn't need to finish her sentence.

Around that time, Marcus met someone, too—a girl named Anna who'd grown up in Cedarburg and whose parents owned a tiny bed-and-breakfast there. He met the parents and it turned out the father had a passion for vintage muscle cars. For the first time in his life, Marcus had a father figure who was interested in his pursuits, and he warmed to the old man as quickly as he had to the girl.

That spring at the commune, we nailed handmade bird-houses to trees and spent hours watching titmice braid their nests. In late April Rafe became concerned about one nest in particular, insisting that the smallest of the newborns was getting squashed beneath his siblings, and that the mother bird couldn't get food to him.

"It's Nature," I told him. "Let her take her course. She knows what to do." Others in the camp responded similarly. Still Rafe continued to monitor the nest, and to pace around in a cagey way that unnerved me. When the young titmice finally fledged, I took down the nest and found it empty, utterly smooth.

"See," I told my brother. "They all made it out. He was fine." Rafe took the nest out of my hands. His face was white, filled with dread, and instinctively I stepped back even before he'd begun to work at the twigs and threads with his finger-tips. A few seconds later he pulled the nest apart and we saw the suffocated baby buried there. When the smell wafted up to meet us, Rafe dropped the nest and walked away.

Late that night, long after the fires had died out, I swore I heard the single note of a harmonica. The next morning Rafe told me that he was leaving the commune. He needed a real job, he said. He couldn't live like this anymore. Some of the campers accused him of cowardice, of abandoning the Earth. He shrugged and packed his things. Pablo was living with a girlfriend in Milwaukee then and he invited Rafe to sleep on their couch until he found something. He had a job installing internet and cable in people's houses, making just enough to pay the bills, and he claimed he'd scaled back on everything but his cigarettes.

Pablo's girlfriend got pregnant, then left him with the baby soon after it was born. He accepted these circumstances with surprising stoicism, and I think this, too, was a wake-up call for the rest of us. He and Rafe rotated their work schedules so they could watch the baby. Frida and Andrei sent them whatever little money they could. Pablo's runaway girlfriend had taken their only car, so Marcus stepped in and used another connection to help find Pablo a replacement. He was working as an inventory inspector at a used-car retailer then.

About six months after Rafe left the commune, I hitched a ride to Milwaukee with my few possessions stuffed into a backpack. I went to Frida's first, begging a place to stay for a few weeks until I figured something out. She told me it was fine, she was hardly at her apartment anymore now that she was going up to Green Bay on the weekends to be with Dan. From her I learned that my brother was working a night job as a street sweeper, cleaning up the parking lots at a big local mall.

I don't know why I did it, but one night I asked to borrow Frida's rattletrap car, and I drove out to that mall after all the stores had closed. I switched off the headlights and watched from a distance as Rafe drove his little white truck up and down the lots, stopping at the storefronts too so that he could jump out and grab the bags from the outdoor trash bins. I followed him for the entirety of his shift. By the end of it, by the time he'd driven off, I was crying.

I called Andrei. "I want in," I said.

By this point, Andrei had returned to his journeyman training program and finally earned his card. He picked up a job nailing trim in a commercial building in the city and so for a while there we were all within easy proximity of one another. We began to meet sporadically as a large group, sometimes over dinner at someone's cramped apartment or in a noisy cafe on the outskirts of the city. Those interactions were strained, full of weird pauses and non-sequiturs, for our routines were like ill-fitting clothes; we tugged at them, adjusted them, trying to make them fit again, but something always rode up and exposed us. Inevitably we would hurry away disconcerted, exiting the house or restaurant to attend to separate and sometimes imaginary duties. But we were trying.

It wasn't a steady climb. When Lonnie and Lissa died within a year of each other, and when we discovered that my mother had passed also, way out in Oregon on some mountain road we'd never seen, we faltered. Rafe almost returned to the commune. Marcus nearly destroyed his relationship, begging Anna to dump him for someone better. Andrei and Pablo flirted with the bottle again. Frida and I talked late into the night about marriage and how we just didn't see the point, even as Dan was beginning to hint that he wanted to spend the rest of his life with Frida.

But we rallied again. Andrei took control of the house he and his siblings had inherited—no one else wanted anything to do with it—and resumed renting it to vacationers for extra income, which he distributed equally among Frida, Pablo, and Marcus. Rafe stuck with his job. Dan proposed; Frida accepted. Andrei called me with a proposal of his own: "Keep Frida's apartment after she goes. I'll help you with the rent if you'll agree to start a program at one of the community colleges. In a couple of years, you can get a real job and you won't need my help. Deal?"

The old arrogance, the yearning to be the artist in the atelier, was still there. For about ten seconds I flirted with the idea of returning to the commune. Or I could get some lowly job at one of Milwaukee's art galleries . . . I'd begin to paint again, and my gift would finally emerge, and they would all see it . . .

Andrei said, "Are you still there, Abra?"

"Okay," I said. "Deal."

I scanned catalogues for a week. The different trades clattered around in my head like marbles: *HVAC repair, human resources, computer science, accounting, horticulture, supply chain management.* Dreary for their orderliness, they were just words that had nothing to do with me. At night I paced my tiny kitchen as I argued with Andrei in my head. Did he understand that I was about to give up not just my dream, but dreaming itself, the mental vagrancy that was my choicest indulgence? Did he really expect me to bear it, the harsh light of this new life scattering my idea of myself like fog? And what would be left behind—what would be revealed—when the mist disappeared? I still believed that it was worse to be a real fragment than an imaginary whole.

But one morning I woke up with the word "optician" on the tip of my tongue. I found it in one of the technical college catalogues next to a picture of a human eye. Also known as ophthalmic assistant, the caption explained, this position involved pre-screening, specialty testing and the dispensation of glasses and contact lenses to patients . . .

I didn't allow myself to think about it too closely. I applied and enrolled. I took my classes, studied my textbooks, learned the intricate anatomy of the eye. Sometimes after a long night of studying I would dream of Rupert and jolt awake in a cold sweat. But I kept at it.

Frida married Dan and moved to Green Bay. Andrei met a woman named Meri on the Mariners' Trail boardwalk and within a year they were renting a house in Manitowoc. I met Gary at the community college where he was completing a degree in landscape design. Pablo and Rafe continued to live together until they met the women they married, and then they moved into small houses in Sheboygan. There,

Rafe trained to be a home inspector and Pablo entered union schooling to become a plumber.

Marcus and Andrei had their quiet weddings. Gary and I got married at a courthouse, then rented a small place in the city with a balcony overlooking Lake Michigan. We rarely fought over the course of our short marriage, but we did fight about that balcony. He wanted a lakeview and I didn't. In the end I gave in, but would only stand on that balcony in the black of night, when the Lake easily could have been a vast cornfield or an empty highway.

We all met for holiday dinners, everyone coming out either to Frida and Dan's house or else to Marcus and Anna's place. Sometimes spouses came along and sometimes they didn't. It wasn't until after Andrei's divorce and his takeover of the old house that we began to meet again at Lonnie and Lissa's. I think the only reason we were willing to do this was that Andrei was alone there, and we owed him for helping us climb out of our respective pits.

My father, sober now, would walk over from next door to join us. He was still working as a realtor but had begun writing what would be his award-winning novel, and in those last few years before he died, he blushed when he spoke of it. "It's the real thing, this time," he told me. "It's killing me, that's how I know." He never criticized us for our emotional distance after Jeffrey's death. It seemed that our occasional phone calls, our lunches with him in Milwaukee or Sheboygan when he came to visit, were more than he'd hoped for.

In a curious way, we were similarly neglectful of our own families. On the surface it didn't appear to be so; we were all obsessed with working long hours, with providing, with anticipating needs. We were quick to fill cracks in our driveways or to repaint fading kitchen cabinets, but our spouses accused us one by one of being silent and inscrutable, so immersed in external improvements that we failed to be true companions of the heart.

I know it wasn't just me because I watched it happen between Andrei and Meri, and because Frida sometimes called to confide that Dan was pleading with her to open up, to be *intimate outside of the bedroom* and because Marcus' wife once took me aside at a dinner to ask me point-blank how to make him talk to her.

"He's working so hard for us," she said hastily. "Don't think I'm not grateful. It's just . . . sometimes he's there, but he isn't. You've known him your whole life. Maybe you can tell me . . . "

Pablo's wife made a similar appeal to Frida, who relayed the conversation to me over the phone and admitted that she'd had no answer for her sister-in-law. Mandy, Rafe's young wife, was materialistic and easily distracted by his efforts to save money and improve their home. But even she let drop the occasional remark: "At least I always know where to find him at night, even if it's not in our bed. He's either mowing the lawn in the dark or scraping out the gutters."

We were overcompensating, immersing ourselves in externals to escape the alternative. I felt it in all of them and even now I have a visceral memory of that frantic need to take care of things. I'd clean up after my husband when he made it clear he didn't expect me to, or I'd wash his truck by hand, or organize his sock drawer, or write birthday cards to his mother and sister long before they needed to be posted in the mail. At those rare family gatherings where spouses and children were in attendance, my cousins were always the ones washing dishes or refilling drinks or preparing car seats for departure. How many times did I see one of their wives, or Frida's husband, reach for a quick hand-squeeze only to be casually diverted by a sudden need to clear the table? How many too-quiet or else too-loud drives home did they share after those meals? It was always one or the other with Gary and me—silence, or else chatter as superficial as the family's talk over dinner, to-do lists drawn in the air and idle prognostications of the weather. Over time these routines became so ossified that there seemed no hope of changing them.

Most likely it was the children that held most of their marriages together. In any case, Andrei's couldn't survive, and neither could mine. After my divorce, I moved into my tiny place in Chicago and saw the family only at those big holiday gatherings. Meanwhile Marcus, Rafe and Pablo raised their children, and Andrei went on restoring the old house and keeping watch over my father.

Those last few years before my father's death were quiet. Only rarely did we reveal to one another that something was still deeply amiss. There were inexplicable breakdowns— Marcus weeping over a transmission dying in a beloved car, Pablo walking out of the house one Halloween when his son asked to be taken to the pumpkin float up in Two Rivers, Frida bursting into tears while making Jell-O for a July 4 dessert . . . Andrei calling me from a Home Depot where he'd gone in to buy a replacement blade for his table saw but had wound up in the restroom instead, sick at the stomach.

"I need you at the lakeshore tonight," he said. "Promise me and it'll at least get me back to the house."

Once, in a Walgreens with Rafe picking up soda and ice for a get-together, I lost track of him for a while only to find him standing stock-still in the toy aisle. His eyes were closed and he was holding a cheap plastic rattle cupped in his hands. I backed away and didn't mention the incident when he rejoined me in the checkout line. He returned the favor one afternoon when he was in Chicago with his wife for an anniversary lunch. They dropped by the Sears Optical where I worked, and when I choked up in the process of fitting glasses to an eleven-year-old boy's face, he politely turned aside with his hand at Mandy's elbow and pretended to be fascinated by a display of sunwear.

No one ever spoke Jeffrey's name, or Rupert's—at least, not in front of the group. To do so would have been to betray a tacit but critical confidence. As a family, we had a contract.

Andrei came the closest to breaking that contract. It began with a dream he had, in which he was an indolent prince who'd abandoned his father's kingdom and was living in luxury in some faraway land. His father sent him a letter asking him to return and till the earth, because the crops were dead and the people were starving. The following morning, Andrei called to tell me he'd made up his mind to start writing. He would resume his late-night studies, sign up to audit courses . . . "Only now," he said, "I'm going to keep one hand off the wheel."

But determined as he was, he continually faltered. Over the phone he'd berate himself: "I can't. I try, but I can't. How can you give shape to the thing you most want to keep . . . insubstantial? How can you animate the thing you most want to bury? Everything I put down is an evasion. If it's pretty, it's just there to distract . . . even if there's depth, it's more like a hole in the floor I've dug out for myself so that I can fall in before I go any further. It's all fucking lies."

"There's a path around all that."

"I can't find it. I definitely can't *blaze* it."

"Yes, you can." Did he have any idea what it took for me to encourage him this way? I was terrified of what might come of it, and I didn't understand it. Even then I wanted only an anodyne, while he seemed bent on willful suffering. Survival depended upon an averted gaze, I wanted to tell him. Numbness. But in these moments, as of old, I'd be possessed with love for him, and recklessly I would say, "You can, Andrei. You *will*."

He kept at it. The first poem he allowed me to see was something I couldn't bear to read twice, and yet its closing lines followed me around for weeks: *I say, good riddance to the pittance that is my talent, and God forbid I should live in a half-way house between my love and its object.* The poem took up residence in me like some creature that had slipped in through a back door left ajar, and the sense of it in my house troubled me with deja-vu until it occurred to me that all the stories Andrei and Jeffrey had loved as children had begun this way. Whether as the rusty sword roused from its long sleep or as the infant birthed in a forgotten stable, truth was wise enough to enter our cluttered consciousness via the slyest means. Given time to watch its progress up the road, how many of us would permit it past the steps and into the hall? How many of us, even if somehow unafraid, could believe we had room?

Now and then I unfolded an easel in my sterile apartment kitchen and attempted to paint. But no matter how vibrant my colors, the final product always seemed inert. I could not paint faces—ironically, the eyes were beyond me—so I tried to instill my pines and birches with spirit instead, to no avail. Even my flowers looked like paint-by-numbers. Eventually I stopped. The canvases gathered dust under my bed.

I kept my routines. I went to work, ran my errands, slept alone. I saw the family on holidays and birthdays. I stayed away from the Lake and filled my evenings with the chatter of television or with pop music that was safe in its banality. I was losing days and even months as easily as buttons or socks, but that was exactly what I wanted, and I imagined myself content.

And so twenty years passed after Jeffrey's death, and taking a bird's eye view, one might have said that the six of us journeyed successfully out of tumult and into relative peace. We had almost convinced ourselves that all was forgotten, that all was well, until my father collapsed at the banquet and cried out for Rupert.

The plates beneath the earth's surface are always shifting, their slow battles imperceptible beneath our feet but enacting the planet's greatest dramas—the melting of glaciers, the formation and collapse of mountains, the migrations of men. I believe it is the same within a family, only sometimes the shifts are not silent and arctic in their pace but sudden and savage. And while my family's tragedy is now twenty years behind us, the fissure has been held closed only by the butterfly keys of time, and deep gaps remain. We have reformed our lives from the outside in, but it's not enough. The proof is in our mindless chatter at holiday meals, in Andrei's divorce and mine, in the fact that that my cousins and brother have never spoken the truth to their spouses or closest friends. We're still like those kids at confession, saying everything except the one thing that matters. But where would we begin? Where can I?

The rain has diminished, and I stand motionless on the soaked lawn between our two houses. I know I should go down to the lakeshore, to Andrei. But I still can't move. I haven't been to Point Beach since my cousin died. What possible good could it do? It is too late to do right by Jeffrey, and to walk those sands would be only a torment, for I fear that God will be all too close there, the insistent wind his breath at my neck.

Like Andrei, I'm afraid to believe. I have failed in faith for the same reason I have failed in art: I prefer a comfortable bewilderment to a hard clarity. I like to imagine truth as the skeins of a dandelion, weightless and ethereal and too tenuous for any earthly mind to grasp. I like to imagine that the question we have asked for centuries is forever unanswerable. And yet, standing here in the predawn, I suspect the answer has always been as close to me as the family with whom I've lived.

I cross the lawn to Andrei's work-area and lift the heavy tarp covering his miter box and table saw. I breathe in the scent of cedar sawdust and long afternoon labor. Then I start down the path to the lakeshore—the path he's illuminated with his tea lights in glass. When the tea lights vanish, I reach out to tap trees for balance as I wind my way north. I stumble, catch myself, lurch forward again past the ghosts of old landmarks and the dark freshets of Molash Creek. Startled animals dart from their hiding places. Droplets of rain patter from the canopy to soak my shoulders. In the last stretch before soil gives way to sand, I come upon the cluster of massive conifers that could be a gathering of monsters or giants, and I falter beneath them. I tilt my head back to find pale stars shimmering behind the mandala of the pines' highest branches. I hike on.

It is 5:15 in the morning when finally I emerge from the forest's darkness onto Point Beach. The light here is just beginning to shift from blue to rose, and a mile of washed-up rubble coruscates beneath the nascent sun. A lot of it is just trash, but there is also driftwood, and all his life Andrei has come down after a storm to salvage it. I find him crouched at the water's edge, clad in a deep green parka. He's tugging at something snared in the shallows.

"Andrei," I say, and he turns halfway. Mica mirrors across his forehead as though he's run silty water through his hair.

"You come for some free wreckage?" he asks. His tone is measured, carefully devoid of hope.

"I came for you."

I kneel on the sand at his side. A quartet of birches twenty yards behind him flushes gold; birds call out as shadows tremble and disperse. I realize he's not struggling with a piece of wood after all, but with a massive old rope half-buried in the sediment.

"Might be from a cargo vessel," he mumbles, not looking at me. "Their stuff washes up sometimes."

"What are you going to use it for?"

He shrugs and keeps pulling. "Nothing. Not a damn thing." He's straining, hurting his hands.

"Andrei," I say again. "I want—I want—"

And I stop. It's not about what I want. I say, "Let me help you."

He goes still, a strange look flickering across his face, like he's remembered something. Then his hazel eyes find mine. I answer the plea there by wrapping my hands over his, which are still clutching the rope. I lean in and kiss him deeply. He makes a sound in his throat, and it is a chanter's first daunt-less note, an epic's beginning. Gently I release his fingers from their grip one by one, until we've let the rope go.

ACKNOWLEDGMENTS

Many thanks to J. Bruce Fuller and to everyone at Texas Review Press for the care they have shown my work. Thank you to my brother, Jimmy Trahan, who has supported my journey for fifteen years, and to Geol Greenlee, my mentor and friend, who carries the fire. Most of all, I want to acknowledge ten souls whose courage, kindness, and forbearance rerouted my life in 2023: Treveno Campbell, Jay Cormier, Jason Desrochers, Brent Frazier, Bill Henry, Si Keomongkout, Rodney Lyons, Joe Maine, Dave Mitchell, and Ralph Thompson.

ABOUT THE AUTHOR

ELIZABETH GENOVISE grew up in Villa Park, Illinois and earned her MFA in fiction at McNeese State University in Lake Charles, Louisiana. She has been the recipient of an O. Henry prize among other honors and has published five collections of short stories: *A Different Harbor, Where There Are Two or More, Posing Nude for the Saints, Palindrome,* and *Lighthouse Dreams,* as well as a novella, *The Numismatist.* She teaches literature and writing near Knoxville, Tennessee.